descended

ingrid j. adams

three bees
— press —

Printed in Australia

Cover design by Bea Brabante

Illustrations in this book are copyright approved for Three Bees Press

First Printing: April 2023

Second Edition: March 2024

Paperback ISBN 978-1-7635034-0-3

eBook ISBN 978-1-7635034-1-0

Distributed by Three Bees Press and Lightningsource Global

 A catalogue record for this work is available from the National Library of Australia

descended

for some, the veil between
realms is stretched thin...

For Xay.
Because lights out is just
another beginning…

warning

You're about to step back in time to the 1990s, when the insults were slurrier, society was more laid back but less tolerant, and kids had unsurveilled freedom. No mobile phones or social media meant trials, tribulations, and mistakes mostly stayed at the scene of the crime, and political correctness was a largely theoretical concept not many abided by. If you think this book may go places that aren't productive for you to immerse yourself in at this time, please feel free to set it aside. I don't believe in spoilers, but you can visit ingridjadams.com for a list of triggers.

not a child of the 90s?

Then here's a QR Code I prepared just for you. Amongst other things, it will take you to a Spotify playlist (entitled 'descended · one') so you can play along at home. Because 90s (and 80s) music was so angsty and awesome — I hope you agree.

prelude

manly, new south wales, august, 1995

Reinenoir was hungry.

Ravenous in fact.

But it wasn't food she needed.

The night was pitch black, the only sounds the cracking of twigs beneath her feet, the rustle of shrubbery. The scent of leaf litter and fragrant wattle filled the air. By the time she arrived at the edge of the clearing, her eyes had adjusted to the dark. In its centre sat a circular altar draped in deep purple satin. A young woman lay upon it, unmoving, unconscious, her platinum pixie cut dishevelled, her rumpled navy scrubs barely concealing the generous curves beneath.

A nurse.

Reinenoir smiled.

Four tall white candles stood around the altar. She watched as a small figure stepped forward, stretching to light them, the candlelight flickering over her jet-black bob, her square jaw, her creamy skin. It was her Maiden. Reinenoir heard a sound then, and her gaze shifted to the tree line from where a great hulking mass was emerging, the shadows seeming to run and drip from him as he rose up behind the nurse, towering over her to block the meagre moonlight. Artax. Most of his face was obscured by the satiny hood of his dark purple cloak, a cloak that matched those worn by Reinenoir and her Maiden.

The nurse stirred, shuddering as Artax's breath hit her. She groggily raised the back of her hand to cover her nose and Reinenoir knew too well the stink that filled her nostrils; a stink reminiscent of the deep rotting stench of fetid guts.

"Leave the ressst to me, Maiden," Artax lisped, opening his hand. There on his palm, a small pale flame sprang to life.

The nurse blinked and looked again and Reinenoir smiled to see the disbelief in her expression. The flame was burning higher now, cupped between his sharp black nails. He swept his arm in a circle and the sea of tealight candles that rimmed the clearing ignited in its wake. Reinenoir edged back into the shadows, happy just to watch. For now.

The clearing was ringed by pale gums, their luminous branches stretching eerily into the infinite blackness. Artax stood over the nurse, the Maiden beside him. He pushed his hood back enough that the candlelight strobed over his face. The nurse recoiled. His lips were pierced with silver rings, his chin adorned with a black stud, and protruding horizontally from the bottom of his nose was a large silver bolt. Resin skulls plugged the gaping holes that stretched his earlobes to his chin. Every inch of visible skin was a tapestry of black tattoos, the whites of his eyes inked to dark pits. He held the nurse's gaze and slowly opened his mouth; a forked tongue protruded to deliberately lick raven lips.

The nurse scrambled back on the altar, but Artax pushed her roughly in the chest, holding her down and drawing an athame from his robes. The ceremonial knife was golden, its crooked blade decorated with runic markings. She gasped as he held it to her throat.

"You move, you bleed," he hissed.

Reinenoir made her entrance then, gliding from the tree cover.

"Don't damage the merchandise, Artax." She pulled her hood low. All her victims ever really remembered of her were her lips and nails, painted the same shade of haemoglobic red.

"Of coursse not, Lady Reinenoir," Artax said ingratiatingly, withdrawing the dagger from the nurse's neck. He and the Maiden bowed to Reinenoir, joining in unison to greet her, "Blessed be the evening, High Priestess."

Reinenoir nodded with disinterest. She moved straight-backed to stand at the nurse's head, with Artax and the Maiden flanking her.

"What do we have here?" she asked, placing a small hand on the nurse's cheek. At her very touch the young woman gasped, tried to pull away, and Reinenoir knew she could feel the black emptiness swirling through her, creeping into her every pore.

"It's an empath, my lady," the Maiden replied, a heavy accent clinging to her words, "but it's not trained and is oblivious to its true power."

"Interesting," Reinenoir replied, moving her hand to the nurse's chest. The young woman immediately began to choke and splutter. Reinenoir regarded her blankly for a moment or two before casually removing her hand. The nurse gulped air deep into her lungs. "This is just what I need to strengthen my collection. Excellent."

The nurse tried to sit up, to protest, but the Maiden flicked a hand in her direction, and although she didn't come close to touching her, the young woman was thrown roughly back onto the altar, pinned down by an annihilating weight. She couldn't move, she struggled to breathe.

"Please," she rasped, but the Maiden closed her fist and the nurse's mouth snapped shut in response. Panic-stricken, she tried in vain to part her lips, raising her fingers to claw at her mouth and the Maiden laughed callously.

"I don't have all night," Reinenoir said impatiently. Their juvenile games tended to irritate her. The Maiden opened her fist to release the nurse from her hold. "Let us begin."

A reverberating sound filled the air then, as the three of them began to chant, the resonance so powerful the nurse shook. They started moving around her, raising their arms up high. Around and around they went.

"No!" she whispered, her eyes wide, her breathing rapid. "Please stop. Let me go. I have a family, people who need me. My name is Essie…"

But they only moved and chanted faster. As they spun around her, her eyes began to roll, glazing, deadening. She fumbled her hands to ward them off, to protectively cover her chest, but she was already too weak. They suddenly stopped their flurry and Reinenoir stepped forward to stand in front of her. Reinenoir spread her arms wide and threw back her head as a swirling vortex opened over her sternum, iridescent streams of inky bioplasma unfurling from within, coiling and twisting like great writhing snakes to hook into the nurse's chest.

Reinenoir knew just like the others before her, the nurse would be feeling a crushing pressure in her heart, in her lungs, as if they were being vacuumed out through her solar plexus – as if Reinenoir was sucking the very life out of her, pumping all that she was, from deep inside her body.

Because that's exactly what she was doing.

Her loss was Reinenoir's gain.

When the nurse's head lolled to one side and her eyes drooped shut, Reinenoir smiled broadly, breathing heavily, cheeks warm, as her hooks retracted and the vortex spun shut. "Woo!" She shivered with a coursing rush. "Well done," she nodded to the two of them. "That was just what I needed."

She spun on her heel, heading for the edge of the clearing. Just before she disappeared into the bush, she glanced over her shoulder.

"Get rid of that, would you, Artax? And go hunt me another. And quick." She narrowed her eyes before adding, "You know, time is running out. And I need to be prepared. For him."

five years earlier....

chapter one

something to believe in

manly, new south wales, march, 1990

indigo

Indigo crossed his arms and leaned back in the heavy mahogany chair, long legs sprawled out in front of him.

"Why are you always in my office, Wolfe?" Mr Hargreaves sighed. The headmaster eyed him wearily.

Indigo shrugged his broad shoulders and glanced out the second-storey window, barely registering the panoramic views over Manly Beach and beyond. The rolling lawns and manicured gardens of North Head Grammar sat vacant. Everybody was in class.

Between them on the headmaster's imposing desk sat a crumpled pack of Benson & Hedges.

"We've spoken about this repeatedly," Mr Hargreaves continued. "You know, the other kids look up to you. Every time you're caught smoking, I have to deal with a barrage of copycat incidents. You're fourteen-years-old, Wolfe, lay off the cancer sticks."

Indigo continued to stare out the window, now absently tracing a finger over the sharply pressed crease in the thigh of his charcoal trousers, the same trousers every boy in the school wore with a white button-down shirt and a navy-and-grey-striped tie. He smoothed his hand through the back of his dark blond hair, still slightly salty from his morning surf. He wished he was surfing right now.

The headmaster slammed his palm down on his desk and Indigo jumped. "Look at me when I'm talking to you, Wolfe!"

Indigo turned his attention to the headmaster who was looking a little worse for wear these days, his face lined, his hair shot with grey. Mr Hargreaves' students always joked that what he lacked in chin he more than made up for in nose.

"Sorry, sir," Indigo said, flashing his most charming smile. Indigo knew no one could resist that particular smile. "Won't happen again."

Yeah right!

The headmaster stared at him for a moment or two before sighing again, his shoulders slumping as he opened a desk drawer and rummaged around inside. He came up with a piece of paper, a form Indigo was more than familiar with. He scribbled on it, then slid it across the desk. "You know the drill. Have your guardian sign this and return it to me."

Indigo nodded as he reached for the page, swallowing a smile. He had forging Edita's signature down to a fine art.

"Just because you don't have to work to get top marks doesn't mean you can slack off, Wolfe," Mr Hargreaves said. "So pull your socks up and start setting a good example for your peers!"

"Yes, sir," Indigo said, suppressing an eye roll.

Business out of the way, the headmaster's demeanour shifted. Indigo knew what was coming.

"When's that mother of yours next in town?" he asked, his sudden forced casualness cringeworthy. Indigo was more than familiar with the fake nonchalance people adopted when asking about either of his parents. "I think we should arrange for her to come in and see me."

Yeah, he was sure Mr Hargreaves would love that. Just like he'd loved that autographed picture Indigo had gotten him last year. Mr Hargreaves never needed to know Indigo also had forging his mother's signature down to a fine art.

"I suppose she's busy promoting her latest album," the headmaster continued, his sultana eyes glinting. Indigo shrugged again. As if *he'd* know. He hadn't seen or spoken to his mother since he'd left her in Aspen in January. "I heard she might be doing another movie with your father; wouldn't that be marvellous? Hollywood royalty Bernadette

Van Allen and Wilson Wolfe reunited on the big screen after all these years!" The dude was practically getting off at the thought.

Indigo snorted and quickly covered it with a cough. Hell would freeze over before those two ever set foot in the same room again. They hadn't spoken since Indigo was a baby.

"I don't think that's likely, sir," he said. Mr Hargreaves looked so disappointed, Indigo actually felt bad for him. He stood to leave.

He made it two steps before his conscience got the better of him.

"I could get you a signed copy of her album?" he offered, knowing he'd probably regret it. He felt bad for the guy. As far as teachers went, he wasn't that much of an arsehole and he had a soft spot for Indigo. Plus, the man wasn't well. He had chest pain. A lot. Indigo had let his guard down and asked him about it once, suggested he go get it checked out, but Mr Hargreaves had lost his shit and Indigo realised he'd overstepped. It wasn't as though he wanted to know that sort of stuff about people. But he couldn't help it. He just had a way of *knowing*. Like when one of his mates had a sprained wrist or a headache or that time his teacher had that shocker of a toothache. When he was near someone, he felt what they felt in their body, in his. He always had. When he was younger, he'd assumed everyone could. It wasn't until he was older he'd understood he was a freak. So he'd made a habit of keeping his mouth shut.

"Could you really?" Mr Hargreaves breathed. He looked like he was about to have a heart attack on the spot right now. In a good way.

"Sure, why not?" Indigo grinned. The headmaster was so bloody excited, Indigo made a mental note to call his mother's PA in LA and have a genuinely autographed copy sent out.

Mr Hargreaves jumped up and rounded the desk, prattling on about how deserving Bernadette was of the Oscar she'd won last year and how ground-breaking the music video for her latest single was. Indigo's lip curled. Somehow, the more skin his mother showed, the more she was branded empowering and revolutionary. While the headmaster was distracted, Indigo reached for the pack of cigarettes, subtly palming them and slipping them into his pocket. Mr Hargreaves clapped him on the back as he walked him to the door. Indigo towered over the man, as he did most people.

"I don't want to hear about you getting caught smoking again, ok, Wolfe?" he said as he opened the door. The bell rung and doors up and down the hallway burst open. Students began pouring out.

Indigo turned and flashed Mr Hargreaves his most convincing smile before launching into the corridor without looking. He collided with someone – hard. Books went flying as his hand shot out by instinct, catching a slender wrist. He'd always had quick reflexes.

"Watch where you're going!" she snapped as he righted her. His eyes met hers, sapphire blue and long-lashed, and he couldn't stop the goofy grin from spreading on his face. It wasn't returned.

"Shit, I'm really sorry," he apologised, dropping her arm and swooping to pick up her books. Her hands moved to her hips as she narrowed her eyes at him. She was wearing her school uniform, of course, navy tartan skirt and a white shirt with a tie that matched his.

He'd definitely noticed Harper Valentine around, because who hadn't? She was wicked hot and she knew it. She pretty much ruled the school. But she was in the year above him in Year Nine and only dated older guys, so he'd never considered going there.

"I'm going to be late for class," she said impatiently as he finished gathering her books in a neat pile.

Before he even knew he was going to say it, the words were out. "Or you could skip class and come for a smoke? Let me make it up to you?"

She stared him down for a moment or two and he was sure she was going to shoot him down. But then she smiled.

"Well, that's the least you can do."

So he tucked her books under his arm and they snuck out to the gardener's shed.

"You got plans for the weekend?" he asked as he cupped his hand around the end of her ciggie and flicked the lighter. She inhaled deeply. The tin shed was gloomy. A ride-on mower was parked in one corner, and an array of well-used gardening tools hung from hooks on the wall above a muddy wheelbarrow. The earthen floor was littered with cigarette butts. He leant his shoulder into the corrugated wall, arms crossed as he gazed down at her. She really was gorgeous, with her long buttery hair, her skin like moonlight. She was fine-boned, like a dainty little sparrow.

"I assume you're going to the Prescotts' party?" she asked, smoke furling from her pouty lips. "I usually see you at those things."

"Yup, I'm obligated to go," he grinned. "Drew's my best mate." Drew Prescott was the youngest of three boys and his older brothers were notorious for their wild house parties. He took a drag of his ciggie as he pocketed the lighter. "You going?"

"No," she said, examining the cigarette clasped between two delicate fingers, "I'm being dragged to Melbourne for the weekend." She stared up at him. "For my uncle's funeral."

"Oh," he said, brows pinching. "I'm sorry to hear that. Were you close?"

"Pfft," she scoffed, eyes narrowing. "No."

He tried to get a read on her to see if that was true, but she was strangely impossible to decipher. Indigo couldn't only feel when others were sick or in pain, he could also sense their other feelings – sad, happy, scared, excited – if they felt an emotion in their body he could feel it in his.

But apparently not Harper's. And that intrigued him.

Right now, there was only one thing he wanted to be able to gauge in her and that was how she felt about him. But his talents had never extended to that. He'd never been able to feel what someone else felt *for* him. He knew how they felt in his presence and could presume from there, but right now, with Harper, he didn't want to make the wrong assumption.

"He's been in a coma for years. He was basically a brainless lump of broccoli," Harper said, her eyes large on his as if trying to determine whether she'd shocked him. "He had nothing left to give; he's better off dead." She finished her cigarette, dropping it to the floor and twisting her toe over it. "But now my parents are making me go play pretend happy families at the vego's funeral."

"Uh, ok," he said, wishing she wasn't such a closed book. "You don't get on with your folks?"

She stared at him in silence for so long he started to squirm. "We're not going to do *that* are we, Indigo?" she finally sighed.

"Do what?"

"Attempt to bond over our shitty parents." And that was the only time she mentioned his parents, alluded to the fact she knew who they were, that she understood they weren't what everybody thought they were.

Indigo was speechless. He never told anyone the truth about his parents – he didn't like to shatter the illusion. Nobody knew Indigo was essentially an orphan, raised by Edita who'd been hired as his nanny when he was a baby and had never left, her role morphing into guardian and housekeeper. Edita and her husband Lukas lived with Indigo at the Van Allen Estate up on Manly's Eastern Hill, but as much as the two of them cared for him, they were more a kindly aunt and uncle than anything resembling parents.

He didn't know how Harper knew that his parents weren't anything like the bullshit public images they projected. But for someone to know the actual truth? He needed that.

"Who are you, Harper Valentine?" he breathed, gazing at her in rapture.

"If I told you, *mon chéri*, I'd have to kill you," she smirked, hoisting herself up onto the rough-hewn workbench behind her, leaning back on her hands, swinging her legs gently as she looked up at him. She flicked her tie over one shoulder, the shirt buttons straining across her chest as she arched back and he gritted his teeth, forcing himself to focus on her eyes. When it came to girls, he was usually pretty good at figuring out what they wanted from him, what with his gift and all, but Harper, she was different. She made him almost… nervous?

In the end, she made it easy for him. She grabbed a fistful of his shirt, drawing him to her, crushing her lips to his, kissing him senseless. Legs clad in knee-high socks wrapped round his waist as she pulled him closer. She drew back after a while, studying his face.

"You really are to die for, Indigo Wolfe," she murmured, fingertips tracing the plane of his cheek. "I could stare at you for hours. Look at this bone structure, your head would look so pretty mounted on my wall," she said, hauling his lips back to hers, "like an exquisitely beautiful work of art."

Ok, that was a bit creepy, but she was so hot and her hands were everywhere and he didn't care.

"Just so you know," she said, releasing his lower lip from between her teeth, "I don't do relationships. I don't do *love*. And I certainly don't do younger guys." She grabbed his hair and yanked his head back, exposing his neck before attacking it with her mouth. "So you'd be well advised not to fall in love with me. It will only end in heartbreak."

So he and Harper weren't in a relationship because she didn't do relationships. Apparently she didn't do younger guys either, but that didn't stop her from doing him every day at lunchtime in the Australian History section of the school library where no one ever went, nor did it stop them spending every weekend together.

Being around Harper was easy in a lot of ways, because Indigo didn't have to make decisions anymore. He was happy to take the path of least resistance for a while. She was strong willed and opinionated and seemed to know exactly what he wanted. And she wanted to be with him all the time.

It was by no means perfect, but he did his best to ignore the imperfect parts. The way she spoke about other people behind their backs was a problem for him. It never occurred to Indigo to be mean to anyone. Because he knew how others were feeling, he often found himself lending a shoulder to someone having a bad day, or to someone in need of a friend. Helping someone else to feel a little better made him feel better. But it pissed Harper off no end.

"Indigo," she hissed one day when he was sitting in the corridor, back to the wall, knees bent up, talking to a Year Seven boy who'd been teased mercilessly when he'd come to school crying because his pet budgie had died in a fit of feathers in his cornflakes that morning.

"Indigo!" she hissed louder, more insistently.

He looked up then and saw her peering around the door to the library, beckoning him urgently. He stood and pulled the boy to his feet, squeezing his shoulder and telling him to come find him if he needed to talk more, before sauntering over to Harper.

"What's wrong?" he asked, brow creasing. She looked livid as hell.

"Why are you talking to that fat-arse loser?" she seethed through clenched teeth, yanking him roughly into the library and dragging him to the familiar dark corner where dusty tomes featuring Ned Kelly, the Eureka Stockade and the arrival of the First Fleet, filled the floor-to-ceiling shelves.

"H-huh?" he stammered.

"That four-eyed pile of lard. Why are you talking to him?" Her eyes glinted dangerously.

"Wow, nice, Harper, real nice," he said. "He's a twelve-year-old kid whose pet just carked it. How can you be so nasty?"

"How can you be such a doormat for all these dead-shit losers who invent excuses to be seen with you? Everyone knows you're with *me,* Indigo. Do you know how majorly my stock plummets every time you hang around with another one of these try-hards?" She shook her head, her long hair shimmering. "You need to stop being so selfish. Think of me for once in your life!"

"Seriously, Harps, are you kidding me?" he snapped. "How can you be so shallow?"

"Oh grow up, Indi! This is what I get for mucking around with someone younger. You're *such* a child!"

"If I'm so immature, maybe you should go find a real man, see if he likes being bossed around," he said, stepping past her to leave.

She grabbed his arm then, wrenching him around and he saw something akin to panic in her eyes. Panic and a vulnerability.

"No need to overreact," she said quickly. "I mean, you're not going to let that dweeby butterball come between us, are you?" she asked, tilting her head. "Because that would be a big, big shame…"

Her hand was snaking up his torso, unbuttoning his shirt, wandering inside, her nails scratching lightly over his pecs. "All I'm asking is that you put me first," she said, her lips now travelling up his throat. "Is that too much to ask? I'm sorry I got mad, but you know I tend to lash out when I'm hurt." She pulled back to pout at him, then leant in to kiss him, her tongue rolling leisurely over his.

He groaned, too distracted now to register what she was saying as she raked her hands up his thighs towards his fly. She knew how to press his buttons and had a way of wearing him down. Sure, she could be exhausting, but she always managed to reel him back in. One upside he found, of being with Harper, was he was always so tired after being around her all day, that he slept like a log at night in his enormous bed in his giant room inside his big old ivy-clad house. There was no tossing and turning and worrying about the state of his life and the world around him, which had consumed so many of his nights before she arrived on the scene.

He ignored the fact she was rude to the teachers. He ignored the fact she spoke down to Edita, that he'd had to ask her to leave his house and she was no longer welcome there. He ignored how quick she was to anger, like when he focused his attention on anyone else. If bitching behind people's backs was an Olympic sport, she could rep Australia and bring home the gold, and that he ignored too.

Afterwards, when the blood was restored to his brain and he could think rationally again, he tried to talk to her.

"We can't go on like this, Harps," he said as he fastened his belt. "I can't do it anymore." He didn't know if he loved her because he didn't know what that would even feel like, had nothing to compare it to. But this whole casual thing was doing his head in. He wanted more.

From her?

From someone.

He could be someone's whole world, couldn't he?

"Do what?" she asked, that vulnerability creeping back into her eyes as she gazed up at him.

"Be on and off with you," he sighed. "Either we're together or we're not. You act as though I belong to you, yet you refuse to put a label on it. I'm sick of all the games. Either you're my girlfriend, or we're nothing."

She went white. She shook her head then, shooting him a look of such revulsion he reeled back. And then she ran. He let her go, gasping in a raggedy breath, his hands trembling as a terrible thought consumed him. Harper had always had a way of just knowing things about him no one else did. She was really intuitive or something, had been from that very first day in the gardener's shed. A sudden wave of nausea rippled through him as he realised she might know the truth about him. That's why she wouldn't commit to him. That's why she was always pushing him away, trying to piss him off.

Could she know the secret he'd kept hidden from almost everyone forever? Why would she want to be with someone like him long-term? Why would anyone? He was damaged goods.

Because feeling other people's feelings, it wasn't the only thing about him that made him a freak.

A slip of a woman in a stiff grey dress opened the door when he knocked. Her face was a map of lines, her salt-and-pepper hair cut to shoulder-length curls.

"Yes?" she asked, peering all the way up at him. "Can I help you?" She had a jaded look about her, as though she'd seen it all and found it wanting.

"Uh, hi there, I'm looking for Harper?" he said, glancing over her shoulder into the foyer beyond. He'd never been inside Harper's house before and was curious about the interior of the palatial estate.

"And you are?"

"Indigo," he said. Her face lightened in a way that indicated she was aware of his existence.

"I am Fernanda." It was obviously in her job description to answer the Valentines' phone, because Fernanda was the one who picked up whenever he called.

"Fernanda! Nice to finally put a face to the name," he smiled.

She opened the door wide and invited him in, leading him to a formal sitting room off the foyer decorated in an austere monochrome palette. The ceilings were high, the furnishings sleek and minimalistic. Indigo felt a wave of loneliness shudder through his gut.

"Can I offer you a refreshment?" He wasn't planning on being there for long. He was done with Harper and her games. He just needed to find out what she knew about him and he'd be out of there.

"Ah no thanks, I'm good," he said as he took a seat on the sable sofa, which he quickly figured had been purchased for appearance, not comfort. She nodded curtly, then left. He glanced around but there wasn't much to look at besides a stack of travel brochures on the glass coffee table showcasing the azure waters and white sand beaches of Tahiti and Fiji. His eyes travelled to the picture-rail behind him, landing on the photo that sat there in a heavy silver frame. He stood and leant in. It was a picture of three little blonde girls, all dressed identically in pretty white dresses, the oldest maybe eight, the youngest probably four. He recognised Harper in the middle by her eyes. She must have been around five or six when it was taken. He frowned. Harper was an only child, so who were the other girls?

When Harper slipped in a few minutes later, she looked far from happy to see him. "What are you doing here?" she stage-whispered, glancing over her shoulder before firmly closing the door.

He crossed the room slowly towards her.

"You won't take my calls," he said, "I wanted to check you were ok. After this arvo." She'd looked so upset when she'd run out of the library. Despite everything, he'd been worried about her.

"You shouldn't *be* here," she said, fingering the tip of her school tie.

"Do you want me to go?"

She glowered at him silently, obviously battling some internal struggle. Before she could answer, the door opened and an elegant, middle-aged woman wandered in, her nose in a brochure for the Maldives. She was blonde and slim, her left arm in a heavy cast. When she looked up and saw them she stopped short, colour draining from her face as she stared at Indigo like a deer in headlights. He could see the heavy bruising around her eye and jaw she'd tried to cover with pancake make-up. He felt a sudden sharp pain in his ribs and realised a couple of hers were broken.

"Mama!" Harper snapped, stepping in front of her mother to shield her from Indigo's view. *"J'ai de la visite! Va-t'en!"*

Harper's mother flinched, then backed quickly out of the room. Harper slammed the door behind her.

"You didn't want to introduce me?" Indigo said dryly.

She stood stock still, staring at the floor.

"Harps?"

He noticed it then, her lip trembling.

"You shouldn't have come here," she whispered. She swiped at her eyes, sniffing. Oh shit. She was crying. All the time he'd known her, he'd never thought her capable of it. He reached for her and she jerked away, turning her back on him. Her shoulders began to shake. He felt terrible. He reached for her again and this time she didn't pull away when he spun her, drew her into his arms.

"I d-don't want you to see," she choked against his chest. He assumed she meant see her cry, so he was taken aback when she said, "I don't want anyone to ever see… what he does to her."

Her voice was so small. He tightened his arms around her as her whole body shuddered. They stood there for he didn't know how long as she sobbed in a way that made it clear she never let go of herself like this.

When she'd cried herself out, he led her to the couch, sat her down.

"Do you want some water?" he asked, peering into her face, swollen and blotchy. She shook her head. "Talk to me, Harps," he ventured, reaching for her hand. "Your mum… Her arm, her face… What happened?"

She stared at a spot on the geometric rug, her expression unreadable. "He hates her," she finally breathed. "He hates her so much."

"Who hates her?"

"My dad. Because, uh, of the accident." Her eyes moved then, landing on the photo of the three girls. "I-I'm not an only child, Indi," she said, her voice so low he had to strain his ears. "I mean, I *am*, but I wasn't always." She swallowed hard. "There was an accident. When I was seven. Mum was driving." Her gaze remained on that photo, glassy and unmoving. "We were fighting, my sisters and I. Ebony was nine, and Reign, she was four. It was my turn to sit in the front, you see, but Ebony the liar said it was her turn, and of course Mum believed her. Mum always believed Ebony, her *favourite child*. So she made me sit in the back with Reign. Ebony and me, we were screaming at each other, and Reign was crying, and Mum was yelling at us to stop. She was so worked up and there was a red light, but she didn't see it. I remember it so clearly, the force of the truck slamming into the passenger side of the car. And then, nothing…"

She closed her eyes, her face impassive. "I think I blacked out, because when I woke up, I was on a stretcher and there were people in uniforms all around me and when I turned my head I saw… I saw two small heaps lying there on the road, covered in white sheets. And I could hear my mother, although I didn't realise it was her at first because the sounds coming out of her, they sounded like something an animal would make." Indigo gripped her hands in his. That she'd gone through this, it made his heart ache.

"Afterwards, Dad couldn't cope. Apparently, he'd always had a drinking problem but had been sober for years. I'd always thought my father was a kind man. But when he's drunk, he's mean. And these days he's mean a lot."

"He doesn't hurt you, does he?" Indigo growled, anger swelling inside of him.

She shook her head vehemently. "It's his only way of coping, you see? After we lost Ebony and Reign… Well, Mum was driving. In his eyes, it must have been her fault. And while Mum always loved Ebony best, I was always Dad's favourite. And I didn't want to ruin that by admitting it wasn't all Mum's fault. And I often wonder, what if I hadn't been fighting with Ebony? What if she'd just let me sit in the front?" She scowled.

"You can't think that way, Harps. It happened the way it happened and you can't change that."

Her head popped up then and she was glaring at him, eyes stormy.

"Why did you have to come here?" she hissed. "Nobody knew! When we moved up here from Melbourne after the accident, we could start again. Nobody knew our tragic tale, nobody looked at us with *pity*. Here, I wasn't the poor little girl who lost her sisters in an accident! Here, I could be whole and strong. I could be whoever I wanted to be! And now you've gone and ruined all that!" Tears gathered in her eyes again and she blinked them away angrily.

He reached for her and she recoiled. He suddenly understood why she was the way she was. It made sense to him now, all of it, her nastiness, her inability to open herself up, to let others in. To let him in. It wasn't anything to do with him or what he was.

Hurt people hurt other people.

"Do you want me to go?"

Her face collapsed then and she shook her head as the tears started again.

"Please don't go," she whispered. "Please don't ever go."

He pulled her into his arms while she sobbed, rocking her gently and whispering to her. His heart went out to her. He could hardly break it off with her now. Instead, he'd stay. Because, for the first time in his life, someone needed him.

Indigo was lounging with his mates in his usual lunchtime spot on the wide sandstone steps of the fountain on the school's back lawn, when he noticed the boy from the corner of his eye. Tall and praying-mantis-lanky, the boy would start to approach, his eyes fixed on Indigo, then veer off at the last minute only to circle back around and attempt his approach again. Indigo and Drew had ditched the class before lunch for a choof in the gardener's shed and he was still a little stoned. He glanced at his mates, some sitting on the staggered steps, others on the grass at the fountain's base, but none of them seemed to have noticed the boy.

He felt a slow smile stretch his face as he watched the boy. He was in the year below, Indigo knew that, and his name was Robbie. Robbie Carlisle. He seemed a nice enough bloke, a little awkward, sure, but there was something about him that Indigo warmed to. He couldn't put his finger on it, but Robbie was different and Indigo had always had a soft spot for different.

Indigo eased himself up onto his elbows, his eyes trained on Robbie who now seemed to be muttering to himself. He held a fistful of paper in one hand as he circled round the back of a building, only to emerge on the other side of the fountain.

Indigo sat up and made eye contact with him and Robbie stopped dead, a blush blooming from his cheeks to the tips of his ears. Indigo lifted a hand and beckoned him over. Robbie stared at him for a moment or two, then glanced over his shoulder, then looked back at Indigo. "Me?" he mouthed, pointing at his chest.

Indigo nodded. "Come here."

Robbie hesitated for only a moment before he began his slow approach, this time coming in for landing. He stopped in front of Indigo and stared at him dumbly. Drew sniggered. Indigo elbowed him. "What's up, mate?" he asked.

Robbie opened his mouth, but nothing came out. He reddened further. He thrust his hand out towards Indigo, who saw the paper Robbie was carrying was a stack of invitations. Indigo reached for them. The minute his fingers closed around the edges, Robbie turned tail and bolted. The boys all burst out laughing.

"Give him a break, guys," Indigo chastised, staring after Robbie. He'd barely glanced at the invites when Harper appeared. "Hey, Harps," he said, stuffing the invitations in the pocket of his navy school blazer. She wordlessly poured herself onto his lap to straddle him, twining her fingers through his hair and kissing him in a way that made everyone in the vicinity shift uncomfortably and look away.

"Get a room," Drew muttered.

"Are you high?" she asked, extracting her lips from his and staring into his eyes, which he knew were probably still a little red-rimmed.

He shrugged. "Barely."

She rolled her eyes. "When are you going to grow out of this bullshit, Indi? You're so boring when you're stoned. Why do you do this to yourself?"

He gazed at her silently. He knew exactly why. But he couldn't tell her the truth – anyone the truth – without giving himself away. It wasn't just something he told people. He liked that people liked being around him, and if he told them, well, they might decide they didn't actually like him. Sure, like wasn't love, but at least he wasn't alone. Indigo was certainly never short of mates. Although it did keep him up at night, wondering how it was possible to have so many friends yet still be so desperately lonely.

Because whenever he was alone, the anger and the sadness and the darkness crept back in. He felt constantly disappointed in himself, like he wasn't good enough, and that was a thought that played in a loop inside his head. He worried a lot, alone in his big bed in his enormous room in the small hours of the morning. He worried about who he was and why he was here and what the point of his life was and if it was ever meant to be easy.

Indigo had grown adept at being who everyone else wanted him to be. He was good at smiling, good at fun, good at making others feel good. But then there were days he was too exhausted to keep up the charade, and on those days, he'd lay his head down on his school desk and close his eyes and wish the world away. Such behaviour would often earn him a chalkboard eraser to the head and an express pass to the headmaster's office, so he tried his hardest to minimise it at school. These days, he only skipped school when the pain he felt in his body was unbearable.

The thing was, to be around people, he had to numb himself. He hated having to feel what everyone else was fucking feeling all the fucking time. Walking down crowded school corridors and feeling the emotions, the pain of every single person he walked past, sitting in class and absorbing his classmates' aches and agonies, at times it was too much. The weed, it helped with that.

The day he realised he had the power to shut it all off was a Saturday arvo when he was thirteen. Drew had nicked one of his older brother's bongs and their stash of weed and brought them over, declaring, "Let's get radical!" with a mischievous grin. They'd waited for Edita to go out, then sat in the pool house, the bifolds thrown wide and spent the afternoon punching cones. At first it was hard not to cough as that deluge of sweet-scented smoke consumed his lungs, but once Indigo mastered that, he'd really liked the way it made him feel, the heavy relaxation that melted through him as the weed descended upon his mind and body with its mellowing caress. It stopped him overthinking. It stopped the judgement playing over and over in his head, the emotion perpetually bombarding his body, leaving only a lazy detachment. It worked much better than booze. When he was stoned his only worry was the quality of snacks available as he and his mates had a laugh over the latest episodes of *Seinfeld* or *Married… With Children*, as they lazed around his pool house, solving the problems of the world.

But Harper hated it. Since that day two months ago he'd learnt the truth about her family, things had shifted between them. It was like her opening up to him had flipped some sort of switch inside of her. He was now officially her boyfriend and that apparently meant he was at her beck and call twenty-four seven. Some days it felt like now he knew her secrets he was irrevocably tied to her 'til the end of time, whether he liked it or not.

"I'll see you at the gates at three, *mon chéri?*" Harper said, climbing off his lap.

"Yeah nah, I was gonna go for a surf with the boys," Indigo told her, wincing, waiting for the fall-out.

She tilted her chin and set her jaw, her eyes boring into his. Most days after school, they went back to her place to hang in the boathouse at the bottom of the sprawling waterfront property. But he'd missed his morning surf and he went crazy if he didn't get in the ocean every day.

Indigo sighed. He knew that look. It meant they were about to have a major blow-out. Nothing unusual about that these days, though. Harper was used to getting her way and when she didn't she lost her shit.

"Did you just *sigh* at me, Indigo Wolfe?" she demanded, eyes narrowing lethally.

His mates had stopped talking, glancing between him and Harper in wary anticipation. They all knew how this would go. A screaming match followed by her publicly dumping him, followed by her ignoring him for the rest of the week, followed by her finding out which parties he'd be going to that weekend and turning up with some hot older guy. She'd then fawn all over her date in Indigo's eyeline 'til he couldn't take it anymore, at which point he'd try to leave and she'd follow him, grab him and drag him into the nearest empty bedroom to make up. And so the cycle would begin all over again.

Drew asked him regularly why he always took her back. But Drew didn't understand. He didn't know the truth, that she needed him, that she was more than what she seemed. Sure, he didn't like pissing her off because the fights that followed totally sucked. But mostly, he wanted to help lessen the hurt inside of her. It was her sadness that had eroded her heart and made her mean. But when they were alone together, she smiled more; she relaxed and opened up. And she wasn't as mean these days. He made a difference to her.

He stood then, taking her hand and leading her away from prying eyes.

"Listen, Harps," he said, stopping under the shade of a Norfolk pine in the far corner of the schoolyard, reaching for her other hand, "we've talked about this. We can't be together all day, every day. I need time to hang with the boys, to surf. You need to not take that personally."

She stared sullenly at the ground, refusing to meet his eye. He squeezed her hands, craned his neck to catch her gaze. "You didn't come over yesterday either," she said softly, blinking hard. She finally lifted her eyes to his and they were hard as stone. "I saw you, you know, in the *carpark*. With that *bitch*."

He exhaled heavily. Great.

"She's not that bad, Harper," he said, struggling to keep his tone even. "And what did you want me to do? It was pouring with rain and she's like, pushing seventy." He dropped her hands, crossed his arms.

"*Not that bad?*" she snapped, voice rising. "What about what she did to us last week? The frigid old *dyke!* I bet she's never blown anyone in her life!" A group of Year Sevens walking past gaped at them, then fell all over each other, giggling as they scurried away.

"Can you keep your voice down?" he said through clenched teeth.

She glared after the Year Sevens, then turned back to him. In a quieter voice she said, "Well, it's true. If I can't get into the library, Indi, I can't finish my assignments and then I'll fail. But that's what the old cow wants, isn't it?" Mrs Critchard, the school's ancient librarian had banned the two of them from the library for life after she'd caught Harper on her knees doing apparently filthy things to him under the portrait of Captain Cook.

Late yesterday arvo when Indigo had been leaving school, he'd seen Mrs Critchard standing by her car in the torrential rain, wringing her gnarled hands and looking bewildered. The carpark had been deserted. He'd stayed back to help a kid from class with his maths homework and was meant to be heading to Harper's. He was already late, but he couldn't just leave the woman standing there. Night was falling and the rain was only getting heavier. As he'd approached Mrs Critchard, he'd been able to feel her rising panic.

"Everything ok, ma'am?" he'd called. A raincoat swathed her bulky frame and a scarf covered her head, but neither seemed to be doing much of a job of keeping her dry.

Relief had flooded her eyes as they landed on him. "Oh! Oh, Indigo, no, it's not. I seem to have procured a flat tyre," she'd said, kicking at the wheel, which he could now see was completely deflated. "There's a spare in my trunk but with my hands…" She'd trailed off as his eyes wandered to her knuckles, swollen and waxy white. His hands tingled and he'd winced, understanding how much hers throbbed.

He'd pushed his soaking hair out of his eyes. He'd forgotten his umbrella again. "Pop the boot for me, will you?" he'd said, moving round the back of the car.

"Oh, are you sure?" she'd asked, following him to unlatch it. He'd quickly located the jack and the spare, hoisting them out and chucking them on the ground.

He'd shrugged his school blazer off, handing it to her to hold.

"Where's your brolly? You're soaked to the bone, you'll catch your death in this," she'd said as he'd knelt down and positioned the jack beneath the car.

His shirt was already drenched through, sticking to his skin. He'd grinned up at her. "I think that ship has sailed. It's not possible for me to get any wetter right now, ma'am."

He hadn't realised Harper had been there, that she'd seen him. But she had and for some reason him helping Mrs Critchard had pissed her off royally.

"I came to get you," she said now. "I knew you were staying late and when it started raining, I asked Jack to drive me back to school to pick you up." Jack was the Valentines' chauffeur. He picked Harper and Indigo up most afternoons. "But when I got there, I saw you. With *her*."

"What, so you just bailed?"

She stared him down.

He pressed his lips together and glanced away, pocketing his hands. It was on the tip of his tongue to tell her he'd sweet-talked the librarian into lifting their ban, but he couldn't bring himself to give her the good news. He knew she was hurt he hadn't turned up at her place last night, but by the time he'd finished with the tyre he'd been filthy and chilled to the bone and all he'd wanted was a hot shower and an Edita dinner. He'd called to tell her he wasn't coming, but she'd refused to come to the phone.

The bell rang, signalling it was time to get to class. "I guess I'll see you tomorrow, then," Harper said. Her voice was soft, but there was venom in her tone. She spun on her heel and stormed off. He wished for the umpteenth time he could feel what she was feeling.

"I'll stop by your place later on, ok?" he called after her. "After my surf."

"Don't do me any favours," she snapped over her shoulder. "Far be it from me to *force* my boyfriend to want to see me."

He sighed again. She seemed to bring that out in him. His fingers brushed the invitations he'd stuffed into his pocket earlier. He extracted them, unfolding the top one so he could read it. And as he did, he immediately knew he really wanted to go to this party.

Because Robbie's name wasn't the only one on the invitation.

chapter two

like a prayer

harbord, new south wales, june, 1990

cordelia

She ducked through the weathered stone doorway and out into the baking sunshine. In her hands was an earthen bowl of food covered by a cloth. She smiled to herself, knowing how pleased he'd be with what she'd prepared for him. She loved nothing more than making him happy. She rubbed her swollen belly as she walked, thinking how much happier they were soon to become, if that were possible. As she approached the apiary she saw him, bent over one of the hives, his back to her. She smiled, as she slipped her shoes off, all the better to sneak up and surprise him. She was so focused on his shirtless form, the muscles straining in his brown back, that when the sharp pain came she cried out, dropping the bowl and grabbing her foot, rubbing at the stinger the bee had left behind. She coughed, clearing her throat because suddenly there was something lodged there. She coughed again as whatever it was grew, constricting and tightening. And her hands. Her arms. Large red welts were growing and spreading. No air. Her lungs burnt. He was coming. She heard him yelling. And then she was in his arms, and they were on the ground, and he was yelling and he was crying, but her throat was swollen shut and there was no air and then, the black…

The door flew open with a bang and Cordelia jerked awake, heart hammering, eyes wide. It took her a moment to clock her bearings, to realise she was safe at home on her bed, to see Robbie hovering there in her doorway, eyebrow raised, lip curled.

"What the…? Were you *sleeping?*"

"Mmmm…" she mumbled, foggy, disoriented. "I-I was just resting my eyes." She eased herself up onto her elbows, blinking the drowsiness away.

"Well come *on*, Cora, they'll all be here soon," he said excitedly, his mood quickly chameleoning. "You need to start getting ready!"

"I *am* ready," she said, smoothing the creases from her white turtleneck crop top.

His delicate nose wrinkled. "Ew. That's not seriously what you're wearing?"

She shot him her most withering look as she slid off the bed, padding over to the full-length mirror on her wardrobe door, head tilted to one side as she examined her reflection. "What's wrong with what I'm wearing?"

"*Jeans,* Cordelia? To our *thirteenth* birthday party? Ew. I can't believe I once shared a womb with you." He pushed his lanky body through the door, deftly stepping over piles of discarded clothes and dog-eared books and magazines and cassette tapes to stand in front of her. He crossed his arms, his brown eyes sweeping her from head to toe. His hair was so crunchy with gel it didn't waver a millimetre despite the vigour with which he clucked his tongue and shook his head.

She clenched her jaw. They were pretty great jeans. "You're the one who insisted I spend all my allowance on them," she sighed as she sank back down onto the end of her bed, a plush confection of ivory and white.

"Well, yes, Calvin Klein warrants every last cent of your savings," he declared, striding to her wardrobe. "Ok, I can work with the jeans. But that top, it's gotta go."

He rummaged through the hangers, muttering under his breath. He yanked out a black bodysuit with a flourish. It was low at the front with a three-quarter sleeve and sat just off the shoulder. "Try this," he ordered, turning his back so she could change.

"Much better," he nodded when he turned a moment later. He made a beeline for her shoe-rack, hands on hips as his eyes moved back and forth past Converse sneakers and thongs and Doc Martens before landing on a pair of black platform heels, totteringly high. He handed them to her, then leant back to study her, chin in hand. "What are we doing about that bed-head?" he asked, reaching to finger the treacle-blonde tresses that tumbled down her back in tangled waves.

She pulled away, narrowing her eyes. "You just get your dirty mitts off my hair." She bit her lip to keep from smiling.

"Tonight has to go perfectly, Cora, you know that," he said, brow furrowed, hands wringing.

She exhaled heavily as it dawned on her the impromptu makeover was his way of keeping the anxiety at bay. "Ok, ok," she relented, reaching to steady his hands. "You can do my hair."

"Yay!" he cried, clapping in delight and she smiled in spite of herself.

Now on a mission, he led her to the white-washed dresser and sat her down, reaching for her brush. He went to work pulling sections away from her face, twisting them and pinning them in place. He left the back down, then eased a few tendrils out to frame her face, brushing the lengths out 'til they shone. He stood back to regard his handiwork, nodding in approval. "I may be seven minutes younger, but I'm majorly wiser when it comes to this stuff."

She rolled her eyes.

"Wherever would you be without me?" Robbie asked, squeezing her shoulders from behind, his eyes meeting hers in the mirror.

"In a lot less danger of rolling an ankle," she shot back, wistfully eyeing the sensible options dominating her shoe-rack.

"Beauty is pain," he grinned, resting his chin on her head. "Hey, Cora?" he ventured, suddenly serious. "I overheard Dad telling Mum you were up wandering the house again last night." He chewed his bottom lip as he regarded her. "Everything ok?"

She absently fingered the ring her mother had presented to her in a box that morning, whispering happy birthday as Cordelia had gazed at the etched white-gold band in awe. "Yup," she said tightly, averting her gaze and shrugging him off. She turned her attention to choosing a lip gloss from her dresser drawer. "Fine."

"I mean, you'd tell me, right? If anything was wrong?" he probed, swatting the lip gloss she'd chosen from her hand and selecting another.

She shrugged.

"It's the nightmares again, isn't it?" His tone was stern.

She stiffened, then quickly composed herself, but his eagle eye didn't miss it.

"Tell me?"

"It's *fine*, Rob. Seriously, I just couldn't sleep."

He narrowed his eyes. "I call bullshit," he said, glancing at his watch. "Bu-ut… I have to go pretty myself up." He backed towards the door. "To be continued," he said, pointing a finger at her. As the door clicked shut behind him she dropped her head to the dresser, her breath heavy, a knot of fear clenching her stomach as flashes of nightmare pressed forcefully into her mind: the sudden sharp sting to her foot, the rapid swelling of her throat, her lungs burning for oxygen.

Last night she *had* been up wandering the house. It was because she'd had the nightmare where she was fixed in place while flames licked and bit her flesh, melting it from her bones, thick smoke choking her so she couldn't scream out the agony. That one always had her flicking on every light within reach and pacing the house for hours.

She lifted her head, gazing vaguely at her reflection in the mirror. Her eyes looked dull. She didn't know if she was excited or apprehensive about tonight. Maybe both. Robbie had begged their parents for a house party, as *anyone* who was anyone had a house party for their birthday. He'd been struggling to make friends at school and seemed convinced this party would change everything.

Robbie and Cordelia had started at the sprawling sandstone campus of North Head Grammar at the beginning of the year. The transition hadn't been too difficult for Cordelia as a lot of her friends from primary school were already there, but Robbie, with his awkward gangliness and a sense of humour you either got or you didn't, as always, was having difficulty finding his place.

Their parents had eventually given in and consented to the party – under the mortifying condition their presence was made to be felt. Robbie had declared he'd die if anyone from school caught a glimpse of an adult at their big bash. Cordelia totally agreed with him. But since it was that or nothing, they'd had no choice but to reluctantly concede.

Cordelia had stood back and allowed Robbie to take total control of the party planning. Until he'd started making noises about renting a karaoke machine.

Cordelia had begged him to reconsider. Karaoke was for old people and a recipe for epic disaster. But Robbie refused to listen to reason. Unfortunately, their parents were going through a phase of being overly supportive of Robbie (an overcompensation for the bullying he was enduring at school), and Cordelia had been outvoted.

Robbie had designed an invitation on the computer and printed it out and the twins had distributed it to their classmates. Their dad had arranged for some of his colleagues from the hospital to come and help him play bouncer for the night and their guests had been informed that nobody would get in without a physical invitation in their hand. So embarrassing.

Cordelia and Robbie had sixty invitations to hand out to their friends. They'd agreed on the first fifty-five guests, but it was the last five they couldn't see eye-to-eye on.

News of what Robbie had done with those five final invites had reached Cordelia before Robbie could tell her himself.

Cordelia knew Robbie had always been in awe of Indigo Wolfe, who was a year above them in school. As far as she knew, Robbie had never spoken two words to Indigo, yet he was always talking about him. But to be honest, most of the school usually was.

"Did you hear Indigo's in Paris again?" Robbie would say to her. "On one of his mum's movie sets, how unreal is that?" or "Did you see Indigo's Reebok Pumps? You can't even get those in Australia yet! I bet his dad sent them from New York."

Robbie tended to get particularly over-excited when there was juicy goss, like the other day when he'd sought her out in the school hallway, grabbing her arm and dragging her against the lockers. "So word is," he'd said under his breath, eyes shining as he leant in, "that Indigo and his mates were getting high at the skate park again last weekend and Sandy Whitcomb attempted to do a Marty McFly and tow himself behind a car on his board, but he was majorly stoned and he wiped out and now he's in hospital!" She'd already heard that from about five other people, but had pretended to look suitably aghast for Robbie's sake.

To be honest, Cordelia didn't know quite what to make of Indigo.

Sure, she got the superficial fascination. Indigo was what you got when the surreally beautiful people of Hollywood procreated. He was absurdly good-looking, tall, with the muscular frame of someone who spent a lot of time in the water.

She didn't really give a crap about the exotic holidays, the new skateboards, surfboards, jet skis and dirt bikes their classmates were always gossing about. Or that he knew how to score bourbon and beer and ciggies, that he had all the latest movies often before they even hit the cinemas, or that his house was apparently like a six-star resort with a pool and a theatre and a gym and limited adult supervision. And who his parents were, yeah, it was cool, but she wasn't blubberingly star-struck like everybody else seemed to be.

She'd noticed he was absent from school sometimes. Migraines, her classmates whispered, headaches so bad they kept him confined to a dark room, but she gathered that was merely supposition. Sometimes she saw him just sitting, gazing into space, a vague stare dominating his handsome features and she wondered what was going on inside.

Her friends had no subtlety whatsoever, gawking at him with googly eyes and giggling when he passed by. But Cordelia just observed him, trying to figure him out. Because beneath all that bravado, she sensed a kind of sadness lurking there.

But she told herself she couldn't be right, that it didn't make sense. People craved being around Indigo; he was trailed by an endless entourage of admirers twenty-four seven. And it sure looked like he got everything he wanted, even though he seemed pretty unaffected by it. Sure, he was playfully cocky, but he wasn't up himself and she'd never heard of him being an arsehole. She'd seen him diffusing punch-ups in the hallways. She'd seen him quietly partnering up with the kids no one else wanted to partner with for school projects.

When Cordelia found out Robbie had accepted a dare from their classmates to give their remaining five invitations to Indigo, she was less than thrilled. But not overly concerned. She knew Indigo and his mates rocking up to a party (somewhere on a messy scale of a-little-smashed to completely-hammered) instantly cemented it as the place to be. But as if he'd come to theirs! It was hardly going to be a major rager and he had his pick of parties.

"He totally called me over, Cora!" Robbie told her, eyes shining. "He said, like, 'What's up mate?'" He frowned then. "And as much as I'd like to tell you that I gave some super slick response, my mind went blank, so I basically threw the invites in his face and cut and run. Not my finest moment," he mused.

"So, is he coming or not?" Cordelia asked. Robbie merely shrugged. It didn't state it was a karaoke party on the invitation, so as far as Indigo knew, he'd been invited to a regular house party. That freaked her out a little. If by some small chance he bothered to show, Indigo would totally bring his mates, probably even his girlfriend, who was stunning as hell but quite frankly scared the crap out of Cordelia. Robbie had just invited the coolest kids in school to a karaoke party and she feared that what he believed could be a triumph might actually be social suicide.

"You can't control other people," her dad always told her. "You've gotta let them make their own mistakes in life because that's how they'll learn." He was totally wise with shit like that. And now their big party was tonight and it seemed she had no choice but to let Robbie sink or swim.

chapter three

i'm on fire

indigo

Indigo lay back on his bed gazing at the invite in his hand, wondering for the umpteenth time if it was worth it. As he'd expected, Harper had been ropeable when he'd told her he wanted to go. But for some reason it wasn't the fact it was a Seventh Grade party, or that Robbie was throwing it that had pissed her off. It was Robbie's co-host that had riled Harper up. Not that she'd say why.

Cordelia.

Indigo thumbed his lip thoughtfully as he stared out a window of his spacious bedroom, his eyes drawn past the expansive backyard to the sun glittering on the harbour below. He'd first noticed Cordelia one lunchtime a few months back. Her friends had giggled when he'd walked by and, instead of ignoring them as usual, he'd glanced up. And sitting there, perfectly still amongst the giggly masses, was an ethereal girl with clear aquamarine eyes fixed so solemnly upon him, her cheekbones high, her lips full. She was wearing her school uniform, obviously, and her hair, a tiger's eye of gold and caramel and blonde, was caught up in a high ponytail that hung in unruly waves over one shoulder. His step had faltered and he'd smiled at her, an instinct really, as he pondered where he knew her from. She'd held his gaze for a moment or two and then her mouth had turned up ever-so-slightly in the shyest of smiles before she'd turned away from him to the girl next to her as if to resume an important conversation his sudden appearance had interrupted.

He'd asked around and found out who she was and who her friends were, and that she and Robbie had only started at North Head Grammar that year. He didn't know why she'd piqued his curiosity so acutely. But occasionally he found himself walking the long way round at lunchtime, passing by where she sat with her friends. He'd stare at her until she'd stop what she was doing and look up at him, and their eyes would meet and he'd smile at her. She never fully smiled back, always giving him that elusive hint of a smile in return.

She didn't run with the super popular crowd, but she seemed to be friends with everyone, unlike her brother, who didn't really seem to belong anywhere except with her. He saw her in the hallways talking to kids from all different years and groups, kids Harper wouldn't be caught dead talking to. He saw the way she hugged her friends, how her hand lingered to warmly stroke their backs, how she peered intently into the eyes of the person talking to her, giving them her full attention, letting them know what they had to say was important.

And she took on anyone who targeted her brother in an instant, hands on hips, eyes flashing. And he felt envious. Imagine having her in his corner!

He saw how close she and Robbie were. He watched from afar one rainy day as Cordelia accidentally dropped her lunch in a puddle, so Robbie carefully divided everything inside his brown paper bag to give his sister half. He watched Cordelia pull Robbie over to sit with her and her friends on days he seemed to be at a loose end. It must be something else, having a twin, someone whose birthright it was to care about you.

So yesterday, when Harper had asked him what they were doing that weekend, he'd told her they'd been invited to a party in Harbord. Of course, she'd wanted to know all the details, and of course she'd deemed the party beneath her and started to arc up. But Indigo had clenched his mouth and shaken his head and told her in no uncertain terms he was going and she could either come with him or find another way to spend her Saturday night. He must have looked determined because for the first time in their relationship, she'd relented with a huffy, "Fine!" He had a feeling he'd be paying for it for a long time to come.

There was a knock at his door and he glanced up. "Yeah, come in."

The door opened and Edita stuck her head into his pin-neat room. "Do you want lunch, Indi?" she asked, her words accent laden. As always, she was dressed in a plain dark dress, her mousey-brown hair pulled back in a severe bun, her face scrubbed clean. The only jewellery she wore was a fine gold necklace, its pendant buried in the deep recesses of her generous bosom.

"Thanks, Edie," he smiled, hooking his elbow behind his head as he re-settled into the soft charcoal linens that dressed his king bed.

"Ok, I will fix you something." He gave her the thumbs up and she shut the door behind her. Indigo smiled fondly after her, wondering for the umpteenth time what he'd do if she ever decided to leave. He remembered the day when he was six, when Edita had sat him down after school and told him she was getting married. She'd been nervous, wringing her apron between thick fingers as she perched beside him on the couch.

"You're not leaving me, Edie?" he'd asked, wide-eyed, his hand creeping into hers. His heart beat a steady thrum as a panic rose to rush in his ears. "If you leave, where will I go?" He knew no one else wanted him, that was for sure. He'd spent time the previous July at his father's place in Manhattan and he'd only seen the man twice those ten days. As for his mother, he'd asked Bernadette as she was last leaving if he could come live with her in LA but she'd wrinkled her nose before replying that her lifestyle was not suitable for a child and he was better off in Sydney. She'd then told him she'd see him in Aspen in January, which meant she wasn't coming home for Christmas again that year. He'd burst into tears then and encroached upon her, his arms held wide, and she'd wrinkled her nose again and side-stepped him, calling for Edita to come and take him whilst decrying the effects of snot on silk.

"No, no, Indi," Edita had said, her eyes warm as she'd stiltedly patted his hand. "I'm not going anywhere. Lukas will move in here." Relief had flooded Indigo's body and he'd collapsed against her, squeezing his eyes shut. "Yes, yes, it's ok," she'd murmured, her hands stiff as she'd awkwardly stroked his hair.

"Ok, good," he'd said, pulling back to stare up at her thoughtfully. "Which room do you think we should give Lukas? The one next to mine is nice and big!"

Edita had smiled, her pale eyes softening with affection. "That's a very kind thought, Indigo, but Lukas will share my room."

"I like Lukas," Indigo had said. Lukas had looked after the gardens on the Van Allen Estate for two years by then and he was always nice to Indigo and let him help with the leaf blower sometimes. He was funny and loud, and he spoke like Crocodile Dundee. Lukas watched Indigo once a week when Edita had her book club meeting and he always made him popcorn and played *Guess Who?* with him. "He makes you happy and I like it when you're happy."

"What do you mean?" she'd asked. "I've always been perfectly happy."

He'd regarded her closely and shaken his head. "No," he'd disagreed. "You've always felt a bit sad inside. The lonely waves, they come sometimes and they take you."

The smile had slipped a bit from her face as she'd reached a rough hand out to cup his cheek. "Extraordinary," she'd muttered under her breath.

That all felt like a lifetime ago.

He crossed his ankles, giving the invitation one more look before propping it on his bedside table. His thoughts moved back to Harper and he wondered if relationships were meant to be this hard, this stressful. He didn't know what was worse, the yelling and the screaming, or when she went all cold and silent like she had yesterday. The silent treatment usually meant something was bubbling under the surface, bubbling and simmering 'til it hit boiling point and inevitably exploded all over him.

The truth was, the bad days with Harper had been outnumbering the good lately. And as much as she'd started opening up to him, he realised he hadn't returned the favour. The truth was, he was too scared. To tell her about the freak show side of him. About knowing everybody's feelings.

He certainly hadn't told her about the disembodied voices he heard.

Maybe he didn't need to. The thing was, he kind of had it under control now — the voices at least — because they didn't come quite so often and they weren't nearly as loud or intrusive as they once had been.

His whole life they'd come in cycles. They'd start far away, a blur of white noise in the background he could block out. When he was small, he'd imagined there was a bubble around him, keeping the voices away, on the outside of it. But as time went on, the bubble would shrink smaller and smaller, the voices coming closer and closer until they were so close they could touch him. A cacophony of noise so loud he couldn't think straight or even function or sleep.

And after those sleepless nights, the voices would get even worse. So he'd tell Edita he was too sick to go to school and he'd lie there all day, his knees curled into his chest, the curtains drawn. Edita would often call his grandmother on days like that and she'd come down to visit, always with a gift for him and she'd sit by his bed and he'd start to feel better. But she hadn't been in such a long time, well over a year now. But the voices hadn't been so bad in that long, too.

He plucked at the bracelet on his wrist, black leather beaded with obsidian and tourmaline, as he wondered what to do about Harper. Indigo had had plenty of girlfriends, but he'd never been in love before, so he didn't know how it was meant to feel. If he was honest, he didn't really know how love itself was really meant to feel. His parents didn't love him, that he knew. It was what it was. He had Edita, but she was really only capable of loving him in her arms-length Eastern European way. Lukas was a top bloke but was more of a mate than anything else. And of course there had been Sarita, but she was long gone.

Sarita.

She'd been his night-time nanny when he was little.

Until Sarita, no one had ever told him he was special – not his mother or Edita. Certainly not the voices. When he was small, he'd gotten along with those voices. But only for a short while, before he realised it wasn't fucking normal, until the bubble shrunk and they got greedy and demanding of him, consuming his every waking hour... And then he'd cry, his head pounding from the agony of the never-ending noise.

He'd sob to Sarita then that they hurt his head. "You have been blessed with so many gifts, my beautiful Indigo," she'd told him when he was three. "Nothing is without its reason, my dear one."

She'd told him not to be ashamed that he was different, because he was special. But she'd also told him not many would understand. "Only tell those you truly trust, darling one," she would say, "those you know will love you unconditionally."

So he told no one but her.

But Sarita had been gone since he was twelve.

And he doubted Harper loved him at all, let alone unconditionally. So he continued to keep his secrets to himself.

chapter four

under the milky way

harbord, new south wales, june, 1990

cordelia

That night, Cordelia's dad and three of his mates gathered out the front of their two-storey grey weatherboard armed with torches to undertake their bouncer duties. They had a clipboard with a list of names they planned to mark off as each kid handed over their invitation. No gate crashers on their watch, they bragged. Dad was usually pretty strait-laced, but his mates had brought a few good bottles of red wine and she overheard Mum scolding them for being three sheets to the wind before the party even started. Cordelia wondered how strict that meant they were going to be. Yet again, she wished Robbie hadn't given those invitations to Indigo. Yeah, she wanted him to come – kind of – but not with all his mates. And Harper. Please, not Harper.

The turnout was good. Bloody good, in fact. She'd heard from a few early arrivals that Indigo had told people it's where he and his crew would be. There were a lot more than the sixty guests they'd invited and Cordelia guessed rumours of Indigo's attendance had prompted the illicit use of photocopiers all over the Northern Beaches to get around the 'Entry by Invite Only' clause.

By eight o'clock the backyard was bursting with teenagers, a lot from the years above, many far too stoned or plastered for how young the night was, others playing the long game with ice-filled backpacks stuffed with Crown Lagers and Sub Zeros, all of them majorly pumped for a big night.

Robbie had squealed when Indigo sauntered in fashionably late with his friends, including his best mate Drew Prescott. Cordelia's stomach dropped when she spotted Harper Valentine, Indigo's hand clasped possessively in hers, her nose wrinkled and her lip curled as she surveyed the party she'd clearly been dragged to against her will. While Indigo was casually fine, his powerful frame clad in a snug white t-shirt, worn jeans, his trademark sheepskin-collared denim jacket and his much-coveted Timberland boots, Harper looked like a freakin' supermodel in a purple mini dress and sky-high patent heels. They stood under the frangipani tree in the back corner of the yard, Harper draped all over Indigo. Cordelia watched as Harper threw her head back in laughter over something Drew had just said. Drew was almost as tall as Indigo, and arguably as hot with his wavy dark hair and his sky-blue eyes. He was a star rugby player and had the crooked nose to prove it.

Indigo unwound himself from Harper and wandered over to say hi to someone Cordelia didn't know. Cordelia glanced around and bit her lip. There were a *lot* of people she didn't know here, a lot of kids she didn't go to school with. She shrugged and turned back to her friends; she was happiest hanging with her people, particularly her two besties: Sian and Peyton.

At the front of the yard up against the house stood the raised stage her dad had helped Robbie knock together over the past couple of weekends. To the right of the stage, in the shadows, sat the evil karaoke machine. Cordelia wanted to put the hose on that thing. Or at the very least, hide its power cord. She'd begged Robbie earlier that night to forget about the stupid machine, but once he had his mind set on something…

"Ciggie?" Peyton asked, producing a pack of Winnie Blues from her purse and offering them around. Cordelia glanced towards the house and shook her head. Knowing her luck, her mum would pop out the minute she lit up, or worse, her dad, who'd lecture her 'til the end of time with a million revoltingly graphic lung cancer stories from work. Sian's boyfriend Will took one, leaning down to touch its end to the lighter Peyton had flicked alight, cupping his hands around the flame. He took a deep drag and slung his arm around Sian's narrow shoulders.

From the corner of her eye Cordelia saw Robbie mince onto the stage, proudly sporting black parachute pants MC Hammer would have died for and a shiny vest in tones of muted red and yellow worn over a black shirt. He was clutching a microphone in his hand. She tried to push her way through the crowd to stop him, but there were far too many people and she could barely walk in her towering heels. She sighed heavily and gave up, returning to her friends.

"Ahem," she heard the microphone screeching in protest. "Ahem. Hello? Is this thing on?" Robbie asked.

Unfortunately, it was.

The chatter of the crowd faded to stunned silence as everyone looked at Robbie. They could feel it in the air: something big was about to happen. A few of the older boys sniggered. The middle-aged balding man who'd come with the karaoke machine and was also proudly in charge of the spotlight, swung it onto Robbie, centre stage.

"What's up, guys?" Robbie continued confidently. "Welcome to our thirteenth birthday party!" He held his arms wide. "Now, I have a little surprise for everyone tonight."

The kids in the audience exchanged amused glances and Cordelia died a little inside.

"What in God's name is your brother doing?" Peyton demanded through the cigarette clenched between her teeth. A look of confusion screwed up her face, creasing her thick foundation. "Did you know about this?" She tucked a bright red corkscrew curl behind her ear and glanced at Cordelia, who exhaled wearily and nodded.

"This is no ordinary party," Robbie paused for effect. *"It's a karaoke party!"* Then, "Hit it!" The man fired up the machine and Robbie launched into an off-key rendition of New Kids on the Block's *You Got It (The Right Stuff)*, complete with dance moves.

The other kids' mouths dropped open in a staggered fashion reminiscent of a Mexican wave as they stared up at Robbie, all arms and legs and feet.

"Not the best choice of song, Rob," Cordelia muttered under her breath as his voice cracked and wobbled, evidence the stuff he had was most certainly very wrong. The karaoke had always been a bad idea. But now it was actually happening, it was worse than anything she could have imagined.

Cordelia heard laughter behind her and glanced around to see Harper and two of her friends standing there, watching Robbie in gleeful disgust.

"Oh my God, this is like, both the best thing and the worst thing I've ever seen," Harper sniggered, her hand covering her mouth.

"It's a complete train wreck," one of her friends added, peeping between splayed fingers. "I can't look away! Why oh why can't I look away?"

Harper winced as Robbie attempted a high falsetto. "Jordan Knight would be turning in his grave right now."

"Jordan's not dead," her friend replied.

"If he heard this, he'd wish he was," Harper shot back with a smirk. "This is the last time I let Indi choose our weekend activities. His taste in, er, *acquaintances* is beyond shocking. Do you know I actually saw not one dad here tonight, but like *four?*"

"Oh my god I know, right?" the friend replied. "Like how *embarrassing*. As if you'd let your parents set foot in your party. And can someone get that tone-deaf loser off the stage before I go all van Gogh and totally rip my own ears off?"

Cordelia could feel the blood draining from her face, flowing into the fists clenching at her sides. She swung around to say something, but Peyton beat her to it.

"Hey, Harper," Peyton snapped, chucking her ciggie butt and stepping towards her. "I know that nose cost your parents a fortune, but why don't you go stick it elsewhere and leave Robbie alone!"

Harper gasped, her hand moving to her nose, her gaze toxic as she glared at Peyton. "I'll have you know I had a deviated septum, you *slut!*" Everyone knew Harper's parents had given her a nose job for her fourteenth birthday, but Harper was determined to stick with the deviated septum story.

Peyton laughed. "Sure you did," she said, hands on generous hips as she looked Harper up and down.

Harper turned her attention to Cordelia, who'd moved to flank Peyton. "Why don't you muzzle your loser brother and your fat-arse bushpig friend here too, while you're at it?" she snapped at Cordelia, glancing up at the stage where Robbie was still singing and dancing his heart out.

A tumble of fury crashed down over Cordelia, her mind awash with so many things she wanted to say to Harper, all jostling for position at once, rendering her speechless. As she stood there, her eyes locked on Harper's, a muffled silence fell to cloak her so all she could hear was the sound of her own breath, the blood rushing in her ears. Harper's eyes grew more and more lethal by the moment, her face whitening considerably, her mouth growing thin and hard with rage as everything else faded away until only the two of them seemed to exist. Cordelia felt consumed, unable to break away. Whatever was between the two of them seemed palpable, a living, writhing thing. And in that moment, she knew exactly what Harper thought of her. She narrowed her eyes, her mind swarming with reciprocal thoughts which suddenly seemed so deafeningly loud.

"Ew, Harps, your nose!" one of Harper's friends suddenly cried out and the connection between them broke. The sounds and sights of the party rushed back over Cordelia. She slowly blinked, shook herself off. A solid stream of blood was spurting from Harper's nostrils.

Cordelia's eyes widened, but before she could open her mouth to offer help, Harper shot her one last look of ferocious wrath, then turned and hurried off clutching her nose, her chin tilted to the sky. Cordelia was reeling, lightheaded, feeling as if she'd been shaken from her body. It suddenly dawned on her the stunned hush that had descended over the party when Robbie got up on stage had morphed into reverberating booing and jeering. She whirled around to see what was happening. Robbie's face flamed red as someone yelled, "Get off the stage, fag!"

Forgetting Harper and her friends, Cordelia pulled herself together and aggressively elbowed her way up and onto the stage, grabbing Robbie's arm and pulling him off and out of sight – but they could still hear the laughing and the heckling, mocking cries of "Loser!" and "Poofter!" ricocheting like bullets.

White spots of fury swarming before her eyes, Cordelia swung to storm back out to confront the crowd, but Robbie gripped her hand in a pincer-like vice. "Please don't," he choked. She turned back to him. He looked stunned, close to tears. "They didn't like it," he whispered, bewildered.

"I told you they wouldn't, baby bro," Cordelia sighed gently. "I may be only seven minutes older, but I'm majorly wiser when it comes to this stuff." She forced a whisper of a smile.

The throng had now joined in a collective stomp-and-clap chant of "Rob the knob!" over and over.

Mum came striding out of the house like a pissed off bohemian goddess, skirts flowing, feet bare, blonde hair streaming. "What in the *hell* is going on out here?" she demanded, the line between her brows deepening.

"The karaoke didn't go down too well, Mum," Cordelia explained tersely. "Like I *tried* to *tell you* it wouldn't."

"It's a *disaster!*" Robbie cried.

Mum stared up at him in shock. "Those kids are out there yelling hateful things and all you care about is that the party's a disaster?"

Robbie's lower lip quivered, his eyes filling as he lowered them to the ground. "They ah…" he stammered, his voice cracking, "they say that stuff to me every day, Mum," he finished.

The colour drained from her lovely face as she swept him into her arms, tears spilling down her cheeks. "I didn't realise it was so bad," she murmured, reaching on tiptoe to pepper his face with kisses. She turned to Cordelia. "Did you?"

Cordelia stared at her for a moment or two in baffled silence. "You knew he was being bullied," she finally managed. "What did you think was going on?"

"It's fine," Robbie said, pulling away and swiping roughly at his eyes, glancing around to make sure no one could see them. "It is what it is. I'm used to it, ok? They say it all the time. I barely even hear it anymore." He peered out around the side of the stage. "It's just… it's just I guess I thought that tonight I'd be able to change their minds about me. That they'd have the best night and then they'd… they'd *like* me." The cracks in his heart were visible on his face. Cordelia put her arm around him, rubbing his back in gentle circles. She didn't have it in her to remind him life wasn't a Hollywood underdog tale.

"Enough is *enough*," Mum seethed as the shatter of bottles being thrown joined the cacophony. "This is getting out of hand. I'll go get Dad and the boys. The party's over. These little shits all need to leave." She stormed off in a cloud of swishing skirts and essential oils.

Robbie turned to Cordelia, stricken. "If Mum and Dad make a big scene and chuck everybody out, we'll never live it down! Like *ever!*

Can't you go talk to them? Beg them not to? We can fix this, we can." He frowned thoughtfully. "Put some music on or something?"

The chanting was getting louder and people were beginning to push and shove. Cordelia was freaking out now. Yes, this would go down as the worst party in the history of North Head Grammar and no one would ever let them forget it, but that paled in comparison to the fact things were actually starting to spiral.

Just then, she saw the crowd parting to let someone through. A tall figure with dark blond hair had pushed his way to the stage and was leaning over to talk to the karaoke machine man.

The next thing she knew, Indigo Wolfe vaulted boldly onto the stage. He stood confidently, feet apart, centre stage and defiantly faced the jeering masses head-on. The noise began to fade, the crowd gradually falling still and silent, staring at him expectantly. With a mischievous grin and a glint in his eye, he gave the man a head jerk, and the opening chords of *Under the Milky Way* filled the yard. Indigo stepped up to the microphone, grabbing it with both hands, and, closing his eyes for a beat or two, he began a performance that arguably rivalled that of The Church themselves. There was a raw huskiness to his voice, a quality that stopped you in your tracks because you felt every word he sang deep in your soul. Robbie felt for Cordelia's hand and squeezed it. She glanced over at him and saw him gazing at Indigo as if he were a knight in shining armour.

The masses stared, enraptured. And then, slowly but surely, people started to cheer. And clap. And then sing along. Indigo was good. He was really good and unlike Robbie, he was effortless. Cordelia glanced out into the party and spotted Harper standing with her arms crossed, her face flushed pink. She'd cleaned herself up, leaving no evidence of her earlier nosebleed. Her mouth was set in a grim line and if looks could kill, Indigo would be dead and buried.

He finished to thunderous applause. He threw his head back and laughed. As the cheering finally began to die down, he gave a playful wink, and the opening beat of *Ice Ice Baby* began to play. Indigo glanced over and made eye contact with Robbie, beckoning him on stage.

Robbie looked at Cordelia.

"Go!" she cried, pushing him towards Indigo, who was now giving Vanilla Ice a run for his money. He had the moves. And he somehow managed to navigate the fine line between irreverent and faultless with perfection. The fact he was having fun with it was infectious and the crowd was eating it up.

A second microphone seemed to launch out of nowhere. Robbie caught it with one hand and fell into step with Indigo. Indigo slowly slunk into backup mode, allowing Robbie to take the lead. By the time they crossed their arms like gangstas, the tide had turned and there was a queue at the karaoke machine.

Indigo grabbed Robbie's hand and held it high in the air. "Let's hear it for my main man, *Robbie Carlisle!*" Everyone clapped and whistled. Robbie was positively beaming.

As they walked offstage, Indigo caught Cordelia's eye and his mouth kicked up in a sexy little smile. She gave him a half smile in return and inclined her head in thanks. His grin deepened and she noticed up close how crazy perfect his teeth were.

Cordelia spotted Indigo and Harper having words under the frangipani tree later that night, culminating in her storming out in a huff, entourage in tow. After that, Indigo ditched his mates for the rest of the night to hang out with Robbie. Robbie was beyond chuffed and Cordelia was convinced he'd wake up tomorrow with a cheek-ache from smiling.

She didn't know how to feel when Indigo stayed behind after everyone else had left to sit around the kitchen table with her family to recap the evening, as was the Carlisle tradition. It didn't seem to bother him at all, hanging out with her parents. She didn't get why he wanted to when she knew his mates had all kicked on to Drew's house.

"Now this, my children, is what we call *real* music," Dad said as he put his favourite Cat Stevens record on with a big smile. "Unlike that dreadful racket I heard coming from the backyard all night." They were enveloped with the comforting strains of *Wild World.* He sat down at the head of the table. "So what did I miss? It almost all went to hell and then it didn't?" he said as he pulled Mum's feet into his lap and began to gently rub her arches. "I was so busy working hard to ensure no hooligans breached the perimeter I missed the main event," he chuckled. His light-brown hair was neatly combed, his tawny eyes intent as he searched their faces.

They stared at him incredulously. "Yeah, you did an amazing job, darling," Mum said, stifling a giggle. "Top notch."

"No one got by you, Dad," Cordelia deadpanned, biting her lip to keep from laughing.

"If our esteemed Prime Minister Bob Hawke's looking for a new security detail, I'm sure you'll be his first port of call," Robbie added. "I've heard he likes a bit of a tipple too."

Dad looked at Indigo. "You got anything to add?" he asked, a twinkle in his eye. Indigo glanced round the table from Cordelia's parents, to her, to Robbie, seemingly unsure how to respond. Her friends always said her family was weird because they actually liked each other and had fun together and she could see Indigo wasn't used to kids giving their parents shit.

"We-elll," he finally said, "aside from the five girls I know of who snuck in under the name BoBo Chen without raising any alarm bells, the six Lucifer Jones' you let slip by, and the four Monet Sallingers no one flagged, I'd say you did a stellar job." His eyes crinkled as he broke into a huge grin.

Dad narrowed his eyes at Indigo, then burst out laughing. "I was wondering how we ended up with so many extra kids back there tonight," he said sheepishly. "So you're saying I don't have a big career ahead of me as a bouncer, then? That I should stick to my day job?"

"Sweetheart," Mum interjected, "we love you dearly, but I think I speak for us all when I say you and your wine-soaked mates were about as useful as tits on a bull tonight."

Dad pretended to look offended but couldn't keep a straight face.

"Let's just say you're lucky Indigo was there to deescalate the situation," she said, "or you might have really had to show us what you're made of."

"Well, all I can say is thank Christ for Indigo because most of those kids were bigger than me!"

"That wouldn't be hard," Robbie quipped. Robbie had overtaken their father in the height department this year, a fact he and Cordelia teased him about mercilessly.

"Well, I for one am incredibly impressed you got up there like that," Mum said to Indigo, her smile fading as her eyes grew serious. And grateful. Things were getting extraordinarily ugly there for a moment." Her silver bangles jangled as her hand crept into Robbie's, squeezing it hard.

Indigo flushed a little as he shrugged modestly, intent on tracing a knot in the oak table with his finger.

"Why *did* you do it?" Cordelia suddenly asked, her gaze curious.

"Just showing off, I guess," he said with a casual laugh. "I mean, all those years my mother made me do all those ridiculous singing and dance lessons. I guess I saw my opportunity to finally put them to use and I took it."

"She wanted to mould you in her image?" Robbie asked.

Indigo shrugged again. "I guess."

"What does your mother do, Indigo?" Dad asked, standing to refill their glasses with homemade lemonade.

Cordelia stifled a giggle as Robbie stared at their father, aghast. Their father would choose a documentary on the life on an earthworm over a Hollywood blockbuster any day and his pop culture knowledge was severely lacking.

"She's an actress, Dr Carlisle," Indigo replied, ignoring Robbie's spluttering.

"Call me Josh," he said. "An actress, eh? Would I have seen her in anything? Mind you, I'm not big on soapies or theatre."

"Um, as *if*!" Robbie gasped. "Are you *serious,* Dad?"

"What?" he said, looking around the table. Mum leant in and whispered in his ear and he pulled back and looked at her. "The one about the time-travelling con woman you dragged me to last week?" he asked. She nodded.

"Oh," he replied, glancing at Indigo, who looked mortified, "oh yes, I do know who she is."

"Don't worry," Indigo said. "I read the reviews. I know it was crap."

"How dare you?" Robbie breathed, squinting at Indigo. "That movie was magnificent! *Your mother* was magnificent!"

Indigo shot him a bemused look.

"You haven't seen it?" Dad asked.

"Yeah, nah," he replied, running his hand through the back of his hair. "I stopped watching my parents' movies in the mid-eighties."

"Well, despite what the critics say," Robbie informed him, "in the court of public opinion, *Time Temptress* is a smash hit! Have you *seen* the box office figures?"

Indigo's lip curled as he shook his head.

"So you must spend a lot of time in the States, then?" Mum asked, standing to open the oven. She pushed up the sleeves of the fine black sweater she wore with a long layered skirt, before grabbing a mitt and extracting the two pizzas she'd made from scratch that afternoon, placing them on the bench to cool.

Indigo shrugged. "I prefer it here, Mrs Carlisle."

"Scarlett," she corrected, looking sympathetic. "Your mother must miss you so much." She cut the pizzas up, drizzling them with pesto and placing them on the table beside a platter of her famous choc-chip cookies, extra chewy, extra choc-chips. "It must be hard having her so far away."

Indigo nodded, but Cordelia saw a shadow flit across his face so quickly it was gone before she knew it. He must have felt her looking at him because he glanced at her then and smiled brightly. A little too brightly. She frowned.

Dad handed him a plate and gestured for him to help himself, and Cordelia quickly moved the subject back to the party.

"Tell Dad about the karaoke, Rob," she urged.

"Yes, do tell," her father said, smiling warmly at his son. "It was all a great success in the end, then?"

Robbie nodded. "It was touch and go for a while there," he said, eyes wide, "but more than one person came to me at the end of the night and said they had the best time *ever* and declared it the party of the year." He puffed his chest proudly as he grabbed a slice of pizza. "So we can all agree here and now that I was right and Cora was wrong," he said, giving his sister a mock-evil smile.

Cordelia scowled, muttering, "Seriously?" under her breath.

"Well," Robbie conceded, "I may have had a little help in winning over the crowd." He smiled adoringly at Indigo.

"A little?" Cordelia spluttered.

"Tell me?" Dad said, and Robbie gave a blow-by-blow description of the evening's antics, a dramatic tale of an underdog finding glory with the help of the brave hero who swooped in to save the day. The way he told it, Indigo practically had a white horse.

Indigo was majorly quick to shrug off all praise showered on him at the end of Robbie's story. He seemed embarrassed.

"How bad's the backyard?" Dad asked.

"It's not totally trashed," Robbie grimaced, "but it will require a little TLC tomorrow."

Her father went outside to inspect the damage, followed closely by her mother and Robbie. Indigo and Cordelia were left alone at the table.

He looked at her and smiled shyly and she was momentarily distracted by his eyes. She'd never seen eyes like his, a soft hazel flecked with infinite galaxies of jade and gold.

"So why *did* you do it?" she asked softly, her gaze serious on his. "For real?"

He hesitated, picking intently at a sundried tomato on his pizza before giving her a resigned frown. "Dunno," he shrugged. "It's like… well, popularity, it's like a weapon, right? And it's a choice, whether you use it for good or for evil. Things were going south pretty quickly and the stuff they were yelling," his eyes darkened, "well, no one should ever have to feel the way those kids make Robbie feel. It's just not cool. At all," he added vehemently, balling a napkin tightly in his fist and glowering. "I just don't know why people have to tear each other down, you know?" he said, regarding her closely. "How can you make someone feel shit about themselves and then just go on about your day? How can making someone else feel shit not make you feel even shittier about yourself?" he said, popping an olive in his mouth and chewing it thoughtfully. "I don't get it." And she could see he was truly perplexed.

"So, your parents are pretty great," he suddenly said. "You're real lucky, you know, nabbing folks like that."

"Well, Mum gave birth to us so we had no choice in the matter there, but yeah Dad, well Rob and I always say someone up there was looking out for us when they sent him to us."

Indigo cocked his head to one side.

"You know he's our stepdad, right? He and Mum got married when we were seven."

"No *way!* I never would have picked it. He's *so* cool."

"Yup, he always jokes that when he found Mum, he got three for the price of one."

He gave her a solemn stare. "Do you have much to do with your real dad?"

"Josh *is* our real dad," she said tightly, narrowing her eyes at him.

"Shit no, that's not what I meant," he said, looking horrified he'd offended her. "I never meant to suggest he wasn't. I meant your… biological father. Where's he? You and Robbie live here full-time, right?"

"He's dead," she said matter-of-factly.

He looked even more horrified, if that were possible. She smiled to put him at ease. "It's cool," she said, "he died before we were born. We never knew him."

"Who was he?"

"No idea. We've never even seen a photo of him. Mum doesn't have any and she refuses to talk about him. His death, well, from what I can gather, it totally screwed her up. She used to cry about him all the time until she met Dad. And then everything changed. Everything got *good.*"

"You really know nothing about him?"

"Nope," she shrugged. "I mean, I've always assumed he had dark hair and dark eyes because look at Robbie, he's a total ring in, so it must be where he gets his looks from. But it's just not worth bringing up with Mum. She used to break down if we so much as mentioned him. And now she's so happy with Dad. They're crazy in love, so I mean, who cares, right? Does it really matter?"

Indigo looked like he was about to say something, but the others traipsed back inside then, Dad playfully bemoaning the state of his lawn, his arm hooked around Robbie's shoulders. They sat back down and her father immediately turned his attention to her. "What about you, darling? I haven't heard much about your night?"

"Yeah, I had fun with the girls," she said nonchalantly, running a fingertip through the condensation on her glass.

"What happened to that boy who was sniffing around you?" he asked. "The one who kept calling here? You know, the one with the hair?"

"Da-ad," Cordelia breathed, dying of embarrassment. She was keenly aware that Indigo was listening.

Mum must have kicked Dad under the table because he suddenly leant to grab his shin, shooting her a quizzical look.

"They're called frosted tips," Robbie said through a mouthful of cookie. "And yes, he was here."

"But we didn't hang out," Cordelia murmured, eyes downcast.

"Why not?" Dad asked, his mood suddenly growing serious. "He didn't do anything to you, did he?

"Of course not, Dad. I just don't like him like… that."

"She's fussy," Robbie said. "She's looking for the one who takes her breath away," he declared, dramatically clutching his chest.

"Yes well, I can't say I'm sorry about that," Dad said. "He wasn't right for you." He looked at Indigo. "Bloody strange hair, I tell you," he said, brows pinched.

Robbie snorted. "No one will ever be good enough for Cora in your eyes, Dad."

"Yeah… well…" he said, his eyes softening as he gazed at Cordelia, "she's my little girl."

An hour and lots of laughs later, Mum stood and stretched. "That's me for the night," she yawned. "I'm off to bed. You coming, Josh?" she asked, reaching for his hand, squeezing it.

He smiled and nodded, standing to draw her near so he could layer light kisses over the faint freckles that smattered the bridge of her nose.

"Gross," Robbie muttered. "Can you guys just not?" Dad laughed as he released Mum and begun to clear the plates and glasses.

"Do you need a lift home, Indigo sweetheart?" Mum asked.

"No, I'm good thanks, I can call a cab."

She nodded to the phone on the wall. "Do you need money?"

"I'll just put it on my Amex," he said as he stood, turning to lift the receiver.

"He has an Amex?" Mum mouthed to Dad, who just shrugged.

After their parents went to bed and the taillights of Indigo's taxi had disappeared into the night, Robbie grabbed Cordelia, his eyes shining as he practically squealed, "Does this mean we're friends with Indigo Wolfe now?"

Cordelia smiled weakly, hoping Robbie wouldn't be too disappointed the next day when, she figured, the balance of power would revert and Indigo would return to his position at the top of the food chain, high above them.

The next morning Cordelia was sitting on the kitchen counter scoffing buckwheat pancakes and catching her mother up on all the real goss from the previous night when there was a tentative knock at the door.

"Are you expecting anyone?" Mum asked, brows knit. Cordelia shook her head. Her mother shrugged and disappeared to answer it.

Cordelia nearly choked on her pancakes when she returned a few moments later with Indigo in tow, a goofy smile lighting his chiselled face.

"I thought you guys might need some help cleaning up after last night," he was saying, picking at a sticker on the deck of the skateboard clutched under his arm.

"Well, that was really thoughtful, sweetie," Mum smiled. "Judging by the amount of broken bottles out there, it seems no one saw the 'no alcohol' clause printed in bold on the invitation," she commented wryly. "Would you like some breakfast? I've just made pancakes."

"Pancakes would be rad, thanks," he said.

"The boys are out back," Mum said, handing him a plate swamped with pancakes, raspberries, and maple syrup.

"Morning, Cordelia." He grinned at her so shyly as he moved past her out the back door, her stomach lurched. She stared after him until she felt eyes on her. She flushed as she met her mother's gaze.

"What?"

Mum just raised her eyebrows and smiled.

Indigo arrived on their doorstep that morning and pretty much never left.

Things at school changed, too.

One day, a couple of weeks after their party, Cordelia and Robbie were leaving the science lab when Tommy Monahagn and three of his neanderthal mates came up behind them. "Well, if it isn't Rob the knob," Tommy sneered, pushing Robbie hard in the back so he stumbled. "Did your sister have to translate the blackboard for you again today, retard? Why don't you learn how to r-r-r-read," he mocked. Tommy's friends were falling all over each other, laughing. Robbie's dyslexia had made him an easy target for other kids his whole school life.

"Get lost, Tommy," Cordelia snapped, trying to position herself between Robbie and his tormentor. "At least Robbie didn't have to repeat the fourth grade!" Everyone knew Tommy's poor scholastic history.

"You know nobody likes you, right, Rob the knob?" Tommy scoffed, shouldering Cordelia out of the way to trip Robbie, pinning him to the ground. "More like Rob-loves-the-knob, ya dirty faggot." He moved in close, his lips almost touching Robbie's cheek. "You should never have been born. You make me wanna *spew*," he hissed. Robbie's lip trembled ever-so-slightly, but Tommy saw. He grinned triumphantly. "You gonna *cry?* Awww wittle Wobbie's gonna cwy like the big girl we all know he is!"

"Shut up, Tommy, you *wanker!*" Cordelia cried, clawing at Tommy's meaty shoulders. "Get *off* him! You're hurting him!" A phlegmy rumble emerged from Tommy's throat as he began the preparation of a loogie with Robbie's name on it.

Tommy's chapped lips parted and a globule of spit oozed from within, as if in slow motion.

"*Stop it!*" Cordelia screamed and for a second there she thought Tommy was going to back off because the loogie paused there, glistening, seemingly hovering still in time and space.

All of a sudden, Cordelia was blindsided by a flash of blond hair and long limbs and the next thing she knew, Tommy was being wrenched into the air and thrown up against the lockers. Even though Indigo was a year younger than Tommy, he towered over him as he thrust a muscular forearm into Tommy's throat.

"I'm so sick of your *shit*, Monahagn!" Indigo's face was a mask of fury as he leaned in until it was an inch or so away from Tommy's, which was growing redder by the moment.

Then he slowly, lethally, whispered, "If you ever fucking well touch him, speak to him, so much as *look at him*, ever again, I will *destroy you.*" He released him then and Tommy fell to the floor, rolling into the foetal position as he gasped for air. Indigo glared at each of Tommy's friends in turn, before putting his arm around Robbie and leading him away.

From that day on, the bullies who'd once made Robbie's life hell lowered their eyes and crossed to the other side of the corridor when they passed him. Robbie started eating lunch with Indigo and his mates by the fountain each day and Cordelia would smile to herself to see Robbie sitting there next to Indigo in the centre of the group, regaling them with tales and anecdotes she could see genuinely cracked them up. It turned out that his epic karaoke party (which to her surprise had launched a stream of inferior imitations) had indeed been the catalyst of change he'd so hoped it would be. Finally, Robbie had real friends of his own. Maybe Hollywood endings weren't always that far-fetched.

Indigo and Robbie became inseparable and the strangest thing was that it didn't feel strange, because the two of them just clicked. Like yin and yang, they were total opposites but complemented one another, Robbie's dramatic theatrics tempered by Indigo's calming stoicism and vice versa. And Indigo totally got Robbie's sense of humour. Robbie's obsession with Indigo's parents faded once he knew the truth about them, his fierce loyalty to Indigo having him declare them dead to him. Cordelia knew he was serious when she found his once-beloved Bernadette Van Allen cassette tapes in the bin.

Her mum often came home to find Indigo rummaging through the fridge, asking what was for dinner and he stayed over so regularly they eventually bought a second bed for Robbie's room. Cordelia was lulled into a peaceful sleep most nights by the sound of them talking and laughing through the wall. It was a nice sound, a sound that somehow kept the nightmares at bay.

One night, a couple of months after their party, Cordelia was going to her room when she came upon Indigo on the phone in the narrow hallway. She figured out pretty quickly he was speaking to Edita, his Lithuanian nanny-cum-guardian.

Indigo took up most of the corridor and had his back to Cordelia, so she waited patiently for him to finish so she could get by.

"Edie, no," Indigo was saying in a stage whisper, coiling the phone cord round his index finger, "I-I really don't want to, ok?" After a pause he continued, "Well no, of *course* I didn't know she was coming into town! As if Bernadette ever tells me anything!" Another pause, then, "The only reason she wants me to go on the yacht with her is because the director she's trying to impress has a daughter my age and she thinks we can all play happy families. Since when has she ever wanted to spend time with me just for the hell of it? She's forgotten my birthday the last two years!" Finally he muttered, "Fine. FINE," through clenched teeth and slammed the phone back into its cradle.

When he turned and saw Cordelia standing there, he froze, his cheeks flushing.

There was an awkward silence.

"Everything ok?" she asked, just to break it.

"Uh, yeah… yeah, all good," he murmured, thumbing his lip. She could see in his eyes that it wasn't, but she didn't press him on it.

"That was uh… that was Edie," he offered, sliding his hands into his jeans pockets. If she didn't know better, she would have sworn he was making conversation purely to alleviate how nervous she felt, standing there with him like that. He was so tall, so insanely gorgeous.

"She's been with you a long time, huh?"

"For as long as I can remember." He leant his back against the wall, knee bent, bare foot propped up against the skirting board. "I read an old article once," he said, "where they interviewed all these people who used to work for Bernadette. It was like an exposé, I guess. Anyway, supposedly when I was a baby, my nanny back then in New York, she used to put earmuffs on me."

"Earmuffs?" She scrunched her nose.

"Yeah, so I couldn't hear the fighting. Apparently Bernadette and Wilson, they used to really go at it. Like, they fucking hated each other's guts there by the end. So one day, Bernadette just packed up all our shit and left. They say she took me to piss Wilson off." He laughed then, sharp and short. "Joke was on her, though. Wilson couldn't have been happier to be rid of us both." She noticed he never called his parents Mum and Dad.

"So we jumped a flight from New York to Sydney, during which it was reported she doped herself up on sleeping pills and I was dumped on some poor unsuspecting air stewardess who couldn't wait to blab to the press about it the minute we touched down." He rolled his eyes. "Bernadette hadn't been back home since before she met Wilson, so my grandmother was waiting at the house for us when we arrived. I was handed straight to her. Bernadette locked herself in her bedroom and declared she was far too humiliated to ever return to Hollywood and she was never setting foot outside ever again.

"Apparently we'd been home mere days before the phone started to ring and within the week she'd accepted a movie role and was back on a plane to LA, leaving me behind without so much as a backwards glance. Grandmother, I'd say, decided raising another baby wasn't for her and quickly hired Edita so she could beat a hasty retreat back to her own life on the north coast." He paused, staring into space. "It's funny, because I feel like I'm the only one who ever read that exposé because it seems to have vanished from existence. God knows who they paid to make that happen."

"How old was Edita back then?"

"Back then?" He raised his eyes to hers, rubbing his chin. "She would have been, what, early twenties? She'd only just arrived in Australia from Lithuania the year before and her English was patchy at best. But she's the eldest of six children and had a lot of experience with babies. I don't remember her being particularly maternal, but she took care of me in her own way. I mean, I remember waking at night when I was like, two, and she was standing over my bed, muttering to herself in Lithuanian while she smoothed my hair and adjusted my covers as she checked the clasp on the amber beads she insisted I wear round my ankle back then. You don't check on someone while they're sleeping if you don't care about them, right?"

Cordelia stared at him. He was looking at her for confirmation, like he really needed it. She really wanted to give him a hug, but fought the instinct. Instead, she smiled, nodded. "How often did your mum come back?"

He shrugged. "Dunno. Maybe two, three times a year? She'd pop back between movie shoots or album tours when it suited her. I remember her swanning in, in a smog of perfume and a clatter of heels and she'd pat me on the head and shower me in expensive gifts before disappearing into her bedroom. She's always liked me to look a certain way, you see, but Edie only ever dressed me in the Chanel and Ralph Lauren outfits Bernadette bought when she was around to insist upon it. And when I got older, well, I'd just chuck the clothes she bought me in the back of my closet and eventually Edie would box them up and send them off to charity."

Robbie stuck his head out of his bedroom door. "Hey, Inds?" he called. "You still gonna help me study for my English test?"

Indigo turned to him. "Sure thing, mate, I'm coming." He chucked Cordelia a grin over his shoulder as he sauntered down the hallway towards Robbie's room. "Shakespeare awaits. I'll see you in the morning, yeah?"

"G'night," she murmured.

That was the night Cordelia started to understand why he'd picked them. Despite his masses of friends, he was actually desperately lonely up there on Eastern Hill with only Edita and her husband Lukas for company. As much as Indigo adored them, they weren't parents. And in reality, all those masses of friends, she wasn't sure if any were allowed past the bright façade to access the real him. She saw now her instincts about Indigo had been right, that he'd become an expert at hiding the fact he was deeply wounded inside.

He kept his word to Edita and went out on the harbour the next week with Bernadette and her A-list friends, but that night he returned to the Carlisle's clearly shaken. Cordelia was in the kitchen helping Mum quickly wash up so she could get to the video she was dying to watch when she heard the back door open. Indigo slunk in, hands deep in his pockets, chin to chest, kicking his Air Max off by rote because her mum didn't allow shoes in her house. When he saw them, he straightened, plastering a big smile on his face.

"Hey, sweetie, how did it go with your mum?" her mother asked, drying her hands on a tea towel.

"Yeah, yeah, it was fine," he replied brightly, the smile on his face competing with the clouding of his eyes.

"Oh, honey, come here," Mum said, pulling him into a motherly embrace. "You're sending my bullshit detector into overdrive."

"You can't lie to her," Cordelia said, leaning against the kitchen counter. "She can sniff it out a mile off. So what happened? Was it bad?"

He flashed a distracted smile. "Yeah, nah, I mean... I dunno," he mumbled as Mum gave him a big squeeze and released him.

"It turns out she only wanted me there so she could pimp me out to the director's daughter," he said lightly, but his voice hitched and Cordelia could read between the lines: the daughter obviously had a crush on Indigo and his presence had been at the director's request, not his mother's. "Bernadette ignored me the whole day. Which is fine," he rushed on, "I mean, I haven't seen her in six months, why would she want to take time out from chugging martinis, sunbaking topless and flirting with men half her age to have an *actual* conversation with her son?" His smile turned bitter.

"Oh, sweetie," Mum frowned, reaching up to cup his cheek. "It's her loss, I promise you that. She doesn't know what she's missing."

Cordelia didn't know what to say, but her heart broke a little bit for him in that moment. As much as he hadn't wanted to go, she knew he couldn't help but get his hopes up every time one of his parents threw him a crumb. All she could think to do was invite him to watch her movie with her in the hopes it might take his mind off things (she didn't realise 'til after that it was a pre-release his mum's PA had sent from LA he'd brought over for Robbie; Indigo had probably already seen it, but he didn't say anything).

So she made him some toast, remembering to spread the Vegemite on disgustingly thick and they sat down together to watch *Ghost*. It was a little awkward at first as technically he was Robbie's friend, and the two of them had never hung out without Robbie there as a buffer. But Robbie was out with their dad and wouldn't be back for hours. Cordelia was very aware of the nearness of him on the couch, of the static of his leg touching hers whenever he shifted in his seat.

"What do you think happens when you die?" he asked her after Patrick Swayze had disappeared into the celestial light and the credits rolled.

"Uh, I dunno," she replied, turning towards him, "it's not something I've ever really wanted to give much thought." She swallowed hard. "I mean, I don't think this is all there is and that when we die, it's like lights out and it all just fades to black... But who knows?"

An unexpected tumble of images and feelings bubbled their way to the surface, highlight reels of nightmares she'd tried to forget. Suddenly, it was almost like she could feel her throat swelling and constricting, like she could smell the smoke charring her lungs. She coughed reflexively as she shoved it all back down deep, shook it off.

"You ok?" he frowned, his expression tinged with worry.

She forced a smile and nodded, chucking the ball back in his court. "What do you think happens?"

He stared thoughtfully at her before replying, "I don't believe there's a heaven and a hell, that's for sure. I mean, I don't think demons come and carry you off to the underworld if you're a shitty person, what's the point of life, of living and growing and evolving, if we simply get categorised as good or bad when we die? I mean, we've gotta get another chance to get it right, right?"

"What, like reincarnation?" she asked.

"Maybe," he shrugged. "I wonder if we get to make requests."

"What would you ask for? If you could design your own life?"

"Different parents," he replied without hesitation. "Parents like yours." He smiled sadly. "You guys are so lucky. You have everything."

She cocked her head to one side. "No one has *everything*."

"Josh and Scarlett sure seem to. I mean, you realise no one else's parents slow dance in the kitchen like yours do, right?"

"They don't have a baby," she told him.

"They want a baby?"

"So much. She was just eighteen when she had us, don't forget. She's only thirty-one now. She should easily be able to have another baby with Dad, but it just doesn't seem to be working for them. Every month I hear her crying at night and I know it didn't happen for them again."

"Oh," he said, "I didn't realise. But at least they have you guys, right?"

She smiled. "That's what I've overheard Dad saying to her, 'Look at the two beautiful children we do have'. But I don't think it's the same thing. Of course she has us, but it doesn't make her want another baby any less," she shrugged.

She caught his gaze then. "I can't tell you how many kids at school think you have everything. They'd kill for your life."

"Well, you know what, Cora? They can take it. Because the reality is my parents don't want me and they don't give a crap about me." His attempt at a light tone failed dismally, and he choked on the searingly honest words. "I spent half my childhood fantasising that I was adopted, that my real parents would swoop in one day and reclaim me. Do you know how it feels when there's nobody in the world who loves you unconditionally the way a mother or father is meant to? I mean, it's their fucking *job*, right? If you're gonna have a kid, the first rule is just to love them, right? But mine didn't seem to get the memo. Your parents, they would die for you. Mine? They'd sell me a hundred times over for an Oscar nomination."

As he spoke, he plucked at the black leather string beaded with obsidian and tourmaline, which was a permanent fixture on his wrist. Cordelia had asked him about it once and he'd shrugged elusively and placed a protective hand over it. All she knew was he never took it off. She crossed her legs up under herself and listened quietly as he continued, his tone growing sharper. "But what's the use in complaining, in blaming *them*? *They've* always been the way they are. Look at today, for example, it's my fault. *I'm* the fucking idiot. I knew Bernadette didn't want to spend time with me. I mean, she never has before, right? But *still* I went. And I guess I had these *fantasies* in my head, these... these pathetic *illusions* that this time she might want to hear about what's happening in my life, you know, that this time it might be different. But it never is."

He smiled tightly then, his cheeks flushing pink. "Whoa. I'm sorry," he apologised with a grimace.

"What for?" she asked, tilting her chin, frowning.

"I-I don't know where all that came from. I sound like a fucking tool. I shouldn't have dumped all that on you." He regarded her closely, a pleat forming between his brows. "I don't know what I was thinking." He shook his head almost imperceptibly, stared fixedly at the ground.

"It's ok."

"No, it's not." He exhaled sharply through his teeth. "You don't understand. I... I don't say this shit out loud. Like... ever." He raised his gaze reluctantly to hers. "You-you've just got one of those faces, you know?" he mused.

"One of those faces?" she repeated, eyes narrowing.

He reddened further. "Yeah," he grinned sheepishly, "you're one of those rare people you feel like you can open up to, and like, you know... share your ugly with." She must have looked taken aback because he quickly added, "That's a compliment."

It was her turn to blush and she covered her cheeks with her palms.

"Shit," he swore, "I'm sorry." He tipped his head back against the couch and closed his eyes, lower lip between his teeth. "I just meant it's nice to talk to someone without feeling like they're judging you. I'm sorry."

"No. Don't be."

"It's just been a real crappy day," he breathed.

"I won't take that personally," she said lightly.

He sat forward with a start, turning to her, looking aghast. He relaxed when he saw she was smiling. "I meant up until now," he said. His mouth quirked up at the corners.

"It's ok," she said, leaning slightly towards him, "I get it. We all need to vent sometimes." She paused for a moment, feeling a warmth rise up in her cheeks again as he stared at her so intently with those remarkable eyes. "I'm always happy to listen."

"You must think I'm such a dick, complaining I've got it tough." He bent his knee up, resting his head in his large palm. "And you know what? When it comes to material stuff, sure, I've got everything I could ever want. *More* than I could ever want. It seems to help alleviate my parents of any bit of guilt they might feel over their complete and total neglect. A lot of it comes from worrying about what other people think. Like my mother demanding my father's Aspen house two weeks every January and making me go with her, so her friends think she's a decent mother. If only they knew. The minute we arrive, she dumps me on a housekeeper and a couple of ski instructors and I barely see her until it's time for her to hand me my plane ticket so I can fly back home alone and she can piss back off to LA or London or wherever. In her mind, she's got all her maternal duties out of the way for the year by mid-January. Tick." With the flick of his wrist, he drew a big check mark in the air.

"But those photos I've seen in magazines of you and her skiing together?"

He snorted. "You think those are real? She stages those with the paparazzi every year. How else do you think her blow-dry looks so immaculate after a supposed fun-filled day of bonding on the slopes with her beloved son? I've never skied one run with her, ever. I'm just instructed where to turn up and when. Same as when she has me fly across the world to join her on set. If you were wondering, the inside of a luxury hotel suite looks the same in every country."

"I'm sorry," she said, fighting the instinct to reach out and lay her hand on his arm, feeling like she'd be crossing some unseen boundary by doing so.

"You do realise I'm sitting here complaining about how tough it is, travelling the world, skiing in Aspen every year?" he said, meeting her eye with a wry smile.

She didn't smile back. "I don't think you should trash your feelings because of how other people see your life. You have every right to feel the way you do. Dad says we're all dealt different hands in life and we're here to play what's in front of us as best we can." She eyed him thoughtfully. "Everyone has problems, right? In your world, your problems are your problems, and those problems are your world, and I think it's important that we work to, like, make everything right in our own world." She twisted her mouth to the side. "Know what I mean?"

He gazed at her then with such vulnerability her throat clutched her breath. He opened his mouth to say something but Robbie arrived home, bursting into the room in a whirlwind of chatter and movement, completely annihilating the moment. Cordelia smiled gently at Indigo as she stood to go to bed, and he smiled back, inclining his head ever so slightly in thanks.

That night, she lay awake thinking about everything Indigo had confided in her. Everyone was so envious of his life, but she'd seen the reality beneath the gilded surface and the truth was, his ivory tower wasn't so pretty on the inside. His home life was the polar opposite of hers. It seemed to her there had never been anybody who cared how his day went. Anybody who cared if he got wet on the way to school on a rainy day. Anybody to care whether he'd remembered money for lunch or ate his broccoli or got detention. Anybody who celebrated his victories or commiserated his failures. It seemed there had never been anybody in the world who had loved him for him.

And with every fibre of her being, she wanted to fix that.

chapter five

higher love

freshwater beach, new south wales, october, 1990

indigo

She'd made him surf at Freshie. His least favourite break. But it was her local and she'd insisted and he'd done it for her. It hadn't been too bad, actually. Small, but nice. She was fun to surf with; she knew her way around a board, that was for sure. And afterwards they'd sat together on the white sand, chatting, never drawing breath, as the descending sun fired the sky pink and orange and red.

To their right, craggy cliffs rose high above the beach, hardy vegetation spilling from their crevices. Houses and apartment buildings crammed the bluff; each seemed to jostle for their slice of ocean view. To their left, the ocean pool was enduring a pummelling from an endless wash of waves.

He trekked up the dunes to get her an ice cream from the surf club, and when he came back, she was lying back on her towel, hair fanned out, wetsuit rolled down to her waist, elbow bent over her eyes. Her smooth skin looked golden against her dusky-pink bikini top.

"Cora?" he said, holding a Golden Gaytime out to her. She didn't respond. He plonked down beside her, burrowing his heels into the sand. Up close, he could hear the slow and steady rhythm of her breathing. She was asleep. He covered her with his towel and sat there, gazing out to sea, until she began to stir. She sat up with a start.

"Oh shit! Did I pass out?" A blush crept up her cheeks.

"Yup," he laughed, "you were totally KOed." He absently picked up a fragment of sun-bleached shell, turning it over in his hand. "Your Gaytime was melting, so I ate it," he confessed.

She gasped in mock horror. "Some friend you are!"

"I've always wondered if it's true that if you snooze, you actually do lose. And now we know it is." He grinned and tossed her his Caramello Koala. She tore the wrapper open. Caramel oozed out as she bit the chocolatey head off, then passed the rest to him.

She swallowed her mouthful and cleared her throat. "The thing is, Inds, I-I didn't sleep well last night." She stared at her hands in her lap.

"Everything ok?" He hadn't stayed over last night and he wondered if something had happened.

Her clear aquamarine eyes met his.

"You can tell me, you know." He tossed the shell.

Her shoulders dropped and she averted her gaze. "Sometimes," she said in a small voice, "I have these… nightmares."

He frowned. "What kind of nightmares?"

"Dunno. Like, ones that feel so real I can't get back to sleep."

"So it's not always the same one?"

"No. There's a few. They kind of rotate. I've had them for as long as I can remember. I used to hate bedtime when I was little, knowing they lay in wait. But back then, it was the same nightmare, over and over again."

"What was it?"

She took a deep breath, exhaled steadily. "There's this big scary house and I'm always running from it, running for my life." She shuddered. He didn't press her for more details. "Anyway, I'd wake up, heart absolutely pounding and I'd be completely frozen. I'd want to open my eyes, but I'd be too scared to in case I'd brought something back with me. Robbie and me, we shared a room back then, in our grandparents' house and I'd try to scream for him, but nothing would come out."

She looked at him then, eyes searching, as though wondering whether she should say the next bit. Her throat bobbed. "And then…" she said, her voice low, "and then my imagination would kick into overdrive and I'd hear this, like, kind of whispered, layered murmuring."

His stomach twisted. Voices? He knew all about that.

"Mum's room was at the other end of the house from ours and I remember how endlessly black that corridor seemed, how convinced I was it was full of monsters just waiting to grab me. On the nights I felt brave, I'd throw the covers back, and with my eyes still squeezed tight, I'd bolt as fast as I could, my fingertips trailing the walls to guide me to her. Other nights when I was too scared, I'd run the three steps to Robbie's bed and jump in with him, squeezing him so tightly he'd wake up — and you know how hard he is to wake!"

"What would Rob do?"

"He'd cuddle me close and he'd promise me none of it was real." She gazed out at the horizon, lower lip pincered between her teeth. "There was this one night — we must have been seven because it was just before Mum and Dad got married — and the dream had been so bad I was physically shaking. And Robbie, he said to me, 'It's not real Cora, there's nothing in this room except you and me.' And I remember him staring into my eyes by the light of the lava lamp in the corner. And he whispered to me, 'Sometimes when I think I'm asleep, I open my eyes and I'm somewhere else. But then I shut my eyes tight and tell myself it's not real and when I open them again, I'm back here in our room. Because it's *not* real Cora.' And that was the night I realised we all had our imaginary vices and that I didn't want to be a slave to mine anymore. So the next time the nightmare came, I stayed in my own bed. I told myself it wasn't real. I made myself be brave."

"Did it work?"

"I never had that nightmare again, the scary house one." She frowned, dusted a fleck of sand from her knee. "But then the others started." She told him of those nightmares, of bees and welts and suffocation, of being burnt alive, of ships exploding, debris and body parts in the water. They sounded bloody horrific. No wonder she didn't sleep well. She was wringing her hands, twisting and turning them.

He reached out without thinking, twining his fingers through hers to steady them. It felt really fucking nice holding her hand in his. His eyes met hers and suddenly he could barely breathe. God, she was beautiful. She smiled then and his heart lurched in a way it never had before. He dropped her hand and looked away. Robbie was one of his best mates, and Joshua — Joshua had welcomed him into his home, into his family, let him live under his roof. Cordelia was way off limits.

"Come on," he said, standing up and gathering their stuff, "I'll buy you another ice cream."

That night, he tossed and turned, replaying their conversation in his head. That gut-clenching fear she'd described? It was a fear he knew only too well. And the voices? Jesus Christ, he wanted to confide in her the way she'd confided in him, but how could he, without telling her about Sarita? And he couldn't tell her about Sarita without telling her how that had all ended. And if she found out how that ended, would she ever think of him the same?

Fernanda told him Harper was in the boathouse. He headed down the side of the yard, taking the steep stone steps that led to the water, two at a time. As he neared the bottom, he could hear the lapping of the harbour. All he'd told Harper was they needed to talk and he was coming over.

She was lounging on one of the cream sofas that graced the breezy little house with its floor-to-ceiling windows. She was wearing a grey sleeveless cowlneck dress, her cornsilk hair tied back in a sleek ponytail.

"So listen, Harps," he began. But that's as far as she let him get.

"You're breaking up with me?" she whispered venomously.

There was no point in drawing this out. "Uh yeah, yeah, I am," he replied plainly. "You're a cool chick, Harps, but we're just way different."

She stared at him, anger tightening the corners of her mouth. He knew no one had ever broken up with her before.

"You ok?" he asked, peering into her face with concern.

"You're *dumping* me?" she asked. "*You're* dumping me?"

"Ah, that's a pretty harsh way of putting it, but yeah, yeah, it's over, Harper, I'm sorry."

"No," she said, crossing her arms.

"No?" he repeated.

"No," she replied firmly, "this isn't happening."

He half-laughed then because surely she was joking, but when she continued to stare him down his stomach dropped. This wasn't going to be easy. "Listen, Harps…" he said.

"No, Indigo, *you* listen," she interrupted, her demeanour softening. "Why does it matter that we're different? Why would you want someone the same as you? Where's the fun in that?" She smiled coquettishly.

"Uh, there's nothing wrong with being different," he explained. "But you and me? Our fundamental values and life views are poles apart. It's never gonna work," he shrugged. He'd finally understood that what he had with her, it wasn't love. The thing was, he just didn't feel good about himself when he was around her and he'd begin to think that maybe, just maybe, he deserved more. "You're a gorgeous girl, Harper. You're never gonna struggle to find someone else."

"I don't want someone else," she pouted, sliding smoothly towards him on the couch, reaching out, tracing a finger down his bicep. She leant forward and began to run her lips up the curve of his neck, and before he knew what was happening, she was unfastening his shorts, wending her hand inside.

"We're so good together, *mon chéri*," she whispered against his lips. "I need you, Indigo. I love you. You're the only one who's ever come close to knowing me. Please don't leave me, I love you so much, tell me you love me too…"

Oh God, she was making this so difficult. But he had to be tough. It wasn't fair on her to let this go on when his heart wasn't in it anymore. Maybe it never had been. He stiffened and pulled back, grasping her forearms and gently pushing her away. "Ugh, Harper, you're exhausting!" He stood up and backed towards the door, hurriedly buttoning his shorts. "I just don't have the energy for this anymore! You don't *love* me. Some days I question whether you actually even *like* me. You're constantly trying to change me and all we do is fight! It's never gonna work between us, Harps. I'm sorry, I truly am. I never meant to hurt you…"

That was when her walls bricked up. "*Hurt* me?" she spat, standing to glare at him, her lovely face flushed with fury. "*Hurt me?!* You wanna know about *hurt*? Oh, you'll know all about *hurt* once I'm finished with *you!* You're an *arsehole*, Indigo Wolfe, a *total fucking arsehole!*"

"Ok, we're done here," he replied curtly, turning on his heel to leave, thankful she'd just made it easy.

"Just so you know," she screamed after him, "I'm telling everyone *I* dumped *YOU!*"

Wow. It was real easy now. Is that all she truly cared about? Fuck this shit. It was so over it wasn't funny. He stopped and slowly spun to face her. She was breathing heavily, so angry she was blinking at an incredible pace. "You do what you gotta do," he said with a shrug.

"It's those fucking Carlisles, isn't it?!" she shouted. "Ever since you started hanging round *them,* you haven't had time for *me!* What's so good about their homely little cottage, anyway? It doesn't even have a *pool!*" She was so bloody shallow he could explain it 'til the cows came home and she'd never get it. He turned his back on her and walked out. "They're not like *us,* Indigo."

"Exactly," he muttered.

"If you think I'm ever going to forget this, you've got another thing coming!" he could hear her yelling after him. "I'll get you back for this, Indigo! I never forget! I'll get you back for treating me this way!" She wanted to hurt him. They were just words. She probably didn't even mean them. *"Va te faire foutre!"*

He just kept walking.

Indigo scooped up his board and waded out of the ocean. The surf was on fire today, which was what he'd needed after how crap things had gone with Harper. He felt bad; he did. He never wanted to be the cause of someone's heartache. But she had issues. Issues he'd thought he'd be able to help her through. But she never wanted to deal with them, had rejected his help time and time again. If she wouldn't get out of her own way, there wasn't much he could do. Having her admit to him last weekend it had been she who'd driven that nail into old Mrs Critchard's tyre that stormy afternoon, had been the final straw. He couldn't be with someone who thought that was ok.

And yes, maybe she'd been right. Maybe the Carlisles had rubbed off on him. But shouldn't he want to be with people who made him want to be better?

He jogged up the dunes to the outdoor shower, twisting the tap, tilting his face up to catch the spray. He was heading over to the Carlisles after this and he still didn't know what to do. After Cordelia's confession the other day, he'd been tossing up whether to tell her about the things he felt, about the voices, about Sarita. But he'd never told anyone about the feelings, about the voices, except Sarita.

One of his earliest memories was of lying on his back in his cot, his small feet in his chubby hands, as he gazed up into Sarita's face. Her skin was as dark and smooth as night, her hair was magnificent, hanging to her waist in a myriad of twisted braids, her eyes deep pools of coffee, love and kindness always to be found there. Her lips permanently hinted at a smile even when she talked of things that made her eyes sad.

She would tell him how special he was and her words made him feel good. He'd started to believe maybe if he tried his hardest to be really good and really special, his mother might stay a little longer next time she came to town.

Sarita was the one who'd been with him when he'd found Banjo, a beige puppy with black-tipped ears and toes. He was only four when Banjo came to stay and Indigo still remembered how cross Edita had been when she'd followed the trail of muddy footprints to his room to find Banjo under the rumpled covers of his bed with him.

Edita had shouted in her thick accent while Indigo held tight to Banjo's neck, refusing to let his new friend go. She'd had one of her headaches that day. She hadn't mentioned it, but Indigo knew, just the way he always knew, by the throbbing in his own temples. Edita had eventually thrown up her hands in defeat and let him keep the dog, muttering that a child needed something to love.

The next day, when Indigo had come into the kitchen to find Edita petting Banjo's head and feeding him scraps of bacon, he knew she was won over. Banjo's whole body was wriggling in delight as she spoke to him affectionately in Lithuanian and placed the fatty morsels upon his pink tongue.

"*Geras berniukas,*" Edita was murmuring. "*Yummy bekonas.*"

Man, how he'd loved that dog. His death a couple of years back had hit him really hard.

Banjo was exactly what Indigo needed and Sarita had known that. She was always there to soothe him and sing to him when he was feeling sad or lonely and couldn't sleep. One night he'd lain in bed sobbing his five-year-old heart out because he was the only child at school who'd had no one show up for Mother's Day breakfast. The pungent scent of geranium had filled his nostrils as Sarita appeared, sitting upon his bed, placing her hand on the small of his back.

"I h-had to sit all b-b-by myself Sarita and the other k-kids and their mums… their eyes were s-so sad when they looked at me," he'd bawled into his pillow. "Now *everyone* knows n-nobody loves me!"

"Nobody loves you? I do. So much. Can you not feel how happy I am when I'm with you, darling one?" she'd said.

And even though he could, there were other voices whispering otherwise. "No!" he'd cried, turning to sit up. "I can't! You don't!"

"Indigo," she'd said calmly, "focus on me. Deep breath in, ok? Just like we practiced."

He'd looked at her feral-eyed and shaken his head stubbornly.

"Indigo."

He'd gazed at her forlornly, then attempted a shaky breath deep into his lungs.

"Good, baby, that's good. Now another," she'd coaxed, over and over until he was calm. "You control your breath, you control your body," she'd reminded him. "Now tell me, what happened to the note your school sent out about Mother's Day?"

He'd stuck his bottom lip out. "I put it in an envelope and my teacher helped me post it to Bernadette's house in LA. She didn't write back, but I thought… I thought she *might* come. That she might surprise me like the mums do on TV. They always come. But not my mother. *I hate her,* Sarita! I *hate* Bernadette!"

"I'm sorry no one was there for you today, but this mother of yours, you know you were born unto her for a reason. We've talked about this, haven't we? To hate is a waste of energy."

Indigo nodded. "I chose my mother and father before I was born because this is the life that will help me… become who I need to be." He knew the words by rote. But he didn't fully believe them. Why would anyone choose parents who would make them feel so sad inside?

"You're exactly where you're meant to be, Indigo, and you're doing so good. And tell me, darling one, what if you'd given that note to Edita?"

He'd screwed his face up for a moment, then said, "She would have come."

"Why?"

"Because she cares if I feel sad."

"Why?"

"Because... because she... she loves me a little, I guess."

"As do I. And Edita – well, I know she doesn't always show it, but Edita would lay down and die for you." She'd smiled her beatific smile then. "Beautiful one, I know how much this hurts, but all these feelings, all these experiences, they're going to make you so strong and so wise, and that strength and that wisdom are going to help make you into such a special person."

"But why don't *I* have a family, Sarita? Everyone has one but me — a mummy and a daddy, and brothers and sisters." It hurt his heart so much that his father didn't want him, that everything in the world was more important to his mother than him.

"You do have a family," Sarita told him. "You have us."

Sarita, she just knew things. She was the wisest person he'd ever met. She always knew just what he needed, when he needed advice, when he needed her comforting silence. Sometimes she'd tell him tales of adventures she'd had, so many adventures it was as if she'd lived a thousand lives.

As Indigo grew older, Sarita stopped only coming at night. The sunny backyard of the Van Allen Estate had gardens to rival the Botanic Gardens and a lawn the size of a park that overlooked the harbour below. Indigo loved to lie out on the grass with Sarita and watch the little white boats straining at their moorings, the seagulls coasting over the waves; the children crouching in the lapping tide with their buckets and spades. He found if he lay perfectly still bees, ladybugs and sometimes even dragonflies would come and land upon his hands. He would watch them in silent fascination as they crawled up and down his arms, their tiny wings and legs tickling him as he suppressed his giggles. In summer, the cicadas would arrive; his favourites.

By the time he was seven, Indigo had gotten used to seeing his mother just two or three times a year. He no longer sobbed when she left, with no more than an air kiss goodbye. She never hugged him for fear he'd wrinkle her couture or mess up her blow-dry.

The year he turned ten, she'd flown home to spend the holidays with him but had gotten a better offer the day before Christmas when the director she was dating sent a private jet to whisk her off to Hawaii. Indigo had sat at his bedroom window watching Lukas load her matching Hermés luggage into the car.

"It's ok to feel sad, my dear one," Sarita had said, appearing at his side to lay a gentle hand upon his back.

"I'm not," Indigo had shrugged, staring blankly out at his mother climbing into the car, her blonde French twist disappearing from view as the driver closed the door behind her. And he meant it. When he looked at her now, he just felt nothing. He was done trying to please her, done with all the activities she demanded he do, the tennis lessons and the guitar lessons and the singing and dancing and acting classes she insisted upon like some absentee stage mother forcing him to be what he wasn't. The last thing in the world he wanted was to be anything like her.

"Is that really how you feel?" she'd asked, looking deep into his eyes.

"She doesn't feel sad, so why should I?" he'd said vacantly, his attention drawn back outside. Although he'd never been able to feel how other people felt about him, in his mother's case, it was more than obvious.

"Darling boy," she'd said, "it's important you acknowledge those feelings, but know they are not yours."

He'd torn his gaze then from the car disappearing round the bend and merely shrugged at her. "It's easier like this," he'd scowled, shrugging Sarita's hand from his back. "Lemme alone," he'd whispered, refusing to look at her again. She'd left. Not for good that time. He hadn't known then their days together were numbered. Or that she'd leave because of him.

When Indigo arrived at the Carlisles' that afternoon, Cordelia was lying out on a bohemian looking rug in the front garden, making the most of the spring sunshine. She was sprawled on her stomach, long shapely legs bent up, bare feet dangling. Open in front of her was one of the Sebastian Winters novels Scarlett was always going on about.

"Hey, you," he called, ducking through the banana palms and birds-of-paradise to join her on the small patch of lawn.

"Hey, Inds!" Her whole face lit up as she sat up and pushed her cherry-red sunnies onto the top of her head. She looked super cute in cut-off denim shorts and a black and white polka-dot camisole, her wild hair swept over one bronzed shoulder. She dog-eared the page to mark her place before chucking the book aside. "What's news?"

"I broke up with Harper," he announced, sinking down opposite her on the rug, leaning back on his hands.

"Oh no," she said, tenting her hand over her eyes. "Are you ok?" Her full lips turned down at the corners as she gazed at him.

"Yep, totally, it was time," he said, launching into a blow-by-blow.

"And what, you're just gonna let her get away with telling people she dumped you?" she asked when he'd finished.

He snorted. "I couldn't give a shit what she says. If that's what she feels the need to do, then whatever. She can tell people what she likes."

"She might start spreading rumours you're a really bad kisser," she teased, a smile blooming at the edges of her mouth. "Or worse!"

He grinned. "Maybe I am a bad kisser," he said, nudging her foot with his.

"That's not what I've heard," she giggled.

"What have you heard?" He cocked an eyebrow at her.

"Let's just say your reputation precedes you."

Oh shit.

She thought he was a sleaze.

"Oh my God, Inds, we all know you're *amazing* at everything," she teased, hitting him on the shoulder. "Word is you're perfect, right?"

He wasn't perfect.

Far from it.

She knew that didn't she?

The smile faded from her lips. "What's wrong?"

He realised his face had tensed up. "I-I uh, I wanted to tell you something, Cora," he blurted and he must have looked serious because she leant towards him, those angel eyes intent on his. "Listen, it's about the other day… That stuff you told me…" he trailed off, chewing the inside of his cheek.

"You can tell me anything, you know that, right?" She placed her hand lightly on his. It tingled where she touched.

He knew that. So he did. He told her about feeling everyone's feelings. About the voices that'd come and gone his whole life, about how they weren't that bad anymore because the bubble, it'd been holding fast for so long now.

When he was done, she stared at him thoughtfully. "So I gotta ask," she finally said, "how am I feeling right now?"

Without hesitation, he described everything he felt in her down to the tiny papercut in the crease of her right index finger. She was quiet for a while and then she had more questions. Of course. Questions about the feelings and emotions and pain. And then questions about the voices.

Were they inside his head or outside of it?

Both.

How many voices were there?

So many. Too many.

What sort of things did they say?

Anything. Everything. Sometimes they told him about shitty things they'd done. Sometimes they told him shitty things about himself. Sometimes they just talked shitty, endless nonsense.

How come they come and go?

No fucking idea.

Do you talk back to them?

As if! He'd almost given himself an aneurism trying to ignore them.

You said they don't really affect you anymore. When was the last time you heard them?

It'd been at least a year, when he thought about it, since they'd caused him trouble. Maybe more. The bubble felt so big these days; them trapped on the outside of it so he barely registered they existed anymore.

Where did they come from? Were they... dead people?

That was the big question, the one he couldn't answer.

Not once did she ask him if he'd imagined any of it, or suggest there was anything wrong with him. She just listened with an open mind, without judgement.

"So this Sarita," she ventured, finger moving through the fringe of the rug they shared, "she was the only one you talked to about this stuff?"

He nodded.

"But she's gone now?

Another nod.

"What happened?"

He took a deep breath. "The last day I ever saw her, I was twelve. It'd been a bad day, that day," he said, the memory of it bringing a wave of emotion. "Bernadette was meant to be coming home, but she'd just called to say she was going to St Tropez instead. So I took her Porsche out for a joyride — as a big 'fuck you' to her I guess — but Edita caught me, went ballistic and sent me to my room where the voices started up again. I'd learnt a few ways to shut them up by then. One of them was by stealing vodka from the liquor cabinet in Bernadette's room."

Her eyes widened. He'd realised by then that not feeling, felt good. Blissful even. Not feeling and not caring. Because when he let feelings in, he just felt anger. And sadness. Angry and sad more than he should. Although he'd become an expert at hiding it outside the safety of his room.

"Anyway, I was lying on my bed, totally hammered, feeling pissed off and hard done by and extremely sorry for myself. I remember being pretty pissed at Sarita actually, because she'd been coming by less and less and I took that really personally. I was so out of it I hadn't even realised she was there until Banjo raised his head from my chest and started to wag his tail.

"So I opened my eyes to see her standing over me, hands on hips, looking not angry, but disappointed, which we all know is so much worse." He rolled his eyes. "So she just starts laying into me, telling me I was better than this, that she couldn't help me when I did foolish stuff like this to myself, that I was destined for much greater things — she'd always had high hopes for me, old Sarita," he sighed.

"I remember this wave of fury just crashing over me, because of course nothing was ever my fault and the whole world was out to get me." He forced a wry smile. "So I started mimicking her, which was a totally mature response." He'd been such a dick back then. "Funnily enough, that didn't deter her. She sat down beside me on the bed and continued to talk so softly, so calmy to me: *This wasn't who she'd taught me to be, I was behaving like a coward, I'd never learn and grow if I kept this up and so then what was the point, I was wasting my life, all this opportunity...*

"But man, I didn't want to hear it. So I snapped at her to go away, because I was so fucked up she couldn't help me. No one could. Anyway, she continued to berate me until I totally lost it. I guess I just didn't want to feel the things her words made me feel. She was like Jiminy bloody Cricket, always chirping at me. It was too much. *She* was too much."

"What did you do?" Cordelia asked.

He closed his eyes then as the guilt and shame washed over him. No one knew except him and Sarita.

"I'd like to remind you I was completely plastered," he said, cracking his lids to gaze at her. "Not that it's much of an excuse. By this point, I was so consumed with fury I was actually seeing double…"

"That could've been the booze," she murmured with a weak smile.

He chuckled. Even at his lowest point, she could coax that out of him. But he grew solemn again as he braced himself to finish. "I screamed at her: 'Fuck *OFF* Sarita! I don't want you in my *fucking life anymore!*'" His hands clenched into fists as he added in a small voice, "And I pegged the empty vodka bottle at her."

Cordelia was just staring at him. "Wow," she finally managed.

"It didn't hit her. But yeah," he shrugged, "it worked, because she left. Left for good. Left me with Edita and Lukas and every so often Bernadette, but I couldn't talk to any of them the way I'd been able to talk to her. And that was that." He didn't tell her that Sarita's voice of reason didn't leave. He saw her in his mind's eye, her mouth wide and smiling, her clothes wild and colourful, fuchsia, violet, lilac, magenta. In his mind, she never changed, never grew older. Sometimes he wanted to beg her to come back to him, but he never did. He couldn't stand how wildly disappointed she'd be in what he'd become.

"Um, so yeah," he said, scrutinising Cordelia's face, trying to gauge what she was thinking, "I just wanted to tell you… all of that. I kind of felt like I owed you a secret. After what you told me the other day." He knew he didn't have to ask her not to tell anyone. She never would.

"You thought I'd understand?"

He nodded.

"I do," she said. "And I'm thankful, because now you know you always have me to talk to." And in that moment, his heart felt so full he was almost dizzy. Being around her was just so easy. Like they'd known each other forever.

The next morning he woke up in Robbie's room, in the bed Scarlett had gone out and bought just for him, with a smile on his face. Yesterday had changed everything for him in every way. Yesterday he'd finally told someone else the whole truth about himself. And he hadn't been judged, or ridiculed, or belittled. And it felt fucking good.

sixteen months later....

chapter six

perfect day

harbord, new south wales, february, 1992

indigo

"So he was gardening *naked?*" Indigo said, leaning forward, brows hitched.

"Well, so he claimed," Joshua grinned. "And *apparently,* he just happened to trip over a rake and fall arse-first into the carrot patch."

"Ewwwww!" Robbie cried, scowling across the table from Indigo to Joshua. "Can we just *not*, over dinner?"

Joshua laughed, reaching to cup Robbie's neck. "But you guys haven't heard the best part," he said, eyes twinkling. "When we removed the carrot, we discovered that it was *peeled.*"

"Oh my God, *GROSS*, Dad!" Robbie squealed, as everyone else burst out laughing. "There's a time and a place for such tales!"

"Never did have the stomach for my work stories, this one," Joshua said, widening his eyes affectionately at Robbie.

"Yeah, well, butts and guts don't exactly pair well with roast lamb and *carrots*," Robbie grumbled, dramatically dropping his knife and fork and pushing his plate away.

"He does have a point, Dad," Cordelia chimed in, wiping her eyes. "Your stories *are* pretty gross. Often hilarious. But always gross."

"Are you guys kidding?" Indigo cried. "His stories are *awesome!*" He'd never been able to understand the twins' lack of enthusiasm towards their father's tales from the ER and operating theatre. He personally couldn't get enough; the human body was a fascinating puzzle.

"I think," Scarlett said, easing up from the table to refill the gravy boat, glancing from Joshua to Indigo, "that we can leave the bowel obstruction stories 'til after dinner." She grimaced.

"My own family, turned against me," Joshua bemoaned, a twinkle in his eye. "Thank God I have Inds or I'd think no one cared about my day."

Scarlett dropped a kiss on the top of his head on her way back to the table. "I care very much about your day, darling," she grinned, "once I've finished eating. You know my stomach is weaker than usual these days." He grabbed her and pulled her onto his lap, kissing her cheek and rubbing her rounded belly with his palm.

"May I be the first to say ew, again?" Robbie said, staring at them in disgust. "There are children present, you know?"

"What did your obstetrician say today, Mum?" Cordelia asked, slicing into a chunk of pumpkin.

"Ten tiny fingers and ten tiny toes," Scarlett smiled, placing her hand over Joshua's on her stomach. "Our lives are going to descend into complete chaos in just a couple of months."

"It's so going to be a girl," Robbie said.

"As much as I'd love a little sister," Cordelia said, "it's a boy."

"I think it's a girl," Scarlett said, smiling up at Joshua.

"Absolutely," he agreed.

"It's definitely a boy," Indigo said, eyeing Scarlett thoughtfully. Ever since she'd announced her pregnancy, all he'd been able to see in his mind's eye was a baby boy, blond with brown eyes.

"Is this a betting situation?" Robbie asked, rubbing his hands together.

"What are we betting?" Joshua asked.

"Nappy changes," Scarlett suggested. "Whoever loses is on nappy duty for the first month."

"Agreed," Robbie said. He turned to his sister. "Cora?"

"Totally," she said.

"I'm in," Joshua said. They all looked at Indigo.

"You three are going to be up to your elbows in baby wipes," he laughed.

Robbie glanced at his watch and jumped up. "Oh my God!" he cried, rushing his plate to the sink and hurrying into the rumpus room. "Are you guys coming?" he called as they heard the TV go on. "It's started!"

Indigo and Cordelia exchanged amused glances across the table. He stood and leant to pick up her plate as she grabbed an armful of glasses and took them to the sink. She turned to her mother. "We'll clean up after *90210*. You go put your feet up."

"I'm pregnant, sweetie, not ill," Scarlett said, smiling at Cordelia. "You cooked such a beautiful meal, clearing up is the least I can do."

"Go sit, I can do it now," Indigo said to Scarlett, turning on the tap to rinse the dishes. "I'm sure Robbie will catch me up. Blow. By. Blow," he added, a ginormous grin breaking through his mock scowl.

"Cordelia! Indigo!" Robbie was now screeching. "You're missing it! Poor little hymenly-challenged Andrea wants West Beverly to give out free condoms, and Donna's mum is having none of it! You've gotta see this!" *Beverly Hills, 90210* was everything to Robbie and it was unfathomable to him anyone would willingly miss a minute. Posters of its stars papered his walls and Cordelia was constantly teasing him for having ripped off Jason Priestley's hairstyle, sideburns and all. Indigo had learned long ago that he was expected to be seen but not heard during *90210*, and witty commentary was definitely frowned upon.

"It's so not worth it," Cordelia said with a roll of her eyes and a killer smile. "Listen to him. If he gets any more high-pitched, he'll upset the neighbour's dog again. Let's just wash up after." She put her hand on his arm, ever so casually, and his stomach flip-flopped. He grinned at her, nodded dumbly and followed her into the rumpus room. They sat on the couch with Robbie between them.

June would mark two years since Indigo became a fully-fledged member of the Carlisle family. He'd been there for Christmases, birthdays, Sunday breakfasts and Easters. He stayed over at least four nights a week. Most Friday nights Robbie would sleep over at his house, often with Drew or one of their other mates. Cordelia joined them regularly enough that she had her own honorary room there, but sometimes she'd leave them to their boys' night and go stay at Peyton's or Sian's.

Indigo was suddenly surrounded by people who genuinely cared about him. They felt his successes and losses as if they were their own. They made sure the brown lunch bag left on the kitchen counter for him each morning before school was nutritionally balanced and packed with care. They made sure he had an umbrella in his school bag on the days the sky looked grey and threatening. They gave him pointed looks if he asked to be excused from the table before his plate was clean of vegetables.

They would be there for him in an instant if he needed them, no questions asked. And when he was around them, he didn't hurt. He still felt what other people were feeling, but it was more a fleeting sensation that quickly passed than the lingering burden it once was. And the voices, well, they'd remained at bay outside the bubble, so far in the background he'd almost forgotten they were there.

He loved the Carlisle's cosy two-storey bungalow with its cluttered kitchen and its ringing laughter and the fragrant freesias that appeared in vases all over the house in the spring. It was ingrained with the smoky saccharine scent of the incense Scarlett burnt day and night and when Joshua was home, the soundtrack of his old familiar records played constantly in the background — Bob Marley, Cat Stevens, and Meat Loaf. This was a real home filled with real love. For the first time in his life, Indigo felt truly seen, truly loved for who he was, flaws and all. They were everything — Joshua, Scarlett, Robbie. And Cordelia.

The moment *90210* cut to an ad break, Robbie turned from Cordelia to Indigo, his eyes shining. "Oh my God, did Brandon *seriously* just shame Andrea for never having gotten *laid*? Does he honestly not realise how bad she wants to give *him* her carnal treasure? Sure, she's an uptight, stalkerish pain-in-the-arse, but..."

As Robbie gushed on, dissecting every ounce of drama that had occurred over the last twenty-five minutes, Cordelia caught Indigo's eye in amusement and he knew exactly what she was thinking. He furrowed his brow and mouthed 'carnal treasure?' and she pressed her hand to her mouth, her body shaking with silent laughter, her eyes twinkling.

He composed himself, turning his attention to Robbie, so passionate in his pontification, but before long he was looking back at Cordelia. She was his favourite thing to look at.

She was twisting a button of the oversized grey cardigan she wore draped over a black slip dress, intently nodding along with Robbie who still hadn't drawn breath. She must have felt Indigo staring, because she looked up. When their eyes met, he winked and her lips quirked up. She tucked a loose strand of hair behind her ear, that tiger's eye hair. He longed to bury his face in that tumbling palette of blonde and caramel and gold, to run the lengths through his fingers.

Her smile widened as she held his gaze, and he was transported back to a coral island in Fiji he once stayed at where the sea had been the most heavenly shade of pristine aquamarine. That was the hue of her eyes.

The truth was, he'd found Cordelia captivating from the moment he first saw her. There was just something about her that drew him in, always, at first, as that sweet elusive girl sitting with her friends in the quadrangle. And now, she'd grown up these past couple of years. His eyes skimmed her slender frame, lingering on the gentle curves she so frequently bemoaned. What with the waifish Kate Moss and her heroin chic look being revered and emulated around the globe, boobs and butts were totally out of fashion. But he'd never much believed in fashion.

The kind of beauty Cordelia possessed was timeless. A beauty that transcended physicality. Because there was so much beauty in her infuriating tenaciousness, in her sweetness and strength, in the way she loved her family and friends with a ferocity Indigo had never before seen in his life. And she *got* him. She saw beneath the cocky front he put on for the world, and he could be vulnerable with her. He let his guard down when he talked to her and he loved the way she listened, her eyes so serious on his.

All the girls he'd met since her seemed colourless.

For him, there was only her.

But to say the actual words?

He couldn't.

Her family was his family. They were his world. And he couldn't risk that. The Carlisles were phenomenal, and if people that phenomenal valued him, he must be worth something. Josh and Scarlett had welcomed him into their lives, treated him like a son. He could lose everything, lose her friendship, which meant everything.

So he said nothing. Just being near her, dissecting movies together, laughing with her until he couldn't breathe, surfing with her, sitting together at the dinner table, was enough.

Well, it wasn't. But it was because it had to be.

After *90210* finished, they discovered Scarlett had sneakily cleaned up the kitchen, so they settled back on the couch to watch a video. As always, Robbie insisted on choosing. As always, Indigo said he didn't care, as long as it didn't feature either of his parents. As always, Cordelia was happy to watch anything. And as always, Robbie passed out before the movie *Point Break*, was half over. Indigo looked forward to these nights because ever since they'd first watched *Ghost* together it had become an unofficial tradition – he and Cordelia staying up talking long after the TV had faded to black.

"So after all that, he just un-cuffed him and let him go out there and surf his way to certain death?" she asked incredulously as the waves crushed down on Patrick Swayze, and Keanu Reeves threw his badge into the ocean and stalked off into the fifty-year storm. She went to the video machine and pressed stop, then began to rewind the tape.

"Yep, you heard Keanu. He knew he wasn't coming back. That swell was epic. No one's riding that and coming out the other side." He'd seen *Point Break* at the movies with Robbie but it had been her first viewing.

"And like, if they're not gonna spring for Aussie actors to play the Aussie cops," she said as she sat back down, "could they at least scrounge up a dialect coach?" He threw his head back and laughed. She regarded him closely for a moment or two. "He just let Patrick Swayze kill himself," she said, gaze wandering to the blank TV. "Like, seriously?"

Indigo shrugged. "It's kinda poetic, right? Because he said early on that he was willing to pay the ultimate price for the ultimate high. He believed it wasn't tragic to die doing what he loved, and Keanu knew that."

She tucked her endless legs up beneath her and turned to him. "I don't know if, after everything he did, he deserved the death he wanted. For him, prison was a much worse fate. And to be honest, I think he's a bit of a wanker, claiming a death that's the result of self-indulgent risk-taking is in any way noble. It's not like he died for some great cause or trying to save someone he loved or anything." Fuck, he loved the way her mind worked.

"How many of us actually get a death that means something?" he asked. "Listen, if it makes you feel any better, it'd be a pretty gnarly way to go, being totally crushed like that. Although they do say drowning's meant to be quite peaceful."

"Who're 'they' and how could 'they' tell anyone that if they're dead?" she asked, raising a sceptical eyebrow.

"Dunno," he chuckled. "Ouija board maybe? Possibly a séance?" Her shudder was almost imperceptible. "So Pres's party on Saturday night, you coming?" he asked.

"Why the sudden change in subject to Drew's party?" she frowned.

"I know this stuff, like, wobbles you out." He could sense her churning fear.

"Can you stop feeling my feelings?" she said with an exasperated eye roll.

He shot her a cheeky grin.

"Fine," she sighed. "Yep, you're right. The thing is, whether dying is your choice or not, what bigger change is there than death? And you know I'm hopeless with change." Her expression turned serious as she drew her knees into her chest. "Even if you weren't scared of dying, wouldn't you still be scared of not seeing your friends and family again? Like if I were paddling out into surf I knew for sure was going to take me out, I reckon all I'd be thinking is how much I'd miss Mum and Dad and Robbie and Peyton and Sian and…and… you…" she finished, her cheeks flushing slightly. She was suddenly intent on examining the antique band she wore on her right hand, the ring he knew Scarlett had given her on her thirteenth birthday.

"I made the list, did I?" he said lightly, his heart leaping.

She looked up at him, her eyes huge on his. "Of course you did," she said, the flames rising higher in her cheeks. "You're one of my best friends, Inds." She exhaled steadily. "We see each other every day. I mean, you're *always* here. I've kinda gotten used to having you around. I guess I'd miss you if you suddenly weren't in my life… So yeah, I would feel sad if I never saw you again." She smiled shyly then and teased, "Just a tiny bit," holding her thumb and finger apart a couple of millimetres.

He swallowed deeply and nodded, forcing a grin over the myriad of conflicting thoughts juddering through his head.

"Don't just leave me hanging. You could say you'd miss me too," she huffed, her eyes twinkling. "Am I on your list?"

The irony was the very thought of not being around her made him want to die. He knew if there was such a thing as the afterlife, he'd beg, borrow, and steal to spend it with her. If reincarnation was on the cards, he'd sell his soul to ensure he met her in the next life. He opened his mouth to tell her she was the person he'd miss the most in the whole wide world before reason crashed in, reminding him he was merely caught up in the moment and that was no excuse to give himself away.

"Yeah, yeah, I guess you'd make the cut," he said nonchalantly instead.

She grinned brightly then, although he could see in her eyes that he'd hurt her, but he didn't know how to make it right. So instead, he quickly changed the subject again. "So, *are* you coming to this party at the Prescotts on Saturday or not? Pres's dad's out of town and as usual it's really his brothers' party, so it'll be super hectic, but I have to go, of course…"

"Dunno," she shrugged. "Depends if I'm in the mood to hang around a bunch of mega-wasted guys daring each other to do the stupidest shit I've ever seen. Those parties are like a front row seat to Darwinism in action."

"Remember when they dared each other to snort wasabi?"

That laugh of hers, the way it illuminated her whole face, the way she raised her hand to cover her mouth, it was completely endearing. And of course then she snorted, as she always did when she really got going. She immediately reddened. Indigo laughed so hard Robbie actually jerked in his sleep. They both froze, but he re-settled quickly back into his rhythmic snoring.

"Those girls they hang around with are completely intimidating." Her voice was low.

"How so?" Indigo asked, perplexed.

"I don't know," she replied, staring at a spot on the couch as she shifted uncomfortably. "They're all like, so thin and beautiful and glamorous."

"Yet they hang around watching a bunch of crazy jocks play beer-can dodgeball," he argued, trying to capture her gaze.

"Besides," he said, making his voice as casual as possible, "look at you, you're a knockout, what are you worrying about those girls for?"

She raised her eyes slowly to meet his, searching his face.

She mustn't have found what she was looking for because she rolled her eyes and smiled, the moment having passed. "So you're saying I should come to the party?"

"Shit yeah you should. Who else will stop me skateboarding off the roof into the pool?" he grinned.

"You would have cracked your head open!"

"I would have made it," he said cockily.

"Guess we'll never know."

"Robbie's going to stay at mine after, you should too. That way, you don't have to worry about your curfew." He leant forward excitedly. "We could take the jet skis down to Palmy for a Box Head session on Sunday morning? Surf's meant to be pumping, there should be some good ten-to-twelve-footers coming through."

"Death on a stick out there, mate," she quoted, shooting him a heart-stopping smile. "I'm in."

On an unseasonably hot March night six weeks later, Indigo awakened to Joshua shaking his shoulder.

He sat up with a start. "What's wrong?" he muttered blearily. "What time is it?"

"It's about four. Scar's been in labour all night. Her water's just broken. We're gonna head to the hospital," Joshua said calmly.

Indigo jumped out of bed and started pacing, unsure what to do or where to go. "Is she ok? What do you want us to do? How can I help?"

Cordelia appeared in the doorway in tiny black floral shorts and a black cap-sleeved t-shirt. "Mum's fine," she smiled, as Joshua squeezed past her to check on Scarlett. "She's been amazing, but the contractions are pretty close together now, so Dad thinks it's time to go."

She glanced over to where Robbie was snoring loudly, his mouth wide, and giggled.

"We'll go on ahead, but if you wanna try and wake sleeping beauty over there, we'll see you guys at the hospital?"

"What, like now?"

"No rush."

Indigo nodded. "Good luck."

"Good luck to you too," Cordelia grinned as she turned to leave. Robbie was an incredibly deep sleeper and they all knew rousing him was no mean feat. He'd found in the past that grabbing Robbie's nose and holding it tight was the most effective method. He'd go with that.

Robbie was majorly distressed at the thought of what was happening in the blow-up paddle pool in that delivery suite, so it fell on Indigo to distract him. Together they paced the hospital corridors, pilfering rubber gloves to make balloons and seeing if they could tip the vending machines to score free chips and chocolate bars.

They'd eventually settled on opposite ends of the couch in the waiting room, stretching out so their feet overlapped in the middle. They must have fallen asleep because the next thing Indigo knew, Cordelia was cupping his cheek and whispering to him that it was all over. He gazed up at her, wondering if he was dreaming, her face so close to his, the jasmine-and ylang-ylang scent of her hair heavenly.

"We're off nappy duty," she was saying.

"It's a boy?" he murmured, a slow, sleepy grin on his face.

"It's a boy," she said and he jumped to his feet and swept her into a hug, swinging her around. She felt so good in his arms he never wanted to let her go, her body moulded perfectly to his, her head nestled under his chin. As he stood there holding her, butterflies came alive inside his stomach, their wings beating a steady thrum he felt everywhere. An orderly rattled by with a trolley then, jolting him back into the now and he released her, stepping back and awkwardly sliding his hands into his pockets.

Cordelia grinned a wicked grin and leant down over Robbie, pinching his nose and crying, "Oh my God, is that Luke Perry?!"

Robbie sat bolt upright, open-mouthed, his head swivelling back and forth like a plaster clown in a sideshow carnival game. "What? Where?" he demanded, bleary-eyed.

"Oi, sleepyhead," she said, "you're officially a middle child."

"The baby's here?" he said, jumping to his feet. "What is it? Is it ok? Is Mum ok? What time is it?"

"A boy, he's divine. Mum's exhausted but over the moon, and it's just after ten."

"That was a long labour," Robbie mused as they headed for the delivery room.

"Not really," Cordelia said. "He's been here for a while. You two just looked too cute to wake, practically spooning there on the couch together."

"Spooning?" Robbie spluttered. "We were not!"

"I borrowed Dad's camera," she grinned. "I have photographic evidence."

They entered Scarlett's room and there he was, Matthew Jack Carlisle, a baby so wanted and so longed for, a baby seven years in the making, a baby so beautiful, they were all instantly smitten, no one more so than Indigo. The moment the small sweet-smelling bundle was placed in his arms, he was overwhelmed with emotion. "Great choice, Matty, joining this family here," he whispered. "You must be one clever little guy."

After Matty was born, Indigo never wanted to leave the Carlisle's house. Matty was a colicky baby and it seemed everyone was grateful to have an extra set of hands around to rock him or take him for a walk or wander the corridors with him in the wee hours of the morning when he refused to settle. Indigo was quickly dubbed the baby whisperer, because only in his embrace would Matty strop screaming bloody murder, would stop drawing his little legs up into his chest and balling his fists so tightly. Indigo would lay Matty across his chest and rub his small belly, always knowing exactly where it hurt, often falling asleep himself, one large hand held securely over the baby's body. Sometimes he'd hold Matty in his arms and gaze down into his huge brown eyes and pictures would come into his mind and he swore it was Matty trying to communicate with him.

They were all so distracted the September after Matty was born that Indigo wasn't expecting it when Robbie finally poked a toe out of the closet. They'd been hanging in Robbie's room discussing who was going to a party at Drew's that night. Indigo didn't want Robbie to figure out how he felt for Cordelia, so he always went out of his way to talk about other girls. Robbie was sprawled on his bed while Indigo was simultaneously doing sit-ups and listing all the girls that were going to be there when Robbie cleared his throat and said, "So listen, Inds, I-I don't really care which girls are gonna be there tonight. Because… because I don't really *like* girls. Well, not the way *you* like them I mean… You see, the thing is…" He'd taken a deep breath and sat up before adding a big blurty, "I'm gay."

Indigo froze mid-sit-up and looked at him intently, unsure of what to say. Although it had remained unspoken up until now, it had always been the most obvious thing in the world to him. It was one of those things that just was and he'd never given it much thought.

"Did you *know?*" Robbie squeaked.

Indigo merely shrugged and jumped up, tapping Robbie so he shuffled over and he could sit beside him. He grinned broadly and nudged him with his shoulder. "Listen, man, I might have had an inkling…" He slung his arm around his friend, hugging him close. "I bet it feels good to finally say it out loud, though."

Robbie hung his head. "It's not fair, Inds," he whispered. "You know what they used to call me at my last school?"

Indigo shook his head.

"Vegemite."

Indigo frowned.

"Because a little bit goes a long way," Robbie mimicked. "I've always been the awkward kid nobody gets. Then I was the dyslexic kid. Now I've gotta be the gay kid, too. Why do *I* always have to be different?" He bit his lip, his eyes filling.

Indigo turned his head to stare at him, searching for the right words. "Rob," he finally said, "it's true. For as long as I've known you, you've been different from everyone else. But you know what? That's my most favourite thing about you." He started playfully listing all the guys who would be at the party, (although he was very aware that when it came to guys their age, Robbie was very much alone in the openly gay department), before circling back round with a nonchalant, "Wanna talk about it?"

High school was a hetero vacuum and Indigo felt Robbie's isolation. So after the big coming out he'd gotten fake IDs for Robbie and Cordelia, and the next February when his mother was in town performing at the Mardi Gras Afterparty she'd gotten him tickets. Drew had come too and they'd worn glitter on their bodies and faces and danced on podiums and bonded with fabulous drag queens and Robbie had connected with people who made him realise he wasn't weird or unusual or alone — he was just in high school.

It was so crowded that night, Indigo had to hold Cordelia's hand to lead her through the throng and it was so loud he'd had to lean in real close to talk to her. She'd looked smoking hot in that shimmery midnight-blue mini dress that clung to her curves, taller than he was used to in ankle-breaking high stilettos.

When his mother was lowered from the ceiling onto centre stage, clad in the most miniscule pair of white fringed hot-pants and matching bralette, head adorned with sparkly devil horns, he felt himself shutting down, withdrawing into himself. But then he'd felt Cordelia's hands slide into his and all that existed in that moment was her, those wide eyes locked on his, holding him steady. And then he barely registered Bernadette up there, all adoring eyes on her as she belted out a pitch perfect rendition of *Dancing in Heaven (Orbital Be-Bop)*. She strutted and shimmied, living up to her moniker 'Goddess of the Gays', effortlessly performing the most complicated of dance moves like the freakin' superstar she was. Her back-up dancers were a bevy of super-cut men whose sculpted torsos glistened as they twirled her and spun her high up over their heads. And through it all, she didn't miss a beat, continuing to shake her arse while the enraptured crowd screamed and whistled.

"Meh," Cordelia said, faking a yawn. "She's not all that."

And he laughed then, his heart swelling because she had his back. She was a terrible liar, but it still made him feel better. Her face was alight all night as she watched Robbie, finally in his place with his people, realising there was a whole wide world out there outside of his suburban little existence. Robbie had his first kiss that night and he'd made a lot of new friends.

Because Drew and Indigo had industriously bartered their shirts to a brazen admirer in exchange for some little pink pills, the four of them were still a little high when they'd left the afterparty, so sleep wasn't on the cards. Robbie had protested when they'd directed the taxi to Jump Rock near Indigo's house, refusing to participate as they'd kicked off their shoes and stripped down to their underwear, scrambling down the rocky outcrop by the light of the wan moon to reach the highest platform. Robbie had gathered their clothes as Indigo and Drew had front flipped off the cliff into the darkness, hitting the inky ocean six metres below, followed quickly by Cordelia, who leapt off after them. The water had felt amazing on their skin and the three of them had swum until Robbie began to freak out, yelling down all the ways in which they could die, his list heavy on sharks and prehistoric giant squid. So they'd reluctantly picked their way out through the razor sharp oyster shells and clamoured over slippery rocks back up the cliffs to placate him and do it all again.

When they got back to Indigo's they'd jumped in the pool, swimming and laughing and solving the problems of the world while the Violent Femmes warbled from the outdoor speakers 'til the sky turned pinky-grey. They were in the hot tub lazily passing a joint when Edita came out and whisper-yelled it was almost five in the morning and they'd better get to bed before they woke Bernadette, who'd arrived home an hour before them. Indigo knew his mother would be well KOed under a heavy veil of Valium but they did as they were told anyway, subtly stashing the joint and apologising to Edita, who shook her head and muttered in Lithuanian, bustling about fetching freshly laundered towels for them. Edita was always on edge when Bernadette was in town, but her bark was worse than her bite.

The next morning, Indigo barely flinched when his mother swanned down with her luggage and announced she was returning to LA a week early. He'd filled the void she'd created in his life and her power over him was now non-existent. So he bade her goodbye and left before she could, heading back to the Carlisles with Robbie and Cordelia.

When Indigo looked back, the thing that shocked him the most was it all ended as quickly as it had begun. Almost three years of utopia, almost three years of being an honorary Carlisle, he thought it would last forever. But he was soon to discover nothing ever does.

chapter seven

if I could

cordelia

Cordelia had gotten used to having Indigo around. And of course he'd kind of grown on her. Maybe more than kind of. Underneath that cockiness and those ridiculous bronzed good looks was so much more.

Ever since the night he'd first opened up to her about his parents, they'd grown closer and closer — he'd even confided his biggest secrets to her — until one day she realised he was the best friend she'd ever had.

She recalled that day so clearly. She'd been fourteen and the guy she'd been dating had dumped her for not wanting to take things so quickly and she'd come home in tears. Not because she was heartbroken — she hadn't been that into him to begin with. He was the type of guy who suggestively pushed your head down towards his crotch when you were making out, the type of guy who seemed to have about thirty-two fingers on four hands, every one of which felt wrong on her body yet continued to wander no matter how many times she said no. But his break-up tirade had included insults like 'frigid bitch' and 'prick-tease' and she'd been feeling incredibly fragile when she'd arrived home planning on slinking up to her room before anyone could see the state she was in.

But just as she was about to open the front door, she'd heard footsteps coming up the pathway behind her, and then, "Hey, you." She'd frozen, not wanting to turn around, dying at the thought he might see her cry.

But her shoulders were shaking and, of course, he noticed. "Cordelia?" Indigo had said softly, coming up behind her. "What's wrong?"

She'd shaken her head, still not turning, not trusting herself to speak.

"Look at me," he'd said, but she'd known if she did, it would be the end of her. She'd felt his hand on her shoulder then and he'd gently spun her to face him and when she'd seen those beautiful eyes of his peering into hers, edged with so much worry, she completely lost it. He'd drawn her into his arms, holding her while she sobbed and when she'd calmed down a bit, he'd led her to the porch steps, pulling her down to sit beside him.

"What happened?" he'd asked, tenderly brushing the tears from her face with his thumbs. So she'd told him, even though his face had darkened like thunder as she blurted out every nasty slur that had been hurled her way, even when his hands had clenched to white-knuckled fists by his sides and his jaw set in such a way she'd known if her ex were there, Indigo would have made him regret every word.

"What's wrong with me, Indigo?" she'd whispered.

"What's wrong with you?" he'd breathed. "Fucking hell. *Nothing.*" He'd put his arm around her and pulled her close. "You, Cordelia, are perfection." He'd kissed the top of her head, then rested his chin upon it. "Anyone who makes you feel anything less isn't worth a minute of your day, ok?"

She'd sighed a deep, shuddery sigh and shrugged.

"I'm serious," he'd said, pulling back so he could stare her in the eye. "He's not worth your tears. He's just some silly little boy who doesn't even know himself yet, let alone you."

"How do you know?"

"How do I know? Because if he knew you, if he truly saw you, he'd never be stupid enough to let you go. He's not the one, Cora."

"The one?"

"The night of your thirteenth birthday party, Rob said you were looking for the one who takes your breath away."

"You remember that?"

"I remember everything."

She'd leant back into the crook of his arm, nestling her head on his shoulder, suddenly realising she could barely catch her breath. There in his warm embrace, heady with his scent, she'd wanted the world to stop turning so they could stay that way forever. She'd been fourteen then and by fifteen she'd noticed the constant stream of well-formed women who revolved in and out of Indigo's life had slowed to a trickle. And then one day she realised there had been no one for months.

Yet she never got up the courage to ask him why. She'd seen the girls he'd dated. He was so experienced, so worldly. Why would he ever be interested in her?

Cordelia often lay awake at night, marvelling at how much their little family had evolved over the years. Once it had just been her, Robbie and Mum, and then Dad, and then Indigo and now Matty. She was so blessed to be so completely surrounded by people she adored. Sometimes her heart felt so full it could burst.

Matty's arrival meant Indigo was around even more. And Indigo was so good with him, a real natural. When she was holding Matty and Indigo walked into the room, Matty would lunge out of her arms, throwing himself towards Indigo. She couldn't really blame him. When Indigo walked into the room, she had the same inclination.

She and Indigo spent more and more time together, surfing before school and on the weekends or hanging out with Robbie and his mates or hers. He got a motorbike for his birthday the year he got his licence and the two of them would often jump on it and ride up the coast. Her dad hadn't been happy about the bike and it hadn't helped when Robbie had joked it was the safest thing she'd ever have between her legs. For weeks on end, her dad's work horror stories around the dinner table followed the same theme: patients who'd been scraped off the road after motorcycle accidents and brought into his ER. But her mum had talked him around as usual and in the end he'd had to admit he trusted Indigo's judgement and skill. After all, Indigo had been riding motocross since he was ten and knew his way around a bike.

Cordelia loved riding on the back of that bike because she had no choice but to wrap her arms snugly around his waist and press herself tight up against him. She'd lean her cheek against his shoulder, dizzy with the sandalwoody-sea-on-a-summer-breeze scent of him. She'd squeeze her eyes shut tight as her senses went into overdrive. It took all her strength to resist slipping her fingers beneath his shirt to trace the contours of his lightly sculpted abs.

Then there were all those nights they ended up watching TV together, her counting the moments until Robbie started snoring garishly on the couch beside them, his mouth wide and snarling. One night, despite insisting they watch *My Girl*, Robbie had nodded off, as was his way. Cordelia happened to glance over at Indigo to see him wiping his eyes.

"Are you crying?" she exclaimed, widening her eyes at him.

"It's sad, ok?" he laughed through his tears as he plucked at the leather beaded bracelet on his wrist. "The kid died. And he doesn't have his glasses. He can't see without his glasses." He regarded her dry eyes and said, "What, are you made of stone?"

"I'm just not much of a crier," she shrugged. "Unlike *you*, you big cry baby," she giggled, poking him in the ribs and handing him a tissue. What she really wanted to do was hug him. "I think we should wake Rob up so he can see his big tough mate sobbing over a PG-13 movie. I mean, there go all his grand plans of making you watch *Beaches* with him. If you can't handle *this,* there's no way you're ready for *that!*"

"Piss off," Indigo chuckled, "I can totally handle *Beaches.* And you just keep your big mouth shut, Cordelia Carlisle. I have a reputation to protect here… I kinda rely on the fact that no one's game to mess with me," he said, eyebrow cocked. He leant in towards her, eyes earnest. "You know I'm not big into violence. So I kinda need for people to not be *willing* to fight me. Although we all know I'm pretty good at it," he shrugged.

"Yeah," she said with a roll of her eyes, "you're totally the wind beneath my wings."

She loved that she could make him laugh, really laugh. She knew nobody teased him the way she did and he seemed to find it funny that she had the audacity. "I'd totally mess with you," she said, holding up her fists and cocking her head to one side. "You wanna take it outside? I could give you a black eye. Maybe knock out a couple of those perfect teeth, give you a bit of street cred?"

He laughed that deep belly chortle that threw his head back and doubled his whole body over. Eventually she started giggling at him laughing, until they were both rolling around, simultaneously laughing and shushing each other so as not to wake Robbie. He didn't even care that she snorted when she laughed. In fact, it only seemed to make him laugh harder.

He caught her gaze then and the way he looked at her... it made her feel so much. When he looked at her that way, it made her feel beautiful. And it had for some time now.

And that night, something was burning there in his eyes and for a moment she let herself believe it was the intensity of the flame he carried for her. It took everything she had to stop herself from reaching out to trace the plane of his cheek, to touch his lips, to utter the words that would change everything. But then a large snarfle escaped Robbie's throat, bringing her crashing back to reality, and the reality was that she and Indigo were just friends. The very best of friends, but just friends, nonetheless. And so she made an excuse about being tired and went to bed, pushing away the fact that every time she said goodnight to him, every time she walked away, it hurt.

indigo

That stolen moment was so fleeting it was almost as though it never happened, but Indigo had felt it, had seen it in her face. But then Robbie had shattered their reverie and she'd flushed and looked away and he wondered if he'd imagined the whole thing. He wished so hard in that moment he could feel what others felt for him. He knew she felt happy when she was around him, but so did a lot of people. She'd stood up quickly and said she needed to go to bed and he was left watching *My Girl* with Robbie snoring loudly beside him.

Every fibre of his being yelled at him to go after her, to knock on her bedroom door, to enter that private sanctuary of hers and confess his feelings to her and damn the consequences. It was torture being so close to her, yet so far. That afternoon, when she'd wrapped those slender arms around him as they'd ridden down to Avalon, he'd barely been able to concentrate on the road with every contour of her beautiful body moulded against his. Most nights he dreamt of her and in those dreams she was his and life was perfect. But when he woke, reaching for her, aching for her, he always realised too soon that he lived in a reality where they were just friends and he couldn't just run his fingers through the lengths of her hair any old time he wanted, or touch those crazily kissable lips of hers or hold her near.

Not being with her it was driving him insane. She'd burrowed deep in his heart and expanded within its chambers, consuming it in its entirety so there was barely space for anything or anyone else. He half rose to follow her upstairs but then sat back down again, then just as he was about to get up again, he heard the front door open and close and Joshua appeared looking weary.

"Oh good, I was hoping you were still up," he said, flopping down beside Indigo on the couch. He had a rolled-up magazine in his hand.

"How was work?" Indigo asked.

"Yeah, fine," Joshua said distractedly, then, "Listen, Inds, er, have you er…" He twisted the magazine in his hands as he spoke, "have you seen this yet?" he finally asked, unfurling the magazine and showing Indigo the front cover.

Indigo stared at it and shook his head. Joshua held it out and he reached for it tentatively, staring down at an image of his father's face. *'Wilson the Lone Wolfe,'* the tag line read. *'Hollywood's Ultimate Absentee Father Neglects His Pack.'*

"What is this?" Indigo asked, feeling slightly sick. He hated it when his parents were in the press and all the attention it brought.

"Read it," Joshua said, placing a firm hand on his shoulder, squeezing reassuringly. "I need to go take a shower. We'll talk after, ok?"

Indigo nodded dumbly, flicking through the pages with shaking hands until he came to the article. There was a picture of him, a recent one too, which creeped him out. Who knows which bush they'd hidden in to get that? He closed his eyes as a feeling of dread washed over him. And then he opened them and began to read.

It turned out that exposé was just the beginning. March of 1993 must have been a slow news month because the whole thing blew into a complete and utter media shitstorm. Wilson Wolfe's career revolved around his image as an all-round good guy and loving family man. But someone had leaked the truth and now the press was hounding him, branding him a fraud, calling him a truant father and accusing him of being neglectful of his kids. He was torn to shreds by the media, his reputation in tatters. Wilson's PR manager went into damage control. As his four older sons were now well into their twenties and thirties and he had no jurisdiction over them, Wilson and his entourage set their sights on Indigo, by then seventeen-years-old, still a minor and a ready solution to their problem. If Wilson could get custody of Indigo and move him into his home in New York, he could start to claw back his image.

Bernadette, who was honeymooning on the Amalfi Coast with the twenty-something husband she'd met on her latest movie set, didn't bother to respond to Wilson's petitions for custody until he reluctantly dangled the transfer of the title of his beloved Lake Como villa into her name, at which point she was quite willing to sign Indigo over to his father.

Indigo barely knew the man whose name resided on his birth certificate. He knew he was the source of his trust fund and the child support cheque that arrived each month; he knew the big empty house in Aspen he rattled around in two weeks a year belonged to his father, and when he was younger there were the ten days every July he was sent to New York to stay in Wilson's penthouse with Ana Maria the housekeeper. He'd read articles in which his father declared his love for and closeness to all five of his boys (whom he never saw), but Cordelia was the only one he'd ever told how hurt and angry his father's hypocrisy made him feel.

Things happen quickly for someone as influential as Wilson Wolfe. It was only a matter of weeks before Indigo was ordered to pack his things and move to New York.

Indigo couldn't believe his father could just fucking come in like this and destroy his whole universe, that he could tear him from the only family he'd ever known. The megalomaniac piece of shit! Indigo was powerless. It broke him to bits that he had to leave Australia and everyone in it. Her.

He put on a brave face but already he was beginning to withdraw into himself, his smiles growing more forced, the insomnia and anxiety he hadn't seen in years slowly creeping back in. The day he left, Scarlett prepared all his favourite foods for lunch and they all sat down to eat, stoic and reserved. Indigo caught Cordelia looking at him across the table, and he knew she could see straight through it all, that she could see how he was falling apart inside, and he didn't want her to see that, because he knew how hard she'd worked over the years to put him back together, to make him whole, to help him reframe the way he saw himself. He'd grown to like who he was in her eyes and right now, seeing someone else reflected back at him in those clear aquamarine pools, he couldn't cope with that. Not one bit.

cordelia

Indigo was leaving for the airport that night so had spent the day at her house, withdrawn and quiet, but savouring his last moments and saying his goodbyes. Cordelia swore she'd seen tears in his eyes as he'd bounced Matty on his knee and held him close, inhaling his sweet baby smell.

They knew their time was almost up when Indigo went to change for his flight, emerging in jeans and a blue plaid flannel shirt, his hair neatly combed, navy Converse on his feet, his trusty denim jacket slung over his arm. And then his driver arrived to collect him, luggage already piled high inside the black sedan, and it seemed it was all happening way too soon. Mum began to cry. Dad was stoic as he pulled Indigo into a bear hug and held him tight, not letting go for a long time. Robbie buried his face in Indigo's chest, then fled to his room, slamming the door behind him. He later told Cordelia that was the moment he understood friends could break your heart too.

It was Cordelia who walked Indigo out to the car where the driver waited discreetly behind the wheel. Her stomach churned as tears threatened to spill down her cheeks. She could barely fathom that this was it. That in a few moments, he just wouldn't be there anymore. Two steps down the driveway, he suddenly grabbed her hand and pulled her into the shadows of the banana palms at the side of the house. And she was in his arms. And she could barely breathe at the very nearness of him; his face inches from hers, his whole body pressed to hers, the electricity palpable. All those months and years of wanting, of wondering, of adoration…

"Cordelia," he whispered, his thumb caressing her lower lip, his eyes bright on hers.

Her breath caught in her throat. Her heart was beating so fast.

And then his lips were on hers, gentle at first until she was kissing him back and then, not gentle, a snatched moment of perfection on what felt like their last day on earth. Nearly three years of yearning, loving, culminating in one perfect kiss. His hands were in her hair, his tongue gently persistent against hers. No one had ever kissed her like this; she could live and die inside this kiss.

When they finally broke apart, they were both breathing heavily.

"I've always loved you," he whispered as he slipped the leather beaded bracelet off his wrist and onto hers.

And then he was gone. Gone. Gone before she could catch her breath and gather herself and tell him that from the very depths of her soul, she'd always loved him too.

chapter eight

disarm

manhattan, new york, april, 1993

indigo

So he left them, left her, and he boarded that plane with the most portable of his worldly possessions packed into the hold below and he was broken. Angry. Angry. Angry. And so broken. Everything changed when he left Sydney; *he* changed. It was like the protective coating that had cocooned him for so long, that had kept him sane and safe, had been ripped off and he was left raw, exposed, vulnerable. His whole world shifted on its axis and he was thrown from dry land, propelled into the darkest depths of the ocean where there was nothing to cling to and it seemed impossible not to drown.

He'd made up his mind to hate New York, to hate his father, to hate everyone and everything. So upon arrival, his first order of business was to find a reliable dealer who could supply him with weed whenever he wanted it, sometimes pills and coke, stuff he'd merely dabbled in for fun in recent years because he hadn't needed it. But now he did. He started drinking on the weekends, and then every day. He spiralled and spiralled until he'd funnelled himself swiftly and deftly into the depth and breadth of his misery without spilling a single drop.

And Cordelia. Well, he'd left Cordelia with nothing. Nothing but that one aching kiss, both first and final, forever scorched upon his lips.

The night he'd had to leave Sydney, leave her, had ripped his heart to shreds and undone the very last bit of him. To know that endless love had been there all along, right there within his reach and then to have to let it go, unexplored, unresolved, largely unspoken... It had been his demise.

She'd been so beautiful that night. When he closed his eyes, he could see every detail so clearly, her hair cascading down her back in a wild spill, those angel eyes tinged with such sadness. It made him want to cry just to think of them. She'd been barefoot in a little white dress, her legs long and tanned, her embrace so warm, her lips so generous and soft.

But now he was all alone, lying on his side in his big bed with its rumpled navy sheets, eyes closed, a pillow hugged to his chest. His stomach hurt so much from feeling everyone else so acutely. He had his headphones on, totally immersed in Guns N' Roses' *Patience*, when he felt the energy in the room shift. He split his lids to see the imposing form of Ana Maria looming over him. Night had fallen and she reached to switch on a lamp. He blinked, his gaze sliding listlessly to her round face. She looked majorly pissed off, but she always did. Her mouth was forming words he couldn't hear. He dragged his headphones off.

"Mr Indi," she was saying curtly in her lilting Jamaican accent, "phone call. Miss Cordelia again."

He squeezed his eyes shut tight and shook his head.

Ana Maria sighed heavily. "I cannot keep lying to the poor girl and telling her you're out, Mr Indi."

"Just do it. Please," he murmured. He felt tears prick his eyes. The person he'd been with Cordelia was not the person he was anymore. If she could see him now, she'd be so disappointed in him. They all would be. So he'd done the only thing he could. He'd cut off all contact with them. He never took their calls. He read all their letters, devoured them over and over, yet he never replied. And their letters grew fewer and farther between, and their attempted phone calls had dwindled to once a week, then to once a fortnight.

"Fine," Ana Maria snapped coldly. "But you better be going to school tomorrow and not be laying round this apartment all day again or I'll be telling your father." She spun and huffed out of the room and Indigo reached under his bed for the bottle of bourbon he'd stashed there. He was all alone again. All alone and so lonely. It covered him like a shroud and he felt himself withering more and more each day.

Indigo fit in well at his new private school on the Upper East Side. His whole life, he'd always had his pick of friends and now he purposely sought out those who would only judge him on the surface. Because of who his father was, the teachers turned a blind eye if he slept in class or wagged school or turned up drunk or stoned. As the swirling darkness descended upon him, growing thicker and denser, he merely went through the motions.

The worst thing was that here in New York, the bubble that had kept the voices at bay these past few years had popped. And they'd barrelled back in, whispered at first, then louder and louder, so many telling him he wasn't good enough, that he was useless and worthless and weak. And his father tended to agree with them.

Indigo hadn't been the good compliant son his father had naively expected and Wilson Wolfe wasn't used to not getting what he wanted. His go-to coping method, when things didn't go his way, was to behave like a petulant child.

"Indi!" Wilson screamed. Grey light bathed Indigo's room; it must be morning. He could hear his father storming through the sprawling Fifth Avenue penthouse he shared with four staff members and now Indigo.

"Indigo!" Wilson yelled as he flung Indigo's bedroom door open and tore the curtains back, then yanked the covers off his bed. He kicked the stereo system beside Indigo's bed and the Smashing Pumpkins abruptly stopped singing *Disarm*.

"Go 'way," Indigo mumbled, curling into the foetal position and squeezing his eyes shut.

"Get up!" Wilson barked. "I want to talk to you, boy."

Indigo opened his eyes and glared up at his father standing over his bed, hands on hips, face like a thundercloud.

"Why?" Indigo snapped, pulling a pillow over his head.

Wilson leant over and wrenched the pillow away. "Listen, I don't give a damn if you drink my bar dry, Indi. I've turned a blind eye to the pilfering of my coke and pot, but I draw the line at wanton destruction!"

"Whaddaya talking about?"

"I'm talking about the cigarette burn on my brand new damask sofa! That thing cost more than your tuition for a year!"

"Well, you were ripped off, Wilson. That thing is ugly as shit."

Wilson's face turned an ugly shade of puce. "That's enough lip out of you, boy! I hold my meetings in that room. How do you think it makes me look, having a sofa that's been clearly vandalised in my home?"

"It wasn't me," Indigo said, surly, climbing out of bed and pulling a t-shirt on over his Calvin Klein boxer briefs.

"It wasn't you?"

"Nope," he replied, folding his arms, scowling.

"So who was it, then?"

"Dunno."

"Oh, I see. I suppose it was a member of my staff then." His lip curled as he surveyed his son. "I guess I'll just have to interrogate them all and fire the one I suspect as the culprit." He turned to leave the room.

"Fine," Indigo sighed. "It was me. But for fuck's sake, it was an accident, ok? I fell asleep smoking a spliff. It's just one small hole. Put a pillow over it or something."

"Put a… put a *pillow* over it?" Wilson spluttered, advancing on him, fists clenched. "What sort of second-rate establishment do you think you're living in here?" He came close enough that Indigo could see the scars from his latest facelift, could see the silver roots beneath his dyed blond hair. "I rue the day I brought you to live here. I really do. You're a spoilt, ungrateful waste of space!"

"Yeah well, you only have yourself to blame for that!" Indigo snapped. "You think I *want* to be here?"

He hadn't heard one kind word from the moment he'd set foot inside Wilson's home and it had worn him down like icy water on sandstone. He'd come to believe he was what his father said he was: nothing. And he'd gradually lowered himself to meet his father's expectations. Cordelia had spent years slowly, gently building him up, but the bad stuff was easier to believe.

"I'm too old for this shit," Wilson said. "Why I agreed to a fifth child is beyond me. I must have had rocks in my head. I don't know what I did to deserve a son like you. Why can't you be more like your brothers? Letting your mother raise you was pure stupidity, I suppose, that self-centred ditz couldn't raise a sea monkey!"

"You don't even know me," Indigo spat. "And *you're* the one who made me come here!"

Wilson snorted. "Well, that sure was a mistake, but what's done is done. If I send you back now, the media will have me for breakfast. Just finish out the year and I'll give you your passport back, then I don't care where you go. In the meantime, you keep to your part of the apartment and I'll keep to mine. I don't want to see you. I don't want to hear you."

"Fine, let's start now," Indigo said, gesturing to the door.

Wilson spun to go, but his step faltered and he turned back. "Ana Maria showed me your SAT scores," he said, studying his son through narrowed eyes.

"She had no right," Indigo growled.

"Did you pay someone to sit it for you?"

Indigo snorted, crossed his arms. "Nope." Why would he bother?

A sliver of softness relaxed Wilson's scowl. "But they were almost perfect scores." He sounded bewildered. Dumbfounded?

Indigo shrugged. He barely remembered taking them. "I thought you were leaving?"

Wilson's face hardened back up. "You're late for school," he barked, pivoting to leave. "And take a shower. You smell like a bar room floor."

The moment Wilson slammed the door behind him, Indigo melted back into his bed and squeezed his eyes shut. He hated it here so much. He hated that his father brought out the arsehole in him.

He was just so *tired* all the time. The darkness encased him like thick choking smoke, devouring all oxygen and light so it was impossible to shake. He clenched his hands into fists, curling his knees to his chest against the constant churning tearing at his insides, like shadow fingers clawing at his gut.

'*You're a worthless piece of shit.*'

His eyes sprung open, but there was no one there, of course.

The voices. He'd first started noticing them again on the plane over, but they'd been so quiet, almost like a hum of white noise, he'd managed to ignore them. But they'd slowly grown in clarity and annunciation, so now there was no doubt they were there.

Sometimes they were inside his head, other times outside of it, and they varied, by gender, by accent, by intonation. They told him things, things he didn't want to know, things he didn't want to hear, like the one now that forced its way in, to tell him in great detail exactly how she'd killed her twin sister and stolen her identity.

With every cell of his body, he wanted to crawl to the phone and call the number he knew by heart. He wanted to hear her voice on the other end of the line; he wanted to beg her for help. But for her sake, he couldn't. He loved her far too much to sully her with his poison, for he'd learnt now how contagious that poison was. So instead of calling her, he rolled a joint and decided to stay in bed for the day.

He thought of re-reading one of her letters for the umpteenth time, but he knew that today her beautiful words would just make him feel sadder.

In October, Wilson flew to his latest movie set in the Bahamas, so Indigo had free rein of the penthouse. Wilson had commandeered a villa in the Caribbean which he expected Ana Maria to run, so he took her with him. They wouldn't be back until after Christmas. Indigo couldn't stand the staff hovering over him, so he told the rest of them to take leave with full pay.

He wandered listlessly through the apartment. Love did not exist within its walls. It was cold and austere, all marble and sapphire and navy and gold. His father was proof that money couldn't buy taste.

The separation he felt from others, from the world in general, was a chasm so great it seemed unfordable.

He'd graduated in June and now spent most of his days in bed, curled up in a ball, the lonely waves crashing over him. When he could muster the energy, he allowed the acquaintances he'd made to coerce him out at night, dragging him to clubs or parties or underground raves, readily numbing himself with whatever was on offer: drugs, booze, female attention...

And then it was back to his bed where he could lie and stare at the ceiling all day, or at the grey-blue walls when that grew tiresome. He was just so damned exhausted he could barely move and everything hurt so much. He wasn't used to living so far from the ocean, so far from nature. New York was so busy and crowded and as the days went by, he grew more and more consumed by its seamy darkness. Sometimes he'd dream dreams dripping with damaged souls in so much pain it was like he could feel the whole city crushing him. When he awoke, he'd imagine he could feel every single one of them and it hurt so bad, it hollowed out his insides and he couldn't make it stop.

He hadn't fucking asked to be privy to the most private thoughts of a nameless, faceless crowd and he wished and wished and wished to shut it all out, that suffocating misery. Whispers for help. Shameful confessions. Chilling secrets. Demands for assistance he had no way of giving.

He'd find himself dozing off and then he'd dream again. More and more, he dreamed of dying and the blissful nothingness that came with it. It scared him, how much he liked those dreams.

But then he'd dream of Cordelia, so beautiful she was like sunshine for his soul.

'Come back to me, Indigo,' she'd say. 'Come back and I'll make it ok.'

And he wanted to go to her so badly. But he couldn't. She'd be so ashamed of him, of what he'd become. He had to let her go. Because there was no longer any hope for him, there was no way his life was ever going to get good again.

He'd lay in bed clutching his hands over his chest as though gathering the damaged pieces of his heart together, trying to stop the warmth of her love seeping from the cracks. He'd barely register that his pillow was wet with tears. And then he'd sleep again.

He'd awaken to the voices, a mishmash of static so overwhelming he didn't bother trying to figure out where one ended and the next began. He would merely lay and let the deluge wash over him.

There was one voice though, that was louder than the rest, one that would repeat over and over:

"You are nothing."

"You are worthless."

"You are toxic."

"You are unlovable."

And he would lie there, eyes blankly staring, and murmur catatonically:

"I am nothing."

"I am worthless."

"I am toxic."

"I am unlovable."

One day, the hallucinations began. He'd catch movement from the corner of his eye and he'd swivel his head towards it, but no one would be there. But then one time he turned and there was an old woman there, ranting and sobbing in a language he didn't understand, and from then on it was relentless, the constant parade of people who seemed to appear in his bedroom then disappear just as quickly. Strangers standing over him, wandering through the hallways, materialising behind him in the bathroom mirror. But he could ignore the sight of them. He merely had to close his eyes and they were gone. But the sound of their pleas and accusations and confessions was harder to ignore as it joined and merged with the cacophony of nameless, faceless voices he was picking up like a defective radio. The bad things they told him eroded his faith in humanity.

He'd lie immersed in the chatter, hands jammed over his ears, although that barely did anything. Loud music helped to drown them out sometimes. They weren't all bad. There was one sitting there in the background, soothing and melodic, telling him he was special and important, but it grew fainter and fainter, drowned out by the ones that confirmed what he already knew: that the world was shit and he would never be good enough.

Sometimes they told him the world would be better off without him in it, and as time wore on, he found he tended to agree with them.

chapter nine

nothing compares 2 u

harbord, new south wales, april, 1993

cordelia

The Indigo-shaped hole in the Carlisles' lives was palpable.

Cordelia lay awake at night thinking of their eclectic, ever-changing little family. First her and Robbie and Mum, then Dad, then Indigo, then Matty. And now not Indigo. Her heart was no longer full.

It took Mum weeks to stop reaching for a third brown lunch bag each morning before school and at least two months of throwing out leftovers to adjust to not cooking to accommodate Indigo's enormous appetite. She no longer knew what to do about the huntsman spiders that frequently wandered into her house; she'd always left them for Indigo, who would expertly scoop them up with his bare hands and gently release them into the garden.

Dad had to get used to the polite nods and smiles he now received from his family when he talked about work, rather than Indigo's enthusiastic barrage of questions.

Matty, now a year old, was undeniably unsettled after Indigo's departure, sleeping a lot less and crying a lot more in the weeks that followed. They could see his little eyes searching the doorway in the afternoons when Robbie and Cordelia walked in from school, waiting for Indigo to stride in and sweep him up in his arms and blow raspberries on his tummy as he always had.

When she wasn't at school Cordelia holed herself up in her bedroom, drowning her sorrows in tragic love ballads. In those first weeks it seemed no one but Sinead understood that nothing compared to him, but as time slowly passed her attitude adjusted with Mariah's suggestion he'd possibly never been anything more than a vison of love, until eventually Vanessa Williams convinced her that there was hope, that they'd get their happy ending because she was the best he was saving for last. Those gals made her feel like she wasn't all alone in this, that she wasn't a pioneer in heartbreak.

Robbie was moody and snappish and Mum had to remind him more than once that he wasn't the only one who was hurting, because it seemed for all of them Indigo's absence was a raw, physical thing.

Whenever they called him, they were told he was out. At first they wondered if his father was holding him hostage, keeping him from his old life, his old friends. So they'd gone to see Edita, who reassured them she'd spoken to Wilson's housekeeper and Indigo was ok, but the faraway look in her eye and the set of her jaw made them think otherwise. They'd written to him too, but hadn't received so much as a postcard in return.

He consumed every inch of space in Cordelia's mind, so there was room for nothing else. She'd always known he had a dormant melancholy inside of him and she worried desperately that it might have awakened to consume him. Because as far as she could tell, Indigo had completely shut down and derailed. He'd shut them all out.

Even her.

Whom he'd loved.

Always.

Or so he'd said when he left.

A knot of nervousness developed in her abdomen so large and twisted that the very thought of food turned her stomach.

"I think we should speak to Dad," she said one night to Robbie as they sat down to watch a video together. "Ask him if we can fly over there and see him?"

"Fly over there?" Robbie replied with a scowl. "Why would we fly all the way over there?"

"Because he needs us."

"Pfft, yeah right," Robbie scoffed, shifting on the couch to face her. "He needs us so much that he hasn't picked up any of our calls or answered *one* of our letters. He's probably found some new family to infiltrate and doesn't need us anymore." When Robbie was hurt his defence mechanism was to turn nasty and Indigo's abandonment had wounded him deeply.

"That's not true," Cordelia objected, her cheeks flushing. They weren't *that* replaceable – were they?

"Then where *is* he, Cordelia?" Robbie sighed. "He knows where we are. If he needed us, he'd call."

"I-I don't know," she said, teeth digging into her lower lip. "But I know something's not right. This isn't like him."

"Or maybe we never knew him at all. Maybe he's over there hanging out with the spawn of movie stars and he no longer has time for the ordinary likes of us."

"You know he's not like that," she said, leaning in solemnly close. "He's our friend. It's our job to be there when he needs us. We owe him that much."

"The only thing we owe Indigo Wolfe is a standing ovation," Robbie said with a roll of his eyes. "I mean, his parents are actors, right? It comes naturally to him, obviously. He had all of us fooled."

"You don't mean that," she said softly, tears welling in her eyes.

"Listen," Robbie sighed, reaching his arm around her, "what happened between the two of you before he left – the things he said to you… I hate to be the one to bring this up, but I think you need to consider the fact… the fact that he might have met someone else and he's too gutless to tell you… or any of us," he said gently.

Cordelia felt herself stiffen. It wasn't as though the thought hadn't entered her mind, but she'd been doing a spectacular job of pushing it away. Hearing Robbie say it out loud, though, she could no longer deny the possibility.

"Do you really think he could have forgotten me so quickly?" she whispered, her chest hollow, aching.

"A few months ago, I would have said no way. But now… I don't know what to think anymore, Cora. I just don't want to see you sitting here pining away for him indefinitely." He pulled her in close, kissed the top of her head.

"But… but he told me he loved me," she said, lip trembling.

"And I don't doubt for a second that he does. But it's not as though you guys made any promises to each other."

"I didn't think we had to," she replied softly. There had always been so much unspoken between her and Indigo. She just assumed that when he said that he loved her, he meant he'd love her forever. She assumed that kiss was the start of something, not the end.

She lay in bed that night, her fingers moving over the beads of the bracelet that was now a permanent fixture on her wrist, as she battled between her head and her heart. Her head chastised her for being stupid and naïve, telling her of course he'd moved on. Someone like Indigo was never going to stay single for long. But then her poor battered heart chimed in, reminding her that she needed to keep her faith in him, that what they had was deep and true and once-in-a-lifetime, that the boy she knew wouldn't just casually move on to someone else.

When Matty began to coo and chatter, she went and fetched him from his room, bringing him into her bed with her, kissing his small bald head.

"I don't know, Matty," she said absently, "do *you* think he misses us?" Matty tilted his head so he could look intently into her eyes, as though he could understand her. "Even if he doesn't love me, I know he certainly adored you." She stroked his chubby cheek. Matty grinned at her, flashing his two tiny bottom teeth.

"I wanna fly over there so much," she murmured. "I have this feeling of dread in the pit of my stomach telling me something isn't right. But what if I get there and he's with another girl? Imagine how stupid I'd feel…" And so the battle between head and heart raged on.

"Cordelia?"

She glanced up at the sound of her name, drawing her eyes from the ocean, grey-green and rough, to meet his.

"I thought that was you," he said in his solemn way.

"Hey, Drew," she smiled, moving her surfboard and wetsuit aside as he sat tentatively down on the sand beside her. He leant back on his hands and tilted his head up to catch the sun's dying rays. She absentmindedly swept her damp hair over one shoulder, roughing her fingers through the ends in an attempt to dry it off a little.

"It's cold once that sun starts to go down," he said after a while, glancing at her in her skimpy white shorts and black bandeau bikini top. "You ok?"

"I'm fine," she said, but the goosebumps on her arms and legs gave her away. He grabbed the navy-and-white striped rugby jersey draped over his shoulders and handed it to her. She smiled gratefully and pulled it on. It was warm from his body and smelt of the spice of his aftershave.

"How've you been?" he asked, turning his piercing blue eyes to her.

"Ok," she shrugged, shyly meeting his gaze. "You?"

"Yeah, fine, I guess. Missing my best mate."

"Have you heard from him?" she asked tentatively.

"Nope," he said, giving her a tight smile. "You?"

She shook her head, averting her eyes. "Should we be worried?" she asked softly. "About Indigo? Do you think?"

Drew hesitated, his eyes unfocused as he gazed at the horizon. "Honestly? I don't know. In the past, when he's been away with one of his parents, he's stayed out of touch. I think it's hard for him, you know, to hear what's happening back here when he's miserable over there."

"*Is* he miserable?" she asked, digging her toes into the sand, still warm from the sinking sun.

"He's always miserable when he's with Bernadette or Wilson," he shrugged.

She nodded because she knew that was true. She turned to look at him, his profile backlit against the hazy pink sky. He had a nice face, his nose slightly bent, his jaw strong. His brown hair was thick and wavy.

"You haven't heard *anything?*" she probed. "What he's doing over there? Who he's… who he's hanging out with… and stuff?"

He turned to look at her then, his gaze serious. "I haven't heard a word in six months, Cordelia. So if you're asking me if he's seeing anyone, I honestly don't know."

She felt her cheeks flush and was thankful for the fading light. "Wolfie's never been much for the telephone or letter writing," Drew told her.

"How can he just vanish like this?" she said. "It's like he's been abducted by aliens or something."

"And taken to the centre of the earth," Drew mused.

"H-huh?"

"Hollow earth, it's a thing," he said, turning to look at her. "It's where a lot of the beings we consider aliens come from."

She stared at him, eyebrow cocked. Drew was always ready with a weird and whacky hypothesis no one else had ever heard of. She knew this quirky side of him was one of the things Indigo loved most about him, with the two often heatedly debating whatever theory Drew was into any particular month.

"Any photos you've seen of the North and South Pole have been doctored. Look into Admiral Richard Byrd's Arctic and Antarctic expeditions. He discovered enormous holes at both poles which allowed access to the inner earth. Byrd's adventures within have been quite well documented."

"And what's inside?" she asked, her curiosity piqued.

"Continents, a central sun, species we consider extinct like dinosaurs... And a race of super humans, descendants of the Lemurians who founded Atlantis. They're a highly advanced civilisation, a lot more advanced than us."

"So they know about us, but we don't know about them?" she challenged.

"Of course. They originated on the earth's surface before discovering it was hollow and moving in there. Their technology's incredibly sophisticated and the majority of UFO sightings are them visiting us. If you don't believe me, do your own research. I can lend you some books."

"Uh, yeah, ok," she said, because so much of her *wanted* to believe in a world of magic and madness. She needed to believe in something bigger than her, that there was *more* to the world, so she quietly loved anything that challenged her reality, especially a good mystery (although this one seemed particularly far-fetched). Her father once told her no one had ever grown more intelligent or worldly by remaining in the confines of their own belief system and she felt in her bones that, of all there was to know, humans only knew the tiniest of fractions.

"So, my dad's staying at his girlfriend's this weekend. My brothers are having a party, if you and Rob wanna come?"

"Yeah, Rob's mentioned it." Aside from school and surfing, she'd barely left the house in months.

"So, come?" he said. "It would be good to see you guys. Sian will be there with Will, and you could bring Peyton, too." Drew played rugby with Sian's boyfriend, Will.

"Yeah, maybe," she said, flashing him a small smile.

He grinned back and her eyes were drawn to the dimple in his left cheek. He stood up, dusting his hands off on his shorts. She made to give him his jersey back, but he held his hand out to stop her.

"You can borrow it. Return it to me on Saturday night. It will give you an excuse to come."

She nodded. She was freezing and wasn't keen to part with it, anyway.

"Thanks, Drew," she said softly and he gave a little wave as he turned to trudge back up the dunes.

After a few steps, he turned back. "We all miss him, Cordelia. He can make you feel like the centre of the universe when you're around him and coming down from that can be pretty hard. But you have to find a way to find your feet outside of him, regardless of whether or not he comes back." He shot her a sad little smile and shrugged before turning on his heel and walking off.

Drew's words stuck with her and she did end up going to his party that weekend. Dressed in low-rise jeans and a monochrome bandana top, she took Peyton and Robbie with her as well as the rugby jersey she'd washed and ironed to return to him. As much as she hated to admit it, she had fun that night with Peyton and Sian and her other friends, more fun than she'd had in a long time. She'd forgotten how good it felt to relax and hang out. She barely saw Drew all night, but as she was leaving, he appeared out of nowhere, grabbing her arm and telling her he had something for her. He handed her a calico bag. Inside was a stack of books.

"As promised," he grinned, his dimple deepening. "Take a look at these and let me know what you think." She thanked him and left, thinking it'd be a while before she got around to them. But that night she lay in bed tossing and turning, unable to sleep. She found herself switching on her bedside lamp and reaching for the bag, sorting through the dog-eared books within until she found the one on hollow earth.

The next week when she bumped into Drew in the corridor at school, she asked him if he was keen on hopping a flight to Antarctica to see the hole at the South Pole for themselves, and it had made her laugh, how chuffed he was. She had to admit she found his quirkiness refreshing. And she found it amusing, that he was this super popular rugby player who believed aliens had crash landed in Roswell, who was convinced JFK was assassinated by the elites because he was in the process of disbanding the Federal Reserve Bank and improving America's monetary system.

The truth was his whacky theories, they gave her something else to think about other than Indigo. Imagining all those possibilities gave her perspective, made her problems seem smaller because if there was so much more to the world, then what did she have to worry about in the scheme of things? When thoughts of Indigo, always accompanied by gut-churning worry, began to slip into her mind, she'd turn her imagination to the super civilisation dwelling inside of planet earth, or to Area 51, or to wondering which intergalactic species really built the pyramids.

Robbie never wanted to talk about Indigo, but Drew was happy to and Cordelia needed that. It was nice to have a friend she could share Indigo stories and anecdotes with, who seemed to miss him almost as much as she did. By no means did Drew fill the void that Indigo had left. They weren't the type of friends that hung out one-on-one, always in a group or at school, but he certainly knew how to stretch her mind. And slowly, with time, she wasn't so gloomy and glum all day, every day. She still woke up each morning with a roiling in the pit of her stomach, her mind consumed with worries over Indigo, but she'd grown adept at pushing them aside, forcing herself out of bed and going about her day.

One day in late November, she awoke in the early hours, arms flailing, her body drenched in sweat. She'd been dreaming of whispering shadows and ghostly presences, of tumbling through darkness, of meandering black water hard as concrete. A new nightmare, different to the others somehow.

She sat bolt upright, clamouring for her bearings. It was still dark out. She heard movement downstairs, the murmur of the television and she realised her dad must be home from the hospital. She slid out of bed, padding to the door, aware her skin was slick, her hair damp. Heart pounding, hands shaking, she made her way downstairs.

"Dad?" she said, as she reached the doorway.

"What are you doing up, darling?" he said, swivelling on the couch to look up at her. "What's wrong?" he asked when he caught sight of her.

"I-I had a nightmare," she said. Without warning, tears filled her eyes. He held out his arms and she dove into them, burying her head in his chest, enjoying the safety of his embrace. He smoothed her hair and rubbed her back.

"You haven't had one in so long I assumed you'd outgrown them. Wanna talk about it?"

"I... I don't really remember it," she realised. "I just remember how it made me feel." Her stomach dropped and she shuddered. She pulled back to look him in the eye. "I can't shake the feeling we need to go to New York. I can't explain it and I know it's not logical, but please, can we go? See Indigo?"

Her dad pulled her close, kissed her forehead, seemingly deep in thought. "Your mother and I have been talking about taking a family holiday after Christmas. I can take time off then. Mum's been angling for Hawaii, but I s'pose we could fly to New York first, even if just you and I go and then meet the others in Waikiki on the way home."

She nodded emphatically, throwing her arms around his neck. He chuckled and squeezed her tight. "Thanks, Daddy," she murmured.

He kissed the top of her head. "To be honest, I'd like to check on Indigo myself. I'll call my travel agent in the morning." He'd always drummed into her and Robbie that family came first, second and third, and to him, Indigo was family.

She felt like her throat had been released from a chokehold, like she could breathe easy again. Whatever was going on with Indigo, she had to see for herself. No matter what he was doing, or who he was with, she knew it was the not knowing that was stunting her life. And no matter what fanciful concoctions her mind threw her way, deep down she couldn't shake the feeling that something dark was looming. The Indigo she knew needed her.

chapter ten

paint it, black

bear mountain bridge, new york, november, 1993

indigo

The bridge was deserted, but that was to be expected at three in the morning. Indigo was glad of it. It meant no witnesses, no good Samaritans, no saviours. Leaving the keys in the ignition of his father's Ferrari, he stumbled from the car. An empty vodka bottle rolled out the open door and smashed on the pavement by his feet. He glanced back at the apparition sitting in the passenger seat, a Japanese-looking guy who'd talked non-stop in his surfer-bro drawl for most of the car ride, and shook his head in apology. The guy nodded gently, a sad smile upon his face, then vanished.

Indigo pulled up the hood of his thin sweatshirt and ducked his head as he walked slowly up the pedestrian walkway, ignoring the biting chill that ate through to his flesh. He barely felt it. The truth was, he felt so much of everything else, there was no room for something as trivial as the cold. A light dusting of snow swirled through the air, floating sprinkles of white fluttering to break the darkness. It vaguely entered his mind that it was too early for snow, but the thought wandered from his mind as nonchalantly as it had entered it. What did he care?

He reached the centre of the bridge and stopped. This was as good a place as any.

He reached out and placed his hands on the railing, gripping it hard with white knuckles. His fingers were already growing numb. He peered over the edge. He could hear the frosty Hudson meandering its way below. He couldn't see it, but he knew it was down there, wide and deep and ugly, muddy green.

It would do.

The frigid water was a long way down. One hundred and ten metres. Three hundred and sixty feet, down, down, down.

The damned voices were getting louder. They never shut up. Never. Teasing him, taunting him, torturing him. It was never-ending. They whispered, they chattered, they yelled and screamed and demanded of him day and night. But he would have the last laugh. He would shut them up. For good.

'Don't do it.'

    'Do it.'

       'Don't do it.'

         'Do it.'

            'Do it.'

              'DO IT!'

He'd lost himself so spectacularly that he was nowhere to be found. Wave after wave of loneliness and sadness and desolate emptiness rippled up from his stomach into his chest where it sat like a barbell, crushing him so every breath he drew was short and shallow.

He shook his head. The human race was a cesspit of anger and hate and misery. He couldn't stand feeling it anymore. It was too much, too much, too much. He was sick to his stomach every damned day with the palpable hopelessness that radiated through his body.

He was done.

    His whole life was an agony he had no say in and no control over.

    Until now.

    He was taking control back.

He released the railing and took three big steps back. The voices in his head were deafening now, the clawing in his gut crippling. He grimaced and set his jaw.

And just like that, he propelled himself forward, his hands meeting the icy railing to vault his body gracefully up, up, over the side of the bridge, his long legs easily clearing the fence.

And then he was out in the whistling darkness, the frigid Atlantic wind slicing his face like a thousand knives, his rag doll body tumbling over and over, the voices so loud, the feelings all encompassing.

He didn't see the concrete blackness of the water rising up to meet him. All he saw were images, an effervescent collage of his life speeding pell-mell through his head. So much bad, so much pain. But now, in this moment, he saw it – he knew there had been so much good, too.

The last thing he saw was a face. A face so beautiful and ethereal and true. A face that brought him warmth and comfort. Cordelia.

He was speeding through the darkness, into nothingness. And then, at the very end, it felt almost as though his rapid decent slowed somewhat, paused even, before the big hit.

And then there was nothing. No more to see. No more to hear. No more to feel.

Just peace.

chapter eleven

queen of the night

the covenstead, somewhere below north fort, manly, new south wales

reinenoir

Somewhere on the periphery of her consciousness she could hear her Maiden singing softly in that native Balinese tongue of hers, the melody a bridge back to the present. Reinenoir stumbled, gripping the narrow wall of the tunnel for support.

"Is everything alright, my lady?"

She barely registered her Maiden was speaking.

"Lady Reinenoir?" The Maiden stepped around her High Priestess to peer into her face.

Reinenoir gasped a shuddery breath. "Did you feel it?" she panted, narrowing her eyes as she shivered.

"Feel what?"

"The shift," she murmured, fist to her chest, leaning heavily against the wall.

The Maiden closed her eyes for a moment or two, then nodded. "But does that mean…?"

"An interference in the timeline. We've jumped the tracks." Turmoil furled through Reinenoir's body as she set her jaw. "Where is Artax?" she demanded, hands now clenched at her sides.

"In the armoury, I think," the Maiden said. She eyed Reinenoir cautiously, clearly ruffled at the site of her usually cool and collected mistress so shaken.

"Go fetch him!" Reinenoir ordered. "Tell him to meet me in the barracks at once!" She swept off down the tunnel, meagre light illuminating the mottled concrete of the domed ceiling and walls.

She reached her destination and began to pace, gliding back and forth across the floor of the dim room, her purple robes rippling in her wake. Her heart was thumping loudly as her mind raced to examine all the possibilities over and over. She stopped dead, staring at the wall, wide-eyed, stricken, as she realised a large part of her felt relieved, that she could breathe easy. That realisation brought with it ice cold fear. She pursed her lips, chastising herself, trying to convince herself this was by no means how she wanted things to go. Because that would mean that after all this time, after everything, she could still succumb to the weaknesses of the flesh she thought she'd left far behind.

Artax sauntered in a few minutes later, the Maiden in tow. He leant against the doorframe, crossing his arms over his bulbous belly, regarding Reinenoir silently with those witching-hour eyes. He'd removed the hood of his robes, exposing himself in all his glory, his squat bald head a swirl of black ink, two small fleshy horns protruding from his forehead.

"I need you to look," she demanded, stepping towards him. "It didn't happen as it was meant to, as we saw it. You assured me our contribution would be enough to persuade him." She turned and began to pace again, as the Maiden moved wordlessly to a chair in the corner. "But I felt the jolt, as if the whole world shifted. Not that any of the mindless masses out there are any wiser to the fact their whole reality just morphed."

Artax continued to regard her, his head tilted to one side, eyes slitted. "You're pleasssed," he finally said, a smirk curling his metal-pocked lip.

He'd wandered inside her mind. How dare he! She shoved him out, shrouded her thoughts.

"*Pleased?*" she snapped venomously. "I am *far* from pleased! How *dare* you question my loyalty and commitment!" She thrust a threatening palm out towards him.

The smile twisting his black lips, vanished. "I apologissse, my lady," he said, bowing his head. "I misssspoke."

'If you enter my mind without permission again, I will end you,' she projected into his head.

"You know it'sss not persssonal, my lady," he said with a wave of his hand. "Merely a force of habit."

She pinned him with a venomous stare. "I called you here because I need you to look. Can you see what happened? Did he have a change of heart?"

Artax closed his eyes, his face blank. He was quiet for some time. "No," he eventually said, "he went through with it."

"So why did the timeline shimmer?"

Artax stepped forward, reaching out towards her, looking her in the eye. "Sssee for yourssself," he said. She closed her eyes, and as his hands touched hers, a series of images projected into her mind, like pictures on a movie screen.

When it was done, he released her and she stepped back, bending to clutch her abdomen, her breath heavy. She managed to right herself, her back straight, her eyes flashing.

"No," she whispered, looking to Artax for reassurance.

"I'm afraid ssso," he shrugged.

"What is it?" the Maiden asked. "What happened?"

"There was an interference. It didn't go as we saw it," Reinenoir said, her knees weak. "And now," she swallowed hard, "it's all different. They've changed everything."

And the worst part was, it was stirring up feelings within her she'd thought were long dead.

chapter twelve

under the bridge

bear mountain bridge, new york

indigo

Peace was fleeting.

Not everlasting, as he'd so desperately hoped.

Indigo didn't know how long he'd been unconscious, but he was suddenly aware of the frozen mud of the riverbank like cement beneath his back, the scent of damp and moss in his nostrils. And the pain. Every fibre, every cell in his body was screaming in pain.

The overwhelming agony coursing through him indicated he was still very much alive.

Someone was touching him, torturing him, pressing down on his already bruised and busted ribs. He tried to cry out, but he could feel a force rising in his throat, gushing, propelling its way out of his lungs, out of his poor broken body. With a violent hack, he rolled to one side, retching up dirty river water.

His lungs betrayed him, reflexively gulping the frigid night air deep, deep down, gasping for the oxygen they had been deprived of.

A voice drifted over him, deep and soothing "That's it, buddy, that's the way, just breathe, just breathe." He could see someone kneeling beside him on the river bank, feel them rubbing his back.

He tried to draw his knees up to his chest, tried to find a position to make everything hurt less, but he could barely move. He cried out, screaming with all the pain, all the disappointment, all the agony, all the hopelessness, all the failure.

"Why?" he choked. *"Why?"*

"Not tonight, buddy," came the gentle voice. "Not on my watch."

Indigo could feel the blackness closing in on him again. He struggled to turn his head to see his unwelcome saviour, but all he grasped was a blur of tanned skin and dark hair before the darkness came again, taking the pain with it.

Somewhere, sitting just out of reach on the periphery of his awareness, floated a blurry mishmash of blue scrubs and white coats and unfamiliar faces and rattling gurneys and long sterile corridors punctuated with blinking fluorescent lights.

The next time Indigo woke up, he knew he was in a hospital. The smell of antiseptic that assaulted his nostrils and the gentle bleeping of unseen machines were a dead giveaway. At least there was no pain. In fact, he felt nothing. Nothing at all. He'd not felt nothing in a very long time. It was blissful to not feel.

His eyelids fluttered, slowly parted, revealing his surroundings. Cracked ceiling, water-damaged cornices, peeling paint. An IV in his right arm, pumping God only knew what into his vein. The source of the blissful nothingness, he assumed.

His left arm was encased in a heavy cast from wrist to shoulder, his right leg bore a matching one, thigh to toe. His chest was bandaged — who knew what was underneath all that? There was no pain to give any indication.

"Pain is the body's messenger," Scarlett had always lectured him. "Its job is to tell you when something isn't right inside. Every time you silence it with medication, you're shutting down the means of leading yourself to the source." He smiled drowsily, clumsily, affectionately, at the memory.

"You think you're so smart," he murmured to his pain, "but I've found a way to shut you up now. You're not the boss of me anymore." Indigo's eyelids drooped so he could barely focus. *This is good shit.* He smiled, leaning his head back on his pillow and closing his eyes.

"Hello?" a voice rang out.

Indigo's eyes snapped open. He frowned pensively. He glanced dopily around, but all he could see was a scuffed wall and a closed door to his right, and a thin blue curtain that hung from a rail to the left of his bed. His stomach dropped in fear. Were the voices back?

"Yo! Hello?" the voice came again. "Hey, man, you awake over there?" American, with a hint of inflection he couldn't place. He'd never heard this voice before.

"*What?*" Indigo demanded. "What do you *want* from me?" He was still groggy but could feel himself getting sharper.

Silence.

Then heavy breathing that made him realise this disembodied voice actually *had* a body. "Wow. I was just tryin' to say hey and officially welcome you to room fourteen," came the hurt reply. "You been outta it for days."

"Who are you?" Indigo asked, slowly turning his head back and forth to shake off the fog.

"I'm your roommate, man. The name's Luis Martinez." Pause, then, "Soooo, I'm assuming the reason you're pissed is cos you've just awakened to the stark realisation you still here?" Luis spoke quickly and Indigo struggled to keep pace.

"Still here?" Indigo asked softly.

"Yeah, *here. Alive.* Look, if that's what it is, I totally get it. I felt the same way when I woke up. This here's a pretty small psych hospital, man. You and me, room fourteen, we the kamikaze patients."

"Kamikaze?"

"The nurses talk, man, and I got nothin' to do all day but listen. You and me, we the same. We both failed to leave this shitty life on our own terms."

"Oh," was all Indigo could manage.

"So I gotta know, because it's the mystery of the whole hospital. You came in with no wallet, no ID, there's no missing persons reports out on you. Everyone wants to know who you are. I see you got a accent, man, you from England or somethin'?"

"Australia," Indigo replied drowsily. There were no missing persons reports out on him. Had his father not realised he hadn't come home?

Not the doorman? No one? Indigo gritted his teeth bitterly. He vaguely recalled his father being in the Bahamas, but he didn't know when that was or how long ago.

"How long have I been here, Luis?"

"Here?" Luis replied. "You been here, like, ten days. But you was brought in by ambulance from somewhere south of here where you had some operations and shit, so I hear. I dunno how long you was in that hospital for."

"What's the date?" Indigo asked quickly, his panic beginning to override the drugs.

"Dude! It's nearly Christmas," Luis laughed. "*Feliz Navidad*, it's December nineteenth."

Almost a month. He'd been gone almost a month and no one had even bothered to report him missing.

"Where are we?" he whispered.

"Oh, we in upstate New York, but way up north. Almost in Canada. This is where you go when no one wants to know about what you did," he said darkly. He sighed. "But it's a good place. Staff are real nice. Food's ok."

"Where are you from?" Indigo asked, needing to anchor to something certain.

"My daddy's from Puerto Rico," Luis replied. "And my maamaan's from Afghanistan. But now they live in Jersey. Apparently, me tryin' to take myself out is the most shamefully humiliatin' thing that's ever happened to them." He paused for a moment. "They didn't want their friends or the rest of the family to know. So once I was well enough to travel, they sent me up here. They told everyone I followed some *chica* down to Florida. My maamaan comes to visit me once a month," he added, "to continue her interrogation and castigation."

"Your father?" Indigo asked.

"He ain't ever come once." Indigo could hear the pain in Luis's voice. Paternal rejection. It was a hurt Indigo knew only too well.

"I'm sorry to hear that," Indigo said, meaning it.

"So what's your name, man?" Luis asked, changing the subject. "Everyone's been takin' bets on who you are and where you from.

Don't think anyone guessed Australia though," he mused. "You a long way from home."

"My name's Indigo. Indigo Wolfe."

"Really? That your real name, man? Cos it sounds like some made up shit."

"Nah, yeah, it's my name alright," Indigo replied, almost smiling. The faceless, body-less Luis on the other side of the curtain was a pretty likeable kind of guy.

"How old are you?"

"Seventeen," Indigo replied.

"I'm eighteen," Luis told him. "My birthday was a couple of weeks back." He paused, then asked, "If you Australian, what're you doin' here in New York?"

"Um, my father's American. I was living at my mum's place in Sydney, but things changed custody-wise and I had to go live in Manhattan with him."

"And you hate the bastard, right?" Luis probed.

"How did you know?"

"Just a feelin'," Luis said, sounding somehow amused and sorry at the same time.

Footsteps approached, briskly clipping. The scuffed white door eased open and a head poked in. She was probably in her forties, rather plain, with a large forehead and a broad mouth edged in terracotta lipstick. Her hair, brown with bold yellow streaks, was caught back in a butterfly clip. She was wearing a nurse's uniform, crisp blue, neatly ironed.

"Our mystery man's awake!" she cried, her smile brightening her whole face. "Welcome back!"

She fussed around him, checking his pulse and IV. "I'm Jenny," she said brightly. "Can you tell me your name, tater tot?"

"His name's Indigo Wolfe and he's from Australia!" Luis called from the other side of the curtain.

"Hey, pickle, shush over there with your big ears," she scolded good-naturedly. "Now," she continued, "Indigo Wolfe from Australia?" She placed her hand on his forehead and peered into his eyes, hers full of concern.

"Yes," Indigo whispered. Her presence was comforting.

"How are you feeling, Indigo?" she asked.

"Numb," he replied honestly.

She laughed a tinkling laugh. "I'm going to get your doctor in to see you in a minute. He'll be able to adjust your medication now you're awake." She regarded him admiringly. "My, my, look at you. Your eyes are open, all that swelling's gone down. You need a good shave, but you're quite the looker, aren't you?"

"Hey!" Luis called out. "I heard that."

"You're still my number one guy, Luis, my darling. No one is as handsome as you," she smiled, winking at Indigo. "How old are you, honey?"

"Seventeen," Indigo croaked.

"*Seventeen?*" she cried, the blood draining from her face. "You're a *minor?*"

"We're almost the same age," Luis declared.

"We just assumed…" she trailed off, worry gathering in her eyes.

"What?" Indigo prompted.

"We just assumed you were in your early twenties. When you arrived here, your face was so swollen, we couldn't even tell what you looked like so we couldn't put out a description of you. All we could give the authorities was your hair and eye colour and approximate age, which we said was twenty-three. I'm afraid we've been looking for your family in all the wrong places. Oh dear," she said, putting her hands to her cheeks.

Indigo tried to shrug but realised he couldn't move his shoulders. He winced.

"Careful now, honey," Nurse Jenny tsked, "you've got a broken collarbone, amongst other things, so you need to take it easy."

"I may never shrug again," Indigo murmured. "What else is wrong with me?" He suddenly had a terrible thought. He looked towards the end of the bed, concentrating hard. Both his big toes wiggled. Relief flooded through him.

Jenny saw and smiled gently at him. "You're all good in that department," she reassured him, placing a hand on his shoulder. He noticed her eyes flit momentarily in Luis's direction before coming back to rest on him. "So your leg was broken in three places, your arm in two, you had six broken ribs, a broken collarbone, both cheekbones were fractured and you had a deep laceration to your forehead."

Indigo instinctively raised his hand to the bandage across the left side of his head.

"But don't worry," Jenny continued brightly, "I'm told you were very lucky that an excellent plastic surgeon was on call the night they brought you in. You *will* have a scar, but it won't be large." She leant forward and added with a mischievous grin, "And don't worry about that, either. Chicks dig scars."

Indigo tried to shrug again before remembering he couldn't. This would take some getting used to.

Jenny picked up his chart and scribbled a few notes on it. "I still can't believe how lucky you were," she commented as she clipped her pen back to her top pocket. "Someone was really watching over you that night, tater tot. One of your ribs did puncture your right lung, but they managed to fix that in surgery. Your spleen was ruptured but you still have it." She looked up and smiled at him. "So no permanent damage." Her smile faded a bit. "Well, no permanent physical damage."

"Why am I here?" Indigo glowered. "Luis has already told me what this place is."

She perched on the edge of his bed and peered into his face. "Look, honey," she began, taking his hand in hers, "you were brought into the ER of a hospital south of here in a dreadful state, from what I'm told."

"By who?"

"Doesn't say," she replied, flipping through his chart. "But there's a note here saying whoever it was took care of all your bills and continues to do so, so a very good Samaritan, I'd say. The doctors down there stabilised you, patched you up, and kept you there for a couple of weeks. But once all your scans came back clear, it was decided there was nothing else they could do for you, and, well, I suppose it was decided that you were better off someplace like this, where we'd be able to help fix the parts of you that still needed fixing."

His cheeks flamed. They thought he was crazy. He hadn't given a thought to what might happen to him if his bridge jump didn't succeed. The enormity of it suddenly began to sink in. He'd tried to kill himself. And failed. People were going to find out. He'd given them his real name. They were going to call his father.

"There's no need to be embarrassed, honey," Jenny reassured him, gently smoothing his hair off his forehead. "We all need a little bit of help from time to time."

"Please don't call my father," Indigo suddenly burst out, gripping her hand tightly in his, panic rising in his chest. Why hadn't he lied about who he was? Fucking drugs. He could have given them a fake name, put his age up, they would have just let him walk out of there and he could have just slipped back into the world as someone else, someone new. "Please," he begged, eyes desperate, "you can't, you can't," his breathing suddenly ragged, suddenly out of control, suddenly out of his grasp. He began to pant, his chest palpitating with a frenzy. He couldn't get any air.

"I-I can't breathe," he gasped, his hands rising to his throat. "I can't breathe." He was dying. Maybe he would get his wish after all.

Jenny jumped up and rushed out of the room, returning with a paper bag in hand. She pushed a button and the bed raised him to a seated position. She placed the opening of the paper bag over his nose and mouth.

"Indigo," she said, her voice calm and soothing, "you're just having a panic attack. Breathe into this for me, tater tot. Come on, you can do it."

Indigo looked at her wildly, but did as he was told. In, out, in, out, the bag deflating and inflating, rapidly at first and then slowing as his hysteria subsided.

Jenny sat with him silently, his hand in hers, her presence a lifeline. Eventually, he gathered himself enough to be able to speak again. "Thank you," he whispered.

"Sure," she said, her wide mouth turning up in that sunny smile again. "Now if you're feeling ok, I'm going to have to go tell the doctor you're awake."

Indigo's grasp on her hand intensified, her touch his anchor. "It's ok," she told him, placing a palm on his cheek. "I promise I'll come right back."

manhattan, new york

wilson

When Wilson Wolfe learned his son was in the hospital and had been for the better part of a month, he was annoyed. Quite frankly, he'd thought the boy had found his passport and simply run off back to Sydney and had told his staff as much. He was still angry about his Ferrari, which had been found burnt out near the Canadian border, but not enough to press the police to investigate how it had gotten there. The last thing he wanted was any more media attention right now and he had plenty more cars.

The truth was, once the press furore was over and they'd moved on to another story, he hadn't needed the boy around anymore, anyway. Having Indigo leave had given Wilson one less thing to worry about, had given him back his peace and quiet. The kid was out of control: rude, obnoxious, ungrateful. He came home at all hours completely inebriated, waking up the whole house, often with a different girl in tow, each more beautiful than the next... although Indigo barely seemed to appreciate that.

And now the spoilt brat had gone and made a feeble attempt to kill himself, clearly nothing more than a means of attention seeking.

Wilson was, however, pleased to discover Indigo was in a facility that had grounds large enough to accommodate the landing of a helicopter. He knew his image wouldn't recover if the media found out he hadn't been to see his son, who had been pulled back from the brink of death. It wasn't great that Indigo was in the nuthouse, but Wilson had an excellent PR team, and he knew they'd be able to spin it to make him look good, at least. And the more he thought about it, the more delighted he grew with the situation. All those journos that had torn him to shreds, attacked his parenting, made him out to be the villain. Surely they would see Wilson as the victim in all this, the victim of an ungracious, overindulged, unbalanced child who made a complete farce of trying to take his own life when he didn't get his own way.

So Wilson Wolfe instructed his team to leak Indigo's circumstances to the press.

harbord, new south wales

cordelia

Cordelia awoke with a start. It was a hot, sticky night and her hair was damp against her neck. Her boxer shorts and singlet stuck to her skin. She sat up and reached for a scrunchie, pulling her hair up into a knot on top of her head. She slipped out of bed and moved to the door, compelled to go downstairs but not knowing what was driving her. They were flying out to New York in a few days and she had to step around the empty suitcases Mum had pointedly left in the hall.

She found Dad in the rumpus room reading the paper, *National Lampoon's Christmas Vacation* on the TV on mute. Robbie was sprawled out, asleep beside him. "Hey, Daddy," she murmured, kissing the top of his head and sitting down beside him.

"Can't sleep, darling?" he asked, folding the top of his paper down to smile fondly at her.

She shook her head. "It's so hot," she said, leaning back into the couch and hooking an arm behind her head. "I wish we had air conditioning."

"Maybe next year," he said, patting her knee. "How about we go get you a fan for your room tomorrow?"

She nodded, smiling vaguely. "How was work?"

"Oh, pretty manic," he said with a wry smile. "A few car accidents and a couple of stomach pumpings. It's that time of year."

"I don't know how… " she stopped dead as an image on the television caught her eye. "Oh my God, turn it up!" she cried. Dad fumbled for the remote and hit the volume button so they could hear the newsbreak. They both watched the segment in shock, Cordelia's hands covering her mouth in horror.

As it finished, she promptly burst into tears. Her father moved to draw her into a fierce embrace, rocking her back and forth.

"In what sick world is this entertainment news?" he growled, as Cordelia sobbed harder. "Because his parents are famous, they splash this across the TV?"

"I knew it," she wept, "I knew I should have g-gone sooner, I knew it but I ig-ignored it." She gripped a fistful of his shirt as her whole body wracked and shook. "He was all alone… a-all alone, he had n-n-no one." Imagining how he must have felt, how desperate, how hopeless, she felt as if her heart had been cleaved in two.

Dad continued to hold her tight, murmuring to her and wiping her tears. When he finally managed to calm her down, he kissed her cheeks and went to fetch her a glass of water.

"I'll call and see if I can get us on an earlier flight, darling," he said, sitting down and drawing her into his arms. "And he's alive. That's the main thing: Indigo's alive."

jefferson county, new york

indigo

Upon his arrival by helicopter at the shabby little hospital in Upstate New York, Wilson tried to have Indigo moved to an upscale facility in Manhattan. But Indigo refused to leave. So Wilson threw enough cash at them to take Indigo off his hands for the foreseeable future, then hightailed it back to civilisation.

Indigo liked the small-town doctors and nurses. He liked that here he was part of a community; he liked sharing a room with Luis. There was just something about the modest single-storey hospital that sat in a clearing hugged by forest – peeling walls, cracked ceilings, musty odour and all.

Indigo and Luis had become as close as two people left largely with only each other to talk to, would imaginably become. Indigo had been pretty out of it in the days that followed his regaining consciousness, but whenever he was awake, he'd lain in his bed and chatted with Luis, who turned out to be a pretty funny guy. It amazed Indigo that someone who was so light-hearted and laid-back had wanted to take their own life. Indigo had never asked him why. Because it opened the door to Luis asking the same question of him. So they talked about anything and everything except probably the most important thing.

The day before Christmas, Indigo asked Nurse Jenny if she could take the curtain down between their beds. He and Luis had never laid eyes upon one another and Indigo was getting tired of talking to a disembodied voice. Luis went quiet and Jenny got flustered, refusing his request and muttering a thin excuse about hospital policy and privacy laws.

Indigo argued he had nothing to hide from Luis, plus he was pretty sure Luis had a window on his side of the room and he'd like to be able to see outside, too. He was sick of staring at a shabby blue curtain and a closed door. Jenny went to Luis' side of the room and frantic whispering ensued. She eventually returned to Indigo. "Sorry, sweetie, hospital policy," she said, shrugging her shoulders before leaving the room.

Indigo was quiet for some time before finally asking, "What's going on, man?"

"What d' ya mean?" Luis replied guardedly.

"Hospital policy, my arse," Indigo replied. "What's with the curtain?"

"I don' know what you talkin' about," Luis responded evenly. "You heard Jenny, curtain's gotta stay." He yawned. "Besides, you wouldn't be able to handle looking at my face all day, man. It's a thing of beauty, I tell ya. Much like the sun, you can't look directly at it," he chuckled. "Anyway, I'm pretty beat. I'm gonna catch a nap." And with that, he was silent, but Indigo could tell from his breathing he wasn't asleep. He decided not to push it.

Indigo woke up early on Christmas morning to the glare of sun on snow. He opened his eyes, disorientated, and blinked in shock. Someone had moved his bed overnight. Gone were the bland white wall and door he'd spent the past week staring at, replaced by a large window looking out onto the grounds and forest beyond. Indigo was ecstatic to see outdoors.

"Merry Christmas, man," Luis' cheery voice came from the other side of the blue curtain. Indigo's old side.

"Luis?" Indigo called. "What's going on?"

"It's my Christmas present to you. You wanted a window, you got one."

"B-but what about you? Luis, this is crazy. If we just opened the bloody curtain, we'd both have a window."

"It's cool, man," Luis reassured him. "I want you to have it, honest."

"Well, I don't know what to say. Thank you, Luis."

"Hey no problemo."

"I don't have anything for you," Indigo said.

"It's all good. It's nice to have a… a *compadre* to talk to."

"It is," Indigo agreed. "Merry Christmas, mate."

"Feliz Navidad," came the voice from behind the curtain.

They didn't talk about the curtain again. Doctors and nurses came and went, but Indigo never caught a glimpse of his new friend. Despite his curiosity, he knew he had to respect Luis' wishes. It hadn't taken Indigo long to figure out the constant beeping and bleeping he heard day and night came from machines that didn't belong to him. He deduced that Luis' injuries must be pretty bad, but he had no idea how bad. Even when Indigo graduated from his bed to a wheelchair and was allowed to roam the hospital and beyond, he still never dared touch the sacred blue curtain that encircled Luis's bed like a scarp.

In the frigid depths of winter, the woods surrounding the hospital were cloaked with snow, white, soft, glistening. The muted silence that enveloped the estate was broken only by the occasional trill of an unseen squirrel. Only a few paths had been cleared of snow so exploration was somewhat restricted for Indigo – with his arm useless in its cast, crutches were not yet an option so he was confined to a wheelchair, which, to his frustration, he was unable to wheel on his own. Of all his injuries, it was the broken arm that caused him the most distress as it took away his independence. But he did manage to charm Nurse Jenny into taking him down the wooded trail every day.

It was four days before New Year's and Indigo was returning from his daily roll through the woods with Jenny when he saw a grey Escalade pulling into the hospital's circular driveway. "Stop," Indigo cried. "Please stop!"

Indigo didn't know what it was that made him order Jenny to stop, but something in his voice made her do it. Maybe it was because he'd been expecting this. After all, he'd seen the articles stating filming had been halted on his father's latest project so he could rush to the bedside of his mentally ill youngest son after a suicide attempt. The articles were sympathetic to Wilson, a father overcome with grief and worry over his beloved child, vowing to do all he could to help him get well again. Indigo's slip up wasn't private or anonymous. It was international news.

From their position, they were still hidden by the trees, completely invisible from the driveway. Indigo held his breath as he watched the driver's door swing open and a familiar figure emerge. His whole body flooded with a tumble of joy and dread. *Joshua.* His stomach dropped as his anxiety began to rise. Panic attacks had kind of become his thing since the coma. The passenger door opened and a tall thin frame unfolded from within, well dressed as always. Robbie turned to survey his surroundings, his eyes narrowing as he formed an opinion. Robbie always had an opinion and he always formed it quickly. Long fingers buttoned his dark cashmere coat before he pulled on a newsboy hat, rubbing his hands together to ward off the bitter chill.

Indigo could barely catch his breath, but he held it nonetheless, waiting, waiting, not moving his eyes off the car for even a second. *C'mon, c'mon, c'mon* he urged silently. Surely she would have come too... wouldn't she? He was desperate for even a glimpse of her. But maybe she hadn't come. Maybe she was that angry, or disappointed, or disgusted.

But then the back door slowly opened and there she was, willowy and graceful and glorious. Golden hair a wild cascade, long legs clad in figure-hugging pale blue jeans paired with a white turtle-neck and fawn suede knee-high boots. She reached back into the car for her trench-coat then turned and glanced towards the woods, frowning. He shrunk down so she couldn't see him. But he could see her.

"Friends of yours, tater tot?" Jenny asked.

"Shhhhhh!" Indigo hushed her, holding his hand up. "I don't want them to see us."

Joshua was putting his arm around Cordelia and hugging her to him as they made their way towards the stairs that would lead them to reception.

"Shit!" Indigo swore, as the enormity of what was about to happen hit him. "Shit, Jen, please, you've gotta make sure they don't let them in!"

"But why, Indigo?" Jenny replied, confused. "I don't..."

"Jen! *Please,*" Indigo turned and gripped her hand, his eyes pleading. His breathing was ragged, his face flushed, his eyes wild with panic. "Please! I'm begging you. I can't... I can't see them."

Jenny held her hands up in surrender and strode off. Indigo sat in his chair in the woods, trying to continue breathing in and out, and feeling like the most wretched human being on the face of the earth. *You're trash,* he castigated himself. *You're a coward.* As the initial panic abated, his breathing evened out and his thoughts began to churn in a more rational manner. The guilt he felt hiding out there in the woods whilst he had his family turned away was overwhelming. They'd come all the way from Australia. For him. During the holidays. And he was out here cowering behind a tree, refusing to see them. *What kind of person does that?*

But he *couldn't* see them. He was too embarrassed, too ashamed. Oh God, the shame, it was paralysing. And he knew there'd be questions and accusations and judgements he just couldn't face. They were his reality and he was in no way, shape, or form ready to face reality yet. So he sat out there in the frigid winter air, his toes numb and his cheeks flushed for the forty minutes it took for the Carlisles to accept defeat and leave. Robbie, thin-lipped with fury, Joshua looking dumbfounded and wounded. And Cordelia, wide-eyed and tear-stained as she floated absently down the steps, pulling the black beaded bracelet from her wrist and dropping it in the snow behind her. Three car doors thudded shut and the Escalade revved up and took off, fishtailing down the driveway.

Come back! Indigo wanted to yell after them. But he didn't. He just sat there and watched, craning his neck for one last glimpse of the car as it bumped around the bend and disappeared from sight, knowing that today he hadn't just burnt the bridge between them — he'd taken a grenade and blown it sky high. He'd thought that night on the bridge had been his rock bottom, but this was his Mariana Trench. He felt sick to his stomach. Bile rose up in his throat and he leaned over the side of his chair and retched, his vomit marring the pristine snow below.

So this is what he had become.

Indigo despised himself with a vengeance. All those kids back home who had loved and revered him and put him on a pedestal. Wow, if only they could see him now, cowering out here in all his self-inflicted brokenness. He laughed, its hollow bitterness echoing through the crystal-capped trees. He tasted salt and realised he was crying.

He didn't want to be here anymore.

He tried to stand but fell as he knew he would, face first, into a deep embankment of snow. He gritted his teeth through the shooting pain as he turned awkwardly to lay on his back. He stared up at the bare branches interlaced above him, not knowing where one tree ended and the next began. The snow cocooned him, seeping into his clothes and numbing his flesh.

"Jeepers, Indigo! Honey, what are you doing?" Jenny was back. She grabbed his arms, helped him back into the wheelchair and tucked a blanket over him. She knelt down in front of him and peered into his face, her eyes brimming with concern as she placed a hand on his cheek. He was too cold to talk, frozen to his very core.

"I know you're hurting, tater tot, but we're all here to help you." He pursed his lips and looked away from her. Her shoulders slumped as she stood, moving to grab the handles of his chair. "I've got to get you inside."

chapter thirteen

reckless (don't be so...)

indigo

Indigo lost all sense of time. He stopped going to therapy, stopped interacting with the staff and other patients. As one day bled into the next in an endless cycle of light and dark, he just lay in bed and stared at the ceiling with its fissures and flaking paint chips and creeping circles of damp.

He was vaguely aware Luis had welcomed 1994 with a roommate who was barely there, responding to questions monosyllabically most of the time and pretending to be asleep the rest.

At first, it had seemed Luis was sympathetic to his plight. It was a small hospital and everyone knew what had happened with the Carlisles. But although Indigo barely registered it, a tiny shred of annoyance gradually crept its way into Luis's demeanour, and day by day that shred seemed to tear at his patience, until one day he apparently woke up with a gaping hole of anger he couldn't control anymore.

Jenny had come in to set Luis up for the day before moving onto Indigo's bed, greeting him brightly with a great big "Morning, tater tot!" Indigo had merely grunted. Jenny had yanked the curtain open to let the sunshine stream through the window Indigo had so wanted. Indigo had snapped at her to close it.

Jenny muttered something under her breath and did as he asked, shutting the door with as close to a slam as her professionalism would allow when she left.

Clearly, that was the final straw for Indigo's roommate. "Are you fuckin' *kidding* me, man?" he seethed.

Indigo didn't respond.

"You think what you've *been* through gives you the right to be a total *asshole?* After everythin' Jenny's done for you, that's how you treat her?" His fury, it seemed, had overtaken all his pride, because suddenly Indigo, lying on his back scowling at the ceiling, heard a whirring sound. Then a swish of fabric and the curtain that had always been there suddenly wasn't.

And just like that, the disembodied voice Indigo had come to know and love suddenly had a face. Kind of.

Indigo tried not to let his shock show at the sight of Luis. He mustn't have done a very good job, because Luis snarled, "Yeah, man, *take a good look*, this is what happens when you drive a car at a brick wall at fifty miles an hour! Take a real good look and then tell me what the *fuck* happened in your life that justifies you being such a *fuckin' prick!*"

Indigo was lost for words. He'd wondered what Luis looked like from the very first moment he'd heard his voice. He stared at him, imagining what he'd looked like once. Before. A skinny kid, short, with ebony hair and earnest soft brown eyes. Pecan-hued skin, a pleasant open happy face, a big smile.

Luis sat propped up in an electric wheelchair, his scrawny legs braced on footrests, his left arm hanging uselessly by his side, a hand with just three fingers and a thumb. His body was covered by a baggy grey sweatshirt and black trackpants – who knew what scars lay beneath those.

And his face.

Face?

Half face?

"Oh, Luis," Indigo breathed, pressing himself up on his elbows, feeling light-headed. He wanted to look away, but knew if he did, that would be it for him and Luis. He forced himself to look, to not flinch, to keep his expression even. All his problems paled in significance as he stared at what was left of his friend's face.

Luis glared at him defiantly with his one good eye, the right one. Because that side of his face was ok – a little scarred, but intact. The left side was not. An angry jagged scar encircled what was left of his ear, a few tufts of hair slowly trying to regrow around it. His mouth was slack on that side, a large keloid slicing through his lips from cheek to chin. There was no eye. Just a fleshy socket, patched with grafts.

"Suicide 101, man. When you have a choice of your maamaan's old beater or your daddy's Toyota, don't take your daddy's car just to stick it to him one last time."

Indigo furrowed his brow.

"Airbags," Luis explained. "If it wasn't for those fuckin' airbags, I wouldn't have woken up like this. I wouldn't have woken up at all."

"Are you…?" Indigo pointed to Luis' legs.

"Paralysed? Yup. They call it triplegia. Which means I can't use either of these," he indicated his legs, "or this," he finished, picking up his left arm with his right hand and letting it fall uselessly back to his side.

"Is it permanent?" Indigo asked.

"Who the fuck knows? My spinal cord was only partially severed so they say I should be able to regain some function. But it's been a while now and I still don't feel nothin'." He sighed. "It don't really matter either way, anyway. Not like I wanna go walking around out there in the real world with this mug," he laughed bitterly. "I'm a monster."

"It's not that bad," Indigo reassured him.

"Ha!" Luis scoffed. "You're a shitty liar, man. I seen your face when you saw me."

"Come on, mate, of course I was *shocked*. I wasn't expecting to see you. But now I'm used to it, it's not that bad." He swallowed hard. "Have you… have you thought about seeing a plastic surgeon?"

"A plastic surgeon?" Luis laughed. "La-dee-*fuckin'*-da, man, do you know what a plastic surgeon *costs*? My maamaan stays home to look after my brothers and sisters. My daddy works construction, and even if he *could* afford to help me like that, he wouldn't give me a dime." Luis swallowed hard. "He reckons I asked for this. Says I did it to myself, so I need to live with the consequences of my actions. He believes suicide is a mortal sin, so me goin' and doin' this… well, it's an insult to God and the church, which is unforgiveable in his eyes."

Indigo didn't know what to say. What *could* he say? He knew why a seventeen-year-old kid would steal his father's car and drive it into a brick wall – the same reason a seventeen-year-old kid would steal his father's car and jump a hundred metres off a bridge into the Hudson River.

"Besides, if I had all the money in the world, I'd pay someone to fix my spine, but that ain't gonna happen either, is it? Anyway, I don't think I need to say nothin' else to you, man." He smiled a half smile, as much of a smile as his face would allow. "A picture speaks a thousand words they say, right?" He held his palm out under his chin to frame his face. "I think this picture says it all."

"Thank you for showing me," Indigo said.

Luis paused, frowning. "Hey listen, sorry I was so harsh, but it was... time. You need to snap out of it, man, and start puttin' in the work. Look at you, with your pretty-boy face, your perfectly functionin' body! You can get yourself better and go back out there without scarin' small children. You can keep your failures somewhat private. You have that choice. *Make it.*" He used the joystick on his chair to turn it, starting to wheel back to his side of the room, stopping to close the curtain behind him.

"Don't," Indigo said, holding out his hand in protest.

Luis froze, his hand on the curtain, his back to Indigo.

"Leave it open," Indigo said.

"Are you sure?" Luis asked quietly, his shoulders tense. "No need to be polite for my sake, man."

"I think we're way past polite, dude," Indigo said with a small smile. "I'm sick of the sight of that thing. Leave it open."

Luis sagged visibly in relief. He let go of the curtain.

"Have I mentioned how much I like this for the two of you?" Jenny said, as she bustled into their room. The window was bare, flooding the room with muted winter sunlight and Indigo was sitting up in bed talking to Luis. Talking to Luis and looking him in the eye as he did so. She'd been so happy the day before when she'd walked in to see the curtain down.

After Luis went to physical therapy, Jenny perched on the end of Indigo's bed. "You boys ended up together for a reason," she said, peering into his face. "I think you're good for one another".

Indigo shrugged. "Yeah, he's pretty great, but I'm not sure what I bring to the table." The same old narrative chugged through his head day and night in a constant loop:

'I am nothing.'

'I am worthless.'

'I am toxic.'

'I am unlovable.'

The deep dark despair Indigo was entrenched in was still deafening, pitch black and all-consuming, but after Luis' dose of tough love, a new thought began to follow the old ones like weak sunshine straining through storm clouds:

'But I don't want to be.'

Luis had given him the jolt he needed to motivate him to want to claw his way back into the world, and for that, he was thankful. He committed to his therapy, to doing the work he needed to get better. He knew it was going to be bloody hard, but what was the alternative?

"Dr Marks tells me you've asked to stop seeing him," Jenny said one day, trying to catch his eye.

Indigo nodded, staring intently at the waffle blanket that covered his legs.

"Do you really think that's wise, honey?" she asked, placing her hand gently over his.

"He and I, we don't see eye to eye."

Dr Marks was a weary psychiatrist in his late sixties who'd seen it all and refused to waver from his go-to treatment protocol. He insisted Indigo needed to remain highly medicated, that he was a danger to himself and quite possibly others, and that he suffered from schizophrenia, clinical depression, and, most likely, psychosis.

Indigo vehemently disagreed and the two of them parted ways. Dr Bellamy was only a resident, but she was keen and passionate and, while she was regarded warmly by her patients, the general consensus amongst her colleagues was that her treatment methods were experimental, reckless even. Indigo knew in his bones she was the right doctor for him. She was always ready with a bright laugh or sympathetic smile, always open to venture down a road less travelled.

She wanted to focus on his depression.

Indigo felt comfortable in her presence and knew he didn't have to hold back. He could tell her anything and everything. And he had a lot to tell. Once the floodgates opened, everything poured out in a disjointed tumble. His parents. His childhood. The voices. The hallucinations. The feelings. The dreams. The Carlisles. The bridge. Cordelia.

But he grew frustrated when he couldn't get his thoughts straight. He couldn't remember the details properly doped up on his meds, so he began furtively cheeking them. But the more he reached for the light brimming on the edges of the haze in which he'd dwelled for so long, the more he was reminded of why he'd jumped in the first place.

Everything he'd jumped to escape returned, and with a vengeance. His dark thoughts were all-consuming, the voices were louder and more insistent, and the lonely waves of despair crashed over him, pounded at him, crushed him with their relentless brutality.

He was terrified. He was convinced he was going nuts. But Luis was there to reassure him that a common trait of people who were nuts was that they *didn't* know they were nuts. Luis was a rock for Indigo during those dark days. Indigo was constantly muttering to people who weren't there, curled up in the foetal position, hugging himself in despair. Luis never flinched. And he never complained when he was woken at night by his roommate's cries of terror, or when Indigo yelled at someone – no one – to shut up and go away.

Indigo talked and talked to Dr Bellamy, yet all the talking didn't stop the voices or the feelings or the visions. Dr Bellamy suggested hypnosis to regress him, to clear the bad memories. It was heavy going and took everything he had. He usually slept for hours after a session. Time marched on, his physical body began to heal, his casts came off, and in their absence, his independence grew. He was able to venture out and wander the woods alone, and eventually run its twisting paths each morning, rebuilding his muscles, regaining his fitness.

He'd always found nature incredibly soothing and healing. And while he preferred the ocean and desperately missed the beaches back home, there was something comforting, nurturing, about the forest.

Indigo awoke in late March after a particularly heavy hypnosis session completely disoriented. It must have been late afternoon or early evening, as the sunlight had faded to shadow. He could feel the night encroaching. At first, he thought it was the music that had woken him. Luis often forgot to turn his boombox off when he left the room. Indigo lay, too groggy to open his eyes. He knew the song that was playing. It was Phil Collins, singing about a lifetime of waiting, of anticipation, (or was it actually dread?) of long-awaited moments… *In The Air Tonight*, that was it.

He lay there, letting the music wash over him, suddenly realising he felt… peace.

Aside from the radio, the room was silent for once. No voices whispered at him or yelled at him or demanded of him. Nothing hurt. The loneliness and despair that had resided in his belly for so long were almost excruciating in their absence. The pounding that had beaten a steady agonising thrum in his head for so long now had stilled. He nearly felt like *himself* again. He was almost scared to open his lids, but then he felt a hand close over his and his eyes sprung wide.

He stared at her. *Was it really her? Had she finally returned to him?* A rush of emotion overcame him and he felt his eyes well up as he gazed into hers, deep, dark, soulful, doused with affection.

There she was, in all her glorious beauty, draped in magenta and violet, her hair magnificent, endless serpent-like braids hanging to her waist. Her scent, heady geranium, intoxicated his senses and brought all the good that had dwelled within his childhood rushing back.

"Sarita," he breathed.

And she smiled her joyous smile, that smile he remembered so well from his youth, that lit up his days and nights and comforted him when he felt unloved and abandoned.

"You came back," he whispered.

"I never left, darling one," she replied.

His brow creased in confusion. "You *did*," he said accusingly. "You *did* leave me! When I was twelve!"

"No, Indigo. I've always been right here with you. It was you who chose not to acknowledge me anymore."

Ice trickled down his spine.

"What do you mean?" he whispered. He was scared. Scared of something. He didn't know what, but something that was just there, out of his grasp, out of reach… and it scared him senseless.

"I've been watching over you as best I can. I never left, not even when you stopped listening, stopped seeing and started to self-destruct."

Indigo's stomach plummeted. It was all unravelling.

"Sarita?" he gasped, reaching out for her, desperately trying to cling to her. Sweat beaded and dripped off his forehead.

"I never left you, dear one. I *could* never leave you. Don't you remember how often I visited you in your dreams?"

Luis wheeled into the room, his eye widening in concern when he saw Indigo.

"*Luis!*" Indigo rasped. "Luis, can you see her? *Is she there?*" He pointed wildly at Sarita at his bedside, pleading, hopeful.

Luis wheeled himself closer. He put his hand on Indigo's arm and looked him straight in the eye. "There ain't no one in this room 'cept you and me, man." He reached over and turned his stereo off.

No. Indigo howled then, in agony, in despair, in sheer disbelief.

What was real anymore? His reality had been stripped to its very core. He was crazy. He was! His mind spun back to those times of innocence, to a childhood debunked with one sentence. So he was crazy always, even back then. Had he always been crazy? Yes, he had. He was batshit crazy.

"*Indigo!*" Sarita demanded. "Look at me!"

He lowered his chin to his chest and squeezed his eyes shut, covering his ears with his hands. He reached for the Walkman he kept beside his bed and shoved the headphones tight over his ears. He pushed play and turned the volume all the way up. The Rolling Stones' *Paint It, Black* filled his ears.

He drew his knees up to his chest and started rocking back and forth.

"Go away," he moaned, "please, just go away." Warm tears splashed from his eyes as his childhood tumbled through his head. What had been real? The memories came hot and fast through his mind, burning, clawing, blazing a new reality in their wake.

Luis looked alarmed in a way he hadn't been before. "I'm gonna go get someone, man," he said, turning his chair and whizzing out of the room.

With his hands jammed over the headphones, Indigo couldn't hear her anymore. He lifted them slightly. Nothing. He lifted them more. Still nothing. He removed his headphones and opened his eyes.

There she sat, patiently, calmly, on the edge of his bed.

"Indigo," she said, hands folded delicately in her silken lap.

"You're not real," he breathed. "You're in my head."

"Indigo," she said again in her gently lilting voice, a voice he had adored from the first moment he heard it, a voice he had associated with love, and comfort, and security. But it had all been a lie. "Indigo, if I was in your head, not even that music would be able to drown me out."

He gazed at her, blinking at the realisation of what she was saying.

"I'm not in your head, Indigo. I'm here. I'm real."

"B-but Luis couldn't see you. Only *I* can see you."

"Yes, but that doesn't mean I'm not real. It just means you're special."

Tears clinging to his lashes, Indigo stared at her, desperate for reassurance. "I'm not crazy?" he asked hoarsely.

"No, darling boy. You are not crazy. Just very gifted. And you've lost your way. Don't you remember all our lessons? All the work we did together?" she said, leaning in towards him.

"Who are you?" he whispered, looking her up and down as if seeing her for the first time.

"I'm a guardian, Indigo."

"A guardian?"

"A gatekeeper between worlds. You and I have known each other a long time, dear one," she smiled. "We've been together many lifetimes. Although whilst you have always had a physical body, I have not."

"I don't understand."

"When you were born, you weren't just dumped here in this world all alone, no one ever is. Every person on this earth is assigned a guardian whose purpose is to watch over them, to liaise between your world and ours on your behalf. I am yours. Most are completely unaware of the presence of their guardian, the voice that whispers in their ear, the one who holds them steady when times are tough. Some experience their guardian as a feeling, an inclination, often only having contact with them in their deepest state of dreaming, the memory never brought back to consciousness. But not you, my beautiful one. You've always been able to see through the membrane between worlds. You were always aware of me, seeing and hearing me in my true form. And I've always been here, guiding you, watching over you, trying to help you find your way to the path you're destined to follow." She smiled gently. "But you seem to have forgotten everything I've taught you."

"I've missed you," he confessed, looking Sarita in the eye, "so much." He swallowed hard. "Please help me."

"Of course, dear one. That's what I'm here for. Your time at this place is nearly done. Someone will be coming soon to take you away from here. You will know it is right when you see them. But until then, you must try to remember all that I taught you."

Indigo stared at her.

"So many of the feelings you've had, so much of that pain, and that sorrow..."

"Isn't mine," he finished for her. "But it still hurts like hell."

"Yes," Sarita confirmed, "but it doesn't have to." Her smile was soft.

"But the voices..." he ventured. "The voices and the visitors and the never-ending noise..."

"Everyone is aware of the basic senses: touch, sight, sound, taste and smell," she explained, "but you, dear one, your senses go beyond that. You have senses beyond the physical: higher senses." Her eyes crinkled joyously. "You are an empath, Indigo, which means you're incredibly tuned in to other people's feelings and emotions and bodily symptoms. And why it's particularly hard for you is because you are also telepathic and clairvoyant."

"I don't understand," he groaned, scrubbing at his eyes with his fingertips.

"You will, eventually," she said gently. "You were born with the ability to feel very deeply what other people are feeling, to hear what others are thinking, and to hear and see those of us who are not of your world."

"Not of my world?"

"Yes. We the discarnates."

"Discarnates?" he repeated, nose wrinkling.

"Discarnates are souls without physical bodies, some of which are guardians." She laid her hand over his. He glanced down at it, frowning, pulling away.

"If you don't have a body, how come I can feel you when you touch me?"

"Because you are so incredibly sensitive, my darling one. I may not have a physical body, but my soul is made up of a force that is real, that you have the ability to sense."

"Why me?"

She regarded him serenely for a long moment. "Do you remember the day you met Banjo?"

Indigo couldn't help but smile at the mention of his beloved dog. "Of course," he replied, his voice full of warmth. "Man, he was one cute puppy."

Sarita didn't smile back. "Think harder, Indigo," she instructed, reaching for his hand. As her fingers touched his, a rush of memories flooded over him. The squeal of brakes. The pitiful yelp. The tiny, twisted body. And the blood, scarlet and sticky and warm.

Light-headedness came fast as the blood drained from his face. "Oh no," he murmured, knuckles white as he gripped fistfuls of blanket, "that's right… I remember now…" He'd been outside playing on the driveway under Sarita's watchful eye when they'd witnessed Banjo dumped out the window of a passing car. He'd managed to limp up onto his clumsy puppy paws just as another car had come speeding up the rise. Indigo had cried out too late and Banjo had disappeared up under the wheels. The car had driven away.

Indigo had run as fast as his four-year-old legs could carry him, pressing the button so the wrought-iron gates that guarded the entrance to the estate slid open and he could run out onto the street. He tenderly picked the puppy up, cradling him in his arms. His tears had mixed with Banjo's blood as the little dog had looked up at him, eyes rolling, limpid with terror. Sarita had taken Indigo by the elbow and led him off the road. "Help him, Sarita!" Indigo had begged, sobbing. The little dog was in so much pain, was so terribly scared, Indigo remembered feeling every ounce of it.

"Indigo," Sarita had said, kneeling down in front of him and taking his face between her palms, "you help him."

"I don't know how," he'd cried.

"Yes, you do," she'd reassured him sternly. "You always have. You can make him better."

So Indigo had sat with the poor broken puppy in his lap and closed his eyes, and remembered everything Sarita had ever taught him, remembered everything he'd ever known forever. He knew right where it hurt and exactly what to do. And when he opened his eyes, after a length of time had passed he didn't know how to measure, Banjo was nestled securely between his knees, his breath rising and falling calmly, rhythmically, in his little chest. He was whole and healed and warm with life. If not for the dried blood on his coat, Indigo would have thought he'd imagined the whole thing. Indigo recalled how content he'd been in that moment, how proud of himself he'd been. How proud Sarita had been, smiling at him with the strength of a thousand suns.

As the memory faded, Indigo opened his eyes and looked at Sarita perched beside him on his bed, his hand clasped in hers. "How did I do that?" he asked in wonderment. And how had he not remembered how he'd really met Banjo?

"It's what you've always done," Sarita told him. "Lifetime after lifetime, you've perfected your skill. Indigo, my darling boy, you are a healer." She smiled, tenderly touched his face. "All you hear, all you feel, all you see… none of that exists to torture you. Harness your higher senses and you will realise all your sensitivities are there to help you help others. Take back control of your life – you have the power."

"I'm not crazy," Indigo murmured, looking deep into her eyes for affirmation.

"Not in the slightest, dear one. But tell me, Indigo, that puppy, that accident, is there anyone in your life now who reminds you of Banjo?"

Indigo regarded her incredulously as she glanced at the empty bed on the other side of the room. "Not Luis?" he breathed.

Sarita smiled her magnificent smile and inclined her head in a slight nod. "Do you think there may be a reason you and he were placed in the same room? That maybe you were meant to meet him? And he you?"

"I'm meant to help him." His stomach flip-flopped.

"His guardian has been asking you for help, but you haven't been listening."

Indigo laughed bitterly as a sudden anger swelled to consume him. "Oh yeah? I haven't been *listening*? Well, how in the *fuck* am I meant to hear them over all the others? I mean, I'm assuming Luis' guardian isn't the one telling me I'm worthless and to go slash my wrists, right?" He grinned maniacally. "Maybe it's the one who's been confessing to me her child's real father is her husband's brother? Surely it's not the sicko who comes every night at midnight to tell me in great detail how he tortured and killed his wife and where he *buried* her body?! Tell me Sarita, is his request somewhere amongst the deluge of shit I've been forced to listen to for *months — years —* on end!?" He was yelling now.

Sarita caressed his hand. "Deep breaths, dear one. Remember, you control your breath, you control your body." He scowled but obeyed, inhaling and exhaling steadily. "We have plenty of time to help you gain control over your telepathy and your clairvoyance," she assured him. "But you won't be here for much longer, darling one, so you have to help Luis now."

"But... but how?"

"Trust in yourself. Listen to your intuition. You will know what to do. And I am here to help you."

"But he's so messed up," Indigo said softly, his lack of confidence overwhelming.

"Not all wounds are meant to be healed," Sarita told him. "We can only do what we're meant to." She rose to her feet, leaning in so her face was centimetres from his. "I know you can do this. You were born to do this, darling one."

When Nurse Jenny rushed into his room a few moments later with a frantic Luis hot on her heels, she was confronted with a calm and collected Indigo, sitting up in bed, a look of determination on his face.

"You crying wolf, pickle?" she asked Luis with a sidelong glance. "He sure seems fine to me."

The next couple of nights while Luis slept, Indigo sat at his bedside trying to figure out how to help him. He spent half the time second guessing himself, clumsily fumbling his way through. The childish innocence and trust he'd possessed when he'd healed Banjo all those years ago was long gone and hard to recapture. His mind was a very noisy place these days, brimming with self-criticism and uncertainty. But Sarita was constantly at his side, communing with Luis' guardian, advising Indigo in her delicate way.

When Nurse Jenny knocked on his door the next afternoon to tell Indigo someone was there to see him, he swore his heartbeat increased tenfold. "I know you've said no visitors," she ventured, "but he was very insistent."

Sarita had promised someone was coming. Indigo traced a finger absently over the white stripes that ran the side of his navy Adidas tracksuit pants as he regarded Jenny. He took a deep breath, then stood shakily from the craggy armchair beside the window in which he'd been reading the Eckhart Tolle book Dr Bellamy had given him. He pulled on a matching tracksuit top, zipped it brusquely to his chin, then ran a hand through his hair. He nodded at Jenny, "I'll see him. Where is he?"

"Outside, in the back garden," she replied, brows shooting up in surprise he'd agreed so readily.

Nerves flickered inside Indigo's belly as he exited the hospital and strode out into the grounds, scanning the lawn for his visitor. It would be April soon, and the snow that had blanketed the ground for much of his stay, had largely melted away. The spring sun was slowly resuscitating the brown grass back to green, and while the trees were still bare, Indigo knew they wouldn't be for long. He spotted a lone figure on the far edge of the grounds staring towards the entrance to the forest. His back was to Indigo.

As Indigo drew closer, he saw the man was quite tall, broad-shouldered yet slender, his thick dark hair longer on top, cropped closer at the sides. He was wearing a black leather jacket, combat boots and faded black jeans. As Indigo approached him, the man turned, and Indigo was jarred with a jolt of recognition.

"Hey, buddy," the man said, his voice warm and slow. "Remember me?"

chapter fourteen

fire and rain

indigo

"It-it's you," Indigo breathed. He searched the man's dark brown eyes and there was something so familiar there, familiar in a way he couldn't put his finger on. He had regular features, his face kind, his smile warm. There was a calmness to him, a laid-back demeanour that made Indigo feel immediately at ease in his presence. He looked to be in his early forties.

"Indigo, my name is Diego Matias Sebastian Rafael," he said, holding out his hand, "but you can call me Raf." Indigo took it and Raf clasped his other hand over the top, holding it warmly. "So you *do* know who I am?"

Indigo nodded. "Of course I do. I've spent months being angry at you..." he trailed off.

Raf grinned, eyes crinkling, "Yeah I know. And now?"

"Now?" Indigo replied thoughtfully. "I'm grateful to you. I owe you everything." He stared at Raf, holding his eye. "You saved my life." He took a deep breath, his exhale unsteady. "Thank you. Thank you for pulling me from the water and bringing me to the hospital."

"You're most welcome," Raf said, grin deepening. His warmth was infectious. Indigo couldn't help but feel as though he was an old friend in whom he could confide all his secrets.

"How did you even see me jump? It was so dark that night."

"That's not a story for today," Raf told him firmly, "but if you feel ready, I want you to come with me, buddy. They've done all for you they can here, they can't help you anymore, but…"

"But you can," Indigo finished for him, never surer of anything in his life.

Raf nodded. "I see you, Indigo. There're parts of you that only someone like me can help you with."

"Like what?" Indigo asked, teeth denting his lower lip.

"The voices?" Raf said simply.

Indigo inhaled sharply. "The pain?" he ventured, his voice small.

Raf nodded.

"And the… the visions?"

"You're gifted," Raf shrugged. "Your higher senses are… very highly developed." He slid his hands into his jacket pockets and regarded Indigo quietly. "You're able to see, hear, and feel things that other people can't."

Indigo nodded.

"Me too," Raf confessed. "We're different, Indigo," he said, quickly adding, "That's a *good* thing." He placed his hands on Indigo's shoulders and gave him a smile so kind it was impossible not to return. "You're just out of control. You need help. You need guidance. I want to help you. Let me help you?"

Indigo straightened his spine, his answer coming before he had a chance to think. "Yes."

Raf nodded. "I'll pick you up tomorrow morning."

As they said goodbye, he realised he would be sad to leave Luis and Jenny and Dr Bellamy, who had all done so much for him these past months. They had cared for him and nurtured him and done all they could to make him feel loved, to feel valued.

The three of them had saved his life just as much as Raf had.

They wouldn't want him to leave, he knew that. They wouldn't understand. They might even try to stop him.

Tonight was his last night to help Luis. He was going to have to work quickly. He needed to make it count.

luis

The next morning, Luis awoke and yawned, stretching his arms up over his head. He was drowsy. He'd been sleeping so heavily lately, as comatose as if he'd been floored by a heavyweight opponent. And his dreams were incredibly vivid — of flying, and running, and jumping, and Indigo. Indigo was always there in those dreams, surrounded by a warm golden glow that swirled to envelop Luis like a comforting embrace, seeping through every bit of him, into his very tendons and bones.

Forgetting himself, drowsy and disoriented, believing he was still in that dream, Luis sat up and swung his legs over the side of the bed, sliding off and padding gingerly to Indigo's bed to tell him about his dream before it vanished into the ether.

But Indigo's bed was cold and vacant, neatly made with an air of finality. And there was an envelope propped up on the pillow, addressed to him. Luis glanced up and realised the whole side of Indigo's room was empty. Reality began to dawn on him and his stomach dropped like a stone.

He reached out for the envelope and gasped when he realised he was reaching with his left arm. And then he looked down and realised he was standing. And that he had walked. He'd walked from his bed to Indigo's. He'd walked across the whole damned room!

He began to holler.

chapter fifteen

dreams

harbord, new south wales, april, 1994

cordelia

"What're you reading, honey?"

Cordelia was sitting cross-legged on the couch, her nose in a book. She glanced up at Mum, tiny in a short burnt-orange dress with long floaty sleeves, her unruly blonde hair caught back in a loose braid.

"It's one of those weird books Drew gave her," Robbie interjected from his place in front of the television on the other couch. "It's probably about aliens or something." His eyes were glued to the TV and he didn't look up, but his tone was judgy.

"Aliens?" Mum said, her stacked bangles clinking as she straightened the couch cushions, then plonked down next to her daughter, tucking her legs up beneath her. "Since when are you interested in aliens?" Matty toddled in and climbed onto Cordelia's lap. She kissed his head and ran her hand absentmindedly through his golden curls.

"It's about the Salem witch trials actually," she said, throwing Robbie a greasy look. She shuffled Matty around on her lap, moving him to the crook of her arm.

Her mother leant to pick her own book up from the coffee table. She held it up so Cordelia could see the front cover. It was the latest Sebastian Winters novel. "If you're wondering what to read next, I'll be done with this one soon. I can't put it down. You'll love the heroine. She's got real *spunk.*"

Cordelia smiled. "Geez, Mum, does Dad know you're obsessed with another man?" she teased. Her mother was always raving about the best-selling paranormal mystery author.

Mum grinned and laid a hand on Cordelia's cheek. "It's nice to see you smiling, sweetie."

Cordelia shrugged her off. "Please stop fussing, Mum, I'm fine."

"Ha!" Robbie said from the other couch, his gaze still on the television.

"*Shut up,* Rob!"

Matty looked curiously from Cordelia to Robbie.

"You've hardly been fine," Robbie said, glancing over at her. "You've pretty much been a zombie since we got back from New York."

"Have not," she said, burying her face back in her book, trying to pick up where she'd left off.

"Um hello?" Robbie said. "You didn't leave the house except to go to school for like two months. You barely left your room, you pretty much stopped eating…"

Cordelia clenched her jaw, trying to ignore him.

"That's enough, Robbie," Mum chastised, and from the corner of her eye Cordelia saw her flash him a look. "We were all pretty low after New York. You weren't firing on all cylinders yourself. The main thing now is Cordelia has decided to move on with her life."

Mum smiled encouragingly at her and Cordelia felt a wave of guilt. After Indigo had refused to see them at the hospital four months ago, she'd been a complete mess. The hurt and rejection had been completely overwhelming. All she'd done was lie in bed all day with saltwater leaking from her eyes. She'd completely lost her appetite, her stomach so filled with a writhing ball of nervous apathy, there was no room for food.

She oscillated between desperate sadness and bitter anger. When she thought of how hopeless Indigo must have felt to do what he did, she was overcome with such devastation she thought her heart might physically crack and bleed out. But then she'd think about the fact he didn't call her, that he didn't ask for her help or tell her what was going on, and she'd grow more and more furious with him. And the fact he'd had them turned away after they'd flown all that way to see him… well, that hurt more than anything.

Peyton and Sian would come over and sit on the end of her bed, trying to cheer her up, but even they got fed up with her despondency after a couple of months. One Sunday a couple of weeks ago, she'd been looking for a library book she'd forgotten to return when she came across the bag of books Drew had lent her behind a pile of dirty clothes under her dresser.

She'd sat down on her bed and opened it, gingerly reaching inside to pull out the stack of musty, battered books she hadn't looked at since last year. She'd put aside the couple she'd read, then started to flip through the ones she hadn't, perusing the back covers to glean a little more information about which particular far-out theory each explored. One specific book had piqued her interest and she'd lain back amongst her pillows and begun to flick through it. It wasn't until it grew dark outside that she realised she'd spent the whole day reading. She'd forgotten how those books took her mind off things, gave her something else to think about and fixate on.

The next day at school, she'd tracked Drew down and apologised for having had his books for so long. His dimple had popped when he'd grinned and assured her it was no problem whatsoever. He'd then asked her which ones she'd read, which had led to an in-depth discussion on the Mayans and how prepared they should be for the world ending in 2012 and he'd been late for rugby training.

The next Saturday night, she'd allowed Peyton and Sian to convince her to go to a party with them. So she'd washed and straightened her hair and donned a red plaid miniskirt and a black crop top, and gone out with her friends. Drew had been there, making out with some leggy brunette in the corner. It had seemed strange being at a party, Faith No More's *Epic* vibrating from throbbing speakers, everyone drinking and laughing and having fun when she felt like her whole world had caved in. She went outside because she suddenly couldn't breathe. She wandered over the back lawn and sat quietly in the shadows, leaning back on her hands and staring up at the moon.

"You hanging out here with all your mates?" a voice said behind her. She turned and smiled when she saw Drew walking towards her, a bottle of VB in each hand.

"You've come up for air, have you?" she teased, leaning to adjust the strap of her black studded ankle boot.

"Huh?" he said, reddening slightly when he realised what she meant. "Oh yeah, you know, just a bit of fun," he shrugged. He took a swig of his beer and sat down beside her on the grass. He offered her the other one and she took it. "So," he said, staring straight ahead, "you read any more of my books?"

"I have," she said, "and I have questions." And so began a lively discussion on the mud floods of Tartaria that continued for so long that by the time Peyton came to find her to tell her they were leaving, most of the party had cleared out. Cordelia checked her watch and told Peyton she'd meet her out front in five.

"What happened to your friend?" Cordelia asked Drew, looking for the leggy brunette in the dwindling throng.

"Oh shit," Drew said, looking stricken as he realised what he'd done. "Oops," he grimaced. "I was meant to be getting her a drink..." He cupped Cordelia's wrist so he could glance at her watch, "... like two hours ago." He shrugged then. "Oh well, she didn't believe in UFOs. It never would have worked out, anyway."

Cordelia laughed. And it felt good to find something genuinely funny again.

"Hey, are you into *The X-Files?*" he asked suddenly.

"I've never seen it," she admitted.

"*Whaaat?* It's seriously the best show ever made. Come over next Friday, watch it with me. I'm sure I'll be able to convert you."

She nodded as he pulled her to her feet, then leant to kiss her cheek goodbye. She headed out the front to find Peyton and Sian. They were sitting in the gutter under a palm tree, waiting for her. She sat down beside Sian, crossing her legs at the ankles.

"So what's going on with you and Drew?" Peyton demanded, leaning across Sian to fix Cordelia with a penetrative gaze.

"Wh-What?" Cordelia stammered. "Nothing! We're just friends, nothing more."

"Sure," Peyton replied, tucking an orange curl behind her ear. "You keep telling yourself that." She reached into her bag for a lighter and a pack of ciggies, fishing one out and flicking it alight.

"Seriously Peyts? It is possible to just be friends with a guy, you know?"

"Not one as hot as Drew Prescott. He's a total spunk rat," Peyton shot back, smoke flaring from her nostrils. "Those dreamy blue eyes, that cute little dimple, that totally sexy broken nose…"

"You think his *nose* is sexy?" Sian interjected, her face scrunched in confusion. "Like, how can someone's *nose* be sexy?"

"I dunno," Peyton shrugged. "It makes him badass or something."

"He's, like, not as hot as Indigo," Sian said, her long raven hair falling sleekly over one eye as she leant forward. "But no one is. Indigo's *brutally* hot."

Peyton shot her a death stare. "Seriously, Shi?" she said through clenched teeth. "We agreed not to mention the 'I' word."

"Oh," Sian said, flushing and glancing at Cordelia. "Oh yeah, I'm sorry, Cee."

"You don't need to wrap me in cotton wool," Cordelia said, absentmindedly twisting her ring around her finger. "I'm fine." Although the very mention of his name had been like an electric shock. "I'm not interested in dating anyone at the moment, and I don't think I will be for the foreseeable future."

"I'm just saying," Peyton said, dragging deeply on her ciggie, "if Drew makes a move, you should totally go for it."

"Yes, we know," Cordelia said lightly, "you think his nose is hot."

Sian started to giggle.

"Oh, come on!" Peyton said. "*All* of him is hot."

"Well then, I'll set the two of you up," Cordelia offered.

"Psh, no thanks. I've got my eye on someone else." She winked. "Anyway," she said, leaning forward again, "now Shi's already broken our pact and brought him up, what do you think Indigo would think about you and Drew going out? Like, you wouldn't be the first of his girls Drew's dated."

Cordelia rolled her eyes. "Firstly, I have no intention of going out with Drew. Secondly, please don't refer to me as one of Indigo's girls ever again, and thirdly, who did Drew date after Inds?"

"Harper Valentine!" Peyton announced.

"Harper Valentine?" Cordelia repeated. "Now that's a name I haven't heard in a while. Didn't she just drop off the face of the planet a couple of years back?"

"Yeah, apparently she like, moved away after her parents died," Sian said.

"Oh yeah," Cordelia breathed. "That was *awful*." She could still see the headlines — '*Murder-Suicide in Mosman*'. "Poor Harper."

"Well, if it makes you feel any better, I heard she got *quite* the inheritance," Peyton said, eyes shining, stubbing her ciggie out on the curb. Peyton loved nothing more than a bit of gossip. "She's probably living on the French Riviera or something." She paused thoughtfully. "Remember what a bitch she was at your thirteenth birthday party? All that shit she said about Rob?"

"How could I forget?" Cordelia murmured, images of Harper storming off with blood streaming from her nose, running through her head.

"But hang on," Sian said, rummaging through her purse and pulling out a can of Impulse. "When did she date Drew?" She popped the cap off and proceeded to mist herself with the sickly-sweet body spray.

"Right after Indigo," Peyton said, fanning the fumes and coughing.

"I doubt it," Sian said. "Wasn't she totally obsessed with Inds? Like, she wouldn't let anyone near him, right?"

They both looked at Cordelia. "I don't know!" she said, throwing her hands up. "I mean, he told me she got pretty nasty when he broke things off with her."

"Hang on," Peyton said, "*he* broke up with *her*? I heard *she* broke up with *him*?"

"He *dumped* her. But who *cares,*" Cordelia said, shaking her head. "It was like four years ago. What's the big deal? And I never heard the Drew thing."

"Oh," Peyton said, screwing up her face, "maybe they didn't date. It could have been that they were just shagging. Ask your sister," she said to Sian.

"How would she know?" Sian asked, a look of confusion twisting her fine Eurasian features.

"*Der,*" Peyton said, "she was in Harper's year?"

"Oh yeah," Sian grinned, smacking a hand to her forehead. "Ok, so... tell us, who *is* he? Who've you got the hots for?"

Peyton mimed zipping her lips and shook her head, a mischievous glint in her eye.

"Who?" Sian cried, hitting her lightly on the arm. *"Tell us!"*

"Ah, here's our cab," Peyton said, climbing to her feet and waving it down.

"Peyts!" Sian called, jumping up and following her. "You can't just drop a bomb like that and not tell us..."

"Just because you've dated the same boy like, *forever* doesn't mean you have to live vicariously through me," she laughed.

Cordelia smiled softly as Sian tried to coerce Peyton's crush out of her all the way home. It was nice to feel normal again, even if it was just for a few hours.

The next week when she saw Drew at school, he'd asked her again to come over Friday and she'd agreed. She was actually really looking forward to hanging out with him.

That Friday, Dad dropped her at Drew's.

"What time do you want me to pick you up?" he asked as she kissed his cheek and opened the car door.

"Oh, it's ok. Drew said he could drive me home after."

"Ok. Just call if anything changes. Have a good night, darling." Cordelia knew he was so happy to see her getting out and about, he would've driven her to the moon if she'd asked.

She walked up the weed-pocked path and knocked tentatively at Drew's front door. She'd been to plenty of parties at this house, but that was always with about a hundred other people. She heard heavy footfall and the door flew open. There stood Drew, broad-shouldered in a Nirvana t-shirt and grey trackies, his dark hair damp from a recent shower. He smelt of shampoo and his usual aftershave. Pearl Jam's *Better Man* drifted from somewhere inside the house.

"Are you ready to have your mind blown?" he said with a wide grin, dimple deepening. He was clutching a worn-looking VHS tape in his hand, 'X-Files' hand-written on the label.

He ushered her in and down a narrow corridor past the kitchen and into a living area containing two black leather couches and a technical looking entertainment system flanked by CD towers. The house was untidy, discarded shoes and items of clothing scattered throughout, dishes piled high in the sink, one lone shrivelled apple in the fruit bowl. Drew's mum had walked out on his dad a few years back, leaving him to raise Drew and his older two brothers on his own. Cordelia gathered tidiness wasn't a priority in this house of four men.

He asked her to sit, indicating the couch opposite the TV, chivalrously dusting what looked like chip crumbs from its seat. He silenced Pearl Jam with the flick of a button as he knelt to insert the video into the player, then flopped down on his back on the other couch, elbow winged behind his head.

"Your dad and brothers are out?" she ventured, twisting a button on the denim jacket she wore over a little floral dress.

"Yup. Dad's always at his new girlfriend's place and the boys are at some party. You wanna drink or something?" he offered.

"Yeah, ok," she said, and he hit pause on the remote and disappeared into the kitchen. He returned with a bowl of popcorn and a couple of bottles of water, handing her one. He offered the popcorn and she took a small handful.

They watched the first couple of episodes, Drew expertly fast-forwarding all the ads, and she had to admit she was hooked. He looked over to her. "So? What do you think?"

"Can we watch another?" she asked.

He sat up, elbows braced on his knees and gazed at her. "You really like it?" he asked, and he looked so happy she burst out laughing.

"It's a really good show," she admitted.

"It is. Because it promotes existential conversation about the paranormal." He leant forward in his seat. "You see, you've gotta have an open mind, Cee. Everything you know about the history of the world you were taught from an approved syllabus. Who do you think controls that syllabus? Controls that information?"

She arched an eyebrow at him and smiled as she listened to him pontificate about aliens and ghosts and government cover-ups. He was super smart and there was something about his passion that she found enchanting.

After she'd grown tired of challenging him, as it only seemed to fuel him further, he led her out to his car and opened the passenger door for her.

"What do your footy mates think?" she asked him as they drove. "Of your… beliefs?"

"Oh, you know," he laughed, "they're always paying me out. But it's all good. I'd rather think for myself than just believe what I'm told to believe by the education system and the media. True intelligence comes from questioning everything."

"What are you going to do next year?" she asked him. "When you finish school?"

They were stopped at a red light and he turned to look at her. "I'm gonna study Medicine."

"Are you really?" she asked, unsure whether he was pulling her leg.

"Yup. I'm going to infiltrate the establishment and shake it up from the inside," he grinned. "Anyway, I'm hoping to get in off the back of my rugby, so we'll see what happens."

"That's awesome," she said, surprised and impressed.

It amazed Cordelia how quickly her friendship with Drew deepened. They didn't hang out every day, or even every week, but they didn't need to. Whenever they saw each other, they just picked up where they'd left off. Some days at school, they had lunch together, and he always had a new book to lend her or a show to recommend. She saw him out at parties goofing around with his rugby mates and chatting to pretty girls, but he always made the time for a deep and meaningful with her. His had grown into a friendship she valued.

chapter sixteen

where the streets have no name

sedona, arizona, june, 1994

indigo

Indigo had never met anybody who didn't own a TV until Raf. But what he did own was a book collection to rival the local library. Three walls of his enormous study played host to ceiling high bookshelves housing works of fiction, non-fiction, textbooks, encyclopaedias, history, romance, mystery, fantasy, sci-fi, adventure, self-help… Books on any topic Indigo could want for.

"Help yourself," Raf told him when he wandered by one afternoon to see Indigo perusing the shelves.

Indigo turned. "You got a lotta books, man," he said with a hitch of his brows.

Raf chuckled as if at a private joke and continued on his way towards the kitchen. Indigo frowned after him. Raf was proving to be somewhat of an enigma. When he wasn't doting on Indigo, he spent a lot of time holed up in his study, working. And when he wasn't working, he seemed to have a constant stream of visitors from all walks of life knocking on his door. He would greet them warmly, then usher them into the front sitting room, closing the door firmly behind them. They'd usually emerge around an hour later; sometimes they'd be smiling and laughing quietly with him, other times they'd be crying.

Indigo loved Raf's four-bedroom home with its cathedral ceilings and floor-to-ceiling windows. He'd felt like he belonged there from the very first moment he set foot inside. The whole house was masculine in a soft, nurturing way, all rich browns and reds and oranges. The walls were adorned with indigenous artefacts Raf had collected from far and wide.

It had been two months since Raf had brought Indigo to live with him in Sedona, a rugged desert town located smack bang in the heart of Arizona. Indigo had immediately fallen in love with the forest-fringed hamlet with its spiny cacti and hardy desert scrub. More than anything, the awe-inspiring rock formations that towered over the town, crimson, banded with gold, white, and peach, had captured his heart, some jagged and pointy, some smooth and flat-topped, others rising in solitude from the desert floor like prehistoric coral. He'd never seen anything quite like it. He'd never *felt* anything quite like it.

"Sedona is a place of healing," Raf had explained as they'd driven north up the I-17 after landing in Phoenix. "It is regarded as a very sacred and powerful space by the Native American community. In the past, they considered this land too sacred to live within, so they dwelled upon its outskirts, only crossing within for rituals and ceremonies and consecrated events such as birthing. It's said Sedona itself is a giant vortex, and that the very rocks the town was built upon emanate mysterious forces." Raf always spoke slowly, thoughtfully. "You see, the sandstone here gets its red colour from high concentrations of iron, which is highly magnetic ⊠ and it's interspersed and underlain with quartz, which acts as a conductor. The people who live here call Sedona a cathedral without walls."

Indigo had glanced sideways at him.

"You'll see. Or more so, you will *feel*. Everything in Sedona is amplified, intensified, everything you feel becomes magnified. Someone as sensitive as you can live here with acceptance, but you will not be able to hide, least of all, from yourself. There are forces here that will hold a mirror up to everything you need to see. Everything will bubble to the surface like lava. But you will be set free, clean and new and glorious in your imperfection. Scabs will be torn off recent wounds, keloid off to expose the old."

Indigo hadn't known whether to be excited or terrified.

But Raf had been right. Indigo had felt it — the air, thick with ancestral whispering, the town itself seemed to possess a haunting majesty. From what he'd seen, Sedona was a haven for creative and conscious individuals seeking a meaningful existence.

A lot of stuff came up for Indigo his first couple of weeks there. Raf hadn't been exaggerating when he'd said Sedona would expose his wounds. A fragility overcame Indigo, accompanied by such emotion that he felt close to tears almost constantly. It was as though the recollection of everything that had made him melancholy descended upon him all at once. A lot of it was a blur of swirling colour and pain, but Raf was always there, dropping everything to support him, to listen to him talk into the small hours of the morning. Whatever he needed, Raf was there.

He often took Indigo out hiking on Sedona's endless trails. One day Raf led him far off the trail deep into the wilderness through thorny scrub and prickly cacti. They emerged at the edge of a canyon, stony and shaded. High above them, Indigo could see caves carved into the outcrops of the soaring red rocks. All was still bar the breeze slipping through the tree canopy, a faint rustle of leaves and boughs. A man approached them, his black hair flowing down his back, his ears adorned with bone and feather, and Indigo balked to see someone else out there in the middle of nowhere. The man was dressed traditionally, his clothes appearing to be made of buckskin. He smiled beatifically at Indigo who smiled back as the man continued on his way.

"Not so scary, hey?" Raf asked, staring after the man. Indigo threw him a questioning glance. Raf narrowed his eyes at him. "There are Native American ceremonial ruins scattered all around here, Indigo. That man you just saw is a discarnate."

Indigo did a double take, craning his neck after the man who'd disappeared into the forest. "You mean…"

"Most people wouldn't have been able to see him. Only those of us with higher senses. You're highly clairvoyant Indi; seeing discarnates comes naturally to you."

"So you're saying that man, he was… dead?"

Raf slid his hands into his pockets, rocking back on his heels and smiling broadly. "Uh huh," he nodded.

Indigo closed his eyes against the gentle breeze trailing over his face. What he'd thought was the wind in the trees he now realised was the whispering of countless overlapping voices.

"So many voices," he murmured. White noise, the sound track to his life.

"You can't listen to them all at once," Raf said. "Focus on one at a time, hear what each one has to say."

"How do you pick just one?"

"One will always be louder. You'll come to hone your abilities, know by instinct what needs your attention and what's just background noise."

"These voices," Indigo said, "they don't *all* belong to dead people, do they?"

"No," Raf smiled, "telepathy as strong as yours is able to pick up people's thoughts from miles away if they're projecting them loudly enough."

"So when I was in New York…?"

"Yeah, a city that densely populated isn't the most ideal place for a person with unmanaged higher senses like yours," Raf grimaced. "But once you've got a handle on it, you'll be fine." He slipped off his shoes and sat cross-legged on the ground, his back against a fallen log. He looked up at Indigo, hand tented over his eyes. "Let me know when you've had enough for today and we can go home."

"It's always so quiet at your place," Indigo said, as he suddenly realised the visions, the noise, the feelings, largely went away within Raf's four walls.

"Well, there're certain… protections in place over my house," Raf said elusively. "You should get a break from most external forces when you're there."

They wouldn't always visit the canyon. Some days they'd just walk, and during those walks Raf would encourage Indigo to open up. Indigo had spent so long feeling the hurts of others, but he had many hurts of his own he needed to stop hiding from. Raf was a great listener. And although he didn't always say a lot, Indigo found whatever he did say was worth listening to.

On this particular day, they'd hiked up a craggy rock mountain and were resting at its summit, taking in the view from the top. The land had a beautiful emptiness to it that enveloped them, bringing resounding stillness. He had spent the walk telling Raf about being sent to live with his father.

"There was no one there to talk to, no one who cared, and it made me feel… worthless," Indigo said as they sat and looked out at the expanse of trees far below. "I hated my life so much. And I started to hate myself." His voice cracked and he swallowed hard. "I didn't want anyone to see what I'd become, because I thought if they saw me like that, they'd never be able to see me in any other way. I felt such utter loathing for what I'd become and I couldn't see any way to fix that." His heart felt heavy as he stared out at the rust-hued mountains rising from the other side of the valley.

"When times are dark, it's the prospect of brighter days ahead that's meant to ignite some hope," Raf said in his stoic way. "But if we cannot fathom even a shred of luminosity in our future, despair will consume us." Indigo glanced at him as he continued. "When we feel really sad, Indi, we think about it. A lot. We fixate on it, we think about it constantly because that's what we're best at: thinking." He unscrewed the lid from a bottle of water and offered it to Indigo, who took a sip then handed it back.

"It isn't until we understand the need to consciously observe these thoughts and recognise how toxic they are," he said, his eyes now closed, "that we can even start to tackle something as complex as depression. That's why the therapy you undertook in the hospital was so important, because to notice these thoughts, to verbalise them, is how we begin to know ourselves." He opened his eyes and looked at Indigo.

Indigo lay down, the rock hard and warm against his back as he stared up at the sky. "That simple, eh?" he said with a cynical chuckle.

"It takes courage and a lot of damn hard work," Raf said, placing the bottle down and laying back beside him. "You have to stop criticising yourself, stop putting yourself down. But having others offer you unconditional support while you heal is paramount and that is what I am here to do."

"I don't know what to say," Indigo said softly, turning his head so he could look Raf in the eye.

"No need to say anything," Raf said with a gentle smile. "I'm sure you'd do the same for me."

And right there and then, Indigo knew without a doubt that he would.

A couple days later, Raf came home to find Indigo lying on the couch engrossed in the latest Sebastian Winters novel. "Interesting choice," he commented as he plopped down in his favourite armchair, hugging a knee into his chest.

"Yeah well it's been top of the New York Times Best Seller List for weeks so I thought I'd check it out, see what all the fuss is about." Knowing he was Scarlett's favourite author also made him feel closer to home somehow, kind of how knowing someone you loved might be staring up at the same moon made you feel closer to them.

"Are you enjoying it?" Raf asked casually.

"It's actually really good," Indigo admitted, "and I guess you'd agree, considering you seem to have all his books." He glanced towards the study where the top four shelves of one of the bookcases were devoted to the paranormal mystery author. Foreign editions included. "You his number one fan or something?"

"Something like that," Raf grinned with a wink.

Indigo gazed at him questioningly. "What have I missed?"

Raf leant back in his chair, regarding Indigo thoughtfully. He eventually bent forward, elbows on knees, eyes serious. "Listen, Indi," he began, "there's a part of my life I keep very private, that only a small few people know about."

Indigo didn't speak, wondering if he was about to be admitted into what sounded like a miniscule circle of trust. When it came to Indigo, Raf was so generous of his time, his compassion, but not as much of himself.

"When you first came here, you asked what I did for a living," Raf said.

"Yeah and you suggested I should be more interested in who someone is than in what they do," Indigo said lightly.

"I was elusive." He held Indigo's gaze. "The thing is," he began, nodding towards the book Indigo held open in his lap. "Indi, Sebastian Winters... well, it's my pen name."

"Hang on..." Indigo frowned. "What?"

Raf grinned. "Writing is my passion, and I guess you could say I've had a bit of success with it over the years."

"*A bit?*" Indigo blanched, aware of the illustrious career of best-selling author Sebastian Winters, whose identity was notoriously as much of a mystery as the plots of his novels. Until now. "No way," he murmured, "why didn't you tell me?"

Raf shrugged modestly. "Not telling people has become a habit, I'm afraid. I don't like people knowing my business." He drummed his fingers lightly on the armrest before adding, "We all have our damage, Indi. There's a lot about me I keep close to my chest. But I've quickly come to regard you as someone I'd like to... to *let* know me."

Indigo swallowed hard and looked away, mortified his lip was trembling.

Raf was unlike anyone Indigo had ever met and Indigo had felt right at home with him from day one, even coming to enjoy the fact Raf kept a strict vegan kitchen. Raf had a policy of 'you're always welcome inside my home but your shoes are not' which Scarlett had trained Indigo so well for, he didn't feel right wearing shoes inside, anyway.

The thing was, Raf was a bit of a hippie at heart. Granted he was a neat-nick hippie who lived in an immaculate house, who dressed in jeans and button-down shirts, who sported neatly trimmed stubble and stacked woven bracelets and rode a vintage motorcycle (until Indigo came to town and commandeered the bike and Raf went back to driving his navy Mustang). Raf had told Indigo he'd spent months restoring that bike to its former glory in his youth.

"Hey Raf?" Indigo asked later that night over a dinner of vegetable curry at Raf's rustic rosewood table in his bright, airy kitchen. He felt Raf's confession that afternoon had opened the door for him to dig a little deeper.

"Mmmm?" Raf said, laying a napkin on his lap.

"What do you do... with those people? The ones who come to see you?"

Raf smiled. "I help them, Indi."

"How?" Indigo pressed, hand over his mouth as he swallowed his bite.

"The same way I've been helping you. By listening to them. By using my higher senses to advise them."

"Your higher senses?" Indigo repeated. "Like how?"

"We-ell," Raf drawled, "quite often I conduct a hosting session for them, something you have yet to experience."

"What exactly is a *hosting* session?"

"Hosting means I allow my body to be used by a particular discarnate as a means of communication," he said, as though it were the most normal thing in the world.

Indigo frowned as he tucked a strand of hair behind his ear. He hadn't had it cut in a long time and it was now sun-bleached and long enough to touch his collar. "And you host them *how?*" he asked, scooping up a piece of pumpkin with his chopsticks.

"I step aside so they can use my body. I'm basically a conduit for information from the discarnate world to be imparted to this world."

"What sort of information?" Indigo probed, poking at his brown rice.

"Oh, anything and everything. The lay of the future. General knowledge about a specific person, the world, life, death… it's endless really. When someone comes here to see me, information will come through that will help them navigate their life, that will guide them to solve a specific problem or help them find whatever it is they're searching for." Raf picked up his glass of sparkling water and drained it.

"Where does the information come from?"

"Micah is the name of the discarnate I host."

"And he can tell you anything?"

"No," Raf replied, "not anything. The information he imparts is mediated by the guardians."

"The guardians? Like Sarita?" Indigo asked.

Raf nodded.

Indigo frowned. "I don't get it."

"Which bit?"

"Well, how come I can hear Sarita? I can hear other people's guardians and I can hear other discarnates, but apparently I can only hear Micah through you?"

Raf placed his chopsticks neatly beside his bowl and smiled. "There is a hierarchy to the discarnate world," he said, and Indigo balked. "Micah has access to all there ever was and all there ever will be, and he is one of the few discarnates at that level. You cannot see or hear him because he has no form. He is too highly evolved. Next come the guardians, who have access to senior discarnates like Micah, but are mostly here to advocate for their living. The guardians are a lot more concerned with the physical than discarnates like Micah, and hence they're charged with keeping the timeline in check. Then, at the bottom tier come general discarnates which are most common, souls who were most recently living and are still connected to their earthly existences. These discarnates are largely egocentric and self-obsessed and generally do not know how to access higher information. They are not much different to those of us still living, so you'll find they will only want to communicate about their most recent life."

Indigo nodded thoughtfully. "So Micah is more senior than Sarita, but she has control over what he can tell me?"

Raf grinned. "Say I was hosting for you, and Micah was about to tell you something that, by knowing it, would affect your life or the world in a way that would alter things too greatly. Like if you asked how you were going to die, for example, imagine how knowing that would affect your life? So in that instance, Sarita, as a gatekeeper between worlds, would step in and stop him. Micah is allowed to tell you anything that may bring you comfort or understanding or clarification, things that will help steer you through life and ensure you make more informed choices. But he can't tell you things that would disrupt the timeline beyond what the guardians have deemed permissible, or that you're meant to figure out on your own."

"Can you host Micah and let me talk to him?" Indigo asked hopefully.

"For sure, bud. One day we'll get there, I promise."

Raf, it seemed, was on a mission to make Indigo well. There were the subtle compliments given to build him back up that made him feel worthwhile and worthy. "You're good company, Indi," Raf would say, "I really like having you around." And Indigo would feel a spark of warmth flicker in his belly. "You're a really incredible person and I value our friendship." The person his father had seen bore no resemblance to the person Raf saw and that boosted Indigo's confidence.

Then there were their chats over dinner. And the gentle advice imparted whilst hiking. One day they approached a juniper tree in a red-dust clearing, its thick twisted branches sculptural octopus arms reaching into the endless sky. "Can you see it?" Raf asked, pointing to a spot beneath the tree.

Indigo frowned, squinting.

"Some people call them vortexes," Raf said. Indigo had heard people in town mention the vortexes Sedona was renowned for but he'd never experienced one himself. "Others say that because Sedona itself is one giant vortex, these are merely sites of particularly concentrated energy. However you want to think of it, this here is a swirling centre of intense potent power where the earth's leylines cross," Raf said. Indigo knew leylines were the energetic highways that crisscrossed the globe. They were the arteries of Mother Earth transporting the energy that was her lifeblood. "Some vortexes spin up out of the earth, others spin down into it, either way if you can tap into their force you will find it is incredibly powerful."

"But how?" Indigo asked.

"That's what I'm here for," Raf said with a serene smile. No two vortexes were the same, and Raf apparently had his favourites.

"You're ready for this, I know you can handle it." The intense sapphire of the sky above them was almost palpable, the vermilion spires and buttes surrounding them, standing guard, were sheer magnificence. The rounded paddle-like prickly pear cacti were heavy with bloom, orange and yellow and magenta, some plump with fruit. Woodpeckers and gilded flickers flitted in and out of the silvery green desert scrub, winging their way over hardy grasses to land upon flowering succulents only to return to their nests deep within the saguaro cacti. The air was warm and still and silent and steeped in a certain heaviness.

As they approached the juniper Raf indicated a very specific spot where Indigo should sit on the bare earth beneath it. So he sat, cross-legged, the trunk hard against his back. It was a hot day, but it was cooler beneath the tree.

"Can you feel it?" Raf asked, sitting down opposite him. Raf reached his hands out, palms up. A twinge of nervousness tossed Indigo's gut and he hesitated for only a moment before placing his hands on top of Raf's.

The moment his flesh touched Raf's, the twinge escalated to a roiling churn. His body was abuzz, his breath shallow and short as an unknown force began to overtake him, rising from the earth, wave after wave to cocoon him, his only anchor Raf's hands under his. He could feel it emanating through every cell, every fibre of his being and beyond. It was like nothing he'd ever experienced.

"I'm throwing you in the deep end here," Raf said, the corners of his mouth curving up gently, "but it's time." Then Raf closed his eyes and interlocked his fingers through Indigo's.

Indigo squeezed his eyes shut as he was suddenly bombarded with feelings and thoughts and images from his life. Pain accompanied the memories rising to the surface from somewhere deep inside of him where he'd stuffed them all down, forgetting them with his mind but clearly not with his body.

"What is this?" he gasped. "What's happening?"

"I'm using the power of the vortex to expose everything Indigo, everything you've held onto that's lain hidden within. Let it burn through you," Raf soothed as Indigo had dropped his chin to his chest, silent tears of agony running down his cheeks, "and then you will rise from the ashes stronger."

He trusted Raf. So he sat, and he endured, focusing on the steadiness of Raf's grip when he began to lose himself.

"I know it hurts, but everything you've shoved down the deepest needs to come back up, it needs to express itself before it can be released for good and this will help trigger that. Some of this is yours, but a lot of it is not. Think of it like cleaning out a systemic infection. If you simply put a band aid over a deep wound, the infection will flourish and spread and fester beneath the surface, eventually encompassing and poisoning the whole body. You need to lance that wound, slice it open and clean out all the muck, all the venom, all the pus and dead and dying tissue. It all needs to go. Express or regress, Indi, express or regress."

Indigo threw his head back and roared, a primal scream entrenched in suffering from deep within. He was drenched in sweat, wild-eyed, as he relived it all, all the sorrow, all the pain, all the blackness and futility and nothingness he'd experienced in his life, the complete hell he'd endured in his recent New York days, 'til Raf's hands shook in his.

"You are strong enough," Raf said from where he calmly sat cross-legged opposite Indigo. "You are strong enough to bring it all back up so you can experience it one last time. And release it. Cry harder, Indigo, scream louder!"

And Indigo did. And with each tear and each shudder, the poison, the venom, slowly rose to the surface where they seemed to evaporate until finally, Indigo felt calm and strong and centred. Everything was stiller, quieter than it had ever been.

Afterwards Raf urged him to write it all down. And Indigo wrote and wrote, everything that had arisen for him, anything he felt he needed to examine more closely, whether it took days or weeks or years to tackle, he had his list, which he knew might never be complete.

He awoke the next day after a deep dreamless sleep with a smile upon his lips. A true smile. A smile that relayed that new stillness within. He felt anchored to the earth and this anchor fed his strength. He was bathed in a sense of calm, a calm that was rock solid and enduring. He had awoken with a deep knowing he was ready for whatever was to come next.

He swung his legs over the side of the large four poster bed and sat up. The room was big – simple yet cosy and elegant. The ceiling was high and pitched. White walls, a dark wood dresser and bed made with white linen sheets. A large silk rug, textures of red and orange and coral reminiscent of a sunset, covered the floor. He padded to the window and pulled back the rust-hued curtains to reveal the beauty of the woodland beyond. His smile deepened.

He opened the door and made his way to the reclaimed wood and tile kitchen, bright and warm and overlooking the carpet of succulents that surrounded the terracotta tiles that edged the pool, stretching to the forest that bordered the back of the property.

Raf was sitting at the kitchen table, nursing a cup of peppermint tea and reading the paper. "Well, well, well," he said in his slow melodic way, folding the top of the paper over so he could look Indigo up and down, "look at you." He smiled his knowing smile. "How do you feel, buddy?"

"I feel good," Indigo beamed. He grabbed an apple from the fruit bowl and bit into it ravenously. He chewed and swallowed before continuing. "For the first time in so long I'm not anxious or worried or scared, and it's like I'm… like I'm, um…" He faltered, lost for words to capture exactly how he felt.

"Excited for the future?" Raf offered.

"Yes," Indigo said, stopping dead with the realisation, "for the first time in a long time, I'm actually looking forward to what tomorrow may bring."

"Good," Raf replied with a nod of his head. "I'm proud of you, Indi." And Indigo ducked his head and smiled. His heart was no longer quite so empty.

chapter seventeen

glycerine

indigo

The boy's skin was a porcelain so pale it seemed incompatible with desert life. He was around Indigo's own age, with distinctive auburn hair. He always wore headphones and a hint of a mischievous smile upon his rugged face and he always made eye contact and nodded a greeting when their paths crossed. His eyes were a deep pensive brown, framed by thick brows. His jaw was strong, his frame well-muscled, his stride sure and assertive.

As Indigo had grown stronger and more confident, he'd begun venturing out on his own, keen to discover Sedona. He'd rise early each morning and run the trails that twisted through the forest and up the red rock mountains. He usually had them to himself, but occasionally he'd come across the boy emerging through the half-light.

After about a week of casual nods as the two sporadically passed one another, the boy one day flicked a headphone from his ear and winked, "Hey, brother," his grin widening. But he didn't stop and he didn't break his stride. "Hey…" Indigo had replied over his shoulder as the boy retreated into the hazy dawn light. And so their relationship progressed from a nod to a "Hey," to a passing "How you doing?" but seemed to stall there. Indigo had always had more friends than he could poke a stick at, but here in Sedona he only had Raf, and as much as he adored him, he missed having mates his own age.

Most afternoons, he'd take Raf's motorcycle and explore the town and its surrounds. One day he arrived back home to find Raf in the kitchen chopping vegetables for dinner, julienning precise slivers of carrot with a large knife. "You're home!" Raf grinned, and it felt nice, having someone happy to see him. "How was your ride?"

"Awesome," Indigo said as he grabbed a bottle of water from the fridge. Raf's fridge was as always proficiently stacked with glass bottles filled with filtered water. Indigo leant against the kitchen counter and told Raf how he'd ridden over to Oak Creek to climb Bell Rock. He was aware he was smeared in thick orange grime.

"So I've got an off-site consult tomorrow," Raf ventured, glancing at Indigo, "and I feel inclined to take you."

"What sort of consult?" Indigo asked, snatching a piece of carrot and chewing on it as he hoisted himself to sit on the countertop.

"Well…" Raf replied, "the sort I think you might learn a lot from."

"Cryptic," Indigo said, opening the bottle of water and raising it to his lips.

"But I feel you might need a little preparation first. So tell me," Raf ventured, "how would you like me to host Micah for you tonight?"

In his excitement, Indigo choked on his drink, spilling water down the front of his t-shirt. "Are you serious?" he finally spluttered, a huge grin spreading over his face, his body flooding with a mix of trepidation and exhilaration.

Raf laughed and threw him a tea towel. "I take it that's a yes?"

"Yes!" Indigo replied. "Absolutely yes."

"We'll eat in about an hour. Why don't you go jump in the pool?"

"You sure you don't need any help?" Indigo asked, eyeing the mountain of vegetables in front of Raf that needed prepping.

"It's all good, Indi, I got this," Raf smiled. Creating in the kitchen was one of Raf's favourite pastimes. He called it his mad scientist's laboratory.

Indigo threw on a pair of powder-blue Okanuis and went out to the pool. He dove in and swam a lap before surfacing, rolling onto his back and floating in the water which was near-tepid from the day's heat. He missed the invigorating chill of the ocean back home. The sun sunk slowly over the desert, streaking the sky a breathtaking palette of luminous pink, orange and purple.

Indigo had no idea what to expect of his hosting session with Raf. How would it work? What would they talk about? Would Raf simply relay information from Micah, or would he *become* Micah? And Micah, this all-knowing discarnate, would he be able to read what Indigo was thinking? Would Indigo have to censor his thoughts in his presence? Would Micah instantly know everything about him, and if so, how was Indigo meant to feel about that? Indigo was excited, yes, but he was also a little anxious.

That night, after a meal of sweet potato and black bean tacos with cilantro tahini dressing, Raf moved his comfy brown leather armchair so it was facing the couch where Indigo perched. They sat there, the two of them, in the living room, the lights dimmed, the whole world seemingly silent.

Raf smiled and asked Indigo if he was ready.

Indigo nodded, the corner of his lip caught between his teeth.

"Ok," Raf replied with a wink, "I'll see you later then." He rested his hands gently on his knees and closed his eyes. He was silent for a time; Indigo didn't know how long he sat in anticipation. He leaned forward in his chair, transfixed on Raf's face, which was ghostly still. Indigo jumped when Raf suddenly jerked, his hands lifting off his knees, fingers stiff and outstretched, before landing softly back where they'd begun.

"So," he said, his eyes opening to unfocused slits, a small smile playing on his lips, "we shall begin."

Indigo was spellbound. Raf's whole demeanour had shifted, his mannerisms had changed, even his tone and voice were somewhat altered. "It is always, always nice to meet new people, although I'm sure you won't be surprised to know we have met many times before. I am Micah, and this one..." he said, pointing to his own knee — Raf's knee — "...has stepped aside so I can speak with you tonight. Ok, so let me look, let me look," he mused, going silent for a time. Indigo wondered if Micah could actually see him through his half-open eyes that didn't seem to be focused on anything. "Some people I meet are very young souls who have only lived one or two lifetimes," he laughed, "but not you, no definitely not you. You are an old soul who has lived many, many times before."

Indigo frowned as a lifetime of feeling like he'd seen it all and heard it all before, suddenly made sense.

"May I explain to you," Micah said, "what happens when one of those lives ends?"

Indigo's eyes widened. Whoa! Straight into the heavy stuff! Micah certainly didn't beat around the bush.

"So," Micah continued, sitting erect in his seat, his back straight and rigid in a way Raf's never was, "imagine your body has died, you've left it behind and transitioned to the discarnate world. You will still feel like you, you will still look as you did in your most recent life. It is like being born, but this time into our world and it will be celebrated accordingly. You're reunited with your guardian and any other souls who may have decided to wait for you to re-join them in this realm so you can move on to the next life together. These souls may be a family member, a husband, a wife, a parent, a grandparent, a dear friend, anyone really who decided they needed to wait for you rather than move on to their next incarnation without you. So it is like a big, big reunion. You will never, never be alone and unsupported when you die."

Indigo thought back to that night on the bridge, how abandoned he'd felt, how rudderless. And if he'd died? Who would he have spent his eternity waiting for? The answer was obvious. He'd wait for her forever.

"Upon your death, you will emerge into what we call the in-between, and your guardian will have designed your place in this realm in advance for you," Micah said. "It may look like your home, or a hospital, or a beautiful beach or a forest, anything at all, whatever they believe would be most comforting to you at this time. You might remain in this place for mere minutes, or for thousands and thousands of years, depending on how well you are able to let go of your last life. A lot of people die in grief and miss their living loved ones terribly, and they may choose to remain in this place until their friends and family pass over too, at which point they move to their loved one's special place in the in-between to wait for them."

A small hut on a coral island came to Indigo's mind, palm trees and white sand and aquamarine sea, a coral garden to snorkel in, a nice little break for him to surf... that's where he'd like to go. But he'd like company. Paradise meant nothing with no one to love.

"Those in the in-between are still incredibly connected to their old life," Micah explained, "and they are exactly the same as they were when they were alive, with the same emotions, likes, dislikes, fears, beliefs. They just no longer have a body. While all their hurt and physical pain is now gone, they often have much emotional pain and much fear. For those who fear death when they die, the transition is hardest.

"What humans classify as ghosts are those in this in-between place, souls who have crossed over but are so attached to their most recent life that they yearn to remain in the familiar."

Indigo had heard stories of ghosts and hauntings. Who hadn't? Rogue spirits who supposedly terrorised the living. But Micah was implying they were really just misunderstood. Had the manner in which they died been unexpected or violent, leaving them with a desire for resolution? To die suddenly in the midst of a life you were busy living must be incredibly traumatising, incredibly difficult to let go of. How tortured might his soul have been had he succeeded that night on the bridge, having died in so much pain?

Micah was quiet for a spell, regarding Indigo through his slitted lids. Indigo wondered if Micah was reading his mind and immediately tried to quiet it.

"But know that when you die," Micah continued without mentioning any of the thoughts in Indigo's head, "you will be surrounded by discarnates whose sole purpose is to help you transition, to heal you, to support you and help you cross over as best they can."

"Now I know this one," Micah said, tapping his knee — Raf's knee — "wants me to prepare you for where he is taking you tomorrow, so I want you to listen closely..."

chapter eighteen

the unforgiven

indigo

Indigo stared silently out the window, his stomach fluttering as they drove into Phoenix. He reached to adjust the air-conditioning vent. A searing heatwave had hit Arizona and he'd never felt anything like it, being so far from the coast where the heat was so dry it seemed to suck every last drop of moisture from the atmosphere.

"You don't have to do this, you know?" Raf said, shifting his eyes from the road to glance at him. "No sweat, you can just wait in the car."

"Yeah nah," Indigo said, setting his jaw. "I wanna do it." He was apprehensive and maybe even a little scared, but his curiosity overrode it all.

They pulled up outside a grand old house with overgrown gardens and a high black wrought-iron fence. He blinked and looked closer. He could see a sort of writhing inkiness streaming from the house.

"That's it?" Indigo breathed, his stomach flip flopping as he gazed at the three-storey manor, its gabled windows dark.

Raf didn't reply. He didn't have to. Indigo could feel with every fibre of his being that this was it.

"My client's not here yet," Raf said, his eyes on the empty driveway.

Indigo laughed, short and sharp. "I deadset don't blame the bloke."

"His wife's taken their two kids and moved to her mother's. She's refused to set foot back in the house until he's sorted it out. She wanted him to sell it, but he wants to exhaust all other avenues first," Raf said, rubbing his chin.

"And that's where you come in," Indigo said, his eyes drawn to the silent house again.

"So this house was built in the late 1890s, but it's been renovated since then."

"And it started right away?"

"Yep," he nodded. "The night they moved in. My client said they woke up to footsteps in the attic above their heads. At first they thought it was one of their kids, so he went up there to yell at them to go back to bed, but when he got there, it was empty and the dust on the floor hadn't been disturbed. Anyway, this continued to happen night after night, unexplained footfall coming from above them. Then, a few days later, he was at work, the kids at school, his wife at home alone. And she suddenly hears this baby crying. She wonders if it's one of the neighbours, but it sounds really close by, like it's coming from the laundry. So she goes in there and the minute she walks in, the crying stops. And there's no one there."

Indigo stared at Raf, freaked out yet fascinated.

"So this continues to happen," Raf continued. "She hears the baby crying, day after day, but it always stops when she goes into the laundry. By now she's more than a little creeped out. And then, one day, she comes home after doing a big grocery shop and she puts everything away neatly in the kitchen and then she hears the crying again. So she goes to investigate. And of course it stops." Raf paused, glancing at the house. "But then, when she comes back into the kitchen, it's in complete disarray — all the cabinets have been thrown open, all the groceries she's just bought are strewn all over the floor and countertops, the kitchen taps have been turned on and water's gushing everywhere. And then she hears footsteps above her. Anyway, as you can imagine, she got the hell out of there as fast as she could and she hasn't been back since."

"Holy shit," Indigo whispered, pulse quickening.

"So her husband got my number and called me to come take a look because he'd heard through certain channels that I had experience with this sort of thing," he shrugged. "So I've been doing a bit of research, asking around, and it turns out that there was a family who lived here," he nodded towards the house, "in the early 1920s and they'd had a baby, a one-year-old, who'd drowned in the bath."

"No way," Indigo breathed.

Raf nodded. "And then the mother hung herself in the attic."

Indigo exhaled sharply, wondering if it was too late to back out. He was beginning to understand where Raf got the inspiration for his books.

"Before the house was renovated, the laundry used to be the bathroom, and that's where the child died." Raf looked calm as ever.

A knife of fear twisted in Indigo's abdomen. His eyes were drawn towards the house; the writhing blackness was growing thicker, denser. He was about to mention it to Raf when a silver BMW pulled into the driveway and a man got out, short and balding, and made his way towards Raf's car.

"This is him," Raf said, reaching to open his door. He paused and looked at Indigo. "It's not too late to back out," he said, his eyes soft with understanding.

Indigo thumbed his lip and glanced back at the house. He hesitated for only a moment before shaking his head. His curiosity outweighed his fear. He reached for the door handle, climbing out to follow Raf towards the man who was now standing at the wrought-iron gate, shifting uneasily from foot to foot. He didn't seem keen to get too close to the house. Raf shook the man's hand and introduced him to Indigo.

"Let's go," Raf said determinedly, pushing the gate open and leading the way down the garden path past bedraggled rose bushes and unkempt hedgerows. As they approached the house, the storm cloud of darkness enveloping it, began swirling faster, sharp and jagged and menacing.

"It feels disgusting," Indigo muttered.

Raf glanced over his shoulder and nodded tersely. "I know, bud. Hold your ground though, ok?"

Indigo felt the blackness seeping into every pore and he wondered how anyone had lived here for even a moment when the sorrow and the pain were so palpably thick. Raf reached the front door and the man passed him a key. He inserted it into the lock and they heard a click. But when he tried to push it open, it wouldn't budge.

"A little help?" he said, with a glance over his shoulder and Indigo and the client stepped forward and pushed with him. But even with the three of them pushing with all their might, they couldn't get it open.

The client lurched back then, yelling, "Fuck you, you motherfucking bitch!" as he kicked the front window in. "This is *my* house and you're *not* the gatekeeper!" Indigo and Raf exchanged glances and shrugged.

"Well, that's another way to do it," Raf smiled, moving past Indigo to climb gingerly through the jagged opening. Indigo slipped through after him. They both looked back to the client, who took a big step back, crossing his arms and shaking his head.

They moved quietly through a modern sitting room towards the centre of the house, Raf leading the way, Indigo sticking as close to him as possible, eyes darting from floor to ceiling to wall. As he walked, he fished in his shorts pocket for an elastic, using it to scrape his hair back into a short ponytail. He stopped dead when he heard it: the distinct sound of footfall above them. His eyes shot to the ceiling as he grabbed Raf's arm. "We're definitely the only two in here, right?" he murmured.

Raf smiled tersely. "Oh, I wouldn't say that exactly."

A door slammed hard somewhere in the house and Raf's head snapped towards it. "This way."

The client, still watching through the window, called out, "Oh, she's pissed now."

Indigo shot him a withering stare over his shoulder before reluctantly following Raf deeper into the house, emerging into a long hallway. The hallway had cream painted walls and was laid with woven beige carpet. Downlights glimmered above them. But then he blinked and it transformed around him: dark floorboards, pale green walls, gloomy light undulating from a chandelier swinging above his head. He blinked again and it was bright and white again, another step and it was dark and gloomy.

"Uh, Raf…?" he stammered, grabbing Raf's arm again. "Are you seeing this?" The house continued to transform back and forth, one minute as if existing as it had a century ago, and the next, everything shimmering back to the present.

Raf nodded. "Yes. It's because she's close. We're picking up on her clairvoyantly, seeing what she sees. The original house is her in-between."

Indigo took a deep breath and exhaled steadily, trying to still the millions of spider legs clamouring through his gut. It was like being in a strange flickering movie. Her in-between even smelt different, like burning wood, like musty damp.

As they arrived at the laundry, they saw it shimmer and change into a traditional bathroom with a clawfoot tub and a dusty chandelier hanging from the high ceiling, its tiles a murky green. Suddenly, they heard a noise. They looked down and saw a baby in the bath, sitting there in just a few inches of water, a small toy boat clasped in her chubby hand.

"Hey, Raf...?" Indigo breathed, his heart hammering in his chest.

"It's ok, Indi, just breathe," Raf murmured, his eyes glued to the baby splashing around, gurgling happily. And then, right before their eyes, she dropped her boat, and as she reached for it, she toppled over and slipped face first beneath the surface.

Indigo lurched forward, his instinct driving him to pull her from the water, but Raf grabbed his arms, held him back. "It happened seventy years ago, Indi. You can't save her."

They could hear the footsteps again, but this time running, and then the mother burst into the room. Indigo heard himself cry out because she was the most terrifying thing he'd ever lain eyes upon. She flew at them furiously, roaring in their faces, her mouth a cavernous dark hole, her eyes bottomless pits, her pale face distorted. The sheer force of her presence hit Indigo square in the chest so he could barely breathe.

The chandelier above them trembled and shook, the taps turned on full force and the tiles on the walls began to crack, huge zig zags streaking towards the ceiling. Indigo turned to run, adrenalin pulsing through his body, so his hands shook and his heart pounded, but Raf grabbed his hand.

"Hold your ground," he said.

Indigo stayed, grasping Raf's hand and gasping for breath as Raf calmly regarded the discarnate mother raging ballistically.

"Hold your space," he kept murmuring to Indigo. "Stay grounded. She can't hurt you. Stay centred." And as Indigo continued to observe him, he noticed a glimmering white light growing around Raf like a bubble, growing and expanding so it filled the room, a light filled with warmth and brightness and Indigo was able to catch his breath, to gather himself. As the bubble around Raf grew, the calmer the discarnate grew and Indigo began to see she wasn't so scary. She was just a woman, just a mother consumed with grief and guilt. She was scared and she was angry, but above all she was just really, really *sad*. And just like that, she became almost human. She stopped thundering at them, she stopped throwing her darkness at them. Slowly, slowly, she sunk to her knees in front of them, tears rolling down her cheeks.

Raf squeezed Indigo's hand and dropped it as he stepped towards her, sinking to his knees so he could look her right in the eye. He smiled at her. And as he did, Indigo saw another figure appear behind her, a large man with flowing red hair. Her guardian. He knew it the moment he saw him, and he heard the man speaking to him, explaining through both words and pictures, that she had brought so much emotion with her to that place in between life and death, so much fear and grief, that she'd been unable and unwilling to acknowledge him, to let him help her. She was obsessed with her baby's death, that's all she could see; all she could focus on was that trauma, that one trauma that had defined her whole existence. She was too attached to the place in which the trauma had taken place.

But she couldn't ignore Raf who was talking softly to her, explaining to her what had happened to her, what had happened to her baby, he explained that she was safe, that her baby was safe, and that they could be together, and he told her what she needed to do.

"Your baby is not dead," Raf told her, "because there is no death, just transition." He stood and pointed to the bath, to her baby, who was now sitting there happily, playing in the water, and she climbed to her feet and smiled to see that. Raf continued to talk to her until she leant over and picked the baby up, hugging her to her, and her whole energy changed, and with it the energy of the house. It was like a dark cloud lifted, like someone had drawn the shades back and let the sunshine in. Her guardian stepped forward then, and he placed his arm around her and she let him, and then she walked off with him, cradling her baby on her hip, and the three of them just disappeared, literally into the light.

And just like that, Indigo and Raf suddenly found themselves back in the laundry with its white subway tiles and its big shiny tubs and its downlights and its modern washer and dryer. Indigo turned to Raf, unsure of what to say to him. If he hadn't known it before, he knew it now: Raf was a pretty impressive guy.

"Her guardian spoke to you," Raf said as he sunk down onto the floor, back against the wall, knees bent up.

Indigo slid down the wall to sit beside him. "Yeah."

"I'm sure you have questions." It was a statement.

"So what I don't get," Indigo said, "is why you were able to do what her guardian wasn't? I mean, all these years he just sat back and let her terrorise a house full of people?"

"Her guardian had done more than you know, and don't forget, she was his priority, not the house's most recent inhabitants. She was such a damaged soul when she passed over, so traumatised that she had to be treated incredibly delicately. She had no peace whatsoever. She was unable to rest, and hadn't done so in like seventy-odd years, although I believe she was so stuck in that moment, the moment of her baby's death, that that was the only moment that existed for her. She was completely oblivious to everything else, including the passage of time." Raf frowned, his gaze intent on Indigo's.

"He created a whole world for her that mirrored the one she had left. The house she was existing in on that plane was exactly the same as the house she'd left. He kept her there, as it would have been too distressing for her to shock her out of it. She didn't want to accept that she was dead, that she'd killed herself, and that her baby was dead, and she did everything she could to avoid facing any of it, and so she refused to acknowledge her guardian or any other discarnate on that plane. She had so much to accept, so much to deal with and work through. And it was impossible for them to force her." He shrugged. "They are just there to nurture their person as best they can, the guardians and discarnates who meet with immediately departed souls, it's not their job to move anyone onto the next stage until they're good and ready. I, on the other hand, have a lot more freedom to help her."

Indigo nodded, leaning his head back against the cool tiles.

"When you healed Luis, you told me his guardian communicated with you, asking for your help. The guardians are quite senior discarnates, but sometimes they need those of us with higher senses to assist them, to work with them to help their person as best they can. We're a team, them and us, stronger together, able to achieve so much more when we work hand in hand." Raf gave him a gentle smile.

"That woman… that discarnate… and her baby. Where will they go now?" Indigo asked, scuffing the toe of his Converse over a smudge on the floor.

"I would guess right now she needs a little nurturing from her guardian and whichever discarnates chose to meet her when she passed over. But once she's ready to fully leave the physical behind, to cut all ties and attachments… well, in a nutshell, if you think of a coach sitting with his football team and rewatching their most recent game on video, analysing it in detail, discussing what went right, what went wrong, what they could do better, what they learnt, what learning remains… Well that is probably the best analogy for what happens. She'll sit with her guardian and analyse the life she just lived, but she'll also have access to all the other lives she's lived to this point, so she'll do so with the benefit of that knowledge."

Indigo's head spun as he attempted to fathom the sheer volume of information that would need to be juggled. To have all his previous lives laid out before him like chapters of an enormous manuscript, all needing to be reread and unravelled and analysed and examined in order to write the next… Well, it seemed infinite.

"That's so cool," he said, awestruck, his mind spinning. "But then…"

Raf placed a hand on his arm. "We should get out of here before our friend outside thinks we've been devoured by evil spirits and dragged to the underworld," he said, standing up and holding his hand out to Indigo, pulling him to his feet.

Indigo followed him out the laundry, disappointed. He still had so many questions.

"How about I host Micah for you tonight?" Raf asked Indigo as they approached the front door which now opened easily when they pulled it. "That way you can ask him anything you like?"

Indigo nodded enthusiastically.

"All yours, buddy," Raf called out to his client who was pacing the front lawn, wringing his hands.

"She's gone?" the man asked, stopping dead and staring at them as if what he was being told was too good to be true.

"Yup," Raf chuckled, clapping the man on the back as they passed by him. "And we didn't even get slimed."

Indigo lay in bed that night tossing and turning, the sheets twisting and bunching so he couldn't get comfortable. Raf didn't think it was healthy to leave the AC on all night, but for Indigo, the relentless heat made it near impossible to sleep. He should have been exhausted after his foray into exorcisms that afternoon, but he was buzzing. The ceiling fan beat a steady thrum overhead but seemed to do nothing more than move the hot air.

He played his session with Micah over and over in his mind as he rolled to the other side of the bed where the sheets were cooler. "Once you are ready to move on from the in-between," Micah had said to him that evening, his slitted eyes trained on Indigo, "it is time to sit with your guardian and plan your next life.

"Then many other discarnates will come together with your guardian to design the life you have planned in great detail. And once it is complete, your guardian shows you this plan, this map for your next life, and discusses it with you, asks for your input. What I would like you to understand is that this map was designed with much care, and everything upon it was chosen to help you to learn, to evolve, and to grow."

Indigo had wondered what being born into a broken home where he wasn't wanted was meant to teach him. How did growing up feeling unworthy of love ensure growth and evolution? Raf had said growth came from pain, so the answer was apparently somewhere in that.

As if reading his thoughts, Micah had leant in closer to Indigo, bending stiffly from the waist, his face almost stern. "I am trying to make you understand that you were involved in the planning of your life and in the choices taken. Everything that has happened or will happen to you, you had a say in. Your parents are your choice, chosen on the basis they provide you with the environment and circumstances you need to best do the learning you came to do."

At the time he'd just accepted Micah's words, but lying here now, unable to sleep, he wanted to kick his own arse for decisions he'd made before he was even born, and that confused the hell out of him.

Giving up on sleep, he threw the covers back and extracted himself from the sheets, fumbling for his clothes in the dark. He found a pair of gym shorts and yanked them on, then crept quietly out into the hallway. It was too hot for a shirt, or a run for that matter, but he needed fresh air. His trainers were just outside the front door, so he grabbed them as he slipped out. He'd try anything at this point to stop the thoughts churning through his mind on a loop, and attempting to outrun them seemed like his best bet.

chapter nineteen

don't go now

manly, new south wales, july, 1994

cordelia

It was the snap heard all around Manly. The snap that ended Drew Prescott's promising rugby career in one misjudged movement.

That week he'd asked Cordelia why she never came to any of his rugby games, ribbing her about her lack of school spirit. So she was there that day with Sian, standing on the sidelines, rugged up against the July chill, when two enormous Tongans from the opposing team tackled Drew at the same time, sending his leg in two very different directions.

Cordelia heard the snap and the pop. She heard the blood-curdling scream and she saw him go down and not get up. When the crowd parted, she saw him lying there in the mud on his back, clutching his knee, writhing in agony. She saw his foot facing the wrong way and bile began to rise in her throat. Tears sprung to her eyes as she watched him loaded onto a stretcher and bundled into an ambulance.

He was taken to Manly Hospital where her dad made sure he got the best orthopaedic surgeon they had. Cordelia went to visit him the next day. He'd had surgery that morning and she wasn't prepared for how doped up he was.

"Hey," she said, knocking on the open door and sticking her head into his room. His leg was bandaged from thigh to toe and his eyes were closed. They flickered open at the sound of her voice and he gazed drowsily at her, seemingly willing his eyes to focus.

"Heyyyyyyyyy," he drawled, a slow dopey grin spreading over his face when he realised it was her. "Come and… sit."

She perched gingerly on the side of his bed, being careful to avoid all the wires and tubes.

"How are you?" she asked, peering into his face. He was chalky pale. He looked terrible.

"I've been… better," he said, speaking at a glacial pace, "but I'm glad… you're here." He reached for her hand. She grasped it in hers, squeezing it, then pulled a carefully wrapped present from her bag and handed it to him.

"For me?" he asked, eyes wide. "What… is it?"

"Open it," she smiled.

He fumbled clumsily at the wrapping paper, tearing and scratching and eventually winning the battle. "Whoaaaa…" he breathed, staring in transfixed awe at the video tapes he now held in his hands. She'd neatly written *the truth is out there…* on the labels in green marker.

"I realise you've already seen season two," she quickly explained, "but I know your brothers recorded over some of your *X-Files* tapes so I thought you might like a refresher while you're holed up at home with…" she indicated his leg.

"Come here," he slurred, holding his arms out wide, a broad grin on his face. She ducked into his embrace, allowing him to squeeze her. "Thanks, Cee… I love it," he said when he finally released her.

"Where's your family?" she asked, glancing around the room.

"Oh," he said slowly, feeling for her hand again, "Dad's away. Deacon was here before… to sort out the… paperwork, but he had to go." He smiled at her again, his eyes glazed. "But all that matters… is that you're… here. That face of yours… is enough to cheer anyone… up."

She blushed. "Do you want some water?" She dropped his hand and reached for the jug beside his bed. She lifted it and filled a cup for him.

"Is it… filtered?" he slurred. "Or are you trying to… kill me with fluoride?"

Drew had a thing about fluoride, but so did her mother. She picked up the cup and sniffed it. "It's definitely not filtered," she said, pouring it back into the jug. "I'll go find you some bottled water." She stood to leave.

He grabbed her hand again. "Don't go. I always feel so... happy when you're with... me." He stared into her eyes with an intensity that made her glance away. "Beautiful Cordelia," he murmured, "the only... person ever to humour me and... read my books." He went quiet for a minute before adding, "Besides Wolfie, that is... but we certainly can't... rely on him these days... can we?" He laughed slowly, his head lolling. "God knows where he is... Sometimes I wonder... whether he actually was abducted by... aliens," he mused, his eyes adopting a faraway look. "Take me to your leader," he said in a robotic voice.

Cordelia glanced over her shoulder towards the door. "I should really get you that water..."

"No!" he cried. "Don't leave me, Cee. If you stay, I'll... tell you a secret?"

She looked at him warily, then shrugged. "Ok," she said tentatively.

He beckoned her in close, so she leant in. He smelt of antiseptic and soap. Not his usual scent. "Ok, but you can't... tell anyone, ok?"

She nodded.

"Now cross your... heart."

She drew a cross over her chest.

"Ok," he said, "here's my... secret, but you can't tell... anyone, especially not... Cordelia. I don't want her to... know I'm in love with... her."

Cordelia's breath snared in her throat and she felt the blood draining from her face. She suddenly felt light-headed.

"What?" she whispered, pulling back so she could look him in the eye.

"I love Cordelia," he repeated. "She's so... kind and beautiful and so smart and open-minded and we can... talk about all these theories... and ideas... and... and concepts for... hours and hours! She's the... perfect woman."

"I don't know what to say," she mumbled, pulling away from him.

"Ok, but just don't... say anything to Cordelia because if she... knew she probably wouldn't want... to hang out with me anymore."

He stopped talking then for a moment and just stared at her, his eyes fluttering, his whole upper body swaying.

"Hang on," he whispered, "you *are* Cordelia! I can… see your m-m-mesmerising eyes!" He bit his lip then as he regarded her. "Ok, ok, here's the… deal," he said, holding up a finger. "Just don't tell… *you* what I just told *you*… ok?"

She stared at him dumbfounded before realising he really was that out of it. "Ok," she agreed, standing up and gathering her things.

"Phew," he said, leaning back on his pillow, "that was a… close one. Crisis… averted." His eyes were beginning to close, his breathing evening out. Within moments, he'd passed out. She ducked out and bought him a couple of bottles of water, then crept back into his room, leaving them beside his bed while he slept.

She felt tears welling in her eyes as she hurried for the exit, hoping not to bump into her father or anyone else she knew. She spied her dad's best friend Essie in her nurse's scrubs, emerging from a room down the end of the hall and quickly turned the other way. She adored Essie, but she'd never been able to lie to her and she wasn't ready to talk about what had just transpired.

Why couldn't anything in life ever just be simple?

She was grabbing some books from her locker between classes a week later when she heard the voice behind her. "There's only one person I know who'd bring me bottled water and *X-Files* videos in hospital."

She froze as she felt her cheeks flush. She didn't want to turn around. "Oh yeah," she said with a forced laugh, rummaging intently through her locker, "you know me."

"Thanks, Cee, you're a legend. I'm sorry I was unconscious when you came by. When I woke up, your dad told me you'd been. It would've been nice to see a friendly face."

She turned. He was perched on a pair of crutches, his bandaged leg hovering off the ground. "What?" she said.

"I said I'm sorry I was KOed when you came by," Drew said, smiling apologetically. "Between the anaesthetic and the morphine, well… I just hope I wasn't drooling," he joked with a grimace.

"Oh," she said, her mind whirring as she examined his earnest face. "Oh, no, no, you were fine. Sleeping like a baby." She smiled hesitantly. If he had no recollection of what he'd said post-op, maybe he hadn't even meant it.

"Well, thanks for coming by. I'm sorry I wasn't a better host."

She closed her locker, tucking her books under her arm. "You going to the science wing?" she asked. He nodded. "I'll walk you. Do you want me to…" she offered, indicating the books he was trying to juggle along with his crutches.

"Oh," he said, "yeah, it's my first day back. I guess I haven't quite got the hang of all the logistics yet."

She took his books from him and walked him to class. She hadn't told anyone the things he'd said that day at the hospital and now, she realised, as she was the only lucid witness, she never had to. Things could go back to the way they were.

Except they didn't. Drew was in a lot of pain after his accident. The meds his doctors prescribed just weren't cutting it and Cordelia could see on his face how much he was suffering. He pushed through with school and his studies; his HSC exams were looming and he had to ace them now more than ever, considering a rugby scholarship was off the table.

He went on a mission to find alternative methods to treat his pain. He came around and sat with her parents to pick their brains. As her mum was a naturopath and her dad was a doctor, he felt he was getting the best of both worlds. He explained he couldn't concentrate on his studies with the meds; they made his brain too foggy, but that without them the pain was unbearable. They suggested acupuncture and kinesiology, which did alleviate his symptoms enough that he could at least study. Mum knew of a lady in the Blue Mountains who was a psychic healer who everyone raved about. He made an appointment to see her but couldn't get in until October, a couple of months away.

Cordelia arrived at his house one day just as Sandy Whitcomb was leaving. Like Drew, Sandy was in the year above her at school. Sandy's family could buy and sell most of Manly, but with parents who didn't believe in giving handouts to their kids, he'd found his own way of making a living. He'd been diagnosed with ADHD in Year Eight and prescribed Ritalin, but instead of taking the Ritalin himself, he'd sold it to his classmates, who paid handsomely for the high. And so began his career as the school dealer.

"G'day, Cordelia," he said as he walked past her out to his car. He was small and weedy with unkempt, curly hair, but what he lacked in stature he made up for with his endless confidence and giant personality. Sandy was incredibly loud, thick-skinned, and, although his smile was more upper gum than tooth, it was always plastered across his sunny face.

"Hey, Sandy," she said, as she made her way to the porch. "Drew?" she called as she stepped through the door.

"In here!" He was sitting on the couch playing Nintendo, his feet propped up on the coffee table. Metallica's *The Unforgiven* was blaring loudly from the speakers in the corner.

"What was Sandy doing here?" she asked casually.

"Huh?"

She leant to turn the music down. "I said, what was Sandy doing here?"

"Getting his arse smashed in *Super Mario*."

"And?" she said, staring down at him.

He sighed, paused his game and nodded to the couch beside him. She sat.

"It's just a bit of weed, Cee. It takes the edge off so I can sleep at night."

"I thought the acupuncture was working?"

"Look, yeah it is, during the day. But at night the pain gets really bad," he explained, twisting the cord of the controller around his thumb. "The weed helps me sleep. If I can't sleep, I can't study."

"You didn't say anything. I thought the pain wasn't so bad anymore." She felt a little hurt he'd kept this from her.

"Yeah, well, I didn't want to worry you."

"I'm your friend, Drew," she said, and she saw a shadow flit through his eyes. "You can talk to me."

He shrugged. "It's no big deal."

But she knew that it was. His knee hadn't healed the way they'd expected it to. "Are you still going to physio?"

"Yeah. But it takes time and in the meantime it hurts like hell. Hey," he leant down and picked up the second controller and offered it to her, clearly wanting a change of subject. "Wanna play?"

"You only like playing me 'cos you always kick my arse," she grumbled, reluctantly taking the controller.

"You know," he said after a couple of rounds, one of which he'd let her win, "I've been doing heaps of research on cannabis. Did you know tonnes of ancient civilisations used it for its healing properties? And it's a really effective pain reliever. It's a kinda miracle drug."

"Maybe," she replied, "but possibly not the kind that Sandy sells." She put the controller down and stretched her arms up over her head.

"Yeah, his may be a little THC heavy and a little CBD light, but it still does the trick. What've you got against Sandy?" he asked, standing up and limping into the kitchen.

"Nothing. He's fine."

"Then what's with the attitude?" he called as she heard the fridge open.

"I don't have an attitude," she insisted. "Sandy's just a bit of a loose unit, that's all. I mean, I didn't think you hung out with him like that."

"It was just a couple of rounds of *Mario*," Drew said, hobbling back and handing her a bottle of water.

Everyone knew the stories about Sandy. He'd always been *that* kid – the one who'd taken his mum's Range Rover out for a drunken spin when he was fourteen and been arrested after opening the door to vomit as he'd zigzagged his way down the freeway, not realising the cops were behind him. He was the kid who went on a family holiday to Thailand, downed a magic mushroom shake and promptly disappeared. (He was found two days later, on a neighbouring island which he'd apparently swum to, living with a bewildered local family in their hut.)

"Hang out with whoever you want," Cordelia said, narrowing her eyes. "It makes no difference to my life." She leant her head back against the couch. "I thought we were meant to be watching *Quantum Leap*, anyway?" she said, changing the subject. Much to Drew's disappointment, she just hadn't been able to get into *Star Trek*, but she had to admit she'd grown quite invested in *Quantum Leap's* Sam Beckett's time travelling misadventures.

"Yup, we were," he said, picking up the remote. She could tell he was pissed off.

In November, when Drew asked her to his Year Twelve formal, he played it down, saying he wanted to go with a mate so he could relax and have fun. He'd been a lot better since his visit to the psychic healer in the Blue Mountains. He hadn't said much about it when Cordelia asked, just muttered something about it being 'woo-woo stuff'. She was interested and had pressed him for a blow-by-blow, but he'd clammed up and hadn't wanted to talk about it.

As she got ready for the formal, it crossed Cordelia's mind that in another world, she might have been going with Indigo. If he were here, he would have just finished his exams too. She wondered if he'd gone to his prom and if so, who he'd taken.

Her bedroom door crashed open and Robbie sauntered in.

"Need some help?" he asked.

She was sitting at her dresser with rollers in her hair finishing her makeup.

"Which earrings?" she asked, holding up two pairs, meeting his eyes in the mirror.

"Those," he nodded, pointing to the black beaded dangly ones. "And hair down." He picked up the dress he'd helped her choose and stared it up and down, nodding in approval. It was made of fine velvet in a green so deep it was almost black, long and fitted with slits up both thighs.

She began to unwind the rollers from her hair, soft, bouncy curls unfurling down past her shoulder blades.

"Let me help," he said, coming up behind her and removing the back ones. "I'm thinking Nicole Kidman at the Oscars this year?" he said as he ran his fingers through her locks. "She looked fabulous, right?"

"Yeah, but she had Tom Cruise as an accessory."

"Speaking of dates, are you excited to go with Drew?" he asked as he worked on her tresses. "He's got a good two feet on Tom Cruise."

"I guess," she said, teeth working over her lower lip. "We do have fun together."

"I'm sure," he murmured, attacking her roots with a teasing comb.

"Not too big," she protested as she dabbed on some lip gloss.

"So, is tonight going to be the big night?"

"Big night?"

"The night you finally give Drew a bit of a kissy, kissy, squeezy, squeezy?"

She gave him a withering look in the mirror.

"Oh, Cordelia," he cried dramatically. "Oh dear sweet, sweet chocolate-covered Cordelia!" He grinned wickedly then, crossing his arms as his tone changed. "Cut the act, this is me you're talking to *womb-mate!* I've known you longer than anyone and we both know you're not stupid. And therefore you *cannot* tell me that you haven't noticed Drew's completely, obsessively into you."

"He's not!" she said hotly, standing up and crossing her arms back at him. "We're friends! We have the same taste in books, we share ideas…"

"Oh!" Robbie cried sarcastically. "So it's a meeting of the minds, is it?"

"It *is* actually smart-arse," she snapped.

"Bull. Shit. You think it's a meeting of the minds. The only things he wants meeting are his sweaty, writhing body and yours."

"Shut up, Rob," she said through clenched teeth.

"I mean, come on, level with me, Cora, like, you *do* know how he feels about you, right?"

She hesitated and he saw.

"Ooooh, something's happened," he said, sitting down on her bed and patting the spot next to him. "Sit 'n' spill," he ordered.

Her shoulders slumped as she sat, finally telling him what had occurred the day she'd visited Drew in the hospital after his knee surgery.

Robbie's eyes gleamed. *"I knew it!"* He regarded her serious expression. "So," he ventured, "do we like him too?"

"I don't know," she said. "I-I kind of feel… disloyal to—"

"Don't say it," Robbie interrupted, holding his hand up. "Don't even *think* his name. You owe him *nothing*. Zilch. Zero."

"I know that. I do. But then on some level, deep down, to be with someone else feels kinda like cheating on… him," she said, lowering her eyes.

"Cora, we haven't heard from him in like, forever," Robbie said. "New York was almost a year ago. You shared one kiss a million moons ago. For all we know, he's never coming back. Don't waste your youth and beauty pining away for him. Because one day you'll turn around and you'll be old and saggy-titted and bitter and twisted and alone."

"Gee thanks," she said, widening her eyes at him. It had been more than a kiss. A hell of a lot more. But she wasn't getting into the depth of what she'd shared with Indigo, with Robbie right now.

"Look," he said, putting his arm around her and hugging her close, "alls I'm saying is, live a little. I know you loved him — we all did — but he's gone, Cora. He's geographically untouchable. Drew's a babe and he's a great bloke. You could do a lot worse, you know. You deserve to be happy." He gave her a final squeeze and stood up, pulling her to her feet. "And speaking of geography, he'll be here any minute, so let's get you red carpet ready!"

Despite her apprehension, Cordelia found herself having fun once they arrived at the formal. Drew was the perfect gentleman, holding doors open for her and pulling out her chair and constantly asking if she needed anything. He was fun to dance with, even with his gammy leg, and as they took a break from the dancefloor to sit outside and chat, she found herself thinking what a nice smile he had. It was that damned dimple.

"Thanks for coming with me tonight," he grinned as they sat out on a garden bench beneath a star scattered sky. Music drifted across the lawn from inside, the Smashing Pumpkins singing *Tonight, Tonight*.

She smiled back, somewhat shyly. "Thanks for asking me. I've had a great time."

"There's no one else I'd rather have taken," he said, reaching out and tentatively taking her hand. And she let him. His palm was warm and smooth.

He gazed into her eyes, and the way he was looking at her, her stomach fluttered. He began leaning in and she didn't pull away, allowing him to brush his lips gently against hers. She closed her eyes and let him kiss her, found herself kissing him back.

And as quickly as it began, she pulled away. "I'm so sorry," she said, jumping to her feet, pulling her hand from his. "I can't. I'm sorry. I'm so sorry." He looked crushed and she couldn't bear it, so she turned and fled. She found a phone booth down the street and dialled home. Thankfully, Robbie answered. She asked him to come get her.

While she waited for her brother, she realised she'd run from Drew, not because their kiss had felt so wrong.

But because it had felt right.

And that scared the shit out of her.

chapter twenty

wanted dead or alive

sedona, arizona, august, 1994

indigo

Indigo sped down the road, the sun beating down on the vast red landscape. He revved the bike and kicked it up a gear, the desert flying by faster and faster. He'd grown to love his adopted vintage motorcycle. Riding it reminded him of his favourite bike back in Sydney, the Kawasaki Ninja his mother had bought him after Edita had told her PA his favourite movie was *Top Gun*. It was a guilt present, yet another one for something or another she'd missed. His birthday, if he could recall. Or was it Christmas? Possibly both. Most kids would have gotten the movie on video or a cassette of the soundtrack. Not Indigo. He got Maverick's bike.

His mind wandered to when he and Cordelia used to jump on it on the weekends and ride up the coast. He missed that bike. He missed the beaches. He missed *her*. More and more so as he'd grown well and emerged from the tunnel of inward-looking self-obsession his healing had forced him into.

He'd tried to write to her. To Robbie and Scarlett and Josh too. He'd filled innumerable waste bins with apologies he'd started, but never quite knew how to finish. He'd never been good at expressing himself on paper, he'd always been better in person.

It had been a few weeks since Raf had taken him to the manor and the events of the day still played on his mind. So much so he barely registered he'd left the outskirts of town far behind. He slowed up a bit, glanced around, clocking his bearings, figuring out where he was. Up ahead in the distance, he could see two cars, a white SUV and a beat-up brown sedan. He squinted at them as he drew closer. They were both stopped in the middle of the road; the SUV parked at an angle, blocking the sedan's path.

He decelerated as he approached, wondering if there'd been an accident.

He pulled to the shoulder and climbed off his bike, then walked up alongside the brown sedan to the open driver's side window. No accident, it appeared. A man sat in the driver's seat, his hand possessively on the knee of the girl beside him. He had greasy brown hair slicked back off his face, a face that was good-looking in a sleazy has-been kind of way. He looked to be around thirty. The girl, a pretty, ample blonde, looked anxious. She couldn't have been more than fifteen or sixteen.

Before he could ask if everything was ok, the door to the other car opened and a guy jumped out.

"Back up, dude," he said, striding towards Indigo and the sedan. His American accent was cadenced with the inflection of someone who'd grown up amongst surfers. He had high chiselled cheekbones and a shock of jet-black hair that hung past the collar of the white button-down shirt he wore over pale pink shorts. He was the epitome of fit, his caramel skin stretched taut over lean muscle. Indigo guessed he was in his early-twenties.

Indigo squinted. He'd seen this guy somewhere before, but try as he might, he couldn't place him. "Everything ok?" he asked.

"Not really," the guy replied as a woman climbed out of his car to join him. She looked to be in her late-forties, short and cuddly with a peaches and cream complexion and stiffly permed blonde hair, her sunny face framed by a short, blunt fringe. Her pale pink t-shirt, complete with giant bedazzled flower, was tucked into a blue gingham skirt that fell to her calves, revealing a pair of hot pink scrunchy socks worn with white tennis shoes.

"Sasha?" she called to the guy, her eyes darting nervously from the sedan to Indigo.

"I got this, Dawn," Sasha replied. Indigo looked from Sasha to Dawn, trying to figure out what they were to one another. They were a mismatched duo if ever he'd seen one.

"You don't wanna get involved in this, honey," Dawn called to Indigo. "You should go."

Indigo shrugged and returned to his bike. He swung a leg over it, reaching for the ignition. Whatever was going on here was clearly none of his business.

"Get out of the car, Skeet," he heard Sasha say to the greasy-haired man.

"Do I look stupid to you?" Skeet sneered. Even his voice was greasy. Indigo hesitated.

"Don't make me come in there, eh," Sasha replied cockily, crossing his arms.

"You come in here, I ain't responsible for what happens," Skeet said.

Dawn cried out.

Indigo saw a flash of metal from the corner of his eye. Skeet had a strange golden dagger clutched in his palm, its blade crooked. The girl winced as he held it to her cheek.

"If you harm *one* hair on her head..." Dawn warned, stepping forwards. Sasha grabbed her.

"She belongs to me now. She knows what I'll do if she ever tries to leave me. But I won't hurt her as long as *he* stays back," Skeet called, his voice now tinged with fear. "I mean it, Sasha, I'm watching you."

"How about next time I bring Nash and Aurora?" Sasha said, still clutching Dawn's arm. "Really give you something to worry about, ya?"

Skeet paled but kept the knife to the girl's cheek, although Indigo noticed it trembled.

"Let her out of the car, Skeet," Dawn said, her voice catching. "Please."

"She's a big girl, Dawn," Skeet taunted, having regained his composure. "Old enough to make her own decisions. And she decided she wanted to come with me." He turned to the girl. "Didn't you, bub?"

The girl glanced from Dawn to Skeet, then nodded.

"You're violating all kinds of agreements just by being here, Skeet," Sasha said. "What's Raf gonna do when he hears about this?" Indigo lurched forward in his seat at the sound of Raf's name.

"I ain't violated nothing," Skeet said. A smug smile grew on his thin lips as he glanced sideways at the girl. "Well, almost nothing," he added slyly.

Dawn roared and made to rush at him, but Sasha grabbed her again, wrapping his arms around her and shushing her gently.

"Get out of the car," Sasha said through clenched teeth.

"I never set foot on your turf," Skeet called to them, placing his hand on the girl's knee. "She met me outside of town. I done nothing wrong."

"She's *sixteen* years old!" Dawn screamed. Sasha whispered to her. She looked at him fiercely for a beat or two, then her shoulders slumped and she stepped back to stand by the SUV.

Sasha looked right at Indigo then and although he didn't say a thing, Indigo heard his voice clear as day inside his head: *'You wanna help so bad, fine. I'll distract him. You get the girl.'*

Indigo stared into Sasha's eyes and received the confirmation he needed in the intensity he found there. Another person with higher senses. His telepathy had grown more finely tuned under Raf's guidance and he was now able to discern the messages within the white noise. Indigo inclined his head in the subtlest of nods. He climbed slowly off his bike, taking a step back, out of Skeet's peripheral vision. Sasha started running towards the brown sedan. Indigo slunk around the back of the car towards the passenger side.

Suddenly Sasha shimmered, and an identical clone of him materialised in synch beside him. Just like that, there were two of him, running side by side in perfect unison. Indigo's step faltered. He gaped. One Sasha sprung onto the bonnet of the car, then somersaulted onto the roof, while the other lunged at the driver's side door, yanking it open. Before Skeet could react, one Sasha had grabbed him by the shirtfront and torn him from his seat. The other front-flipped effortlessly off the roof of the car, landing in the dirt behind them.

Indigo refocused, quickly moving to the passenger side door, easing it open and holding his hand out to the girl. She stared up at him, face tear-stained, lip quivering. She looked from Indigo to Dawn, then to Skeet, then shook her head stubbornly.

"Please?" he asked, glancing to where a Sasha had just slammed Skeet hard onto his back on the road. "Just 'til whatever this is, is over?" He grasped her fingers in his, flashed her a winning smile. She relented, allowing him to pull her into the nook of his arm and guide her back around the car.

Skeet clambered to his feet, turning in a slow circle, slashing out with his dagger as the two Sashas slowly circled him. Skeet jutted his dagger at a Sasha, who disappeared only to reappear behind him. Skeet whirled around, his lip curling in a sneer. "Games, Sasha?" he rasped. "Really?"

Both Sashas smiled smugly, shrugging in unison. And then one vanished. The remaining Sasha stepped forward, smiling, beckoning Skeet with two fingers. Skeet lunged. Sasha weaved and ducked in one fluid motion, then leapt high into the air, kicking out, his foot connecting with Skeet's face with an almighty crack.

Skeet staggered back, blood exploding from his nose. He shook himself off, running at Sasha, dagger held high. Sasha scooped a large stick off the ground, wielding it expertly to meet the dagger thrusting down towards him. Skeet continued to strike, but Sasha blocked him, again and again. Sasha was quick and nimble, effortlessly twisting and turning. Skeet was clumsy, panting and sweating. "You're dead, karate kid," he gasped, stumbling towards Sasha, dagger held high.

Sasha back somersaulted out of reach, grinning mischievously as he landed, cocking his head tauntingly. He was just toying with Skeet. Blood dripped down Skeet's chin, his eyes wild.

Indigo guided the girl towards Dawn, giving the brawl a wide berth. But Skeet saw. "You fair weather *bitch!*" he screamed as he spun, hurling his dagger. It was heading straight for the girl's chest with alarming accuracy. Sasha yelled a warning, and Indigo threw the girl out of the way, diving after her. But he wasn't fast enough. He felt a sharp pain as the dagger pierced low on his left side, embedded to the hilt. He staggered, stopped to stare at the stain of red spreading to quickly colour his once-white t-shirt. He gazed up at the others in numb shock, head light. His knees started to buckle as Dawn moved towards him, clutching him in her arms and lowering him gently to his back on the dusty road. She cradled his head in her lap.

"It's ok, sweetie," she soothed, her hand on his cheek. He turned his head to see Sasha leap onto Skeet, pushing him to the ground, holding his forearm to his throat. Sasha no longer looked playfully amused, his fine features marred with fury, his teeth bared.

Indigo's fingers brushed the handle of the dagger, warm and sticky. He felt woozy, his mouth dry as cotton. His eyes searched, found Dawn's, locked onto them. They glistened with comfort.

"Shit, Skeet," he heard Sasha growl, "do you have any idea what you've just done?"

"He got in the way," Skeet gasped defensively. Sasha must have loosened his grip on his throat. "It ain't my fault he stuck his goddamned nose in where it weren't wanted."

"Do you have any idea who he is?" Sasha asked, although his voice suddenly sounded really far away, thick and hazy.

"Nup and I don't give a shit." A snort of derision.

"You don't? Well, let's just say that Raf will, eh? Big time."

"You mean…" Skeet said, all confidence having vanished. "He ain't…"

Sasha must have given some non-verbal response because the next thing he knew, Indigo could hear Skeet promising he didn't know. How could he have?

Indigo was struggling to focus now, confused at what was going on, what Sasha was implying, why Skeet suddenly sounded alarmed. He tried to sit up, to see what was happening, but Dawn held him down and he hadn't the strength to fight her.

"Hold still, sweetie," she murmured, placing her hand over his to stop him grabbing at the dagger. "I'll have you fixed up in a jiffy." With an air of calm, she pulled the dagger from his body, casting it aside and placing her hand firmly over the gushing wound. Indigo gasped as sharp pain tore through his insides. He bit his lip, a cold sweat upon his brow.

"Good boy," Dawn soothed, "that's the way, you're doing so good." She had one hand on his laceration, the other open against his cheek. Her touch was like smooth stones warmed by the sun. Through the haze, he was suddenly aware of a swirling golden light, pink-tinged and glowing as it grew to wreathe him, strongest and brightest around his abdomen.

He must have passed out because the next thing he knew, someone was propping his head up and pressing a bottle of water to his lips.

"You've lost a lot of blood, honey," Dawn was saying. "You need to drink."

He sat up with a start, his hands moving to feel through his blood-soaked t-shirt. It didn't hurt anymore. He lifted his shirt to inspect the wound. It was gone, a faint silver line of scar tissue the only sign it was ever there at all.

He turned to look at Dawn, who was kneeling beside him in the dust. "How did you do that?" he gasped.

"Says the boy who healed a triplegic," she shrugged, smiling warmly.

"Who are you?" he whispered.

"We're friends of Raf's, brah," Sasha said, sitting down beside him. Indigo looked up. Both Skeet and his car were gone.

"Friends?" Dawn said lightly. "I'd say we're family." She looked intently at Indigo. "Raf, Sasha and I, Nash and Aurora, we're kin."

"Kin?" Indigo asked softly, looking from Dawn to Sasha. He was still lightheaded. "Who're Nash and Aurora?"

"So you haven't met them yet? You'll love them," Dawn said, patting his hand.

Sasha raised an eyebrow at her and she grinned wryly. "Ok well, *him*," she shrugged. "You'll love *him* immediately. Her, you'll grow to love in time."

Indigo was suddenly overcome with exhaustion, too tired to even try to comprehend what they were talking about.

"Let's get you home," Dawn said as Sasha hooked an arm around him, pulled him deftly to his feet. Sasha was considerably shorter than Indigo, but he was strong.

"Raf's bike…" Indigo mumbled.

"It's ok, man. I'll ride out with Nash later on and pick it up," Sasha told him. Indigo felt in his pocket for the keys, then pressed them into Sasha's hand as he led Indigo to the car where the girl sat quietly in the back. Sasha helped him into the front seat, buckling him in, then opening the glovebox to chuck Skeet's dagger inside. He climbed into the driver's seat whilst Dawn claimed the seat behind Indigo's. Indigo's head was swimming with questions, but his eyelids felt lead heavy, his head so fuzzy. He leant his brow against the cool pane of the window and closed his eyes for a moment.

"You're in big trouble when we get home, young lady," Dawn muttered behind him.

"Seriously, Mom?" the girl replied. "Don't you think I've been punished enough?"

"Oooh, Reggie my dear, it hasn't even begun," Dawn snapped.

"I'm *humiliated*, my life is *ruined!*" Reggie cried dramatically. "It's not fair! Why do I have to have a Mom like *you?*"

"Yes, I'm a terrible mother," Dawn said evenly, "coming all the way out here to save you from being kidnapped by that monster."

"He's not a monster!" Reggie sobbed. "I love him."

"He just threw a knife at you, dear heart. He's certainly no prize."

"What do you expect him to do when you and your friends corner him like that?"

"You're not seriously defending him?" Dawn gasped. "My God, you're sad about this — when you should be angry." It was a statement.

"Geez, Mom, how about a little *privacy?* There's never any privacy with a mother like you! I bet Sash didn't have a nosey mom like you, always feeling what he's feeling and wanting to *talk about it* and *explore* it and *resolve* it."

"Leave me out of this, Reg," Sasha said, eyes on the road. "My mom's Japanese, ya? If I spoke to her the way you're speaking to Dawn, I wouldn't have seen the outside of my room for a month."

Indigo suddenly registered what they were talking about. "You can feel what she's feeling?" he interrupted, turning his head so he could see Dawn.

Dawn smiled and nodded.

"My mother the *empath*," Reggie snapped. "She can feel what *everyone's* feeling!" She crossed her arms and turned her face to the window. He could see her scowling in the reflection.

"Just like you, Indigo honey," Dawn said softly.

"H-how did you know that?" he stammered.

"Takes one to know one," she quipped.

His gut started to hurt, churning like a washing machine full of pins and needles. He hunched to clutch it with trembling hands.

"Hey, hey, hey, I know it's tough being so sensitive," she said, and he felt her hand on his shoulder. "It was hard enough for me as a girl. I know it can be especially hard as a boy, growing up with all these ridiculous ideas and beliefs about what a man should be."

"Here she goes again," Reggie muttered under her breath.

"I'm always telling my sons that boys don't have to be strong all the time," Dawn continued, ignoring Reggie. "You have just as much right to struggle as the next person! We don't teach you that, and then you grow up and don't know *how* to manage when you do struggle, and don't feel comfortable asking for help because you feel weak when you do. But, Indigo, to ask for help shows incredible bravery."

Indigo turned to face the front, his attention on the desert-scape flashing by, red and orange and sunburnt. His whole life he'd played the role of rescuer and relished it; he didn't know if he had it in him to flip that and ask for help.

"As empaths, we are intimately connected to others, which I know can be overwhelming and painful, especially when you don't understand where their feelings end and yours begin. And with a gift as strong as yours, you are so often overcome with a tidal wave of emotion, a whole city of feeling – literally — that you don't know quite what to do with it. It requires tremendous focus and highly honed skill to manage." He felt her gaze stern on his back.

Indigo thought back to how bad things had gotten for him at Wilson's in New York — the sheer anxiety, the overwhelming loneliness, the constant ache in his chest, how it had crushed him so he could barely breathe. He now knew he'd been feeling the unhappiness, the anxiety, the fear, the anger, the melancholy of everyone around him. Added to his own issues, it was no wonder he hadn't coped. He never wanted to feel like that again. He swallowed hard, shook his head. He was suddenly so shattered he could barely fight it.

He felt her soften then. "It's ok," she murmured. "It's not an impossible feat. In fact, like anything, once you know how, it's easy."

"Sheesh, Mom, give the guy a *break*," Reggie admonished. "I mean, do you blame him for not wanting to hear this? I can't imagine anything worse than being like *you*."

Dawn sighed heavily. "Reggie hon, you're skating on thin ice over murky water. If I were you, I'd pull my head in."

Indigo closed his eyes and when he opened them, they were parked in Raf's driveway and Sasha was helping him out of the car. Raf came striding out wide eyed, brow creased, as he supported Indigo's other side.

"I'm fine," Indigo murmured. "I'm just really tired." They led him to his room, stripping off his bloody t-shirt and laying him on his bed, placing a comforter over him. They left the room and he was vaguely aware of them talking in harried whispers. Raf returned briefly to place a bottle of water on his nightstand and lay a warm soft hand on Indigo's forehead and that was the last thing Indigo was aware of that day.

Indigo was awakened by an unbearable thirst the next morning. He sat up, groping for the water bottle he vaguely recalled Raf replacing on his nightstand when he'd come in to check on him during the night. He found it, twisting the lid off and chugging the whole thing. His room was bathed in dusky grey light, so he knew it was early. He sat up and swung his legs over the side of the bed, dropping his head into his hands. The events of the day before swum back to him and he jumped up, peering down at the faint silvery line that now marred his left side. It was about two inches long and when he ran his fingers over it, it felt smooth.

He drifted into the bathroom, turning the shower up as hot as he could bear it, standing under it until he felt human again. After he'd dried himself off, he dressed in shorts and a tank top, then headed into the kitchen to grab another bottle of water from the fridge. As he passed by Raf's room, he saw it was empty, the bed neatly made and the curtains pulled back. He must have gone to his yoga class already. Indigo didn't feel up to running, but he thought a walk might do him good. He grabbed his Walkman and the Sun Devils baseball cap Raf had given him, then pulled his trainers on, heading out the back gate and into the forest beyond.

He returned later that morning to find Raf sitting outside in the sunshine with a guest. The two men sat at the table beside the pool, a cast iron teapot and two small teacups laid out before them. Raf's face lit up when Indigo rounded the side of the house, and when the other man turned, he saw it was Sasha. Sasha stood, moving gracefully over the terracotta pavers towards him, his eyes tinged with worry, his smile cautious. He wore navy-checked shorts and a mint green button-down, cuffs rolled to the elbow. His thick hair was slicked into a bun.

"Morning, brah, how you feeling today?" He placed a hand on Indigo's shoulder, held another out to him. Indigo took it. Sasha closed his other hand warmly over the top. Indigo noticed he had a tattoo on his inner forearm, eight asymmetrical shapes he recognised as a map of the Hawaiian Islands. "I brought your bike back. I really want to thank you for your help yesterday. I'm real sorry for how things went down, eh?"

"It's all good," Indigo smiled hesitantly.

"Sash's filled me in on what happened," Raf said, producing a third teacup and filling it for Indigo. He gestured to a chair and Indigo sat down beside Sasha. "I'm sorry you got caught up in it all."

Indigo shrugged, flipping his cap backwards. "What was it about?" he asked, looking from Raf to Sasha. "Because I still can't figure out if it was about Reggie or if it was some kind of turf war."

"Both," Raf replied. "Reggie is Dawn's eldest daughter. Unfortunately, her judgement of character is still a work in progress. She's been caught up with Skeet for a while now."

"And Skeet is?"

"Bad news," Sasha grimaced, refilling Raf's cup, then moving onto his own.

Indigo picked his up and took a sip. It burnt his mouth. "You were telling him he violated an agreement? He said he didn't breach city limits or something. What was all that about?"

"Skeet and his er... family," Raf said, "have caused a lot of trouble in these parts over the years. They've been banned from crossing into Sedona."

"Banned how?" Indigo asked, taking another shot at the tea.

"We have our ways," Raf said elusively.

"Where does he live?"

"In a small commune in the forest," Sasha said.

"Commune?"

"Let's just say his father has six wives and Skeet has twenty-eight siblings," Sasha smiled. "Not to mention countless cousins. He's sketchy, ya?"

Indigo widened his eyes. "And Reggie?"

"Skeet's been looking for a new wife of his own," Sasha told him.

"They'd like to add a bit of what Dawn has to their bloodline," Raf added.

Indigo's hand automatically went to his left side. "Dawn," he murmured, "she's pretty special, right?"

Raf nodded firmly. "She certainly is. You've seen that firsthand. Her healing capabilities are pretty phenomenal."

"Yesterday, in the car," he swallowed, "she was trying to talk to me… I was all over the shop and I think I may have come across as a bit of an arsehole."

Sasha laughed. "Compared to Reggie, you were a regular Prince Charming."

"It takes a lot to offend Dawn," Raf said with a big smile.

"Speaking of yesterday," Indigo said, suddenly turning to Sasha, "what the hell was it you were doing with the whole double trouble thing?"

Sasha threw his head back and laughed, his eyes crinkling merrily.

"I wasn't seeing things, right? There were two of you?"

"No, you weren't seeing things, eh," Sasha smiled, nudging him with his shoulder. "It's a little trick I picked up when I was a boy. It's called bilocation."

"Bilocation?"

"It means I can be in two places at once," Sasha said.

"I'm gonna need a little more than that. It's like, what? Your soul splitting off from your body?" he asked, thinking of all the discarnates he'd come into contact with recently.

Sasha's brow puckered. "*God* no, brah. If your soul disconnects from your body, you're dead." He leant in, eyes serious. "So listen, when I look at you, I see… *more* than what most other people see."

"More?"

Sasha tilted his head to one side, regarding him closely. "Tell me, Indigo, what do you think makes you, *you?* I mean, you're not just your body, right?"

"Nope." A couple years back, Indigo had held Banjo tight while the vet put him to sleep. Tears streaming, he'd known the moment the arthritic old dog passed over; he'd felt a distinct shift when everything that had made Banjo, *Banjo,* left. The timeworn body left behind just wasn't him anymore.

"Right on. You're more than a body, more than a soul. You're an infinite force of energy encased in a suit of skin." Sasha reached for the teapot, drained its contents into their cups. "And that intangible force, well, I can sense that and like, read it to get a feel for your vibe, eh?"

"My vibe?" Indigo frowned.

"It's like your own personal radio frequency," Raf explained, "broadcasting everything about you to those of us sensitive enough to pick it up. Round here we call it your biofield."

"Now bilocation," Sasha said, leaning back, "is essentially a projection of your biofield, which isn't restricted by the same parameters as the flesh-and-blood parts of you. So what I do is, I use it to project a replica of my physical body so the bi-lo form has the ability to instantaneously and simultaneously be in a second place."

"Well… shit," Indigo stammered, as he tried to figure out how that was possible. If he hadn't witnessed it firsthand, he wouldn't have believed it. "So those days when you have so much to do, you wish there were two of you…"

Raf chuckled as he stood to collect the empty teapot, heading inside presumably to check on the lunch Indigo could smell fragrantly emanating from the kitchen.

"Exactly, brah," Sasha laughed. "It's come in pretty handy over the years. I've certainly seen more of the world than most twenty-one-year-olds."

"How far can your… selves… go away from each other?" Indigo asked.

"As far as I can think, eh?" Sasha went quiet as his mood turned sombre. "When my grandfather, who was my mentor and best friend, got real sick, I was able to get to his bedside in Tokyo, bringing him comfort as he drew his final breaths — without ever physically leaving Sedona."

"I'm so sorry you lost him," Indigo said.

They sat in silence for a few moments.

"And he could see you?" Indigo ventured, "the… the…"

"The bi-lo me?"

Indigo nodded.

"Yeah," he nodded, "I've been doing this so long that I've achieved the same density in the bi-lo replica as the physical me, eh. But even if I hadn't, you'll find people on their deathbed are very open. All the walls they've built up, all the 'logic' they've spent years perpetuating, suddenly just drops away and all their senses heighten, allowing them to see between worlds and access the matrix of energy surrounding them in its entirety."

"So when you bilocate," Indigo said, gazing at him, "where does your mind go? With the bi-lo replica or the physical you?"

"Well," Sasha mused, "I guess it's like I have one mind in two bodies, ya? I see and feel and know everything that's happening in both locations at the same time."

Indigo regarded him, awestruck. "How did you even figure out you could do that?"

"Dude, my dad was a Buddhist monk – until he met my mom on one of her philanthropic trips to Thailand and ran away with her," he grinned. "My brother and I, we were brought up on a steady diet of meditation and self-reflection."

Indigo's eyes widened.

"Often when I was meditating as a kid, I'd find myself floating above my body, looking down at it, ya?"

"And that didn't scare the crap out of you?" Indigo asked, fingers absently skimming the rim of his teacup.

"Nope. I was never afraid. More fascinated, I think. So I began to experiment. With practice, I found I could control my physical body whilst floating beside it, so I was able to view myself from both perspectives at once. And when I grew bored with that, I began to play around with my bi-lo body. I found that by merely focusing on somewhere, I'd arrive there instantaneously."

"SO cool," Indigo said. "Do you reckon I could do it? That you could teach me?"

Sasha was quiet as he regarded Indigo closely. "Most people like you and me are able to access certain higher senses because we've done so in previous lives, ya? From what I hear, bilocation isn't in your arsenal. I reckon our time together would be best spent in other areas, eh?"

"Our time together?"

"Yup," Sasha said, flashing that grin that lit his whole face again. "Raf reckons you and I should hang a bit. Is that cool?"

Indigo nodded, a slow smile spreading across his face. "I think I like it here," he said shyly. "In Sedona. With people like you and Raf, I feel like much less of a freak."

"Nothing wrong with being a freak, dude," Sasha said, nudging Indigo affectionately with his shoulder. "Freaks are my kinda people."

Indigo's heart swelled. He'd seen Sasha yesterday, with the karate kicking and the back flipping; it was clear he was very accomplished in the martial arts, something Indigo had always wanted to study. He was particularly keen to get his hands on a samurai sword or a staff. This was going to be fun.

"Meditation?" Indigo repeated, unable to disguise the wrinkle of his nose.

"Yup," Sasha confirmed, sitting down cross-legged on the forest floor and indicating Indigo take a seat opposite him in the sun-dappled clearing they'd arrived at after a short hike through the woods. "You must learn to walk before you can run, eh, young Jedi," he teased, a twinkle in his eye.

Sasha owned a dojo in Uptown Sedona and Indigo had heard he was an incredibly accomplished teacher. Visions he'd had of them practicing round kicks and duelling with samurai swords disappeared with a poof, giving way to the image of the two of them sitting like statues on the forest floor chanting 'Om'.

Indigo sighed heavily, trying to hide his scowl as he flopped down opposite Sasha.

A muscle feathered in Sasha's jaw. "Meditation is the foundation of controlling your higher senses, ya? I can teach you nothing until you master it. You need to learn discipline, Indigo. Nobody has any discipline these days," he glowered, picking up a leaf and running it over his palm. "With the higher senses you have, you need that discipline to master them. You need to put the work in and it starts with the basics."

Indigo was sceptical.

The first couple of days he was unenthusiastic, politely obliging Sasha, merely going through the motions. He was frustrated, bored, restless and his arse had gone to sleep more times than he could count. But by the third day he began to see glimpses of that private haven Sasha had spoken of where nothing else mattered, glimpses of slipping like quicksilver betwixt dreaming and waking. And those glimpses fuelled him.

At the end of the week, he finally did it. Indigo found himself sitting cross-legged opposite Sasha in their usual clearing, suspended in blissful warmth, not a care in the world, a tunnel of white light swirling before his eyelids. There was no time or emotion or worry, only space and light and utter euphoria. His whole body tingled as though dipped in a tropical sea and laid out in sunshine. He finally understood the paradox of meditation — he was awake but he was asleep and he was present but he was gone.

He emerged from his trance, his body heavy, his head light, his lips turned subtly up at the corners in the most clandestine of smiles. He slowly, reluctantly, opened his eyes and sighed contentedly as he settled back amongst the pine needles, gazing up at the sun glinting through the branches of the trees above him.

Sasha sat beside him, leaning against the warped trunk of a tree. "Well done," he grinned. "Tomorrow you graduate to meditating on a vortex. Feel good?"

Indigo nodded lazily. "No wonder you're so chill, if you've been doing this since you were a kid."

"Right on," Sasha replied, tilting his head back and closing his eyes against the dappled light. "Meditation forces you to be present, right? My dad always taught us the past is long gone and the future hasn't happened yet, so what's the point of wasting energy on either, ya? All we can control is right now. Not a minute ago, not a minute from now, just right this very second." He turned his head to Indigo. "It's easy to relax, knowing whatever will be, will be — all you're responsible for is following your conscience and your intuition and giving everything you do your best shot."

"Stressing over stuff I could've done differently. That's where I tend to struggle," Indigo admitted. For someone with past regrets as big as his, it was almost impossible for his mind not to go there.

"Yesterday's smoke in the wind, man, it's gone ya, you can't change it, so why waste time worrying about it? And when you're freaking out about the future, you're letting your imagination create scenarios to stress you out, eh," Sasha laughed. "Stressing about that stuff, well, that's the very definition of anxiety. Daily meditation helps you focus on the now, on today."

Indigo gazed at Sasha. He was so disciplined, his life so ordered. Indigo couldn't imagine having it all figured out at twenty-one. He wondered if it was possible for anything to ever rattle Sasha. Surely he wasn't as perfectly chilled as he seemed?

"Hey, Sash?" he ventured.

"Yeah, man?"

"The other day Micah was talking about our lives, saying they're pre-planned."

"Yeah?"

"So, is that why you don't worry about the future? Because your whole life has already been decided?"

"Mmmm… in a way."

Indigo picked up a leaf, folding it along its spine. "Sooooo… every choice I've ever made, every decision, had already been made? I have no free will? Nothing is left to chance?"

"Nope."

"No?" He raised an eyebrow.

"That's not how it works, dude." Sasha's mouth quirked up. "The plan made for your life contains infinite probable realities which allow for you to express free will as you travel through, ya?"

Indigo stared at him, shaking his head ever so slightly.

"So listen, a couple years back, I was at home making dinner. I'd been going through a bit of a sketchy time you see, I'd moved here on a whim and things weren't going great so I was on the verge of moving back home to Hawaii. So I'm cooking away, I'm in the zone and then I open the pantry and realise my then-roommate has chowed down the last of the rice. And I really felt like rice, eh," he chuckled. "So I start poking through the pantry and I see we've got noodles and I think I could probably make do with those, ya. But I'm looking at the package of ramen in my hand and I'm about to open it when I suddenly decide, nope, they just ain't doing it for me, so I chuck those noodles back in the cupboard and I head to the market.

"Anyway, I'm walking up aisles looking for rice, when I hear somebody call my name, ya. I almost fell over when I turned around and saw my old sensei from Honolulu. Turns out his brother had died and left him his dojo here in Sedona." He shifted slightly against the tree trunk. "He'd been here interviewing teachers to run it but hadn't found anyone he'd deemed acceptable and had made the decision to shut the place down instead. He was booked to fly back home the next morning and he'd ducked into the market on a whim to grab some snacks for his flight." Sasha cocked his head to one side, regarding Indigo thoughtfully.

"When he found out I was living here, he immediately asked me to take on the dojo — he and I had always had a special bond and he claimed I was his favourite student, of course." He winked playfully. "So naturally I accepted. And it was one of the best decisions I've ever made. You know how I love that place, brah, how fulfilling teaching is to me." His throat bobbed. "And when my sensei passed away a few months back, he left the dojo to me."

He gazed intently into Indigo's eyes, lips pursed. "Do you understand what I'm saying?"

"Yeah, I think so."

"That night in my kitchen, I could have made do with ramen, but instead I made the choice to go out and buy rice, and having to make that seemingly insignificant choice was always part of my life plan, which contained contingencies for *both* of these probable realities, ya? Think of that decision, whether or not to go to the store, as a fork in the road of my life, one of many." He picked up a stick and drew a line in the dirt, then drew two lines diverging from it. "The planning of your life before you're even born involves having to prepare for every possible reality for you and every other person your timeline may merge with at any point in your life. Your life plan is not a straight line, it is a series of forks that lead to other forks that lead to other forks and so on and so on." Sasha added to his diagram to demonstrate his point, drawing fork after fork. "Make sense?"

"As much as anything around here makes sense," Indigo joked.

Sasha chuckled and nudged him with his shoulder. "You'll come to get used to the weirdness," he promised. "In fact, I'll bet you'll even come to love it, eh."

"Believe me, mate, I already do."

chapter twenty-one

welcome to the jungle

indigo

A week later, Indigo arrived home from the dojo, wincing and clutching his shoulder as he wandered into the kitchen. Now he was on his way to mastering meditation, Sasha had started to incorporate martial arts into his training and Indigo was stiff, bruised, sweaty and dying for a swim.

"Looking a bit worse for wear there, Indi," Raf said with a sympathetic smile. Raf had just arrived home from hot yoga and was drenched in perspiration himself.

Indigo immediately dropped his arms to his sides and shot Raf a grin. "Sasha's a hard taskmaster."

"He tells me you're a natural. And that's high praise coming from Sash." He grinned proudly as he unwound the towel from around his neck and flung it into the hamper as he sauntered past the laundry. "Have you eaten?" He opened the fridge and peered inside.

"Nope," Indigo said, flopping down at the kitchen table and opening his hands to catch the bottle of water Raf threw at him.

"What did you and Sash do this morning?" Raf asked, passing him a plate and fork and placing a platter of sliced watermelon and papaya on the table as he sat down beside Indigo.

Indigo grabbed a watermelon wedge then began to tell Raf about the day's training.

"So Sasha isn't exactly going easy on you then?" Raf smiled.

Indigo shrugged. "Go hard or go home, right?" So Sasha kept telling him.

"You're free this afternoon?"

"As a bird."

"Good. Because I have a little surprise for you."

"What?" Indigo asked, somewhat warily.

"Where's the trust, bud?" Raf joked, cupping the back of Indigo's neck. "It's a good surprise. Dawn's invited you round to her place."

"Dawn?" Indigo said with a frown. "Do you think that means she's forgiven me for the other day?"

Raf stared at him incredulously. "You'd just taken a knife for her daughter. I think she's made peace with you not being super chatty."

Indigo nodded. He'd thought a lot about what she'd said to him and he'd been hoping the two of them might meet again. He poked a papaya slice with his fork. "Hey, Raf? That day... Sash and Dawn, they mentioned some other friends. Nash and Aurora?"

"Mmmm?" Raf said, looking him in the eye.

"Well... Who are they?"

Raf rubbed at the stubble on his chin. "Indi," he said, placing his fork beside his plate, "Nash and Aurora are my children."

"What?" Indigo was taken aback. The only relative Raf had ever mentioned was a father who lived in San Diego.

"Nash and Aurora are my children, the same way Sasha is my son, the same way Dawn is my sister. They are not my blood, but they are my family. The family I have made for myself."

Indigo stared at him, something large and unspoken hanging between them.

"Yes, Indi," Raf said, covering Indigo's hand with his and squeezing it gently, "I have come to regard you as a son too these past months."

Indigo felt as though the air had been sucked from his lungs. He blinked and looked away.

"You and I, we've known each other for many lifetimes. You know that right?" Raf said gently. "Ours is a relationship of soul recognition. That is why it is so easy."

Indigo nodded. "Do you think…?" he faltered. "What have we been to one another, Raf? In the past?"

"I feel a familial connection between you and me," Raf replied thoughtfully, "but what do you think?"

Indigo bit his lip and nodded again as a series of images came to him from nowhere — a desert island. Stacked stone houses. Blue skies and azure seas. An elderly man with white bushy eyebrows smiling broadly at him. Bees. Indigo tried to slow the images down, to grasp them and analyse them, but they were gone just as quickly as they'd arrived.

"If you and I have known each other in other lives, does that mean we were always going to meet now, in this lifetime?"

Raf gazed at him solemnly. "I very much believe so, yes. In my experience, we have a core group of souls we incarnate with over and over again. Life after life, we will always return to these people."

"But doesn't who I meet depend on which forks in life I choose?"

"Some aspects of your life plan are sketched in pencil," Raf said, leaning in, "but others are written in permanent marker, and these are the things which absolutely one hundred percent will happen to you in this lifetime, things which are non-negotiable and which you will always arrive back at, no matter which paths you choose to take leading up to them. The people you are meant to meet, that's written in permanent marker. As is your date of birth."

"What about my date of death?"

"That's more complicated," Raf replied. "It varies from person to person. Some are born with their date of death written in permanent marker. For others, it is dependent on which forks they choose."

Indigo nodded. "So what else is pre-determined?"

"Often pinnacle life events like major illnesses or injuries. In some cases your life partner may be written in marker, but not always. You do not always come here with a soul mate on your life map, which only means that the partner you choose, if any, is left to your free will."

Indigo was instantly distracted by thoughts of Cordelia. Neither time nor distance seemed to have any effect on his feelings for her, on her all-consuming presence in his head. She was his centre, his North Star, and he couldn't fathom the existence of anyone else who could feel like that to him, no matter how far or wide he searched the human race. Cordelia. Until the earth stopped turning he would love her and it sure didn't feel like he had any choice in the matter. Did that make her his soul mate? Did it mean her name was written there across his heart in permanent marker? Because it certainly felt that way. But maybe it was just that way for him.

He thought about telling Raf about her, but he couldn't do it. She was the only part of him he wanted to keep to himself. So many times he'd picked up the phone to call her but had been overcome by so much fear he'd dropped the receiver back in its cradle with shaking hands. An awful thought occurred to him then.

"If someone's your soul mate," he asked, "is it possible to stuff things up with them? To ruin things completely?"

Raf paled then and seemed lost for words and Indigo realised he'd hit a nerve. "Good question, Indi," he finally murmured, and he quickly got up and busied himself with clearing the table.

The sun was high in the fairy floss sky when Indigo parked Raf's motorbike outside the pale pink bungalow set on a quiet street in West Sedona. He checked the address on the scrap of paper Raf had given him, then leant over the white picket fence to unlatch the gate, revealing a pin-neat lawn edged with an undulating palette of wildflowers interspersed with an assault of angel and fairy statues.

The wind chimes hanging from the porch roof sung a haunting melody as a gentle breeze rustled the yard. His tentative knock was met with the sound of hurried footfall, and the door was flung open to reveal Dawn, bubbly and blonde with a grin that oozed pure delight.

"Indigo!" she gushed, pulling him into a maternal embrace. "I'm so excited to see you again, honey." She took both his hands in hers and squeezed them.

"Hey, Dawn," he grinned goofily.

Indigo felt bland in his black cargo shorts and monochrome striped t-shirt next to Dawn in her hot pink high waisted shorts and aqua t-shirt emblazoned with a giant smiling sun.

"How are you feeling?" she asked, leaning back so she could peer up into his face. "Raf's been keeping me updated — he tells me you've been right as rain?"

He nodded, his hand absently moving to the left side of his waist. "I've been good, thanks."

"Come in, come in," she beckoned, ushering him down a corridor lined with framed family photos. Indigo paused to examine a studio shot of Dawn with a man and six children, all smiling brightly. He recognised Reggie immediately.

"The light of my lives," Dawn grinned when she noticed Indigo admiring the picture.

"You all look so happy," he said.

"Thank you, we are," Dawn agreed, squeezing his shoulder. "As you know, we're not perfect," she said, her eyes travelling to Reggie's image, "but no family is."

Indigo still found nuclear families fascinating. A mother who baked birthday cakes and read bedtime stories and made school lunches. A father who taught his kids how to throw a ball and change a tyre, who vocally spectated their Saturday sport, and decorated the house at Christmas time. Holidays that involved road trips and soggy picnic lunches and sibling spats in the back seat of the car, rather than silent first-class flights as an unaccompanied minor and grand yet lonely hotel rooms in Milan or Paris or London. A walk down the corridor at Dawn's revealed the life of a family, a true family in all its togetherness, even beautiful when it was too much.

"I've just made a pitcher of iced tea. Can I pour you a glass?" Dawn said.

"Thanks," Indigo said, taking the proffered tumbler.

They chatted for a while, Dawn explaining that she and her husband Earl had moved their family down from St Louis ten years back. A 'desert change,' she called it. Earl, an ex-banker, now ran a bookstore in town, and their four sons had moved away, a couple at college, a couple out seeking glory. She'd met Raf years back when he'd held a public hosting session at Earl's store and they'd quickly become kin, as she put it.

Indigo shifted slightly on the floral sofa, glancing around the room bedecked in pinks and purples, statues of angels and fairies crammed onto every available surface.

"I just adore angels and fairies," Dawn gushed, noticing his line of sight.

"You don't say," he murmured.

Dawn's laughter pealed out, filling the room. "Reggie feels the same way you do, honey," she giggled. "Says it looks like heaven threw up in here."

Indigo burst out laughing. She leant forward and pulled her hair back to show him the little angel tattooed behind her ear.

"Now tell me, the things I said to you the other day, they frightened you, didn't they?" she asked, shifting closer to him on the sofa. Indigo shrugged.

"Don't be nervous," she said, taking his hands in hers. "Can't you feel this is a safe space?"

He nodded but his stomach was churning.

"As you may have gathered from Reggie, God love her," she rolled her eyes affectionately, "once I've set my mind on helping someone I'm full steam ahead whether they like it or not, so if you don't want me to lay my hard earnt wisdom on you speak now or forever hold your peace."

He nodded tersely. "Go for it."

"I'm going to teach you how to manage your empathy, Indigo. I know it can make life hard, but for healers like you and me, it's a true gift, once you understand how to use it."

Without warning, Indigo's eyes welled up and his throat constricted. The idea of working through this suddenly felt insurmountable. And she'd called him a healer, as though they were equals. He pulled his hands from hers and covered his face in embarrassment.

"I know, heavens to Betsy, I know," Dawn murmured as she pulled him into her arms and stroked his back. They sat that way for a time, Indigo didn't know how long, her rocking him and caressing his hair. After a while she reached behind him to pluck a tissue from a pink crocheted box. She handed it to him.

"I'm so sorry," he said with an embarrassed smile, "I don't know where that came from."

"In this house we never apologise for our emotions," Dawn said with a wag of her finger.

Indigo nodded.

"Now," she continued, clapping her hands together, "*you*, my darling boy, *you* are an empath," she smiled, raising her jiggly arms up in the air in celebration. "Yay!" she cried. "Welcome to the club."

Indigo couldn't help but laugh at her reaction. "Yay," he repeated meekly, unenthusiastically, raising his hands only as high as his shoulders.

"Stop that," she scolded lightly. "You have a gift, and you need to recognise that. Us empaths," she said, her hands in perpetual motion as she spoke, "we need to know how to switch off the barrage of feelings coming at us twenty-four seven. Because if we don't know how to stop feeling all the sadness and despair and suffering and pain of those around us, it can contribute to depression." She paused there, reaching for his hands again and peering deep into his eyes.

"It's getting easier for me," Indigo admitted, "but I do still struggle sometimes with recognising what's actually mine and what isn't."

"Know how you feel when you're just *you*," she said earnestly. "I know Sasha's been teaching you meditation, and that's an invaluable part of it, to quiet the body and mind. And you need to work on your own issues. The stronger you get, the harder it is for other people to affect and influence you, and I think that's the key to all of this — you can't control the external so you need to focus on what you can control — you. Your thoughts and feelings and attitudes and responses."

Indigo nodded. It was comforting to sit with someone who really understood.

"Now," she said, standing up and holding a hand out to him, "come with me." She led him to a sunny room at the back of the house. It contained two comfy armchairs, a massage table covered in mauve faux fur, a padded stool, and a white wooden cabinet topped with incense, candles, and a menagerie of crystals of all shapes and colours. Glass doors opened up onto a small courtyard complete with a lily-padded koi pond, and of course more angel statues.

"Slip your shoes off and lie down, honey," she said, indicating the massage table. "Face up," she ordered, as he lay back on the table and she adjusted a pillow under his head. She moved the stool to the top of the table, cupping his head in her hands. She closed her eyes and took a deep breath.

Indigo immediately felt super slothy. He shut his eyes and allowed her to do whatever it was she was doing to him. "The wound on your side looks great," she said approvingly. She was quiet for a time after that. "Tell me about your clavicle," she murmured after a while.

Indigo hadn't told anyone that the collarbone he'd broken when he'd jumped off the bridge had begun to give him trouble lately, especially since Sasha's martial arts training had turned vigorous. It hadn't helped that he'd landed a back somersault badly yesterday. He admitted as much to Dawn.

"We can fix that," she said confidently. She was quiet a while longer before commenting, "Gee whiz, you've given that liver of yours a good bashing! That will need a good cleaning out. And your spleen has a lot of scar tissue."

"You can feel all that?"

"Sure can. Plus, I can see it. I've honed my higher senses to such a degree that not only can I see inside your body, but I can see your biofield and the disturbances within it." For the next hour, Indigo faded in and out of consciousness, at times mindful of a spreading swirling heat in his chest or his abdomen, at other times consumed by a hazy nothingness.

When he finally came to, he was aware of a comforting hand on his forehead. He opened his eyes groggily to see Dawn standing serenely beside him, a soft smile on her lips.

"How are you feeling?" she asked gently.

"Whaaaaaaat?" he murmured, trying to grasp back into reality.

"How are you feeling, honey?"

"Mmmmm… good," he yawned, stretching his arms up over his head. "Really good," he grinned lazily.

"You see how me being an empath meant I knew how to make you feel better today?"

He stared up at her and nodded.

"Now take your time, but when you're ready, sit up and have a sip of water," Dawn advised him, indicating the large glass on the cabinet behind him. "And I'll meet you back in the sitting room."

"You doing ok?" she asked when he joined her a couple of minutes later. She was sitting on the couch, a sturdy leg tucked beneath her. He nodded as he sat beside her.

She gazed at him intently. "I was once where you are now, sweetie. But you, Indigo, I have a feeling that with practice and discipline you'll leave me for dead."

"I don't know about that," he replied, cheeks heating. "What you did today," he said, moving his shoulder up and down painlessly, "and the other day after I got stabbed. Well, I've never seen anything like that." When he'd worked on Luis in the hospital, he'd felt so clumsy, second-guessing every move he made, displaying nothing of the finesse Dawn did in her healing.

"Indigo," she said, leaning in towards him, "I know you're like me, and you don't just feel people's emotions. You also feel their injuries and illnesses and physical maladies."

He nodded.

"And that's why you're such a wonderful little healer," she grinned. "I told you I've heard about your roommate in the hospital. Triplegia's a pretty tricky thing to heal and you did it with no training and without the patient's input. You have true talent, sweetie."

"Yeah, nah, I didn't do it on my own," Indigo objected modestly. "I had a lot of help from my guardian Sarita and Luis's guardian as well."

Her mouth fell open and she shook her head. "Do you know how many healers would kill to be able to access the discarnate? My talents most certainly don't extend to that!"

Indigo shrugged. "And we don't even know if I *was* actually able to make Luis better," he reasoned.

"We do actually. Sasha bilocated in and checked on him. He's walking unaided and has use of both his arms."

Indigo sunk back into the couch and closed his eyes, exhilaration flooding his every cell. He opened them and looked at Dawn. "For real?" he breathed.

"For real."

"Yes," he whispered, then louder. "Yes!" He punched the air in jubilation, then threw his head back and laughed. Dawn joined in.

"You done good, honey," she told him. "You done real good. And now it's my job to teach you to do even better."

He spent hours that night devouring one of the anatomy and physiology textbooks Dawn had given him to study. He recollected sitting around the kitchen table with Joshua, discussing the wonders of the human body and the most captivating of his medical cases, and he felt a twinge of homesickness. His thoughts moved to Cordelia, but he pushed them away. Sometimes it hurt too much to think of her, of how he'd treated her, to consider how justified she'd be in never speaking to him again.

The next morning during his Hapkido training session with Sasha, Indigo's collarbone didn't bother him at all. He couldn't wait to tell Dawn when he saw her that afternoon. For the next week, he lay on Dawn's table every afternoon while she worked her magic on him. A couple of days in and he managed to stay awake during their sessions, and Dawn began to explain everything she was doing to him, encouraging him to discuss every bit of damage.

On the eighth day, Indigo arrived to find Dawn lying on the massage table.

"Your turn now, honey," she grinned, and she talked him through it, teaching him how to scan her body and feel for illness and injury, and eventually to see inside as clearly as if he had X-ray vision. If he wanted to see Dawn's right lung, he could simply focus on that area of her body and see her lung with his own two eyes in as much detail as he wished, as clearly as if he'd sliced her open and examined the organ itself.

He found himself not only describing old injuries in her body, but how they'd come to be. He saw an old, healed fracture in her wrist, and clear as day saw her as a child, riding her bike down a hill as fast as she could go, blonde hair streaming behind her as she hit a pothole, causing her to fly over the handlebars, breaking her radius as she slammed into the pavement.

Sarita also spoke to him during these sessions, whispering what needed to be done for healing to take place. And Dawn's guardian appeared to him, just as Luis's had during those midnight sessions back at the hospital.

He began to see the leylines of Dawn's body, and then her biofield too, hazy at first, and then with intense clarity, and it amazed him, how much a person's biofield could tell him about them: their emotions, moods, attitudes, thoughts, diet, illnesses, injuries, everything was imprinted there under a swirl of colour and shadow. It was a complex blueprint of everything they were.

Dawn was adamant about involving the patient in their own healing process. It was vital to discuss everything that came to his attention in a session with the person on his table. She believed true healing was impossible if the patient wasn't able to acknowledge, work through, and release the issues that had pained them in the first place.

And then there was the most important lesson of all: healing does not always look the same for everyone.

In some cases, Dawn solemnly told him, death is what heals.

She warned him that only a true healer is able to help prepare someone for death, mentally, physically, emotionally. Only a true healer is able to get down and dirty with a dying soul and scream with them and cry with them and rant and rave… and accept. Accept the beauty of death and let go of all the fear surrounding it.

Dawn soon deemed Indigo ready to work with others. She reached out to her network of friends and patients, and Indigo had other bodies to practice on. Word spread like wildfire about the Aussie wunderkind at Dawn's, and before they knew it, he had more patients than he had hours available to treat them. But he loved every second of it. And though it could be exhausting, it never for one moment felt like work and every morning he woke with a smile, excited to start the day.

Indigo rose at five-thirty every morning. Some days he went to yoga with Raf, but most mornings he ran the trails and buttes of Sedona. He found it therapeutic, being completely alone out there, at one with the rough terrain and desolate majestic beauty. It gave him time to think, to let his mind run wild and wander wherever it wanted to go before he'd then quieten it during meditation. And he found his thoughts always returned to the same place.

To her.

To her contagious laugh. Her effervescent smile. The satiny smoothness of her skin. Her golden waves. Her coral sea eyes, so full of heat and light and purity. Her plump rosebud lips… And that kiss. That kiss that haunted him, that nourished him, that played on his mind over and over and over, his lips charred with the memory of the very perfection of that moment.

Cordelia was never far from his mind.

Because for him, he knew she was it. Looking back now, all the girls that had come before and since meant nothing. They had merely warmed his bed and acted as a gauze with which to stuff the deep wounds that bled profusely inside him. Before her, he hadn't known what love was. But now he knew, and it was like nothing he'd ever believed existed.

She came to him most nights in his dreams and he would awaken the next morning raw, aching for her. He missed her vividly. He missed all the Carlisles and thought of them each and every day, but his thoughts of Cordelia were constant. And it broke his heart all over again every time he remembered her face outside the hospital in upstate New York, her cheeks stained by a deluge of tears as she'd discarded his bracelet in the snow.

Everything he'd done to heal himself, everything he'd put himself through to make himself whole, had been for himself, yes. But if he was honest, it had also been for her. To make himself worthy of her, strong for her, clean and free and pure enough that he knew if by some miracle she were willing to give him another chance, he would never hurt her again.

He didn't know if she would ever forgive him.

He didn't know if she still held any love in her heart for him.

But he knew his love belonged to her.

His thoughts were interrupted as the pale, auburn-haired boy appeared round a bend in the trail, his eyes crinkling as he smiled broadly. He ran by, pulling a headphone from his ear as he always did and winked. "Hey, brother." Indigo grinned back at him and returned the greeting, as he always did. One day, he'd stop and introduce himself.

That morning after his run, Indigo hiked far into the forest and climbed up to the top of his favourite red rock formation to sit in the cave carved into its belly. From the mouth of the cave, he had a view that took in the green carpet of trees below him and the banded buttes that stood high like sentries on the opposite cliffs. Directly below him was a perfectly round, flat, smooth circle of rust-hued rock rising out of the trees, large enough to land a helicopter on. It was almost like Mother Nature herself had created a landing pad out there in the middle of nowhere.

He didn't have any plans to meet Sasha, so he decided to do his morning meditation there. He didn't know how long he'd been under for when he was shaken out of it by the sound of voices, their echoey timbre floating up from below.

His eyes snapped open to reveal two people, a petite girl with long ebony hair and skin the colour of burnt mocha, and the boy from the trails, the russet of his hair mirroring the rocks surrounding them. They were deep in conversation as they climbed up onto the landing pad rock. They hadn't seemed to notice him sitting up there in his cave. He was about to call out to them when something inside of him made him hesitate.

The girl must have been in her mid-twenties and was dressed in skimpy black shorts and a cropped halter top, her hair entwined in two complicated braids that started at the crown of her head and twisted down to her toned waist. Her navel was bejewelled, her wrists encased in leather cuffs, her feet bare. Indigo watched as she and the boy walked to opposite ends of the landing pad. The girl leant over the edge of the rock, peering at something just below her. She turned her head over her shoulder and said something to the boy, and he nodded in approval.

Her back was to Indigo as she looked down, her concentration returning to whatever lay below. She reached her right arm out, palm facing up, fingers slightly curled. All of a sudden, a rock the size of a tennis ball shot up from the forest floor below and landed in her outstretched palm. What the fuck? Indigo blinked. The girl casually tossed the rock over her shoulder and held her hand out to catch another and another. Soon a small pile had formed behind her.

The boy called out to her and she gave him the thumbs up, catching one final rock before turning to face him. She stood beside her rock pile, gazing across at the boy on the other side of the landing pad. She said something and he nodded, a look of deep concentration on his rugged face, his dark eyes fixed steadily on the rock in her hand.

They stood facing one another like that, for Indigo didn't know how long. He held his breath, waiting to see what would happen. Without warning, the girl gave the slightest of flicks to her wrist. The rock flew from her hand in a blur of speed, right at the boy. Indigo almost cried out. The rock was travelling so fast it would crush the boy's skull if it hit him.

But before Indigo could even open his mouth, the boy's hand shot forward. Palm out, fingers spread wide, and as if it were happening in slow motion, Indigo saw the displacement of the very surface of the air before his hand as it quivered and streamed like jet wash… and the next thing he knew, the rock had disintegrated into a cloud of copper dust.

Indigo gasped. Before he could regain his composure, the girl threw another rock. And another and another and another. Faster, faster, faster. Each rock was met with the force the boy was projecting from his palm, reducing it to powder and rubble. By the time the final rock was thrown, the air above them hung thick with foggy dust — Indigo could even taste it as he inhaled.

The boy was bent double, holding onto his knees, panting. The girl strode towards him with a water bottle, nodding at him approvingly as she handed it to him. She then flicked a braid over her shoulder, turned and looked directly up at Indigo. He started and shrunk back into the cave.

"It's safe to come down now," she called, beckoning him.

He stood awkwardly and ran his hand through the back of his hair, giving them a sheepish smile. He made his way steadily down the cliff face and hoisted himself onto the landing rock.

"Hey, um, I'm so sorry, eh, I didn't mean to spy," he stumbled. "I'm—"

"We know who you are," the girl cut him off, narrowing her feline eyes as she peered up at him. Indigo noticed her makeup remained impeccable, her eyes highlighted perfectly with black wing-tipped liner and iridescent green eyeshadow. Not a hair on her head was out of place. She hadn't even broken a sweat. The boy, on the other hand, was red faced, his brow soaked in perspiration.

"I'm Aurora. And this is Nash," she said with a hand wave in the boy's direction.

The elusive Nash and Aurora.

"We're old mates," Nash panted, "kinda." His face broke into an exhausted grin. Indigo smiled back and held his hand out. Nash shook it firmly, drawing him in for a macho hug.

"Did you know I was there the whole time?" Indigo asked as Nash released him.

Aurora snorted. "We knew you were going to be there before *you* even knew you were going to be there."

"Huh?" was all Indigo could manage.

"Nash is a pre-cog," Aurora explained, hands on hips. "There's not much that surprises him."

"A pre-cog?" Indigo echoed.

"Like, I'm psychic?" Nash replied. "I can see the future. And access the past. Also—"

"You're English!" Indigo exclaimed, snapping his fingers. He'd thought he'd detected an accent during the few short exchanges he'd had with Nash on the trails, and it had been bugging him he hadn't been able to put his finger on it.

"Yeah, ok, if that's what you took away from my major reveal then well done you," Nash replied dryly. "And if you were wondering, I'm psychokinetic too."

Indigo stared.

"… which means I'm able to harness and project the current from my biofield, as you just saw a moment ago."

Indigo paused for a moment to gather his thoughts. "So… what was that you guys were doing down here?"

"Training. Duelling. Fine-tuning Blaze's precision, accuracy and stamina," Aurora replied with a shrug, glancing at Nash.

"Blaze?" Indigo swallowed a smile.

"I can't even get *her* to stop calling me that," Nash grumbled as Aurora reached to tug the ends of his blazing red hair, "so don't you start."

"Anyway, Raf's been at us to meet you for a while now," Aurora said to Indigo, "so we thought we'd make it memorable."

"And I for one, am *knackered*," Nash moaned, sprawling back onto the rock behind him and closing his eyes.

"Lucky you're so pretty because you're fucking soft, Blaze," Aurora said, crossing her arms and wrinkling her nose.

"So if he's a pre-cog," Indigo ventured, "then what are you?" He looked at Aurora.

"I'm telepathic and telekinetic."

Indigo hoisted an eyebrow at her.

"I can read and project thoughts. And I can move things with my mind," she paused, examining a long shimmery-green-polished nail. "Obviously."

"What sort of things can you move with your mind?" Indigo asked.

Aurora looked long and hard at him. Behind her, Nash's body slowly left the ground and began to rise up into the air. He retained the same position, lying face up, legs crossed at the ankle, arms folded behind his head, eyes closed. He didn't even open them when he groaned, "Cut it out, Rory, put me down." He was floating a good two metres off the ground. "Unless you fancy carrying me all the way home like this? That'd be brilliant."

She narrowed her eyes then and dropped him with a sickening thud.

"Jesus!" Indigo yelled, rushing to Nash's side.

"Shit!" Nash cried, sitting up and clasping the elbow he'd landed on with all his body weight. "Are you bloody barmy?" He glared at Aurora. The gash in his arm was deep.

Aurora rolled her eyes. "He can fix it," she said, looking at Indigo. "Or so I'm told." There was a challenge in her eyes.

Indigo didn't like being manipulated, but thick, oozy blood was dripping rapidly from Nash's arm, thrumming onto the rock below. He guessed the bone was at least chipped, if not fractured.

"What's your deal?" he asked Aurora angrily as he pulled his t-shirt off and held it to Nash's elbow.

Aurora just stared at him, steadfastly. Indigo could hear her voice in his head, just as he'd heard Sasha's the day he was stabbed. *'Stop whining like a little princess and just fucking fix it.'*

"Excuse me?" he growled.

'*The minute Blaze sees that blood, he's gonna pass out, so you'd better get to fixing that arm.*' Once again, he didn't see her speak, but he heard her words in his head. '*Let's see what you're made of.*'

"I'm rubbish with blood, mate," Nash murmured woozily. He began to sway where he sat, then lost consciousness. Indigo caught his head right before it hit the rock. He removed his shirt from Nash's arm and took a deep breath, centring himself. Using his higher senses, he identified the small fracture in the humerus. Once he knew what needed to be healed, it didn't take him long at all. The wound was fresh and easy to work on. Indigo noticed deep jagged scars on the insides of Nash's elbows, old, mottled scar tissue covering veins that had been given a good thrashing at one point in time.

By the time Nash came to, his arm was good as new, the blood spatter on the rocks and his clothing the only indication of what had taken place. Indigo snatched the water bottle from Aurora's hand and passed it to Nash. "Drink," he said.

'*So you are as good as they say,*' Aurora projected at Indigo, hands on hips, head tilted to one side.

"Get the fuck out of my head," he retorted, standing up and pushing past her. "If you've got something to say to me, say it out loud."

"So sensitive," she smirked, taking Nash's hand and pulling him to his feet.

"You broke his *arm!*" Indigo roared, rounding on her. "And for what? To *test me?* What if I hadn't been able to heal him?"

"Raf saved you for a reason," she said. "I knew you had to have talent." Before he could even begin to unpack that statement, she picked up her bottle and stalked back across the rock towards the trail. "I'd suggest you start heading back."

And with that, she strode off and was gone, leaving nothing but bare footprints on the dusty path.

"What's Aurora's deal?" Indigo asked Nash as they moved to a clearing off the trail to take a break under the shade of a gnarled cypress. The sun climbing steadily in the sky beat down hot and dry.

Nash slid down against the trunk of the tree and closed his eyes. "She means well," he sighed. "In Rory's eyes, the end justifies the means. She doesn't always go about it the right way, but at the end of the day her heart's in the right place." He wriggled his back against the tree and dusted a bug off the thigh of his jeans.

"Really?" Indigo snorted. "It sure didn't seem that way back there."

"She knows what she's doing," Nash assured him. "She would never have hurt me in a million years if she didn't have faith in your healing abilities."

"So you trust her?"

"With my life. Look, man, she's prickly, but she'd be the first person to step in front of a blade for you." A big goofy grin spread over his face.

"Ah ok, I get it," Indigo said, nodding as it dawned on him. "You're into Aurora."

Nash's eyes snapped open, narrowing at Indigo. "You think I fancy Aurora?"

"Come on!" Indigo laughed.

He picked up a twig, twisted it over in his hand. "It's that obvious?"

Indigo grimaced and nodded.

"Well, do you blame me?" Nash finally admitted. "Have you *seen* her?" A cheeky glint appeared in his eye. "She's a kick-ass warrior and she's fit as. Look, just don't tell her, ok?"

"You're asking me to keep a secret from someone who's telepathic," Indigo mused. "How exactly does that work?"

"Just don't think about it when you're around her. I never do. In fact, I have shrouding my mind down to a fine art. I can teach you one day if you like." He began snapping the twig into tiny pieces, collecting them in his hand.

Indigo gazed at him sceptically. "Why don't you just tell her? Maybe she feels the same way about you."

"She doesn't," Nash sighed, dropping the bits of twig. "I'm a pre-cog, remember? Spoiler alert: we don't end up together."

"But the future is ever-changing," Indigo argued. "Isn't what you see just one possibility out of many?"

"That is correct," Nash replied, "unless it's pre-determined." He picked up a stone, tested its weight in his hand.

"So you and Aurora? It's still a possibility?"

"With most stuff, I have no way of knowing how much is predetermined and how much isn't." He threw the rock. It landed with a thud in the bushes behind Indigo. "Plus, there's stuff I'm not allowed to see."

"Says who?"

"The guardians. They pull the curtains down around what they want hidden. They're the gatekeepers who filter the flow of information between worlds."

"Whose guardians?"

"The person's I'm reading or mine," he said, fingers drumming a frenzied beat on his knee. "Depending on what sort of information they believe will affect free will, fate and all that fun stuff. But regarding Rory, I know one hundred percent that face is not the one I'm destined to wake up to every day for the rest of my life. Unfortunately."

"I find you people and your rules all very complicated," Indigo sighed, lying back on the forest floor and gazing up through the trees to the cloud-mottled sky above. "I still feel like an outsider sometimes," he confessed.

"Whether you like it or not you're one of us now, brother," Nash replied stoically. "And when you're one of us, you've got a family for life."

The forest was silent, the only sound Nash's almost constant fidgeting. The guy never sat still. "So how did you come to be here in the States?" Indigo asked after a while. "And in Sedona, of all places? I can't imagine this is a particularly forgiving climate for an Englishman... especially one with, er... your... complexion," he finished, eyeing Nash up and down.

Nash grinned a big, lazy grin. "It was a monstrous shock to the system when I first arrived, that's for sure. That being said, I won't hear a word against my moon tan, mate," he said, proudly pulling up his t-shirt to reveal lustrous white abs.

Indigo laughed. "So why here?"

"Simple. Because of Raf."

"Raf brought you here?"

"Yup." Nash kicked intently at a half-buried rock with the toe of his worn brown cowboy boot. "You don't really want to hear the tale of a poor little rich boy nobody wanted."

"Been there, done that, bought the t-shirt," Indigo quipped.

"Well… I guess that's something we can bond over," he grinned, absentmindedly rubbing his right bicep. Indigo glanced down and caught a glimpse of an elaborate tattoo: a hooded skull flanked by leathery wings, its empty eye sockets seeming to glow iridescent blue. It reminded him of the ink he'd seen on gang members in New York. Nash quickly pulled his sleeve down over it.

"How did you meet Raf?"

"Raf rescued me," Nash shrugged, still kicking at the rock which was beginning to loosen from the earth.

"He came to London? Specifically for you?"

"Wouldn't you?" Nash joked, playfully flexing his muscles.

Indigo chuckled. "Did Raf ever say how he knew where to find you?"

Nash shrugged, abandoned the rock. "How does Raf ever know anything?"

"And has he ever told you why?" Indigo pressed on.

"Why what?"

"Why you? Why me?"

"Raf hasn't told you?"

Indigo shook his head. Nash looked at Indigo, and Indigo could tell he was measuring his words. "Wellllll…" he stalled. "I guess you could say Raf collects lost and broken souls and puts them back together."

"The world is full of lost and broken souls," Indigo said, "yet Raf seems to have a knack for finding those with certain… abilities."

Nash shrugged elusively, yet Indigo could see in his eyes he was torn. "We'd better start heading back," he said, climbing to his feet and offering Indigo his hand. "I'm gonna be late for work." The moment their fingers touched, Nash's eyes snapped shut and he froze. When he opened his eyes again a few seconds later, he stared quizzically at Indigo, one brow cocked.

"What?" Indigo asked, as Nash finished pulling him to his feet.

"You're psychokinetic?"

"Psychokinetic?" Indigo balked. "Nope. Why?"

"All good," he muttered. "Let's go." He started telling Indigo about the horses at the ranch he managed outside of town and Indigo understood the subject had been firmly changed.

That evening when Indigo got home from Dawn's, Raf was sitting in his favourite armchair, reading. Indigo grabbed the dinner that had been left out for him, a bowl of felafel layered with tabouleh, hummus, arugula and roasted vegetables, and brought it into the living room with him. He flopped down on the couch opposite Raf, balancing the bowl on his knee while he tucked in.

"This is great thanks, Raf." Raf was such an awesome cook, Indigo had almost forgotten to miss meat. Almost.

"So you met Nash and Aurora today," Raf said, lowering his book.

"Mmmm I did."

"And?" Raf ventured.

Indigo swallowed his mouthful and placed his bowl on the coffee table. "They've got some pretty impressive shit going on, that's for sure. I really like him. But honestly? I'm not so sure about her."

Raf nodded thoughtfully. "Aurora can be a bit of an acquired taste. She doesn't always go about things the way you or I would, which can rub people the wrong way."

Indigo told Raf what she'd done to Nash. "I just don't know," he mused, "anyone who would intentionally hurt their friend, just to test another person… She seems a bit…" he searched for the right word, "cold."

Raf shrugged. "I would always encourage you to make up your own mind about people. But give it time. And an open mind. Rory definitely isn't like other folks."

"How so?"

"Indigo, Aurora is a walk-in."

"A what now?" Indigo asked, pulling a face.

"A walk-in. A soul on the cusp of ascension who wants to return to earth from the discarnate realm as quickly as possible, often for the last time. Sometimes they come back with a specific mission to fulfil, but mostly they have a lot to contribute to the world and don't want to waste time once again being born, battling through childhood, and slowly growing into an adult body."

"There's another option?" Indigo asked incredulously.

"There is," Raf said, bending his knee up and resting his elbow on it. "They look for an adult human who is nearing the end of their incarnation or is struggling greatly with their life on earth and is seriously considering leaving by way of death… And exchange places with them."

Indigo gasped. "How?"

"The old soul walks out, the new one walks in, and a perfectly good body doesn't go to waste. The soul who walks out gets to leave, returning to the discarnate realm, knowing they are allowing the soul who walks into their body to do a great service to the world."

"And this, like, happens all the time?" Indigo asked.

"No," Raf smiled, "it's incredibly rare. In fact, Aurora is the first walk-in I've met, and it's her first time with the process, too. She was granted the opportunity for a specific reason that is yet to come to light." Raf tilted his head thoughtfully, regarding Indigo. "Ask Aurora," he nodded. "I bet she'll tell you her story. And it may help you understand her a little better. She is not as connected to her emotions or invested in outcomes the way most people are. She lives by her gut, not her head. This means she may often seem cold and aloof."

Indigo picked up his dinner again and began to wolf it down. "I'll give her a chance," he promised Raf, who smiled at him as he reached for his book.

chapter twenty-two

walk this way

indigo

"Again!" Aurora commanded, hands on hips in her typical no-nonsense manner.

Indigo flopped down onto his back, panting. He was shattered. The arid desert heat was stifling and Aurora never let up on him.

"Yeah, nah, can't do it," he gasped, propping himself up on his elbows to glare at her.

Her high ponytail hung to her ribs, a cascade of lustrous ebony adorned with tawny feathers and amethyst crystals. She sighed, narrowing her umber eyes at him. "Bullshit," she snapped, examining a blue manicured fingernail. "Get your ass up. Do it again."

He sunk back onto the red earth, staring into the spotless cobalt sky through the trees. Aurora sighed again and strode over, standing over him, her dark skin seeming to glisten under the sun. Tiny black shorts sat low on her narrow hips, her washboard stomach rippled up to a skimpy black bandeau. He'd made the mistake once of calling her a pocket rocket. Once. Never again. Her wrists were encased in crystal-studded leather cuffs, and even in this heat her wing-tipped eyeliner remained perfect, as did her shimmery purple eyeshadow. Aurora the warrior. She never let up. It was his fifth day of training with her and she was a hard task master. She had no time for weakness or negative attitudes.

"I think Sash is expecting me…" he tried. She nudged him with her bare toe and took a long swig from her water bottle. When Indigo still made no move to get up, she upended it on him. He sprung up, shaking droplets from his hair.

"Ok, ok," he said, holding his hands up in surrender. His black tank top clung to his torso, damp with sweat. The water she'd poured over him ran in rivulets through the fine layer of red dust that coated his hair and skin and camo shorts. He could even taste a subtle coating of the rusty powder on the back of his tongue. He was a long way from the beach. God, how he missed the beach.

Nash laughed loudly from his comfortable position at the edge of the clearing where he was strumming softly on his guitar. "Glad it's you and not me, mate," he called as he began a very pointed acoustic rendition of Beck's *Loser* in Indigo's direction.

"Oh, ha-ha fuck off," Indigo muttered as he pulled his hair back from his face, securing it with an elastic. "This is all your fault."

"I'm not even sorry," Nash chuckled. "This is brilliant!" Apparently, the day they'd officially met, Nash had had a vision Indigo was psychokinetic, which he'd later made the mistake of sharing with him in front of Aurora. What had resulted was five days straight of Aurora hurling rocks at Indigo's head while he'd tried with all his might to summon the power from his biofield to deflect or obliterate them under Nash's tutelage.

Aurora had relegated Nash from teacher to spectator when they'd realised his technique wasn't working for Indigo. Yet Nash had still spent the last few days making wisecracks and trying to rile Indigo up, insisting if he got him angry enough, he'd be able to harness the power to make it happen.

"Psychokinesis: you're cocking it up," he cracked from his position of safety. He was incredibly smug not to be in the firing line for once.

"Blaze! You're driving me fucking crazy!" Aurora groaned, massaging her temples with her fingertips. "Can you take it somewhere else?" Her expression softened a bit as she added, "Please?"

"Ok, ok," Nash said, clamouring to his feet. "I'm due back at work, anyway." He slung his guitar over his shoulder and stalked over to his motorbike.

"I'll miss you, mate!" Indigo called sarcastically. Nash didn't turn or break his stride, he just raised his middle finger up over his shoulder.

He reached his bike, swinging his leg over it and revving it loudly, pointedly. He took off in a fishtail of orange dust, heading in the direction of the ranch.

"There's only so much that even I can take," Aurora confided with a tight half smile. A half-smile! The first semblance of positive emotion he'd gotten from her. He'd take it. "This clearly isn't working," she admitted.

"Maybe Nash's vision was wrong?"

"No," she replied without hesitation, "it wasn't. We're just going about this the wrong way. We need to crack this thing," she mused. "Let's take a break."

Indigo followed her over to the rug laid out in the shady spot Nash had just vacated and dropped onto his back on the ground next to her, stretching his legs out and resting his head in his hands.

"Sooooo… can I ask you something?" he began casually. She turned and gave him a withering look and then another half-smile. His second!

"For the love of Gaia, *finally*," she declared, raising her arms up wide to the sky.

"H-huh?" he stammered.

"We both know you've been dying to ask me for days now. It's a relief you've finally mustered the fucking balls, so I no longer have to hear you tossing it around in your mind, trying to figure out how to broach it. It's been *excruciating!*"

"Well, why didn't you just *tell* me days ago then?" he said through clenched teeth.

She shrugged and settled back onto her elbows, staring straight ahead. "Because, princess, I'm not here to spoon feed you." Indigo shook his head, clenched his teeth, trying not to let on how much it pissed him off when she called him that. "You're a big boy. You need to find your own way.

"I walked into this body five years ago," she said matter-of-factly, "when it was twenty-one. The original inhabitant, Lisa, was a very sweet, very lost, very unhappy soul. She'd been cutting herself for some time when I approached her," Aurora explained, pulling up the hem of her shorts to show Indigo the faint white lines etched into the tops of her thighs. "And the series of forks she'd chosen in her life were swiftly leading her towards the end of her incarnation."

"*You* approached *her?*" Indigo interrupted.

"I visited her in her dreams when she was in an altered state of consciousness. The process involved a lot of in-depth discussion with her and her guardian, as both parties had to be one hundred percent sure and committed. All sales are final, as they say." She smirked at her own joke. "She was happy to return home to the discarnate world, so she made one final choice, chose that one final fork that would prove fatal.

"She was driving home from class one day when she got stuck behind a truck. She could have continued to follow it, but it was slow and she grew impatient and chose to swerve around it. That decision meant she arrived home a couple of minutes earlier than she otherwise would have, meaning she entered her apartment just as the shitshow who'd been robbing her was leaving. He was totally strung out and he panicked and hit her over the head with a lamp. She was in hospital in a coma for weeks. Eventually the doctors told Lisa's parents she was brain-dead and recommended they pull the plug."

"My God," Indigo muttered.

"But before they could make a decision she – I – woke up. But here's the deal with walking into someone else's body: your memory is wiped before you wake up so you only have their memories and your intuition to guide you. So I arrived back here with no fucking recollection at all of what had just happened. As far as I knew, I *was* Lisa. I was completely unaware the real Lisa had crossed over into the in-between and I'd just walked into her body. So you can imagine how confused I was when nothing felt right. Nothing made sense. When I woke up, Lisa's boyfriend was sitting by my side, holding my hand, sobbing and gazing adoringly into my eyes... And I looked at him and all I could think was, *what the fuck?* I couldn't stand him touching me. I mean, he was nice enough, cute, but dumb as a box of hammers and he had about as much personality as a wet mop." Her lip curled. "Lisa's parents were there too, but they felt like strangers. Of course, I knew who all these people *were* because I retained all of Lisa's memories when I took over her body — I just felt no affection for them."

"Holy shit!" Indigo commented, manoeuvring onto his side to face her, head propped in his palm. "What a spin out."

"After I left the hospital, I went back to Lisa's life," Aurora said, crossing her ankles and tilting her head towards him. "I hated her tasteless beige-on-beige apartment. I hated her tragic wardrobe, with its turtlenecks and sensible shoes and khakis. And as far as make-up went, the only thing I could find in the whole apartment was one pitiful, unflavoured chapstick."

Indigo cocked an eyebrow at her.

"Law school bored me senseless," she said, wrinkling her nose. "My professors were confused as all hell when I suddenly started failing my courses. I'd been a straight-A student before the accident and apparently had a brilliant legal mind. Now I couldn't give a rat's ass about torts or discovery or jurisdiction. So I dropped out of that stuffy Ivy League school. I started to dress my way and changed my hair," she said, running her hand through her ponytail.

Indigo felt laughter rising and bit his lip to try to stop it. He failed and she glared down at him, eyes flashing.

"I wasn't aware my story was so amusing," she snapped.

"I'm sorry," he said, gasping with laughter, holding up his hands in apology, trying to control himself. "It's just you're this highly evolved soul and one of the first things you do after returning to earth is hit the mall?"

"It might sound superficial," she bit, "but it's the way in which we present ourselves to the world that tells people who we are. And none of it felt like me." She glowered at him before continuing. "It's how I knew something wasn't right. When I changed my appearance, I finally started feeling like myself."

"I get it," he teased, forgetting she didn't like to be teased. "You went to all that trouble to be here, you might as well look good doing it."

"Fuck you," she said, jumping to her feet and dusting her hands off. She turned to walk away. He sat up, gently caught her hand. She spun around.

"I'm sorry," he said, climbing to his knees, dropping her hand. "I was just playing. I didn't mean to upset you. Where I come from, teasing someone is a sign of affection." He offered her a crooked smile. "I want to hear the rest of your story. I'll behave, I swear," he promised, drawing a cross over his heart.

She stared down at him, her face like thunder. He softened his eyes, tilted his head to one side. "I truly am sorry."

"Fine," she finally huffed, shoulders sagging. "But just so you know, I don't understand or particularly like your shitty foreign idiosyncrasies." He had flashbacks to when he'd referred to her as a pocket rocket.

Although he and Aurora both spoke English, they didn't speak the same language.

He moved over on the rug so she could sit beside him again. He bent his knees up, rested his arms on them. She sat cross-legged, staring straight ahead.

"As I was saying," she said stiffly, "I left college and changed the way I looked. I got so damned sick of hearing, 'You're so different!' and 'You're not the same person!'" she said, twisting a strand of hair around her finger. "Despite all her problems, Lisa's public persona had been warm and bubbly, whereas I was... Well, you know that I'm not," she shrugged. "I dumped her dumb bohunk of a boyfriend when I couldn't handle one more mind-numbing conversation with him. And the *sex!*" she shuddered. "For some reason he seemed to think it was a race — and he *always* beat me to the finish line.

"Her parents were nice enough, but I felt nothing for them, so I slowly started pulling away. And don't forget all this time, I had no idea why my life felt so strange to me. I still had no recollection of what had happened. Even my name didn't feel right, so I legally changed it to Aurora."

"Why Aurora?" he asked, wondering what he'd change his name to if ever he felt inclined. Growing up, he'd hated his weird celebrity baby name, but now his name was just his name.

"Because somewhere deep inside me, I just knew that was my name. All the information I had before I walked into Lisa's body was still there, sitting somewhere out there in the unconscious. I just didn't know how to access it or that I needed to. But it was there to guide me when I really needed it, when I followed my gut. One day, I knew I just needed to get in my car and start driving. I knew I needed to leave Boston, but I had no idea where I was going. I just headed south. I found myself aimlessly wandering the streets of Miami, feeling like I was meant to be there, but not knowing why.

"I'd been living there about six months when I first started hearing the voices," she said, her tone even. "They were in my head but they weren't mine, and they were as clear and distinct as if someone was sitting next to me talking to me."

Indigo nodded. He knew exactly how those voices sounded.

"I'd taken a job behind the bar at a club in Miami Beach," Aurora continued. "It was always loud, it was always pumping, and there was always a line around the block to get in. Anyway, it started off slow. I'd hear a customer's drink order in my head before they opened their mouth. I didn't think too much of it at first to be honest. I just assumed I'd been working there so long that I'd learnt to read people. But then things started to escalate." She paused for a moment, narrowing her eyes. "When you can hear the vile thoughts emanating from unevolved assholes…" She shuddered. "Those dickheads got the Aurora Special," she reminisced, as she mimed spitting into a drink. "And as for the insecure thoughts that run through the minds of young women!" She looked pained. "I don't know when female self-confidence died a slow, painful death. When I could be assed, I'd hand them their drinks with a side of 'your butt doesn't look big in that' or 'you're just as hot as she is'.

"One day I was walking through the club when I passed this douchebag chatting up a pretty girl. He wore way more gold jewellery than any man should, but he was hot in a Miami Vice kinda way, you know, way too much hair-gel but obviously charming, and I could tell she thought he was all that. As I brushed past him, I immediately heard his intentions for her and I wanted to puke. I didn't know what to do. I was inexperienced and I was totally alone. So I watched them all night, not taking my eyes off them for a fucking second. Eventually, they headed for the exit, him high fiving his buddies as they left. So I told my manager I was going on break and I followed them."

"You followed them?" Indigo repeated. "What did you think you were gonna do? You're like forty-five kilos wringing wet!"

She shot him a disdainful look. "He took her down onto the beach. She was completely hammered, he'd plied her with drinks and coke and god only knows what else all night." She paused for a moment, her mouth twisting into a grimace, eyes momentarily closed. When she spoke again, her voice was tight. "Have you ever witnessed someone being fucked against their will, Indigo?" she asked, staring him right in the eye.

He looked at her in something akin to offence and shook his head.

"It's something that will never leave you. I could hear her muffled sobs, her pleas, her protests. I could hear her terrified thoughts. Worse yet I could hear his sick-ass deranged ones." She shuddered.

"What did you do?" Indigo whispered.

"Well you know how they say that in times of crisis people find they have superhuman strength? Well this was the crisis during which

I found I had superhuman abilities. I just remember striding towards them, and he was on top of her, his hand covering her mouth, and with all my fucking might I willed him off her. And then, all of a sudden, he was. He shot up off her into the air and was hovering about ten feet off the ground and I realised that my hand was outstretched, holding him up there," she said, holding out her arm to emulate her actions. "I frightened myself with my own power, and I panicked, bringing my arm down and him with it. He landed a bit down the beach, out cold. I helped the girl up, who was too out of it to fathom what had just happened, and dropped her off at the nearest hospital with his wallet so they'd be able to ID him."

She had a distant look in her eye.

"Incidents like these started to occur more frequently – I found myself stepping in on muggings, attacks and sexual assaults. I was *meant* to step in. I fucking hated it, but I didn't have a choice. I didn't know why or how or what the end game was for me and I was miserable as hell." She gave him a sad smile and he could feel how lost she'd been.

"One afternoon," she continued, "when I was sitting at home, I heard a new voice. It was a man's voice, gentle and warm, and it told me to go to a new-age store not far from my apartment building — you know, the type of place that sells incense and crystals and those sickly sweet angel cards? Anyway, I did, and I saw a poster announcing a man named Diego Rafael would be conducting a public hosting session there that very evening." Her face softened at the memory. "I felt compelled to go. The moment I heard him speak, I knew his voice was the one I'd heard in my head earlier that day. And suddenly I didn't feel lost anymore. For the first time since I'd awoken from the coma, I felt like I was somewhere I *belonged*." She dusted a plume of red earth from the rug, a small smile teasing the corners of her mouth. "It didn't hurt that the session he conducted that evening was subtly aimed at me and addressed a lot of the questions I needed answered." Her eyes brightened when she spoke of Raf.

"So I hung around afterwards to speak to him," she said. "Of course as soon as he saw me his face lit up. He was pumped I'd heard his request and come to the store. Raf offered to hold a private hosting session for me, and Micah explained my whole walk-in experience. He said I'd proven I could follow my intuition and that I was ready to hear the truth. I can't tell you what a damned relief it was to find out I wasn't crazy and there was a reason Lisa's life didn't fit me — because it *wasn't fucking mine.* Everything just fell into place for me, and I felt peace for the first time since I'd walked into Lisa's body. I knew my time in Miami was over, so I packed up my shit, quit my job and followed Raf back here to Sedona. And that was that. This is my home, for now, anyway. I'm not sure how long I'll be here on this earth in this body," she said, a faraway look in her eye, "but while I am it's where I'm meant to be, it's where I can do my best work. I know in my gut I walked into this fine-ass body to fulfil a specific mission, but I'm yet to figure out exactly what that is. I have trust though, that when the time comes, I'll know." Indigo found he admired her matter-of-factness.

"Now," she said, leaning forward, dusting her hands off on her shorts, "enough about me. Right now, we're meant to be working on you." She regarded him closely, a thoughtful look upon her face. "I wonder…" she trailed off.

"What?" he asked.

"Clearly Blaze's way of doing things hasn't worked for you. You're different people with different motivations. His was always anger or sorrow because that's what sat in his heart, in his biofield, for so long," she said, and Indigo wondered not for the first time what tragedies lay in Nash's past. "But not you." She snapped her fingers. "Your biofield was never fully consumed by anger or sorrow. Even in your darkest days, you still managed to hold love in your heart." She paused again and stared at him. "For who?"

Indigo felt his face flush. He willed his mind not to go there, but it betrayed him.

"Ahhhhhh, shit yeah, of course," Aurora said, flashing him a knowing look. "I get it, I get it. She's an incredibly beautiful soul. Very pure of heart," she commented in a way that made him question whether she thought that was a good thing.

"Can you please get out of my head?" Indigo mumbled, ducking his chin in embarrassment. He didn't want anyone to see or hear his thoughts about Cordelia.

"Ok, ok, I'm out," Aurora said, holding up her hands. "Remind me to show you how to defend yourself against telepathic intrusion," she said, as if it were the simplest thing in the world. "You need to learn how to shroud your mind."

"So Nash tells me."

Before he could press her on it, she'd moved on. "The thing about darkness," she mused, "is that if you fight it with darkness, you just end up feeding it. To truly defeat the dark, you need to open yourself up to it, embrace it with all the light you have. That unconditional love that sits in your heart? It's what will give you your strength and your power. And you can thank her for that. Your love for her is what inspired your love for you."

"You've lost me," Indigo replied, brow creased.

"Nash's been working on pissing you off, believing it'll motivate you to access your higher senses because, in his experience, consciously generating bioplasma was always linked to his emotions. I assume he's told you about the events that triggered his psychokinesis?"

Indigo shook his head.

"Oh," she said, blinking. "Well, the point is, that's not the right motivation for you." She jumped to her feet and strode back to the pile of rocks they'd been practicing with earlier.

"Come on," she called over her shoulder. Indigo reluctantly made his way back to his place of torture, psyching up to have rocks hurled at his head again.

"When you first started working with Dawn, manipulating energy to heal, it came easy to you, right?" Aurora asked.

"Pretty much."

"This shouldn't be much different, really. I mean, it's the same thing, really, harnessing and honing your electrical field to effect something externally…"

"Nah, yeah, but one's to heal and the other is to harm."

"Is that what's stopping you? You wanna make love, not war, princess?"

He shot her a look. "I-I guess so. I mean, as impressive as Nash's abilities are, let's face it, he's a weapon. And you're trying to make me into a weapon, too. But why? What's the point? To what end?"

Aurora sighed heavily and closed her eyes, obviously deep in thought. When she opened them, she approached him, staring up into his eyes, a serious expression on her face. "I think I need to show you something," she began, "but I want you to promise me you'll keep your shit together."

"Why?" Indigo replied, regarding her with suspicion.

"Because I know now that it's going to be difficult for you to see. But I think you need to, ok?"

"Ok." But his gut was already churning.

"Before I show you, I need for you to understand that this is in the future and I promise you we'll give you plenty of warning when we know exactly when it's going to happen."

"You're already freaking me out."

"Don't be such a pussy," she snapped, reaching her hands out towards him. "This is something Nash showed me a few days ago, and now I'm going to show you." She went to place her hands on his shoulders. He jerked away.

"Hang on," he said, "show me *how?*"

"You, me, Nash, Sasha, Raf, Dawn… we all have psychic abilities, right? Which gives us the ability to share our visions through touching and projecting." She reached her hands out towards his shoulders again. "So if Nash has a precognition and shows it to me, I can project it into your head by merely touching you."

She placed a hand on each of his shoulders. The moment her skin touched his, his whole reality jolted. The red rocks, the desert and the daylight disappeared and all he could see was a beach, a dark beach at night, a beach he knew. It was Manly. And then a series of images that terrified him to his very core, cloaked figures swaying and chanting, a crescent moon, a girl encircled by those figures, trapped by them, helpless and alone. There was a yell and the girl looked up and he saw her face…

"Cordelia!" he cried, wrenching free of Aurora in his panic. The beach vanished in an instant and he was back in the desert, sitting on the red earth where he'd fallen when he'd lost his bearings. He was breathing erratically, his eyes wild as he searched for something to anchor him. "I-I need to go. I need to get back. She's in danger! She needs my help—"

"Indigo!" Aurora demanded, standing over him, hands on hips. "Indigo! Look at me!" He did as he was told because he didn't know what else to do. "You agreed you wouldn't lose your shit," she said matter-of-factly. "So calm the hell down. Now."

He gazed up at her, trying to still his breath.

"This hasn't happened yet. And as I promised you, we'll give you plenty of warning for when it will. If you hadn't fucking panicked and dropped out of it, you would have seen it was you who yelled out. You're meant to be there, so you will be. You need to trust us, ok?"

He nodded again. She pulled him to his feet. "Do you see now why I'm trying to teach you how to defend yourself? There's a lot of darkness out there, Indigo. You of all people understand the world's not all sweetness and light."

"Yup, I'm more than aware of that, thanks," he said tightly.

"Don't you want to be able to defend yourself and the ones you love?"

"I do," he said, mouth set in a grim line.

"Ok, good," she nodded. "So shake it off, ok? I'm sorry I had to show you that, but I had to make you understand why it's so important you master your psychokinesis. But I can't train you when you're full of fucking fear. So take a deep breath in, right down into your belly." He did as he was told. "Now let it go, let it all go…"

He exhaled heavily, trying his hardest to release the emotion the precognition had stirred up. She instructed him to repeat the exercise a few more times, then asked, "You good?"

"I'm good," he assured her.

"Ok, so let's get back to it then." She stalked back to her pile of rocks and picked one up. She turned to face him, throwing the rock in the air and catching it as though testing its weight.

"Close your eyes," Aurora ordered.

Indigo baulked. "Close my eyes? Are you crazy?"

"Trust me," she said. Then added a terse, "Please?"

He took another deep breath and exhaled. He'd seen Aurora break Nash's arm as an experiment. He couldn't even imagine what she was capable of doing to him. But she seemed to know her stuff. And Raf and Nash trusted her implicitly.

He stood, feet apart, facing her, and closed his eyes, cringing gingerly while he waited for a rock to hit him. Nothing happened. He opened one eye.

"I'm not going to throw a fucking rock at you when you've got your eyes closed!" Aurora cried in exasperation, tossing the rock back onto the pile. "I'm not a *complete* bitch!" Her hands were on her hips. "Now, I want you to clear your mind, just like Sash taught you." She was quiet for a beat or two while he closed his eyes and followed her instructions.

"I want you to get into an almost meditative state." He was deathly still. "Now, no thinking. Just feel. Feel what's in your heart. That's it, feel it, let it radiate up and out, let it fill your entire body and beyond. Hold out your hands, palms facing up, and let all that heart energy flow there." He heard her gasp. "Now, very slowly, without deviating from your current state of being, open your eyes."

Indigo calmly did so and looked down. His hands were buzzing, vibrating, the bioplasma streaming off his palms like high summer heat off a bitumen road. It wasn't solid, nor was it liquid, nor was it gas, but it had a density to it that displaced everything around it. His eyes widened, and he looked at Aurora. "Do you see this?" he asked her.

"I do," she nodded. She looked excited. He'd never seen Aurora excited. He wondered if she might actually break a sweat. "Yes!" she punched the air. "I fucking *knew* you could do it!" She held her hand out and a rock flew up into it. "Ready?"

Indigo set his mouth in a straight line and nodded, his eyes fixed steadfastly on the rock resting in her palm.

"Relax a bit," she advised. "You're tensing up again." The next thing he knew, the rock that had been hurtling towards him a moment ago was nothing more than a cloud of dust raining down upon them. He dropped to his knees and held his arms up in silent victory.

"Wooooooo!" Aurora whooped, striding towards him. He threw his head back in laughter. She high fived him. "Shit, yeah! I knew it! I *knew* it!"

"Let's go again," he said.

By the end of the day, Indigo could quite literally obliterate rocks with his eyes closed. He was completely exhausted and Aurora still hadn't broken a sweat.

They met Nash for dinner at their favourite little cantina to fill him in on their day.

"Bollocks you can do it with your eyes closed, you knobhead," he scoffed. He plonked down his beer bottle and sat back in his chair, crossing his arms.

"He can," Aurora confirmed with a smug smile. "You should have seen it, Blaze! He's everything Raf said he'd be and more. I taught him how to shroud his mind in like ten fucking minutes."

"Bloody hell, Indi," Nash grumbled. "If I'd known you were going to put me to shame, I never would have agreed to help you." He absently picked up a coaster, started tearing it to pieces.

"You didn't," Indigo retorted light-heartedly, taking a big swig of iced water and grinning at him.

Aurora sniggered and drained her beer. A big smile spread over Nash's face as he shoved Indigo affectionately on the shoulder. "Yeah well, maybe I should have just taken you out early," he kidded, "left you bobbing around in the Hudson that night."

The smirk died on Aurora's lips and she pinned Nash with a lethal death stare. Nash went ghost white when he realised his faux pas. As Nash's words sunk in, Indigo's grin grew smaller, a sick realisation dawning.

"H-hang on," he said, "what did you just say?" Nash looked down at the table, refusing to meet his gaze. "Rory?" he ventured. And then it came back to him, what she'd said the day they'd first met: *Raf saved you for a reason. I knew you had to have talent.*

"That night on the bridge. Raf being there. That was no coincidence? He knew I was going to be there, that I was going to jump?" He suddenly felt sick to his stomach. "Were you guys there too?" he whispered.

They both avoided his stare. *Were you?* he demanded, banging his palm down on the table.

"Yeah, we were there, brother," Nash finally admitted, raising his eyes to meet Indigo's. He looked wretched. "Did you not ever question how you fell over three hundred feet and survived?"

Indigo stared at him blankly.

"Rory caught you. She slowed you down, broke your fall a bit."

"What?" Indigo looked from Nash to Aurora.

"We needed you injured, not dead," Aurora said.

Indigo could feel the bile rising in his throat.

"Hang on," Nash suddenly interjected, glaring at Aurora, "that's a really poor choice of words, Rory." He turned to Indigo and put his hand on his arm.

Indigo shrugged it off and pushed his chair back, stumbling to his feet. "I've got to get out of here," he choked, heading for the door. He felt as though he was moving under water. His ears were ringing, bright spots danced before his eyes. He pushed his way out of the restaurant and into the night air, gulping deep breaths down into his lungs. He gathered his bearings and started walking.

"Indigo!" he heard Aurora cry behind him. They'd followed him out onto the street. *'Please come back, it's not what you think,'* he heard in his mind. With all his might, he pushed her out and shut her out, used the shrouding she'd just taught him against her. He didn't want her in his head.

Not now.

Not ever again.

They'd let him jump!

He started jogging, heading out of town, taking the backstreets until the houses grew sparser. The darkness swelled as he left the town lights behind. Soon he only had the stars and the silvery moonlight glinting off the rocks to guide him into the desert. His eyes adjusted quickly. It was deathly quiet, desolately so, the energy of the land thick with all that had come before.

He felt rudderless, cut loose in a storm-tossed sea. He didn't know what to think, what to believe. Every fibre of his being had told him to trust Raf. Could he have been so wrong? Sarita wouldn't have pushed him towards Raf if he was dodgy.

They'd all been there that night — Raf, Aurora and Nash. Maybe Dawn and Sasha too? He didn't know. They'd watched him throw himself off a bridge, they'd witnessed his darkest, rawest, most vulnerable hour.

He'd gotten used to the fact there were no secrets in this family, that his suicide attempt was public knowledge. And that was fine. He was man enough to own it. He'd just assumed Raf had been the one to tell them, to give them the full picture they needed to help him.

But that night on the bridge was a picture of which the pieces he was still assembling in his mind, that he was still sorting through, trying to deal with, to heal from. Because he never wanted to be there again. And they'd all helped him so much, they'd brought him back to life. Raf especially.

Before he'd come to Sedona, he'd been terrified of what he'd descended into, but now he was on his way to finding his place in the universe. He'd thought that place was here. For now, at least. But maybe he'd been wrong.

Indigo peered through the darkness as he walked, jaw clenched. It made no sense that Raf, that Micah, would spend so much time on him, if it wasn't genuine. And he knew Raf cared about him. But that night, on Bear Mountain Bridge, it can't have been a coincidence that they all just happened to be there.

"We knew you were going to be there before you even knew you were going to be there," Aurora had said that first day. Indigo's stomach twisted into a million tiny knots. *They'd known.*

They'd been watching him.

But for how long? They'd known he was going to try and kill himself before he had. Yet instead of waiting for him on top of the bridge and trying to talk him out of it, they'd waited at the bottom. And they'd done just enough to ensure he didn't die. When they were capable of so much more.

He thought of all the agony, all the broken bones, the months of rehab and meds, the counselling, the judgement, the pity and self-loathing, he had endured.

He'd counted these people as his friends, his family, his tribe. Obviously, they'd known he had powerful higher senses. He was a weapon. And in the wrong hands, any weapon can do infinite damage.

He was so wrapped up in the assault of thoughts pummelling his mind, he was no longer paying attention to his surroundings.

By the time he felt the presence behind him, it was too late.

Before he could even turn, something struck the back of his head and he felt himself crumple. Just before it all went dark, it flitted briefly through his mind that after all those weeks and months of training with Sasha, with Nash, with Aurora, all it had taken was for him to lose focus for a few moments for it all to have been in vain.

chapter twenty-three

beautiful girl

harbord, new south wales, april, 1995

cordelia

"Who're you drawing today, Matty-Moo?" Cordelia asked, glancing up from the heart she was doodling in pink crayon in the margin of one of his colouring books.

Matty didn't look up from the paper he was furiously scrawling on, his little tongue protruding from the side of his mouth. "Dat's Chati," he said, pointing to a small figure with shaggy black hair. "And dat's Roger, of course," he said, pointing to a long-bearded man dressed in a sloppy pinstriped shirt. Robbie always joked Roger looked like a convict.

"Let me guess," Cordelia said, leaning across the kitchen table, "the one you're colouring now is Care Bear?" He nodded as he drew a pair of knee-high boots on the figure that looked more girl than bear.

Matty was three now and loved to draw his imaginary friends — when he wasn't drawing his 'other' family, that is. He was always sketching them and chattering on about them, his 'other' mother, and his 'other' sister. One day, curious, Cordelia had pressed him on this 'other' family. Matty, almost condescendingly, had looked across the rug to where she was sitting cross-legged peering into his eyes.

He'd sighed heavily, as if the stupidity of mere mortals was too much for him to bear. "My other mother," he'd begun, "had short red hair and lived in a house made of sticks on a green hill. One day she stabbed me wiv a sharp thing, and now I live wiv you." He'd immediately turned his attention back to the little matchbox cars he was parking in his wooden garage, leaving Cordelia to stare at him, her spine tingling.

When Matty was a baby, the one he'd wanted most was Indigo, especially when he was colicky. The moment he was in Indigo's arms, Matty had stopped squirming, stopped crying. In a matter of seconds, he'd started smiling and cooing contentedly. But Indigo hadn't been around since Matty was one, and now Cordelia was the one he wanted most. She was the first to go to him when he had nightmares, kissing his damp forehead and whispering everything was ok, that it wasn't real.

Cordelia adored her baby brother, who captured the heart of everyone he met. Like Drew, who was round at the house more and more these days and could never say no to Matty's requests to toss a footy in the backyard.

Drew.

The day after the formal, she'd called to apologise. He'd been nonchalant, full of bravado, and then they hadn't spoken for a few weeks after that.

When she'd answered the phone one day and heard his voice on the other end, her stomach had done a little flip-flop, her mouth immediately turning up into a smile.

"I got in!" he was yelling down the phone. "I got into Medicine at UNSW!"

"Oh my God!" she'd cried, jumping up and down on the spot. *"That's amazing!* I'm so proud of you! We need to celebrate."

And so she'd dragged Sian and Will and Peyton along to meet him at his friend's house. And they'd spent the night catching up — purely platonically — but she'd found her mind constantly wandering back to that kiss, wondering what it might feel like to kiss him again.

But he didn't try again.

For weeks they hung out, but he always kept his distance.

The new school year had started and Cordelia began Year Twelve and Drew started uni. He continued to live at home with his dad and brothers to save money, so he was still close by in Curl Curl, just a suburb away.

And then one Friday night she'd been over at his house. His brothers and dad were out as they always seemed to be, and the two of them had been making pasta. He'd been giving her the highlights reel from his week at uni when the water began to boil over on the stove top. They'd both lunged for it at once, laughing as their hands overlapped on the saucepan handle. They'd awkwardly turned in unison and somehow found themselves pressed up against each other and just as he'd begun to apologise and back away, she'd reached up and kissed him. She hadn't planned it; it had just felt natural and she went with it in the moment. His lips had frozen beneath hers momentarily and then he was kissing her back, smoothly lifting her onto the kitchen counter so he could wrap his arms around her, drawing her tightly against him.

It had been nice. More than nice.

Robbie had been in his room, thumbing through a *Dolly* magazine, listening to Kylie Minogue, when she'd burst in later that night, swinging her car keys in her hand. When the twins started driving, their parents had gotten sick of juggling cars, so they'd bought a second hand silver Jeep for Robbie and Cordelia to share.

"We kissed," she'd announced, flopping down on the foot of his bed.

"Finally!" he'd cried, throwing his magazine down and sitting up. "How was it? No one did a runner this time did they?"

She'd snatched up the magazine and swatted him. "No, no running away this time. And it was good," she'd said, absentmindedly running her fingers over her lips. "It was really good."

"Details please," he'd demanded, settling back against his bedhead and listening intently as she told him almost everything.

"You're so lucky," he'd sighed, rolling over onto his stomach and resting his chin on the edge of the bed. "I wish I could meet someone. I mean, how am I meant to know if anyone else our age is harbouring homosexual tendencies when they're all still cowering in the closet?" He'd raised his eyes to the poster beside his bed. "If only Luke Perry were gay," he'd said.

"Your very own Luke Perry is out there somewhere, Rob," she'd said. "I'm sure of it." She'd reached out to squeeze his shoulder.

"I wonder what my future boyfriend is doing right now," Robbie had mused. "How can you miss someone so badly you've never met?"

Things with Drew had escalated pretty quickly after that night. The first time he'd officially told her he loved her, she'd hesitated, but she'd quickly come to realise that all love looks different and was special in its own right. The love she had for him was different from that she'd had for Indigo. With Indigo it had been a crazy butterflies-in-the-stomach, I'll-die-if-I-don't-touch-you, lightning bolt kind of love. But with Drew, it was a slow burn, comfortable and comforting like a warm bath on a cold rainy night. He was so sweet and he absolutely adored her. She knew he would never leave her, never hurt her. And he made her smile. They had fun together and their conversation never ran dry.

The next morning, Cordelia fell asleep in her yoga class during śavāsana. Her mother had encouraged her to join her in the practice when she'd been really down about a year ago, and she'd quickly become hooked. They went together every Saturday. She'd even started attending classes in the evenings on her own. She found that yoga high helped her study.

"You're snoring, sweetie," Mum said, shaking her shoulder, and she sat bolt up, glancing round the studio in horror. Luckily, the rest of the class had cleared out. She'd been up late with Matty the night before after another nightmare. It had taken her ages to resettle him. But it wasn't just that. The truth was, she'd been seeing a resurgence of bad dreams herself. Not like the old ones. These ones she branded bad dreams because she awoke from them with an anvil of guilt crushing down on her chest, feeling like she'd just cheated on Drew by dreaming about Indigo. Indigo in some strange Mars-like landscape, Indigo whispering her name, telling her he loved her. She'd almost forgotten what his voice sounded like, but in her dreams she heard it, deep and warm, and it brought chills to her spine. In the light of day, she shook those dreams off, banished them to where dreams go to die, and went about her day.

She lay awake in her bed each night, begging him not to haunt her, to let her sleep in peace, to just let her be happy. Because she *was* happy. She was settled and she was content and she woke up every morning looking forward to the day ahead.

That afternoon, she went round to Drew's. She frowned when she saw Sandy's red Honda Civic parked outside. Drew and Sandy were hanging out more and more these days. As she approached the house, she could hear the strains of Nirvana's *Lithium* drifting from out the back. She sighed heavily as she pushed the door open.

"Drew?" she called as she walked through the house.

"Out here, Cee!" he called back. She stuck her head out the back door and saw Drew and Sandy sprawled in chaise longues by the pool, which was so thick with mushy leaves it resembled cabbage soup. The minute Drew saw her, he jumped up, his face breaking into an enormous grin as he crossed the yard in three strides to sweep her into his strong arms. He brushed his lips across hers. He tasted like smoke. "You look really pretty," he murmured, looking her up and down. She smiled and whispered thanks, smoothing down the hem of the short black-and-white polka-dot dress she wore over a white t-shirt.

"Hi, Sandy," she said, glancing at him lounging there, a bong resting between his thighs. "Up to no good?" she asked, raising a sardonic eyebrow as Drew turned down the volume on the boombox.

"Just hanging out," Sandy said, flashing her his gummy grin. His eyes were bloodshot and bleary. He held the bong out to her. "Choof?" he offered. She shook her head. He passed it to Drew, who placed it on the ground, then pulled Cordelia into his lap, wrapping her in his arms and trailing his lips softly over the hollow of her cheek.

"I might head then, mate," Sandy said, standing up and pulling his car keys clumsily from his pocket.

"Sure," Drew said, nuzzling Cordelia's neck. "See you later, man." He held his hand out and Sandy slapped it on the way past.

"Bye, Sandy," Cordelia said, thankful he was leaving.

"See ya later, babe," Sandy grinned.

The minute the side gate closed behind him, Drew's lips found hers. He gently manoeuvred her onto her back on the chaise longue, covering her body with his. "I missed you," he whispered. She hadn't seen him since yesterday and she'd missed him, too. But she was also a little agitated.

"Productive day then?" she murmured between long slow kisses, his lips warm and strong and utterly distracting.

"Mmmmm?"

"You said you had to study this morning," she said, trying to focus with his hands wandering her body.

"I did. Sandy only got here like an hour ago." He stopped kissing her, pulled back. "I'm not stoned, Cee." She knew by his eyes that he wasn't.

"I know," she said as he bent to kiss her suggestively behind her ear, "but you taste like smoke."

"I had a ciggie to keep Sandy company," he said, his lips on hers again. He eased up onto an elbow, staring down at her. "I only quit smoking for the sake of my rugby career and that's well and truly over." He sat up then. "If I smell, I'll go brush my teeth."

She squeezed his hand and allowed him to lead her inside.

"Have you given any more thought to this ski trip in July?" he asked her later on as they lay on his bed listening to music. Her head was on his chest, her fingers under his t-shirt idly tracing the peaks and valleys of his ribs.

"Yeah, I definitely want to come," she said, her legs intertwined with his, her foot caressing his calf, "but I just don't know if it's the best idea with your knee."

"My knee's fine," he said, his hand roving under her dress and down the length of her thigh. "I'm not going to let it hold me back anymore."

"I don't know. Maybe we should speak to your doctor first?"

"Cee," he murmured, gazing down into her eyes, "I mean, come on, it's fine."

"As long as you're sure," she said, as he pulled her in close and started to kiss her so fervently her insides turned over and she lost the will to argue.

"I'm sure," he whispered as she arched against him and he tugged at her zipper. "I'm sure."

But in the end, being sure meant nothing. Their second day skiing in Thredbo, he hit a mogul too hard and popped his knee. Cordelia was devastated, but she was also angry because she'd known he wasn't ready for this, yet he'd pushed himself and now he was back to square one with his injury.

He needed more surgery. And the pain this time was even worse.

"Why don't you go see that psychic lady in the Blue Mountains again?" she asked him one night as he lay on his bed, tossing and turning, gritting his teeth against the pain while she rubbed his back in slow circles. "She helped last time."

"I'm not going back there," he said through clenched teeth, clasping his knee.

"But last time she helped. Things got much better."

"She and I don't see eye to eye," he said, sitting up and fumbling inside his bedside drawer. He stood and hobbled to the window in his pyjama bottoms, opening it wide and leaning out of it. She heard a flick and saw a flame and the smell of weed instantly reached her nose.

"Yuck, Drew, blow it outside. It stinks," she said, sitting up and fanning the air in front of her. "Your dad's gonna smell it."

"I can't sleep without it," he said as she climbed off the bed, wandered over to him, encircled his waist with her arms and rested her head against him. His chest hair tickled her nose.

He gazed out the window, seemingly lost in the stars above. "I wonder if they're watching us," he said softly.

"Who?"

"Our forefathers. You know, higher beings up there on other planets. The ones who shagged homo erectus to create us. One day they'll show themselves," he paused then, his eyes hardening. "Or not. I mean, why would they want to come back here to this shithole?"

"What do you mean?" she asked, pulling back to peer up at him.

"Look at the human race, Cee. We're a disgrace. War and famine and greed and hate… The unequal distribution of wealth, pollution, deforestation and destruction of the planet… All the wrong people have power. If we're an alien experiment, I'd say we failed."

"There's a lot of good down here too," she said, squeezing him tight. "There's so much love and beauty in the world, Drew. You just need to open your eyes and see it."

"*You* have so much goodness and beauty," he murmured, "and I have so much love for you." He shifted his weight and grimaced in pain, taking another deep drag on his joint. Her heart ached for him, it really did. She hated seeing him in such unrelenting agony. He held the joint out to her and she took it, taking a couple of puffs and passing it back to him. It wasn't the weed that bothered her so much as the baggie of speed she'd found in his desk drawer last week whilst searching for a pen. When she'd confronted him, he'd claimed half his class used it come exam time. It was really the only way to stay awake long enough to cram in all the information he needed to pass first year. He was thinner and paler and jittery and a little moody. She didn't like what it was doing to him and she'd told him that. She didn't know what to do anymore. Aside from just being there for him, she didn't know how to help him.

chapter twenty-four

losing my religion

sedona, arizona, may, 1995

indigo

Indigo was barely coming back to consciousness when he became vaguely aware of voices somewhere nearby. Both male, one older, one younger, the older one was unfamiliar, the other he'd heard before, but he struggled to place.

"I dunno about this," the familiar voice was saying. "You know he's Raf's boy, that he's one of them! Raf weren't happy when he got stabbed on accident, look what he did to us then! Imagine what he'll do when he finds out we taken his favourite kid?"

"Goddamn it, Skeet," the older voice chastised, "we've been through this a hundred goddamned times. I'd rather deal with Raf than *her* any day o' the week. Raf ain't a collector, so you know he won't be drainin' ya biofield 'n' sucking ya powers outta ya goddamn body with one goddamn look!"

Skeet. He knew that name. Indigo was groggy, his head pounding. He felt himself drifting off. No. He had to stay awake. He prised his eyes open and forced himself to focus. It was still dark, so he mustn't have been out long. He was lying on his side in the dirt. He could smell earth and pine. He squinted as his eyes adjusted to the dark. Trees. A fallen log. And he could see the silhouette of two men standing a few feet away. His hands and feet were throbbing. He tried to move his arms and legs, to sit up, but he couldn't. He glanced down. Both were bound.

He struggled against the ropes but realised pretty quickly it was no use. Whoever had bound him hadn't gone easy. They were too tight. He could barely bend his fingers, they were so swollen.

Skeet. The day he'd met Dawn and Sasha, it was Skeet they'd been chasing. Skeet, who'd kidnapped Reggie. Skeet, who'd stabbed him.

"I don't know, Pawpaw," Skeet was saying, "what does she even want with him? Is it cos he's Akasha?"

"Goddamn it, boy," Pawpaw snapped, "ya gittin' too big for ya britches with all these questions and opines. I'm fixin' to smack ya in ya mouth like ya mammy shoulda done had she stuck around some."

Indigo managed to manoeuvre himself to a seated position. He pulled his ankles in tight so he could reach his bindings with puffy fingers. He was beginning to lose feeling in the tips. He started to pick away at the ropes. But as he felt around the lengths, he couldn't seem to find a knot or any sign of a beginning or end to the fastenings.

"Alls I knows is what everyone knows — that when Reinenoir asks fer somethin' you git 'er done, no questions asked."

Indigo's hand slipped on the ropes, scuffling the leaf litter.

"Ah," Pawpaw said, turning towards him, "I see our friend 'ere's awake." He came into focus as he swaggered towards Indigo. He was a slip of a man, narrow rounded shoulders, a swollen pot belly supported by skinny bow legs. He was wearing dirty jeans and a plaid shirt worn threadbare. The crown of his head was bald, a ring of unkempt grey shag protruded from the lower half to hang stringily over his shoulders. "No use pickin' at them bindin's, boy," Pawpaw chastised. "They're done secured with somethin' more than a lick an' a promise." He gave a wheezy laugh, revealing a cavernous mouth sporting more gaps than teeth. The teeth he did have were the colour of overripe bananas.

Indigo glared up at him defiantly. "Untie me," he demanded.

Pawpaw chuckled again, pressing his hands to his hips and swaying back and forth on his heels. "I tell yer, he got gumption this one," he said to Skeet, who'd sidled up to stand slightly behind his grandfather. "Watch 'im," he barked to his grandson. "I'll go tell the others he's roused." He disappeared into the darkness.

Skeet averted his eyes from Indigo as he fished around in his pockets. He produced a book of matches and a crumpled pack of Camels, tapping one out and lighting it. He inhaled deeply, exhaling a steady stream of smoke. He offered one to Indigo who just glared at him.

"Who's Reinenoir?" Indigo asked, trying to flex his fingers to get some feeling back into them.

"What?" Skeet asked, and Indigo swore he paled somewhat.

"You were talking about someone called Reinenoir. Who is that?"

"You bullshittin' me? You don't know her?" Skeet said, taking another deep drag on his cigarette. "Like, honest?"

Indigo shrugged. "Never heard of her."

"Well, she sure as hell knows you," he said, narrowing his eyes. "She's gone to a hell of a lot of trouble to track you down." He regarded Indigo closely. "Surely you knows of her. She from the same parts as you. Infamous these days, she is."

"Infamous why?"

Skeet drew on his cigarette. "She powerful. Crazy powerful." Smoke rippled from his mouth as he spoke. "Fairly new on the scene, but she come from a *line,* she does, a real prominent one. She's grown a damn sight notorious." He squinted down at Indigo. "So what does someone like her want with someone like you?" he said, nudging Indigo's foot with his. "She a collector, so I guess she reckons what you got is worth collectin.'"

Indigo pursed his lips, glancing away. He didn't know what any of them wanted with him, but he knew he had to get away. Suddenly Sasha's voice popped into his head, demanding to know where he was. Indigo focused with all his might on the message he wanted to send back. Skeet stubbed his cigarette out under the heel of his boot.

"What's taking Pawpaw so long?" he muttered, turning and stalking off in the direction the old man had gone. "Don't you be going nowhere!" he called over his shoulder, guffawing at his own joke as he disappeared through the trees.

Indigo was wondering if Sasha had received his reply when he felt a graze of electricity against his arm. Sasha suddenly materialised beside him.

"You ok?" Sasha asked, moving to kneel in front of him.

"I guess."

Sasha looked around, frowning. His face relaxed as he nodded. "I've let the others know where we are, ya."

"No!" Indigo said, sitting bolt up.

"Oh." Sasha stared him straight in the eye, stricken. "Too late, sorry," he smiled apologetically. "We're close by looking for you. They won't be long."

Indigo squeezed his eyes shut. The pins and needles shooting through his hands and feet were being displaced with an engorged numbness. "I can't get out of these." He struggled against his bindings again.

"They're bound with dark magick, brah," Sasha explained.

Indigo blanched. "What?"

"Skeet and his family, they're a dark coven, eh. Their covenstead is about a quarter mile west of here."

"You're fucking with me, right? Their *covenstead?*"

"Their commune. Their evil lair," he grinned, shuffling round to sit beside Indigo in the dirt.

"How many of them are there?"

"More than there are of us, dude."

"How are you so relaxed about this?" Indigo asked, noting Sasha's casual posture, his easy expression.

"Because they're a bunch of inbreds — literally. They aren't too smart and we're more powerful."

"Inbreds? Like they… ?"

"They've always believed they can concentrate and multiply their power and keep their line pure by, er, keeping it in the family, if you know what I mean," Sasha explained with a slight shudder. "They're super sketchy. Anything goes out there, eh. Uncles and nieces, brothers and sisters, cousins…"

Indigo opened his mouth to reply but found himself speechless.

"They've recently begun to realise they may need to introduce new blood to their line, ya. Which is why Skeet was trying to entice Reggie into the fold."

"So, what do they want with me? They were talking about someone called…"

At the sound of hurried footfall he stopped talking and whipped his head around. Despite what had happened between them earlier that night, relief flooded his body when he saw Nash and Aurora emerge through the darkness. Following closely behind were another Sasha and Raf, his expression like ice. The Sasha sitting beside Indigo disappeared. Without breaking stride, Aurora aimed one hand at his ankles, the other at his wrists and his bindings snapped.

Nash held a hand out to Indigo. Indigo ignored it, standing up of his own volition, tight-lipped and cold-eyed.

"If that's the way you wanna be…" Nash muttered under his breath as Indigo shoved past him without a word. His feet were numb and he could barely walk.

"Need some help there, brother?" Nash called after him as he staggered towards Sasha.

"Nope."

"You ok?" Raf asked, placing a firm hand on Indigo's shoulder.

Indigo nodded tersely, avoiding his gaze.

"Move your asses," Aurora said. "They would have felt me disable their magick. They'll be on their way."

Already they could hear the scuffling crunch of heavy steps accompanied by yelling.

"Take him to the car," Raf said in a tone Indigo had never heard him use before. "I'll meet you there." He was white-lipped and fury rolled off him in waves.

"Move it," Aurora chastised Indigo as he limped through the forest as fast as he could on feet plagued with shooting pins and needles.

"I'm trying," he said through clenched teeth. Without a word, Nash hooked an arm around his waist, supporting his weight and dragging him along. Indigo reluctantly allowed it. He heard a loud bang and felt something whistle by his ear. Nash pushed him towards Sasha, who turned to grab him.

"Go!" Nash cried, turning back. Indigo saw Nash's palms were already writhing with bioplasma. "Shall we partake?" he said, cocking an eyebrow at Aurora.

"Totally," she said with a twinkle in her eye. The two of them took off running back the way they'd come. Indigo could no longer see them, but he could hear the chaos behind him.

"Stop," he said to Sasha, who was dragging him the other way. "We should go help."

"Hah!" Sasha scoffed. "Help? Against that lot? I think they'll be more than right, eh."

"But—"

"Indi. You can barely walk. And look at your hands, dude." Indigo glanced down. They were purple and swollen. "You'll be more of a hindrance than a help. Know when to quit, ya? Raf's totally got this. The only reason Nash and Rory are going back is for a play and a sticky beak."

Indigo nodded, his shoulders slumping in defeat as they reached Nash's maroon pickup parked to the side of a dirt track.

"Listen, Indi…" Sasha said, leaning against the car.

"Were you there that night?" Indigo asked, calmly, evenly.

"That night?"

"The bridge."

Sasha closed his eyes for a beat or two. "Yes," he finally responded, "and no."

Indigo looked at him questioningly.

"I'd been popping in on you for a while at Raf's request," he explained. "He'd asked me to keep an eye on you."

"Why?"

"Why?" Sasha glanced at him and frowned. "Because you're very special, Indi. You must know that now, ya?"

Indigo stared at him sullenly and shrugged.

"Nash had seen you on the bridge in one of his visions. He'd seen you jump, and he'd seen you die. And when you died, a light went out in the world. The ripple effect of your death…" He cleared his throat. "Well, we had to intervene."

Indigo stared at him, uncomprehendingly mute.

Sasha's shoulders slumped. "So that night, I was there, yeah." He regarded him closely. "We spoke. In the car. On the way to the bridge, remember?"

"I-I was so wasted, man," Indigo managed. "I don't remember much from that night. Until Raf. Did you try to talk me out of it?"

Sasha looked left, then right, then nodded curtly. "Unsuccessfully, obviously," he frowned. "But at the end of the day, I knew that no matter what, you weren't gonna die. So I left before you jumped."

"Why?"

"You were in capable hands, eh, it would have been purely voyeuristic of me to stay." He swallowed hard, looked down before slowly raising his eyes. "I-I didn't want to see that, Indi," he said in a low voice.

"But Raf was there," Indigo said, "and Aurora and Nash. But not Dawn?"

"No, not Dawn. She wasn't needed."

"Yeah, I know," Indigo bit, "you guys *wanted* me injured, you *wanted* me hurt."

Sasha gazed at him in his serious way. "Nash told me what Rory said, eh. And although it is the truth..." Indigo's eyes widened, "...it's not what it seems. I promise you, everything that was done on the bridge that night was done for your own good."

Indigo opened his mouth, but Sasha held his hand up before he could unleash. "Listen, once we get out of here, Raf will explain everything."

Indigo looked away, scowling, stomping his feet to get some feeling back into them. He eventually lifted his gaze, fixing Sasha. "Sash? You and me, we're mates, yeah?"

Sasha smiled his beatific smile. "Right on, man, I'd go so far as to say we're brothers. Your friendship means the world to me, Indi."

"So you wouldn't lie to me?"

Sasha placed his hand over his heart. "Not in a million years, brah."

"Can I trust Raf?" Indigo asked, his eyes boring into Sasha's, his body feeling all of Sasha's emotions, his mind wandering into Sasha's head.

Sasha didn't even skip a beat. "Yes," he said evenly, honestly, allowing Indigo into his mind. "I promise you. You can trust Raf."

He was telling the truth. And that had to be enough. For now.

All of a sudden, they heard panicked shouting and the night sky behind them lit up in a swirl of green and pink and blue, reminiscent of aurora borealis. Indigo flinched and stumbled against Sasha. "What the hell is *that?*" he spluttered.

Sasha grinned widely. "*That* is what happens when you fuck with Raf's family, eh," he shrugged.

Indigo stared at him, open-mouthed. By the time he'd climbed gingerly inside the car, Raf, Nash and Aurora had reappeared, strolling through the trees chatting casually.

"All good?" Sasha asked as Nash slid into the driver's seat and turned the key he'd left in the ignition.

"Piece of cake," Nash replied cheerfully as he gunned the engine.

"Raf was fucking magnificent," Aurora added, frowning at a chip in her gold nail polish.

"Why they decided to poke the bear is beyond me," Nash said as he bumped the car over the unpaved trail and onto the main road. "Have they lost their minds?"

"Well, if they hadn't before…" Aurora said with a cryptic smile.

Raf still hadn't spoken, sitting in stony silence in the passenger seat.

"They mentioned someone named Reinenoir," Indigo said, eyes flicking to Aurora beside him as she took a sharp breath. "Said they'd rather have to deal with Raf than her." She exchanged a glance with Sasha on her other side.

"Who's Reinenoir, guys?" he asked softly.

Their silence was deafening. Sasha finally replied, "That's what we'd like to know, eh."

"But you know *of* her?" Indigo probed, slowly opening and closing his fingers in an attempt to get some fresh blood into them.

"Yes," Raf said, finally speaking, "let's just say she's definitely come to our attention."

Nash was conspicuously quiet.

"Hang on," Indigo said, "that vision you showed me, the one Nash had of Cordelia being attacked. This Reinenoir's involved?"

Nash didn't say anything.

"Nash?" Indigo said.

"Oh, I didn't realise you were talking to me again," Nash said, his sarcastic tone barely covering the hurt.

"Seriously, man? Can you blame me?"

"Whatever," Nash muttered.

"Just tell me," Indigo said, leaning forward in his seat.

"If Cordelia's the girl you saw in the precognition of the beach attack, then yes, Reinenoir's involved," Nash sighed. "But that's all I know. No one knows who she is. Every time Sash or I try to get near her, she shrouds."

"Shrouds? I thought that only blocked people from reading your mind?"

"Not exactly," Nash said, "Reinenoir's different. She can block more than just her mind, it's like she can energetically camouflage herself. She, or someone close to her, has the ability to dome shroud, which means they pull the curtain down around themselves so they vanish from our radar. Anyway, I don't know what she wants with your Cordelia."

"Great," Indigo sighed, leaning back in his seat and closing his eyes. "I think I should leave. Head back to Sydney."

"Not yet," Raf said firmly, and Indigo's eyes flicked open. "You're not ready. You haven't nearly mastered what you're capable of yet. You'll be of no help to anyone until you have."

Anger roiled in the pit of Indigo's stomach. "You owe me an explanation," he said coolly, his eyes boring into the back of Raf's head. "Skeet and his family? Who are they exactly?" He turned to Sasha. "You said they were a coven, Sash. You didn't mean that literally, right?"

They all went deathly silent. Just when Indigo thought they weren't going to answer, Nash turned, looked him straight in the eye and said, "They're warlocks, man," before turning his attention back to the road.

"They're *what*?"

"Warlocks," Nash repeated. "As Sash said, Skeet's family, they're a coven."

"You're not serious? Like, covens and witches are just fairy tales from the Dark Ages, right?" They had to be messing with him.

"It's force of habit to view history with an air of superiority, Indi," Raf said, his eyes fixed on the road ahead. "We believe our ancestors were so primitive, so gullible, that our modern ways are far superior. But in a time before doctors, witches were healers, they were surgeons, midwives, and psychologists. A witch was an intuitive person of great wisdom people would go to for advice, herbal remedies, healings, abortions, difficult births, and the like. They treated their patients with remedies that had been passed down for generations, remedies deeply rooted in ancient culture."

"Skeet doesn't strike me as someone you'd go to for a home birth," Indigo said, raising an eyebrow.

"Not exactly, no," Raf said with a light chuckle. "But there's a whole other side to witches that's not so prominent in the history books." He shifted in his seat to face Indigo. "You see, Indi, amongst those witches was a much rarer subgroup you'd go to for potions and spells and charms and future telling. This group of men and women were gifted. They were psychic — clairvoyant and telepathic and empathic, amongst other things. Most were adept at seeing and accessing the human biofield," he said.

Indigo leant forward in his seat. "They had highly developed —"

"Higher senses, yes," Raf nodded.

"In its purist form," Aurora said, "these higher senses were passed down through craftist families, from grandmother to granddaughter, mother to son, uncle to niece. Those who inherited their higher senses from their family line were referred to as hereditary witches. A lot of these families claim to be descended from the Water City —"

"Water City?" Indigo interrupted.

"Atlantis," she said. "But of course, there were also solitary witches with no familial ties to the craft, and they would often seek out a prominent coven to study under."

"You see, Indi," Raf said, "that specific branch of witchcraft is still around today. And if you hadn't already figured it out, it encompasses people like Dawn, and Sasha, and Nash and Rory and me and… you."

"*Me?*" Indigo balked.

"Maybe you've noticed we kinda possess abilities that others do not?" Sasha asked, hitching his brows and grinning.

Indigo made a face at him.

"And what do you think you are, Indigo, someone who is able to access such things?" Raf asked.

"Dunno. A freak of nature? I never knew there was a label for it."

"Some do call us witches," Raf said, "and in some ways we are, but in many ways we are not. Yes, we are a subset of the witch and it is where our history lies, but personally, I do not like that label."

"Urgh, I bloody *hate* it!" Nash groaned. "It makes me feel like I'm expected to own a black cat and have a solid supply of eye-of-newt in my cupboard at all times."

"So, what are we?"

"In ancient times we were known as Warriors of the Akasha, but these days we're known simply as Akasha," Raf said.

"Akasha," Indigo murmured, trying out the word.

"We are elite witches bestowed with higher senses, born unto this world to ensure balance is kept — which means we need to leave this planet in a better state than in which we found it." He frowned. "And then there are warlocks like Skeet."

"He's Akasha too?"

"No," Sasha answered, his face darkening, "Warlocks are the opposite of Akasha, our mortal enemy, if you wanna be dramatic about it. They too, have advanced higher senses, but they use their powers for self-serving purposes. That's why Skeet's family are banned from crossing into Sedona, eh. They cause too much mischief. As far as warlocks go, Skeet's family's magick isn't very powerful — it certainly isn't what it used to be."

Nash turned to glance at Indigo. "All the interbreeding," he reiterated, his nose wrinkling. "You wanna picture their family tree as one long spindly branch."

"But there are warlocks out there who *are* powerful?" Indigo asked.

"Very much so, ya," Sasha nodded grimly.

"Reinenoir?" Indigo asked, his breath catching.

Sasha pursed his lips and nodded. "She's notorious for collecting the energy from her victims' biofields, along with any higher senses they might have."

"So when Skeet was talking about her being a collector, that's what he was referring to?"

"Yup. She absorbs their life force and powers, adding them to hers."

Indigo looked up as he realised Nash was turning into Raf's street. "I'm not ready to go home yet," he said quietly.

"That's ok," Raf said, smiling gently at him as Nash pulled up in his driveway. "Come home when you're ready." He reached to squeeze Indigo's knee, then climbed out of the car. "Thanks guys, well done tonight," he said, looking each of them in the eye before closing the door softly behind him.

Nash dropped Aurora home, then the three boys went back to Sasha and Nash's place. Indigo didn't feel much like talking to them either, so he headed quietly into their spare room where he collapsed onto the bed and, after much tossing and turning, fell into a deep sleep.

chapter twenty-five

by my side

indigo

When Indigo arrived back at the house the next day, Raf came striding out of his study, his face creased with worry. Indigo had spent most of the morning at Sasha and Nash's, gathering the strength to come home and face Raf. His head was still swimming with everything that had been revealed the night before.

"Indi!" Raf cried, closing the gap between them in a few quick strides. He drew Indigo into his arms and held him in a tight embrace. Indigo's arms hung limply at his sides as Raf's emotion ebbed over and through him.

"I'm so sorry about last night, buddy," Raf told him. "For all of it. I never want to cause you any pain or give you any reason to mistrust me." Raf released him and indicated the couch. "Please, sit. Let's talk. Are you ok?"

Indigo laughed, short and sharp. "That's a bit of a loaded question, isn't it? Am I ok because I was kidnapped by a coven of *warlocks*? Am I ok because I just found out I'm a member of an elite group of *witches*? Or am I ok because I've just discovered the man I looked upon as a-a *father* sat back and watched me jump off a bridge and did *nothing* to stop me?" He sat stiffly on the couch, arms crossed, and faced Raf, who'd settled himself into his usual armchair.

"I'm sorry, Indi, I truly am," Raf said, his eyes bright.

"Why didn't you tell me sooner? About the Akasha stuff? I mean, that's why you saved me that night, right?" he snapped. "If I was any ordinary person, you would have left me to drown."

"That's not fair. It's more complicated than that, buddy."

Indigo sat back and glared at him.

"Indigo," he said, looking up grimly, "your higher senses, they're so strong, so advanced, back then they'd completely overtaken you. You were overrun with thoughts and feelings and a collective agony that wasn't yours, and when added to all that pain you were feeling so deeply from what was happening in your life, well, that night on the bridge, you were so far gone…" He swallowed hard, gripping the armrest, his knuckles white as he looked at Indigo with an intensity he'd never seen before. "You need to know, it took every last fibre of my being not to step in and stop you from hitting that water. But if you'd come out of that experience unscathed, you wouldn't be sitting here with me today, bud."

"How do you know that?" Indigo demanded, sick to his stomach.

"Because if Aurora had caught you instead of just slowing you down, you would have walked away and simply tried again another day. Nothing would have changed for you. You needed help."

"And you couldn't've helped me without letting me break like, half the bones in my *body?!*" Indigo interjected angrily.

"You wouldn't have listened," Raf argued, templing his fingers under his chin.

"How do you *know that*?"

"Because there was barely any of *you* left!" Raf cried, slamming his hands down onto his armrests. Indigo had never seen Raf lose his composure. "Indigo," he said passionately, "you were so, so broken back then. You'd chosen not to live anymore, for God's sake! We didn't have a shot at getting through to you when you were that far gone." He shook his head, his jaw tight. "You needed to face the consequences of your actions, Indi. When someone just steps in and rescues us, we learn nothing. Sometimes we need to sit in our own mistakes and find the strength to want to save ourselves."

"Yeah, I get that," Indigo snapped, "but I feel like you're dodging the question."

Raf gazed thoughtfully at the ceiling before continuing. "Once you were stable and you were strong enough to fight for yourself, and you had the drive to want to be the real you, that's when we knew we had the capability to help you," Raf said, his face softening as he looked at Indigo who refused to meet his eye. "Mental health, Indi... there's so much we now know about it — the chemical aspect, the emotional aspect, the psychological aspect... and those were the aspects you needed to deal with first. Before we could help you deal with the rarer area we're well versed in — the paranormal aspect."

Indigo set his jaw. He knew Raf bringing him to Sedona was what had saved him: the fresh air, the abundant sunshine, the clean diet and daily exercise. And yes, of course, learning to manage his higher senses.

"There are things you need to know, buddy... Things I think maybe only Micah can explain."

Indigo shrugged, even though his curiosity had been piqued.

Raf leant back in his armchair. Indigo's eyes fixed on Raf's face as he was slowly usurped by Micah. With a jolt, Micah sat upright, stretching his hand stiffly towards Indigo, a soft smile playing upon his lips.

"Ah yes, it is always, always good to see you," he said, gazing through slitted eyes. "Please, allow me to tell you today the story of a young boy and his one true love." By now, Indigo knew Micah was not one to waste time with small talk.

"I want to take you back to a time the world was very different from what it is now. We are looking back around four thousand years to the island of Crete. This was the time of the Minoans. And I apologise here, because most people, when you speak to them of past lives, want to believe they were someone very, very famous in history; Cleopatra or Napoleon or Socrates. They don't understand that just because someone is not remembered in the history books, it does not mean they were not important or their impact on the world was not important. Because every single person throughout history has impacted the lives of those around them, and by doing so, has left their footprint in the sands of time and changed the course of the world in at least some small way." Micah paused for a moment to let that sink in before continuing.

"So it was for the boy in my story today, who was the son of a beekeeper. You may not know this, but the Minoans domesticated bees and this boy helped his grandfather maintain the hives and harvest the honey." Familiar images swum through Indigo's head: an elderly man with sun-weathered skin and bushy white eyebrows, his face a crumpled heap of delight. The grandfather. Grandfather and mentor.

"Like his grandfather before him, this boy, he had a way with bees. His grandfather, who was his greatest friend and confidant, had brought him up to love and respect those bees, and he had a way with them that no one else did. He understood that the fate of bees and mankind were intertwined, and without bees to pollinate the crops and to grow the trees and flowers and plants that were the habitats and sustenance for other animals in the food chain, the human race would struggle to survive. And with that knowledge, he gave his bees the respect and admiration they deserved.

"In all his years working with them, he was never once stung because the bees knew he understood them and was on their side. He kept those bees healthy and met their needs, and from a very young age, he would lie out amongst the hives, letting the bees crawl all over him. He could communicate with those bees, you see, he could talk to them using pictures in his mind, and they with him. The bees knew if they were feeling unwell, they could heal themselves simply by landing upon the palms of the boy's outstretched hands where the energy was beautiful and strong."

Indigo could see the images of the story in his head as clearly as if Micah had projected them onto a movie screen. He could see the immaculately kept hives, the stacked stone houses, the boy's tanned face and large weathered hands as if they were his own. It was all so real he could feel the sea breeze upon his skin, could smell the freshness of the brine carried upon it.

Micah rested his hands lightly on his knees, arms straight, shoulders back, as he continued with his story.

"Word soon got around that this boy could communicate with and heal insects. And the other beekeepers came to him whenever they had a problem with one of their hives, and he would go to their properties, and he would heal their bees, too. And then one day a girl came to see him. She was from a neighbouring community and she was desperate for help. A sickness was spreading through her family's sheep and they'd already lost most of the flock. She'd heard of the boy with the magic hands who healed bees, and she wondered if his talents extended to mammals.

"He was lying out in the sunshine in his apiary when the girl approached him. The boy sat up as she called out to him, and shading his eyes from the sun, he gazed up at her. And the very moment he laid eyes upon that girl, he knew. He knew that until the end of time, the sun would rise and set with her. And she? She knew with a jolt of soul recognition that destiny had led her to him. At his grandfather's urging, he went with her to her property, where he discovered his talents did in fact, extend to other animals. He managed to save the rest of her family's flock. Her father was so, so full of gratitude he agreed to his daughter's pleas to grant the boy her hand in marriage."

A picture washed into Indigo's mind, growing sharper by the moment. The girl with the almond-shaped eyes, so familiar, a tumble of ebony hair hanging to her waist, her body bronzed and athletic. She had the grace of a dancer and a smile that teased at memories he couldn't quite grasp. All he knew was that she made him feel something, this girl, something that felt very much like love.

"And so," Micah said, his expression softening, "the girl became his whole world, and he hers. She moved with him to his property so he could continue to tend to his hives. His family adored her just as he did, especially his grandfather, with whom she developed a special bond. They lived happily together, laughing, loving, playing. And then one day, when they'd been married some time and the girl was pregnant with their first child, she came out to the apiary to bring him his midday meal. He was busy tending to his bees, so she slipped her shoes off so she could sneak up behind him and surprise him. She did not see the one lone bee crawling on the ground, and she stepped on it. As you might know, when a bee is stepped upon, its instinct is to sting. The boy turned as she cried out, and he saw her clutching her foot and falling to the ground. By the time he reached her, her skin was covered in large red welts and she was having great difficulty breathing, grappling at her throat, unable to speak. He took her in his arms, yelling for help. But help did not come. He lay his hands on her, trying to heal her the way he healed the animals, but she was too far gone, too far gone, and it was not to be. She died there in his arms, taking his unborn child with her."

With these words, Indigo felt a physical pain in his chest, the hopelessness of unimaginable loss, of a shattered heart. He clenched his hands into fists, barely feeling his nails digging into his palms as he recalled a long-ago day, sitting with Cordelia on a beach at sunset, listening to her talk about a dream that very much mirrored the story being told to him now. His stomach lurched, the blood thundering in his ears.

"The boy was broken into a thousand pieces," Micah continued, his voice thick with compassion. "The world had shifted on its axis in the blink of an eye and just like that, he'd lost everything. He blamed himself and he could not bear to be around his once beloved bees a moment longer. He carried her body to the edge of the sea and waded out with her to where the water was deep and blue and he could no longer stand, and then he began to swim, still with her cradled in the crook of his arm. And he swam and he swam until he was spent and he could no longer keep his head above water. You see, he couldn't bear to live without her. 'I'm coming, my love,' he murmured. 'Wait for me, I am coming.' And with the girl still clutched tightly in his arms, he went under one last time, allowing the ocean to take him to a place of peace, a place where he believed he and she would continue their journey together forever. As one, they sank to the inky blackness of the ocean floor, and as the water flooded his lungs displacing any remaining air, he vowed to never, never let her go again, to love and hold her there in his arms for all of eternity."

Indigo exhaled shakily.

"When night fell and they hadn't returned," Micah said, "his grandfather went out looking for them. He searched and searched for hours, days and weeks, refusing to give up, even when everyone else told him it was hopeless. You see, their loss, it broke the old man's heart. In fact, a month later, when he was walking along the seashore still desperately searching for a sign of the boy and his wife, his heart gave out there on the pebbly beach and he passed over to reunite with them."

Micah paused to gather his thoughts. Indigo tasted salt and realised his cheeks were wet with tears. He raised his palms to his face, wiping it dry as best he could. He'd felt that story to his very core. He *knew* that story; it was familiar to him in the same way the stories on the pages of the dog-eared books of his childhood were familiar to him. And the love Micah had described? He recognised that love, knew it like the back of his hand.

"You see," Micah suddenly lurched forward as he continued, "the thing about souls who decide to take their own lives is we find it's not the first time they've chosen to return to spirit in that way. The human condition is to repeat experiences you haven't let go of. We find the souls who commit suicide have done so at least once before, if not several times before, the belief that it is a solution to their problems becoming a habit. And believe me when I tell you, suicide is never a solution. It will never solve your problems."

Indigo sucked his breath in sharply through his teeth.

"I believe," Micah said, "that for you to truly make peace with your past and move forward, it is vital for me to explain the timing of death to you. I have just told you about one of your previous lives, and I can see you recognised yourself. You may have even recognised the girl in that story, and the grandfather too, may be familiar to you," he said, tapping his leg — Raf's leg — grinning at his brazen hint. Indigo's head was awhirl. He sure as shit recognised the girl in that story; it was a story he'd heard from her own lips.

"Now," Micah continued, "no matter how it is written, your death is a decision made between you and your guardian. Obviously, this is not done on a conscious level, but no matter how you die, whether it be by murder, from cancer, from a heart attack, from drowning, please know that you agreed to it.

"*But* there is one loophole here." Micah leaned forward from his waist so his face was close to Indigo's. "Just one. And that is suicide."

Indigo gritted his teeth. He had a feeling this was going to be hard to take. He took a steady breath and readied himself, closing his eyes so he could focus only on Micah's words.

"Suicide is the one exception to the rules surrounding death. It is the epitome of the soul going rogue and shutting out its guardian, ignoring their advice and intricate planning. You see, sometimes it seems you may be a little ambitious when planning your life. You may have big, big lessons to learn, so you pack your life full of hardships and sorrow and mountains that, upon approach, just seem too high to climb. Let me say right now, though, that any roadblock or problem in your life, no matter how devastating and seemingly unsurpassable, was thoroughly assessed by both you and your guardian prior to incarnation and deemed surpassable. It wouldn't be there if there was no way around it. That's just not how it works.

"There are always options in place to get through it. But the problem arises when you're down there living that life with all the emotion and all the fears and all the thoughts and distractions that come with being human. And you've forgotten why you're there, in that body, living that life. You've forgotten the fact that you yourself actually agreed to the very earth-shattering devastation you are sitting in right that very moment. And humans are conditioned to view pain as purely negative, as something to dull and mute and sweep under the rug. You humans hate pain, you just hate it."

Indigo pulled a face. It wasn't every day he was disparaged by a discarnate and he wasn't quite sure how to feel about it.

Micah's expression was serious now, his tone no-nonsense. "So when something seems unsolvable, unfixable, and like there's no way out or over or through, and the person feels utterly broken, utterly alone in the dark, well, their thoughts get the better of them and they call time out. They wish to push the reset button, so to speak. They choose to switch off and reboot and start all over again. All. Over. Again.

"Suicide is committed without the permission of their guardian, and without discussion with their guardian," Micah frowned. "Now, despite what many humans believe, I promise you that for those who choose to end their own lives, there is no purgatory, there is no eternal hell. I've already explained to you that you are always met with only love and compassion and support when you cross to the in-between. But — and this is very, very important," Micah said, inclining his head slightly, "committing suicide only means you have to come back and do it all over again. All. Over. Again. And you will indeed have to do it over and over again until you complete what you're meant to complete. And for those who have taken their own lives, with each lifetime, it will grow harder and harder. There is absolutely no escaping it in the end. You cannot go over or under or around, you can only go through."

"Were you ever human?" Indigo asked tightly, unable to hold his tongue, because how could a discarnate who'd never had a body, never lived here on earth, understand how dark and hopeless and desperate a person could actually feel?

"Yes," Micah replied, "although not since the time of Atlantis."

"The world has changed a lot since then," Indigo ventured.

"Indeed, it has. But I have always been here watching, observing, and I can tell you there has always been hate and there has always been pain and there has always been cruelty and death and loss and sickness and war."

After their session, Raf sunk back into his chair, hugging a knee into his chest. "You ok?" he asked, stretching his neck from side to side.

"You were my grandfather," Indigo said.

Raf met his eyes steadily. "Yes."

They were silent for a while. Indigo sensed that Raf would not push him further unless Indigo wanted him to.

"Micah, he… he talked about suicide," he ventured quietly.

"I know, buddy," Raf replied lightly. "Did what he had to say resonate with you?"

"Yeah it did…"

"But?"

Indigo paused for a moment, deep in thought. "But I guess it's pretty hard to hear that everything that went wrong in my life, everything that led me to that bridge that night, was on some level my own choice."

"Of course it is," Raf said with a gentle smile.

"That information, it might have come in handy on top of that bridge," Indigo scowled.

"Would you have listened?" Raf asked, challenge in his eyes.

Indigo opened his mouth to give a sarcastic reply but remembered how far gone he'd been, how out of it, how intent he'd been on ending it all.

Raf glanced at the clock on the wall. "Look, I've got someone coming in a minute," he said, "but I really want to make sure you understand why I did what I did that night?" He looked at Indigo earnestly.

Indigo sighed. "Nah, yeah, I *get* it. But I don't know if I one hundred percent *agree* with it. I'm sorry, Raf."

"Why are you sorry?"

"Uh…" Indigo stumbled, "I guess I'm sorry because for me to disagree with you feels disrespectful."

"How so?"

"Uh, well, you know as well as I do you're way more knowledgeable about this stuff than me."

Raf shook his head. "No, Indigo," he said gently, "I want you to make your own mind up about everything that comes your way. If something I say doesn't sit well with you, then speak up. It means you're coming into your own power and that you're really starting to know yourself. No matter what you think of me, Indi, at the end of the day I'm only human, here, just like you on this lonely blue planet floating through space, trying to make sense of being in this world and in this body."

Indigo shrugged. "Why did you never tell me I was Akasha?"

Raf sighed. "That's a fair question. And to be honest, I'm angry with myself, because I thought I could protect you for longer by keeping you in the dark. It's a pretty big thing to dump on somebody. I was working up to it, waiting for the right time. And I guess last night was it. I realised this morning that who you are, what you are, it was always gonna catch up with you whether I liked it or not."

Just then, there was a knock at the door. They both stood. Raf placed a strong hand on Indigo's shoulder. "Being Akasha means you're a part of something very special, Indi. It means that no matter where you are in the world, we'll always be family. Because we are your soul family, and we are bound by a bond greater than space and time, life and death."

Indigo nodded and Raf squeezed his shoulder.

"Think about what I said," he said as he went to the door. "Take your time. We'll talk again when you're ready."

Indigo always made himself scarce when Raf had people over. He quickly showered and threw on a pair of black pants and a clean t-shirt, then quietly slipped out the back door so not to disturb Raf's session. He climbed onto his motorcycle. He needed a ride to get some fresh air and clear his head.

He revved the engine and took off up the street, heading for Oak Creek Canyon. Aside from running, he did his best thinking while riding, and this ride was one of his favourites. A winding road climbing four-thousand-five hundred sheer feet up a canyon between Sedona and Flagstaff, complete with hairpin turns and switchbacks, the expansive views over steep red rock cliffs, oak foliage and evergreen pines were nothing short of breathtaking.

On his way back down, he pulled over near the mouth of the canyon at a deserted stretch of river upstream of Slide Rock. He stripped down to his Calvins and dived in, stroking powerfully through the clear water. The water was gaspingly icy and prickled his skin deliciously. He clambered up onto a large rock, flat and warm like a pizza stone, and lay on his back, closing his eyes against the sun's rays beating down upon him. Water droplets collected and ran in rivulets off his tingling skin, finding their way back into the creek below. A wayward bee buzzed past him, then circled back to land gently on his chest. He allowed it to rest there, enjoying the feel of its tiny legs as it waddled over him.

As he lay there, the crook of his elbow draped lazily over his eyes, his thoughts drifted back to his conversation with Raf.

Would he have listened if Raf had approached him on the bridge that night and offered him help? Possibly, but probably not. He'd made up his mind and just wanted it over.

But if Aurora had stopped his fall, well, maybe the pure proof in the miracle of his unscathed survival would have been enough to get through to him.

In the end, it came down to whether or not he trusted Raf. And quite simply, he did. After all, he could feel Raf's emotions, hear his thoughts.

Indigo lazily trailed his fingers through the water bubbling past. It was an iridescent blue-sky kind of day, the sun high and blazing with all its might. Its rays on his skin were recharging and rejuvenating him. This really was an idyllic part of the world. But as much as he loved it there, he missed home.

Home.

He hadn't set foot in Australia in over two years.

In his eyes, Sedona, with its soaring red rocks, sculptural cacti and babbling creeks, was a close second to Manly with its white sand beaches, towering Norfolk Pines and roaring surf. Sedona had captured a piece of his heart and he would always be grateful for his time there, but Manly, it was his home.

In Sedona, he was happy and he was surrounded by like-minded people who had quite literally saved his life and given it value.

But he couldn't stay forever.

As great as this life was, there was a shadow looming over it, growing daily in strength and prominence. What he'd done to the Carlisles… cutting them off after everything they'd done for him, when they meant everything to him. Now he was no longer so consumed with himself, with his pain, with his illness. Now it all came crushing back on him and sometimes he could barely breathe when he thought of the hurt he'd caused, of the despicable way in which he'd behaved.

He'd soon have to start thinking about going home to Sydney. He knew his return would be complicated. But he couldn't put it off much longer. Nash's precognition had been proof of that. But there were amends to be made. Explanations to be given. And, possibly most terrifying, true love to be declared.

True love, it seemed, that spanned lifetimes.

He knew now that he'd loved Cordelia in another time and place when they were different iterations of themselves. Different, but fundamentally the same.

He'd lost her then.

He couldn't lose her now.

Indigo rode straight to Dawn's that afternoon where he was due to treat patients. He still worked out of her clinic four afternoons a week, largely seeing patients everyone else had placed in the 'too hard' basket.

His last patient of the day was a five-year-old girl named Daisy who had suffered chronic ear infections her whole life. The infections were so bad she had pus constantly streaming from her ears, and she had permanent holes in her eardrums as a result. It wasn't as simple as patching up the holes and sending her on her way. Indigo needed to work out where the bacteria causing the infection was coming from and why her body had reacted this way.

Daisy's diet wasn't ideal and the environment in her gut was a perfect breeding ground for the bacteria invading her body. Her guardian advised him Daisy was highly clairaudient and she was subconsciously, but purposefully, allowing her body to fill her ears with pus in an attempt to block the messages being conveyed to her from the discarnate world. One thing at a time. He gave Daisy's mother the instructions for her new diet and asked them to come back next week.

When Indigo knelt down to say goodbye to Daisy, she'd thrown herself into his arms and refused to let go, burying her head in his chest and clinging to his neck with spindly little arms.

"Children know a kindred spirit when they see one," Dawn had remarked after Daisy and her mother left. She and Indigo were having dinner together on her back patio. Earl had taken the girls to Phoenix to do some shopping and they wouldn't be back 'til late.

"How am I going to explain to a five-year-old that she doesn't need to be afraid of the disembodied voices she hears?" Indigo sighed. "I mean, it's hard enough for most adults."

"Kids are easier," Dawn told him. "They're much more open and perceptive and their heads don't get in the way all the time. Most adults have been consistently told discarnates don't exist and that hearing voices is a sign they're not right in the head. Children don't yet have these belief systems in place. They're a lot closer to the discarnate world than adults are, as they were a part of it much more recently."

"So, you're saying I can just give it to Daisy straight?"

"Absolutely," Dawn assured him. "She's gifted, so what you tell her will resonate with her."

Indigo nodded thoughtfully as he ate. Dawn had grilled him a piece of fish, which was a bit of a novelty for him these days. Living with Raf, he'd eaten vegan these past months, only having meat when he was at Sasha and Nash's.

"I hear you had an interesting day yesterday, honey," Dawn ventured as she speared a hunk of broccoli with her fork.

"Mmm?" Indigo murmured, his thoughts still on Daisy.

"Yesterday," Dawn prompted him, "I hear you had a bit of a crisis of faith?"

"Are you talking about Skeet?" he asked, reflexively flexing his fingers, which were still sore and a little swollen.

Dawn grimaced. "I heard about that too," she said darkly, "and I can't say I'm not glad that monstrous beast finally got what was coming to him. But I'm actually talking about what happened before that."

"Oh," he said, scowling. "Were you involved, Dawny?" He put his knife and fork down and looked at her. "I mean, I know you weren't there that night on the bridge, but did you know what they had planned?"

"Yes, sweetie," Dawn admitted without an ounce of hesitation. "I knew."

"So you approved?"

"It was the only way." She placed her hand over his with a reassuring squeeze. "I promise you, honey, we talked it through uphill and down dale, and the scenario we went with was the one we kept arriving back at. There was no other way. You've spoken to Raf now, so you know that."

Indigo sighed deeply. "Yeah," he eventually replied, staring at the table. "I know. It just kinda... hurts, you know?" He raised his eyes to meet hers, big and bright and sympathetic.

"I know, Indi," she smiled sadly.

"I just wish Raf had told me from the very beginning," he said, picking up his fork and stabbing his last bite of halibut aggressively.

"You weren't ready then. There were more important things to wade through. If we'd added that into the mix, on top of everything else? Well, it would've been too much. I know this sounds patronising, but it was for your own good. I promise you Raf had every intention of telling you eventually." She paused and regarded him for a beat or two before adding, "Just like he had every intention of telling you *everything*, eventually."

"Yeah, it's not every day you find out you're a member of a secret club of witches," he glowered.

"We don't like that word," she said lightly.

"Yeah, yeah, so everyone keeps telling me."

"Being Akasha," she said, her expression serious, "comes with a lot of responsibility, honey." She stared at him fixedly. "And a lot of danger. Once you know what you are, well, it changes things, right?"

"I guess." Indigo realised she had a point.

"Raf's biggest weakness is his overprotectiveness of those he loves. And you? You especially he has great affection for. He's grown to adore you, sweetie, and if that's influenced the things he's tried to shield you from, well, he's only human."

"What exactly did Raf do?" Indigo asked, "to Skeet and his coven?"

"Raf's retaliation is always swift but fair," she said elusively.

"They were *scared* of him," Indigo said, marrying his knife and fork down the centre of his empty plate.

"Don't mistake Raf's kindness for weakness, Indi. You wouldn't want to be on his bad side. And the thing about Diego Rafael," she said, leaning forward conspiratorially, "is that he's laid back and he's got an enormous heart and he's content with what he has. But I've always felt he's an iceberg: we've only ever seen the tip of what he can do, and there's great power beneath the surface he's yet to fully tap into."

"Why hasn't he?"

"Because he's never needed to. But it's only a matter of time before something motivates him to delve a little deeper and unleash something bigger." She paused to take a sip of her drink. "What he did to Skeet and his coven yesterday, well, it's been a long time coming."

"He didn't like..." He ran his finger across his throat in a slicing motion.

"Raf?" Dawn gasped. "Heavens to Betsy, never! Look, when it comes to the people he loves, you do not want to cross Raf. Because of all he's lost in his life..." she frowned wistfully, "Well, it's only made him hold his kin more dear. But he lives by a strict moral code. He did what needed to be done."

"Which was?"

"Let's just say that although they will forever be warlocks, they will no longer have any recollection of being any different to any other person on the street."

"He wiped their memories?" he breathed.

She nodded. "Not without warning. They knew the consequences of crossing him again."

"But how?"

Dawn placed her knife and fork down and regarded him closely. "I told you, sweetie. Raf has powers not even I can comprehend."

september, 1995

"When's Raf back from San Diego?" Sasha asked, feet propped on the coffee table, eyes glued to the TV. His beloved Cardinals were playing and Indigo knew the fact he was speaking meant it was an ad break.

"Sunday arvo," Indigo replied from the kitchen where he was helping Nash with dinner. Raf had been away visiting his father for the past week and Indigo had really missed him. "I'm picking him up from the airport around four."

Aurora shushed them from beside Sasha on the couch. "It's back on." Her ponytail fell sleekly over her shoulder as she leant forward in her seat, rubbing her hands together, muttering, "Come on, Bird Gang."

Sasha and Nash's two-storey Spanish-style bungalow had become a second home to Indigo these past eighteen months. The house, with its white and brown palette, was heavy on terracotta and wrought iron and exposed timber beams. Sasha's cherished potted succulents and cacti were clustered in small groups all over the living area along with an abundance of candles in all shapes and sizes, most of them never having met with a match.

Nash rolled his eyes. "The sacrilege of daring to speak when the Cards are playing," he said to Indigo, thrusting a platter into his arms. "Those ribs must be done by now." Indigo followed him out under the white stucco arch that framed the back door towards the smoker, where Nash proceeded to lift the lid and lovingly examine each and every rack of baby backs. When Nash had moved to the States, he hadn't gotten into gridiron, but he'd developed a passion for grilling and smoking meat. "Oooh yeah," he said with a big grin, snapping his tongs, "you can call me Grill Master."

"Yeah nah, that's never gonna happen," Indigo said, holding out the platter so Nash could heap the ribs onto it. "Hey, have you ever met Raf's father?"

"Matias? Yeah, he usually comes for Christmas. He didn't come last year because he was on that cruise. He's a nice guy, was totally wild in his youth, so I hear, but he's mellowed out a lot in his senior years."

"He and Raf are close, though?"

"Well, it's just the two of them," Nash said as they headed back inside. "Matias is the only relative Raf has."

"Yeah," Indigo replied. Raf had told him that. "He said his mum hadn't spoken to her adoptive family since way before she died, so he has nothing to do with them?"

"Yup, and Matias lost contact with his family back in Chile when he left there in the fifties or something."

Indigo nodded thoughtfully. "At least they have each other," he mused as he took the dressing Nash handed him and drizzled it generously over the salad.

"Whoa, go easy there, mate," Nash scolded, grabbing the bottle off him. "Raf and Matias are totally different, but they seem to have an understanding. Raf told me once his father didn't speak to him for like two months when he was fifteen because he dropped out of school."

"Raf dropped out at fifteen?" Indigo repeated. "I knew he didn't finish school, but I didn't realise he'd left so young."

"Yeah, he had learning difficulties. Dyslexia apparently. And back in those days, well, you can imagine his teachers weren't exactly sympathetic."

"But Raf... he's a writer! How can he be dyslexic?"

"Well, he's not *anymore*," Nash explained, rummaging through the cutlery drawer. "He found a way to treat it, obviously."

"How?"

"He said he had his brain and primitive reflexes realigned, amongst other things, and he's been able to read and write perfectly well ever since."

"By who?" Indigo asked, roughly tossing the salad. Nash frowned and confiscated the servers.

"An Aboriginal medicine man in the Northern Territory of Australia. And now look at him. He's living, breathing proof you don't need book smarts to be successful. What did Einstein say? If you judge a fish by its ability to climb a tree, it will live its whole life believing it's stupid. Raf's a high school dropout with learning problems, and look what he's made of himself," he said as he reached to retrieve a stack of plates from the cupboard. "I went to one of the best schools in Britain and I never thrived because I wasn't academic and I, like, found it impossible to concentrate." Indigo wasn't surprised, Nash could never sit still. "I preferred to hang out at the stables with the horses than study. Boarding school was totally shit," he said, stirring the barbeque sauce bubbling on the stove top. "The food was seriously rubbish, too. Bangers and mash, spotted dick, toad in the hole…" he gagged.

Indigo wrinkled his nose. "Let's play a game," he quipped. "It's called 'English delicacy or STD'."

"Probably why I was such a scrawny kid," Nash laughed. "That dodgy crap was my only source of sustenance after Father died and my step-monster refused to let me come home on the holidays and… well… you know…" He absentmindedly rubbed at the tattoo on his bicep and Indigo smiled gently, his heart lurching for him. "Anyway," he said, glancing around, "I think we're ready in here. Is the game over?" He craned his neck to see the TV. Just then, the phone began to ring. He snatched it from the wall.

Indigo took over setting the table.

"Oh hey, Nelson." Nelson was the lead guitarist in Nash's band. Nash was quiet for a moment or two then frowned, "Holy shit, mate, you ok?" He listened intently for a bit, toe scuffing back and forth over the skirting board below the phone. "You're kidding me? No *way*. For *that* long? Ok, yeah it's cool, brother, rest up and don't worry, we'll make do, feel better." He hung up and shouted, *"SHIT!"*

"What's wrong?" Indigo asked, juggling a fistful of cutlery.

"Nelson's come off his bike and broken his arm and banged up his head. He can't play tomorrow night." He paused for a moment then shouted *"SHIT!"* again, glaring at the floor. Nash and his band played at a bar uptown a couple nights a week. Indigo had originally gone along to be supportive, but had been blown away because they totally rocked. They had a pretty big following locally and Nash was slipped women's phone numbers and underwear nightly.

"Hang on," he said, gazing up at Indigo. "*You* can play."

Indigo balked. "Not since I was a kid. I'd hardly be able to keep up with you guys."

"Please, Indi," Nash begged, "I know you can do it." He hesitated for a moment and then said softly, "I… I saw you. The other night."

"You saw me?" Indigo replied, brows knit. "I don't know what you're..." But he realised then. "Ohhhhh," he breathed. He felt his cheeks redden. He'd been staying the night at the bungalow a few nights back and hadn't been able to sleep. He'd drifted from the spare room into the living room, where he'd spotted Nash's guitar case lying open on the coffee table. He'd sat down in front of it, gently running his hand down the neck of the instrument before lifting it from its satin bed. He'd loved playing guitar once. Before his mother had made a chore out of it. As he'd held it in his arms, his muscle memory had taken over and he'd began to gently pluck at the strings. And just like that, all those years of guitar lessons came flooding back and he was playing. He hadn't realised he'd had an audience.

"I got up to get some water," Nash shrugged. "I saw you. You're good. And who knew you could sing?"

"Why didn't you say anything?" Indigo asked, ducking his head.

"Dunno," he shrugged. "It kinda felt like I'd intruded on a private moment or something," he said. "That song you were playing, what was it?"

"It's an INXS song," Indigo replied. *"By My Side."*

Nash nodded thoughtfully and Indigo felt instantly exposed. But Nash didn't press him. Instead, he stuck his lip out and turned on the puppy-dog eyes. "Please, Indi?" he begged. "You guys come every week to watch us play. No one knows our set list better than you."

"I'm so rusty, mate. Surely there's someone else?"

"There's not. *Please?* I'll be your best friend?"

"I thought you already were?" Indigo laughed.

"In this life and the next," Nash grinned broadly. "But... I mean, come on, brother, please? Just 'til Nelson's arm heals?"

"I could take a look at his arm?"

"Ha! Have you met Nelson and his super closed mind? No way he's letting someone like you anywhere near him."

"Fine," Indigo sighed, throwing his hands up. "Just 'til Nelson's arm heals."

"Thanks, mate," Nash beamed, kissing him on the side of the face and hugging him tightly. "Did I mention it's good to have you back?"

"I've been home three weeks," Indigo chuckled.

"Yeah, but you were gone a whole month," Nash retorted. "Next time you go to New York, I'm coming with you, especially if a couple of days turns into four weeks again."

"You know why I stayed so long," Indigo said softly, and Nash just frowned, then squeezed him tight again.

By the time Nelson got his cast off six weeks later, Indigo was sad to relinquish his spot in the band and Nash was hesitant to let him. But the truth was he was so busy, his days jam-packed with training sessions at Sasha's dojo and with Nash and Aurora, hosting sessions with Raf, and seeing patients at Dawn's.

Indigo's life had settled into a predictable rhythm. He'd rise at five-thirty to run the trails, occasionally with Nash, and he tried to get out to the Oak Creek to swim at least every other day when the weather was warm, sometimes with Nash, Aurora and Sasha. Nash had gotten him into horse riding and some weekends they'd head out to the ranch for a canter. Other weekends he, Nash, Aurora, Sasha and Raf took dirt bikes out to ride the epic motocross track some locals had built out in the middle of the desert.

But in times of solitude, he found his mind wandered back to Australia. His attention was being pulled there more and more these days. He was growing increasingly unsettled in the States. And just like that, after two-and-a-half years away, he was desperately homesick.

It had been on the tip of his tongue more times than he could count to ask Sasha to look in on the Carlisles for him, but something always held him back. He felt like an intruder somehow, as though he'd lost the right to access them. But he wondered a lot about how big Matty had gotten, how Robbie was doing, how Scarlett and Joshua were. And always, Cordelia.

Was she happy?

Had she forgiven him?

Did she still think of him?

And just when he'd decided he had to talk to Raf and tell him how he was feeling, that his days in Sedona were numbered, Nash appeared on his doorstep one morning in late October, flustered and breathless.

"It's time," was all he said, although he looked heartbroken as he said it.

Indigo nodded tersely.

He was ready. It certainly wasn't going to be easy, going home, facing everyone he'd abandoned, facing a coven of warlocks on his own… But he knew he could do it, all of it. Because this was who he was.

raf

Raf smiled sadly at Indigo over dinner that night. He'd always known Indigo's stay would only be temporary. He hadn't wanted to grow too attached, but it had been impossible not to. Indigo Wolfe had a light inside of him that illuminated everyone he touched. He was an incredible young man, bright, sincere, confident and caring. His energy was infectious. He'd known the boy was gifted, but his talent was beyond anything Raf had seen.

Indigo looked sad, anxious, as he pushed the food around his plate, pale beneath his golden desert tan.

"I know your life is in Sydney, Indi. And although we haven't talked about it, I know your heart lies there too? Cordelia, right?"

Indigo seemed unsure of how to answer. He hesitated, chewing on his lower lip. "There was Cordelia, yes," he finally admitted. "But I'm not sure if there is anymore. I fucked up. I hurt her badly. Her family too. They opened their home and their hearts to me and I threw it all back in their faces." His voice quivered. "I was such an arsehole."

"You were sick, Indi," Raf said gently. "Be kind to yourself."

Indigo shrugged. "That doesn't feel like enough of an excuse. I haven't seen or spoken to them in such a long time. For all I know Cordelia's moved on, met somebody."

"Well, there's only one way to find out," Raf ventured.

"But what if I've built everything up in my head? There's not much that scares me anymore, but this… This terrifies me. I always believed we'd end up together, her and I." He stared intently at a spot on the table. "I'm just bloody terrified that I'll go back home and she'll tell me that she doesn't feel the same way. And I wouldn't blame her, you know… I wouldn't blame her if she hated my guts."

His handsome face twisted into a grimace and Raf knew he was recalling memories he wasn't proud of.

"But no matter how much I prepare myself, if I find that I've lost her, I don't know what I'll do — I'll have to start from scratch, reimagine a whole new future without her and I just don't know how to do that."

Indigo looked drawn and wretched, raking his hands through his hair as he spoke. Clearly, this had been eating him up inside for a while now.

Raf was quiet for some time, contemplating what to say. Dare he reach into the back of his mind, pull that box down from its highest shelf and open it? It had been shut for so long now, packed away, covered in a thick layer of dust.

"I knew a girl like that once," he heard himself murmur, easing up the lid and opening the box a crack. He hadn't spoken of her in close to twenty years. "I actually met her in your part of the world," he said, his voice wavering, and it amazed him that she was still able to illicit such emotion in him. "Byron Bay in the seventies. It was a real trip." He felt a slow grin spread across his face. "And she? Man, was she ever something else." He paused, swallowed hard. "God, how I loved her. I would have stayed forever if I had it my way."

"What happened?"

"We were young and we messed it up."

"Messed it up how?"

Raf shook his head, unable to speak over the lump in his throat. Raf hadn't always been the person he was now. There had been times of great darkness in his life, times he wasn't proud of the person he'd been. But he wasn't ashamed either. He'd never hidden from that part of himself, that troubled youth, because that young man was an integral part of him, the shadow to his light.

"Oh, Indi," he finally sighed, "when you're young, you're so idealistic and rigid and stubborn. Well, I was anyway. I saw the world in black and white, blind to the many shades of grey in between. And love, love is never black and white, especially when you find that person who awakens your soul in such a way that the only way to stop loving them is to stop the very beat of your heart." He leant forward in his chair, his gaze intent on Indigo. "You see, in my case, a love like that was only offered once in a lifetime. And I was young and dumb and arrogant and I didn't fight for it. And I've regretted it every day since. She was my night sky," he smiled wistfully. "My moon, all my stars. To this day, she remains my muse. There's a part of her in every heroine I write.

And I can tell you from experience that I honestly believe it's better to put yourself out there and risk the heartbreak, because at least then you'll know. It's the not knowing that kills you, the wondering."

A muscle ticked in Indigo's jaw.

"There're only two answers in the end," Raf continued, "yes or no. And the thing that young people sometimes find difficult to understand is that no matter how hard you try, no matter how bad you want it, it is impossible to make someone love you." He leaned back, resting his head in his hands.

"What's that saying? The heart wants what it wants? Well, in all my years as a host, in working with human beings suffering through the human condition, I can promise you we have no control over who we love. At times it's unexplainable, it's lawless, it's chemistry, it's destiny, it's kismet. Sometimes we want so badly for it to be written in the stars, but it's just not. And one thing we cannot do is rewrite the stars. Sometimes it's just not meant to be."

"Gee, man, thanks for the pep talk," Indigo said, slumping down in his chair.

Raf couldn't help but smile. *"However,"* he continued, "when a love exists that is meant to be, nothing can stop it. Time, space, life, death, nothing. If it's fate, nothing will keep you apart. When it's meant to be, it will be. In my case, as much as I desperately believed it was, I've come to accept it wasn't. Because if it was meant to be, we would have found our way back to one another. One way or another, fate always intervenes when it's meant to, Indi, because the people in our life, that core group of souls who follow us from lifetime to lifetime, over and over again, we will always find our way back to them, our soul family. For me in this lifetime, my soul family is my Akasha family, and it doesn't include love of the romantic kind, but that's my lot in life and I have so much more than so many and I am grateful for that." He traced his finger through the condensation on his glass as he spoke.

"But for you? This love of yours? She may well be your soul mate, put on this earth just for you, life after life. Either way, you owe it to yourself to find out. And if you truly believe in it, put your ego and pride aside and put yourself out there for it. Because at least then, you'll know."

Indigo closed his eyes briefly, sighed deeply. "I don't know if I can just lay myself bare like that." His voice was low. "I'm scared of getting hurt, of what that might... do to me."

"I know you, Indi," he said, laying his hand over Indigo's. "Look how far you've come. No matter what the answer may be, you are strong enough to play the hand that's dealt."

chapter twenty-six

wonderwall

harbord, new south wales, november, 1995

cordelia

"Cordelia!"

The voice punctured the periphery of her unconscious, sharp and distorting.

"Cora!"

Cordelia groaned and pulled her pillow over her head. She squeezed her eyes shut and tucked herself more tightly into the foetal position. She had her last HSC exam today and she'd been up late cramming.

Her bedroom door flew open with a crash and the pillow was ripped off her head.

Robbie leant in so his lips were almost touching her ear. "Get. Up."

"Go 'way," she moaned, fumbling to shield her face from the blinding light now pouring in through the window from which the curtains had just been yanked.

But it was no use. She groggily opened her eyes to glare at Robbie, who was now sitting primly on the foot of her bed. He was intently grooming his already perfectly styled hair in the full-length mirror that backed her wardrobe door. Robbie's coif still emulated that of his idol, *90210's* Brandon Walsh.

"Next time you're in Beverly Hills, give my best to Brandon and Dylan, won't you?" Cordelia snapped, kicking him from under the doona.

"I wish," Robbie shot back, examining his sideburns and smoothing up the fringe he'd tamed to defy gravity. "Get up, Cora," he said, his eyes still fixed upon his reflection. She hated that he was a morning person – venomously hated it, at that particular moment. "We're going to be late." He was already dressed in his school uniform. Cordelia sat up in bed, waiting for him to finish preening.

"We have to leave in fifteen," Robbie said, his attention now on his tie, which was fashioned into a perfect Windsor knot. "I assume from the grumpy face you still haven't heard from Drew?"

She shook her head. Drew was road tripping up the coast to Byron Bay with some of his uni mates to celebrate finishing his first year of Medicine. The two of them had been like ships in the night lately, her with her exams and he with his. They'd hardly seen each other. And she felt emptier without him. He'd promised they'd spend more time together after exams, so when he'd taken her to a celebratory party and casually broken the news he was leaving on this trip with his friends the next day, she'd been pretty pissed off.

In his eyes it was only two weeks and then he'd meet her in Surfer's Paradise for Schoolies Week (along with every other Year Twelve graduate in New South Wales who was planning on descending upon southern Queensland to celebrate the end of their school career). He'd promised after that they'd have the whole summer together. He'd made her feel like she wasn't a priority to him because he'd barely considered her in his plans, and that hurt because shouldn't she be his everything… or at least something akin to it?

When he'd called the morning of his departure to apologise, she'd been short with him and they'd fought. She'd told him to forget about coming to Surfers, to forget about her, that they should take a break. And they hadn't spoken since.

The truth was, despite it all, she missed him. A lot. She was miserable.

"The big question is, did Sandy stowaway in Drew's luggage?" Robbie smirked.

"Oh ha, HA," Cordelia snapped, reluctantly swinging her legs over the side of the bed and standing up. Sandy Whitcomb and his wares had become a permanent fixture at Drew's ever since his skiing accident.

She was all for a bit of recreational fun, but Drew was becoming a little too reliant on self-medicating and it worried her. His pain seemed to rule his life and he'd become a bit moody and distracted. Things between them just weren't the same. But they loved each other and they could get back on track. It was just a rough patch.

She glanced in the mirror as she stretched. Her eyes were puffy and her hair fell past her shoulder blades in a mane of snarls and knots.

"My *God*, woman," Robbie cried dramatically, clutching his chest in mock horror. "Would you fix yourself up?" He glanced at her in her grey sleep-shorts and black jersey camisole, taking in her tousled tresses and pillow-creased face with a look of dismay.

"I cannot believe I once shared a womb with you," he said, shaking his head. "You're a disgrace." He stood and sauntered to her closet, rummaged through her clothes until he found her uniform, laying it neatly on the bed for her.

"That may be, but I'm *your* disgrace," Cordelia yawned, shoulder charging him with a sleepy grin as she headed past him towards the bathroom. He was opening her top drawer and adding a pair of knee-high socks to the pile.

While she waited for the shower to heat up, she ran a brush through her hair, taming it into soft shimmery waves.

"You can sort your own underwear out," she heard him call as he walked past the bathroom. "Foraging through your bras and g-strings is where I draw the line. Twelve minutes, Cora!" he yelled as he headed down the stairs, presumably to make her breakfast.

Fourteen minutes later Cordelia opened the door to their silver Jeep, balancing a bowl of fruit and yoghurt in one hand and her school bag in the other.

"You can lay off the horn now," she admonished through the spoon clenched in her teeth, climbing into the passenger seat.

Robbie rolled his eyes and slammed the car into reverse. "I'm sick to death of being late because of you," he scolded. "It's beyond ridiculous."

"I'm sorry," she said sharply, steadying her breakfast on her knees while she attempted to subdue her hair with a navy ribbon. "But truly, it's beyond me why you expect anything more from me."

"I guess I'm hoping one day you'll get your shit together," he sighed. Cordelia glanced at him sidelong. Their eyes met and they both burst out laughing.

"Last exam, baby bro," she sighed. "I don't know about you, but I feel like I'm limping towards the finish line here."

"Yup," Robbie nodded as he turned down the beachfront road, opening his window so the car was instantly inundated with a sweet, salty breeze. The warmth of spring had pushed winter out of the air and the tease of summer was upon them.

Cordelia reached to turn up the stereo in anticipation of what she knew was coming. Robbie's new Oasis tape had been playing on a loop for a week now, and he had the tendency to sing loudly enough to overwhelm the Gallaghers when it came to his favourite song, *Wonderwall*. She wasn't in the mood for her brother's overly confident crooning.

Cordelia stared absentmindedly out the window as they passed Queenscliff Beach, trying to ignore Robbie's voice cracking on the higher notes. The surf was on fire and she pouted enviously as she watched a surfer pull into the perfect barrel. The northern end of the beach was shadowed by hunkering cliffs, their faces carpeted with windswept vegetation, their tops thickly laden with apartment buildings. The jutting rocks below gave way to golden sand and turquoise sea, today under a sapphire sky. Beyond the large expanse of beach, a wide pathway lined the grassy embankment that led to the road. As always, it was packed with joggers, cyclists and mothers pushing prams while yelling sternly to small children on scooters blazing a trail ahead.

As they drove past the beach showers, a lone figure drew her eye. She jerked forward in her seat, her heart hammering in her chest, her stomach lurching. Instant recognition caused a cascade of adrenaline to toss her belly and buzz in her fingertips.

He was tall, well over six foot, his hair golden blond, his wetsuit rolled down to the waist of his lean muscular body. He was standing under the shower, his face tilted to catch the spray. His back was to the road, but just as they drove past, he swung around, almost as if he could feel her eyes all over him.

Her window was down and he was mere metres away, so he had the perfect view of her as they cruised slowly by in the halting morning traffic. His eyes met hers, and although she couldn't see them up close, she knew them by heart: soft hazel flecked with iridescent green and yellow.

Azure blue met hazel brown.

Her breath caught in her throat as he held her gaze, unapologetically, unwavering, and that gaze bore so much. She could barely breathe.

It was him.

Of course, it was him.

She'd known it before he'd even turned around.

She couldn't believe it. After two-and-a-half years.

Just like that.

He was back.

Indigo was back.

chapter twenty-seven

again

cordelia

Cordelia spent the rest of the drive to school in a daze, her mind a whirl of tumbling thoughts. *What was he doing back...? Who knew he was here...? How long had he been in Sydney...? Why hadn't he called...? Was he going to get in touch...? Was he back living with Edita and Lukas on Eastern Hill...? And, after everything that had happened... how was he?*

Indigo.

The love of her life, or so she'd once believed. But that was then, and a lot had certainly changed since.

For more than two years, the rumours had swirled rife around his whereabouts. An array of tales had circulated, some taller than others, from someone who'd spoken to someone who'd been told someone had spotted him here or there. An ashram in the foothills of southern India. Heliskiing in the wild mountains of Alaska. Surfing on the North Shore of Oahu. In New York, shacked up in a SoHo loft with a bevy of supermodels. Sedated and quite possibly lobotomised in a Swiss psychiatric hospital. Living in a shack on the beach in Koh Samui. The stories just went on and on.

She'd barely been able to concentrate on her exam and by the time it was over she'd convinced herself it maybe, possibly, hadn't really been Indigo at the beach that morning.

Because how could he have come back and not come straight to her door?

It had been years since she'd last seen him. That surfer could have just been someone who looked like him. His hair had been different after all, long enough now to almost graze his shoulders, blonder, sun-streaked on the ends. Last time she'd seen him, he'd had a schoolboy's haircut, short back and sides. Cordelia tried to ignore the thunder that had filled her blood when their eyes had met. She ignored the fact that she'd know him anywhere, anytime, anyhow.

And most of all, she ignored the irrefutable fact that no one else in the world could stop her heart the way only he could.

"What's up your arse?" Robbie demanded for the fifth time that car ride. It was a harsher variation of the question her friends had asked repeatedly all morning, and Cordelia saw red.

"Just leave me alone!" she snapped, crossing her arms and glaring out the window.

"Psycho," he muttered under his breath. "I gather it's shark week." Snarky shithead.

She threw him a death stare as he pulled into the driveway. She snatched the keys from him, grabbed her board and wetsuit from the garage and headed to the beach. She needed a surf to clear her head.

The ocean was fresh and cleansing. As she paddled out, she asked herself if she was hoping to see Indigo out there. She'd come to Fairy Bower, after all, his favourite break. A wave of guilt washed over her as thoughts of Drew immediately filled her head.

No, the ocean was her place of refuge. This was where she came when she needed to think, to be alone. The swell had died down and there weren't many other surfers out. As she lay on her board, the ocean gently lapping at her toes, her mind wandered back to Indigo.

She was angry at him. Or was she disappointed in him? Maybe both. Yes, a churning mess of furious anger and devastating disappointment jostled inside of her, causing bile to rise in her throat. What he'd done on that bridge that night... She still didn't understand it. And whenever she thought of it, it made her feel physically sick.

The truth was, they weren't friends anymore. They weren't anything anymore. There was a time there when she was naïve and idealistic and she'd thought they'd been everything. But now she knew they were nothing.

He'd cut off all contact and shut everyone out. And that was the bit that hurt the most.

Cordelia knew Robbie had heard about Indigo's re-emergence when he arrived home from the beach the next day and proceeded to stomp around the house, snapping at everyone and slamming doors. She hadn't talked to him about it. She still wasn't ready. If she didn't say the words out loud, it wasn't real. Because no matter how often she told herself him being back meant nothing, changed nothing, there was a constant roiling in her gut that said otherwise.

The mood at the dinner table was unusually sombre that night, the usual joking and teasing and chatter noticeably absent. Dad had come home distracted and withdrawn and had yet to ask anyone how their day was – which was his usual opener.

"Any word on Essie?" Cordelia asked softly, looking from Mum to Dad as she poured Matty a glass of water from the jug on the table.

Dad put his fork down and exhaled a shuddery sigh, exchanging a glance with Mum across the table. Cordelia eyed her father and frowned at how pale and gaunt he looked. She'd recently noticed silver appearing around his temples. He'd been withdrawn lately, distracted, and he'd lost weight. When she'd questioned him about it, he'd made a joke about getting ready for swimsuit season before admitting his Crohn's disease had been flaring up. He'd been working crazy hours lately; she made a mental note to talk to him about cutting back a bit, taking better care of himself.

He smiled sadly. "No, darling, she's still unconscious," he said, his eyes meeting hers.

About a month ago, his best friend and colleague Essie Mathews had left the hospital in the middle of the night after staying late to sit with a dying patient. She was discovered three hours later, unconscious in the carpark. Not a mark was found on her and extensive testing had uncovered nothing, yet she still hadn't woken up. They were all devastated.

"Poor Essie," Cordelia said, chewing on her thumb nail. "I still can't believe it! Do you think she'll wake up soon?"

Her parents exchanged looks again.

"What's going on?" Robbie asked, glancing from one to the other. "What's with all the not-so-subtle looks?"

Dad pressed his fingers to his eyes, massaging them wearily. Mum reached over and took his hand, her bangles jangling melodically. Matty was humming, *You are my Sunshine* quietly to himself as he lined up peas on his plate.

"Three more patients have been brought into the hospital under similar circumstances," Dad said. And he actually looked rattled. "A couple last week, and one yesterday."

"So what is it?" Robbie asked. "What's making them sick?"

Their parents gazed at each other. Cordelia picked up her knife and fork, then put them down again. "We have no idea," Dad finally replied. "I can't for the life of me figure out what's wrong with them. All we know is that it's not contagious."

"Poor Ess," Cordelia whispered, nudging her plate away.

"I spoke to one of my colleagues over at North Shore Hospital," he continued, "and they've had similar cases come in too."

They picked at their food silently, lost in their own thoughts. The only chipper one was Matty, who was happily babbling away about his day at preschool.

Robbie had been scowling at his plate when all of a sudden he threw his fork down with a huff. Their parents looked up at him in surprise. Cordelia, who was helping Matty cut up his chicken parmigiana, was the last to turn her attention to Robbie. She knew in her bones what was coming.

"So I was waiting for the right time to tell you all, but I can't keep it in another minute!" He looked at Cordelia, gnawing on his lip for a moment before he continued. "I heard some very interesting goss at the beach this afternoon." He leant forward, his dark eyes flashing.

His family looked at him expectantly.

"This is going to be hard for you to hear, Cora, but you will *never* believe who's just waltzed back on into town," he continued, glancing around the table. He paused for dramatic effect.

"Who?" Mum eventually asked, because no one else did.

"Indigo."

"*Indigo?*" Dad gasped.

"As in *Indigo,* Indigo?" Mum cried, eyes widening. "As in *our* Indigo?"

"Does anyone at this table actually *know* another Indigo?" Robbie sighed. He glanced around again to gauge everyone's reaction to his momentous news. Cordelia averted her eyes to her plate, keeping her face as neutral as possible. She quickly realised her mistake — she wasn't looking as outraged as he'd expected after his grand announcement. His face fell even further and his eyes narrowed as he regarded her. "Did you *know?*"

All heads turned to her.

"Yes," she whispered, feeling a flush rise up her neck.

"How? *How* did you know?" Robbie demanded.

"I-I saw him," she answered softly. "At Queensie."

"*What?* When?"

"Yesterday morning. On our way to school."

"On *our* way to school? As in, *you* were in the car with *me?*" Robbie's voice was growing more and more high pitched. "And you neglected to say anything?"

"I wasn't exactly sure if it was him," Cordelia replied, still not meeting Robbie's eye.

"Well, that's a load of shit!" he snapped.

"*Shit,*" Matty parroted with a giggle, stabbing a pea with his fork.

"Robert!" Mum admonished. "Language please — little ears are flapping."

"Apologies," Robbie said with a wave of his hand. "But seriously, Cora, *are you kidding me?* I guess this explains why Janet Jackson's been on high rotation the past twenty-four hours. If you promise never to play *Again* again, I might consider returning your precious CD."

"I knew you took it! Give it back!"

"Nope." He crossed his arms.

"Give it!"

"Never."

"Da-ad!"

"Guys!" Dad exclaimed, holding his hands up. "For God's sake! Can we give it a rest at the table? You two are above this petty BS. Enough's enough for tonight, ok?" He slammed his chair back from the table and stood. "You're lucky to have one another. Sort your differences out!" He turned to leave but swivelled back around, his face stony as he pointed from Cordelia to Robbie. "It is your job to protect him, as it is his to protect you. My sister and I… we would have died for one another." A faraway sadness shadowed his eyes. "And I can tell you that if she were still here today, we certainly wouldn't be carrying on like the two of you." He gave each of them a stern look, then went into his study, closing the door firmly behind him. He'd hardly touched his dinner.

They all gaped after him. He so rarely lost his temper.

"He's just really stressed out at the moment," Mum said softly. "What with Essie and everything…" she trailed off, staring at the closed study door and Cordelia swore she saw tears shining in her eyes.

Robbie glared at Cordelia and sniffed. "To be continued."

Cordelia took a deep breath and knocked on Robbie's door.

"Enter," he commanded.

"It's just me," she said quietly, closing the door behind her and perching on the foot of his bed. Robbie was lying on his back flipping through the latest issue of *Cosmopolitan*, Alanis Morissette crowing from his stereo in angst. On his ceiling was a giant poster of a dripping wet Keanu Reeves, his black t-shirt clinging to his muscular frame. The wall beside his bed was still plastered with pictures of the cast of *Beverly Hills 90210*, although they now had to compete with the stars of *Melrose Place* and *Party of Five*.

Cordelia reached over and turned Alanis down.

"I was listening to that," Robbie informed her coldly, not looking up from his magazine.

"Too bad," she replied, tapping his outstretched legs for him to move over. "I want to talk to you."

"There *is* a whole other bed over there," Robbie complained, nodding to the bed that had once been Indigo's. But he was already shuffling over so she could lay down beside him, her head next to his on the pillow. They stared up at Keanu.

She reached for her brother's hand, squeezed it. "I'm sorry, Rob. I know you're pissed at me. You have every right to be. I should have told you. I just didn't know how to feel about Indigo being back. I think I actually went into like, *shock* when I saw him… And then I just didn't know what to think or how to feel, or what it meant."

They lay together in silence, hands clasped.

"What does this mean?" he asked after a while. "For you and Drew?"

"What?" she said, sitting up in indignation. "Why would it mean anything for me and Drew?"

"Um, *seriously?*" he said, winging his arms behind his head. "This is me you're talking to. I've lived and breathed all the Indigo drama alongside of you these past few years. You're going to look me in the eye and tell me that him coming home doesn't complicate things?"

"Why would it?" she said, nose wrinkled. "Indigo moved on and so did I. I'm with Drew now. Drew's been there for me these past two years, even before we were together. He didn't take off and abandon me and not call or write—"

"He kinda just did…" Robbie said, tilting his head and grimacing.

She smacked him on the shoulder. "As if it's the same thing!" She stood, started pacing the room. "I mean, I *told* Drew to go, that we should take a break."

"He's probably drowning his sorrows in young hot—"

"Don't even say it," she said, holding up her hand. "Besides, none of that has anything to do with Indigo. How could you even say him coming home would change things for me and Drew?" she rambled. "I mean, what would that say about me if I dumped my boyfriend the minute *he* came back? I'm not that sort of person, Rob. I'm loyal. I don't hurt people and leave them and not ever call them again! I'm not like that. Despite everything, I love him."

"Who?"

"*Drew!*" she snapped, stopping dead, hands on hips. "I *love* Drew, not Indigo. I *don't* love Indigo."

"The lady doth protest too much," Robbie muttered. "Besides, you already kinda did dump your boyfriend."

"*Rob!*"

"Hey hey, take a chill pill," he said, sitting up, reaching a hand out to her. "I just thought you might want to talk about it. You know you can tell me anything and I won't judge you. Hell, give me something juicy and I'll respect you even more. Come, sit," he said, pulling her down beside him. He shuffled over to make room and she lay her head back on his pillow. "It's ok, you know," he said softly, turning to look at her, "if Indigo coming back's stirred up old feelings for you."

"Well, it hasn't," she said, pursing her lips and glancing away.

"He was your first love, Cora. You're only human. I know *I'm* lying here oscillating between wanting to punch his stupid face and wanting to throw my arms around him and never let go. And I mean, the fact you and Drew have been having problems lately…"

"We had *one* fight," she protested, turning to glare at him. "I'd hardly call that having problems or you and I would be in deep shit."

"Seriously?" he said, swivelling his head to stare at her incredulously. "You guys had a fight a week ago and you haven't spoken since. I mean, you told him to forget about you. Us men are very literal creatures; as far as he's concerned, are you even still together? And what about the whole him-becoming-a-stoner thing? He's very likely tripping balls in a field somewhere in Mullumbimby as we speak."

"Drop it, Rob," she said through clenched teeth. She felt sick about that last conversation she'd had with Drew. She'd lashed out in anger and not even she was sure whether they'd broken up. She certainly hadn't meant to end it. And as for the drugs, that wasn't the real Drew. It was just his pain taking hold and she knew together they could fix it.

Robbie shrugged and reached over to turn his stereo back up. After listening to Alanis bemoan the irony of the world for a bit, he sniggered. "Remember our thirteenth birthday party?"

She bit her lip to keep from giggling. "You were such a dag back then."

"People in glass houses, Cora," Robbie retorted. She nudged him with her shoulder, screwing up her nose in mock anger. "Hang on, hang on," he cried, jumping up and rummaging through his CDs. "You know what song we need right now?" He found the disc he was looking for and ejected Alanis, replacing her and hitting play, turning the volume all the way up. He brandished the CD cover with a flourish so Cordelia could see the title, *Vanilla Ice: To the Extreme.* She burst out laughing. As the familiar beat of *Ice Ice Baby* filled the room, Robbie grabbed a hairbrush off his desk and started singing as he danced around the bed. Memories of that night five years ago, the night their journey with Indigo began, bombarded her mind. She felt herself smiling and caught herself, hardened her face. That was then and this was now. And as far as she was concerned, her journey with Indigo was over.

Despite her resolve not to think about him, Cordelia had barely slept since she'd seen Indigo at the beach a few days ago. It didn't help that Matty was going through a stage of waking every night, screaming in terror at the horrors that haunted his dreams. As much as Mum tried to settle him, only Cordelia seemed to have the magic touch. So she'd taken to sleeping most nights with him in his single bed, his skinny arms wrapped around her neck, his sweet breath warm on her face.

She would lie, night after night, staring at the stick-on stars glowing on the ceiling of Matty's room, thinking of Indigo and Drew, Drew and Indigo, guilt consuming her for doing so... until Matty would start to stir and moan, and then sit bolt upright, his eyes wide in terror, pointing at something unknown at the foot of his bed. So she would shush him, and soothe him, and hold him as he buried his face deep in her chest, his whole body trembling with fear.

Indigo. Cordelia squeezed her eyes shut. All these years later and she could still feel his lips on hers, finally on hers. A kiss such a long time coming, over all too soon. But two-and-a-half years had since passed, with not one word. He'd hurt a lot of people with his actions. His questionable decisions. The aftermath of those decisions.

And now he was back. And he'd had time to surf, and from what she'd heard, time to practice yoga, to run the trails of North Head and

Manly Dam, to grab smoothies on the Corso. But clearly he hadn't found time to see them. Her. Tears streamed silently down her face as she hugged Matty closer. She angrily swiped them away, chastising herself for wasting any more on him.

Not a day had gone by that she hadn't thought of him. Constantly, and then recently, since Drew, intermittently. Five years ago, Indigo had appeared in her life and totally consumed it. But everything since he'd left had convinced her she was nothing more than a fleeting chapter in his life. Certainly not important enough to stay in this world for.

He hadn't called, he hadn't reached out, and he'd certainly never asked her for help. And he must have known she would have done anything for him. That she'd be there, no questions asked. He just had to say the word. But he hadn't. He hadn't said one word.

Not before.

Not after.

Not since.

And now, just as she'd finally moved on, he was back and already turning her world upside down.

chapter twenty-eight

november rain

cordelia

"Shit, Rob!" Cordelia slammed down the receiver of the pay phone and clasped her grey sweatshirt tightly over her black yoga pants and crop top. The sweat that had soaked her clothes and hair during her hot vinyasa class now chilled her to the bone. She pulled her damp tresses into a high ponytail and glanced hopefully towards the spot Robbie had dropped her off, but there was no sign of headlights on the darkened road.

She was furious. Robbie had been desperate to nab the last copy of *Speed* from the video shop and had promised that if she'd let him have the car, he'd pick her up from yoga at eight on the dot. But here she was, standing out in the dark in the middle of Manly Corso at thirty-five past, with no sign of Robbie. She'd called the house four times from the pay phone on the corner, but he hadn't picked up. Her parents had gone away for the night, and Matty was spending the evening at their grandparents' house. She couldn't call them, they'd freak out and make her stay at theirs. Drew was still away, so she'd tried Peyton but had gotten her answering machine, and Sian's phone had been engaged as it always was with her gossipy little sister having a tendency to tie up the line.

"Rob, you dick," she muttered under her breath, as she threw her yoga mat over her shoulder and started off towards home. Luckily, she'd brought her yellow Sony Sports Walkman. She slid her headphones on and turned down the Corso towards the beach. She rewound her mixtape to the beginning because she felt like being serenaded by Guns N' Roses about changed hearts and cold November rain. It was her go-to song when she felt like wallowing.

She sighed in resignation, her anger at Robbie's unreliability dissipating as she accepted it was an easy thirty-minute stroll down the beach front to their house in Harbord, a walk she'd made a thousand times. Walking with her mixtapes was actually one of her favourite pastimes, as it allowed her to lose herself completely. It was the closest she got to meditating.

The ocean, the beach, it was her happy place, and on this unseasonably cool Tuesday night, no one was around. The ocean breeze caressed her face, the comforting scent of salt and sea riding upon it. She inhaled deeply, a ghost of a smile forming on her lips.

A silver sickle of moon hung in the sky, the dull twinkle of the stars above intermittently blanketed by trailing clouds. The road was to her left, but barely any cars passed by. Even the houses and apartment buildings across the road seemed quiet and unlit. Manly was a ghost town tonight. Giant Norfolk pines lined the path, their shaggy branches a thick canopy, their sturdy trunks reaching infinitely into the night sky, each one she passed bringing her closer to home. She could hardly see the low sandstone wall to her right, but she knew it was there, following a good six-foot drop to the sand on the other side.

She was so engrossed in her music that when she was suddenly grabbed from behind, her heart almost exploded from her chest. She cried out, tearing the arms from around her waist and spinning around, wild-eyed, breath heavy.

She was confronted by the crinkled, smiling eyes of Sandy Whitcomb, who was probably taking a break from delivering his merchandise now his best customer was off road tripping with his mates.

"Shit, Sandy! You almost gave me a heart attack!" she breathed, smacking him in his bony chest.

"Sorry, babe," he grinned. "I called out to you a couple of times but you didn't hear me."

"You can't just do that!" she chastised him, her heart still hammering erratically. "Grabbing at girls walking alone in the dark, it's not cool." She glared at him, arms crossed.

"Ok, ok," he said, holding his hands up, "I admit that in hindsight, it wasn't my finest moment." He beamed broadly at her. "Forgive me?"

She sighed heavily. "What are you doing here?" she asked, glancing around.

"Making a last minute delivery, a brother of a mate who missed his flight to Bali this arvo and needed some cheering up. What are you doing walking out here all alone?"

"Rob forgot to pick me up," she said with a scowl.

"I can give you a lift?" he offered, gesturing to his bright red Honda parked down the road. "I just need to make a couple of stops along the way."

"Uh no, it's ok, I'm fine to walk, thanks." She'd seen some of the shady characters Sandy did business with and wasn't particularly in the mood to make a scenic tour of their homes.

"You're completely sure?" he asked, as he glanced at his watch and started backing towards his car.

"Totally."

"Cool bananas," he grinned, giving her two thumbs up as he reached his car.

She picked up the yoga mat she'd dropped in fright and turned to walk off when he called after her, "Hey, Cee!"

"Yeah?" she said, turning back, her headphones halfway to her ears.

"You need anything for the walk home?"

"I'm good, thanks." She rolled her eyes. Sandy Whitcomb, ever the salesman. She waved over her shoulder and continued on her way.

By the time she got to Queenscliff she was so absorbed in her thoughts that when she suddenly stepped into darkness, her stride faltered. She glanced around. She could have sworn this pathway was usually lit. Looking up, she saw the lamps in this section were out. She squinted into the shadows, lifted her headphones an inch or two, pricked up her ears. All she could hear were the waves to her right. She couldn't see them, but she could hear them, rolling in and out, always there, doing their beautiful thing.

She peered around once more, then gingerly stepped deeper into the darkness. There was a feeling growing in the pit of her stomach that something wasn't right, a prickle up her spine, an inkling of being watched. She shook it off, told herself she was being dramatic.

She quickened her pace, eyes darting wildly through the blackness. *One foot in front of the other,* she told herself, *keep moving, keep moving.* She never in her life thought she'd regret saying no to a drug run with Sandy Whitcomb. But here she was, wishing she was safe in the front seat of his car, the pungent aroma of weed slowly seeping into her hair.

The rippling in her gut intensified and she shuddered. She yanked her headphones off and started to jog. The darkness was closing in around her, enveloping her, suffocating her. *Something isn't right.* The trickle of fear swelled to a crippling gush. *Something isn't right.* Her chest began to throb, her breath an erratic staccato as every fibre of her being told her to run.

Something isn't right, something isn't right, something isn't right.

She kicked her thongs off and started running, faster, faster, the panic rising… and then it happened. Her foot snared on an uneven paver. She stumbled, dropping her mat and Walkman. She tried to catch herself, but the shadows were disorienting. Bearings gone, she veered to one side and the next thing she knew, she was falling, falling, falling. It wasn't until she hit the sand, cool and malleable beneath her, that she realised she'd tumbled over the sandstone wall onto the beach below.

She scrambled to her hands and knees, scooted back against the wall, eyes squeezed shut, trying to even her breath. She heard a shuffling sound then and despite how hard she willed them not to, her eyes sprung open. She gasped. A shadowy figure stood over her, petite yet imposing, all the same.

A hood obscured the face, so Cordelia could only glimpse snatches. A strong square jaw. Fawny skin. Straight black hair cut bluntly to the chin. Female.

Her unseen eyes bored into Cordelia, who clamoured shakily to her feet, slid clumsily along the wall, inching away. The woman didn't move, didn't speak. When Cordelia felt she was at a safer distance, she pivoted to flee, but another figure stepped into her path, this one with long mauve hair. A small cry escaped her lips as she stopped short and turned again, but another loomed to block her, this one huge, menacing. She swivelled helplessly in a circle. She was surrounded, outnumbered three-to-one, and although two were quite small, the third was a mountain. Hooded capes of deep plum satin cloaked their identities.

Terrified, she tried to scream, but it caught in her throat, her larynx utterly failing her. She was paralysed. Frozen. Powerless. She didn't know what to do and her brain was of no help, blanking, shutting down, as her hands began to tremble. All she could hear was her breath, an uneven rapid-fire.

Encroaching with glacially slow steps, they ushered her backwards, deeper onto the beach, closer to the ocean, further from the road. When they stopped, she looked down and saw she was standing at the centre of a circle drawn in the sand. Along its circumference sat a ring of small white candles, dark and unlit. The three figures each stepped back to stand at perfect intervals just inside the six-foot circle, silently facing her.

The clouds parted and the tiny crescent of moon cast a sliver of light on the dark-haired woman's face, the hood of the cloak shadowing all but a flat nose and pale, almost translucent lips.

"Artax." Her accent was heavy. "Light us up."

"As you wishhh, Maiden," a low male voice hissed to Cordelia's rear, the words carrying with them the stench of fetid breath. She swivelled as the great hulking figure stepped forward, head bowed under his cloak so all that was visible were a pair of misshapen black sneakers, sloppy on his splayed feet. She recoiled as Artax reached towards her, his plump fingers adorned with chunky silver rings. His hand unfurled to reveal a small, blue-tinged flame dancing on his palm, his long black nails encircling it like a fence of talons. Cordelia blinked. Her eyes must be playing tricks on her.

She stared in horrified fascination as Artax swept his arm theatrically around the circle; the candles lining its perimeter flickering alight in its wake. He crushed his fingers into a fist, extinguishing the flame. Before he stepped back into formation, he slowly, deliberately, raised his head so Cordelia could see part of his face. Black tunnels framed the golf-ball-sized-holes in his earlobes, his ebony lips were pierced with silver hoops, and a large ring protruded from the bottom of his nose. The candlelight shimmered over the assault of graffiti covering his face and neck. A big black stud adorned the first of his wobbly chins. He opened his mouth and flickered his tongue at her. It was forked. She flinched.

"Thank you, Artax," the Maiden said. "Have you received word from Lady Reinenoir? Will she be joining us?"

"I will." The new voice came from behind, female and husky. Cordelia turned. A figure was gliding towards them at a pace that suggested she believed she was worth waiting for. She was willowy and graceful. A cloak of a more vibrant purple hid so much of her face that all Cordelia could see was a pair of full, sin-red lips. She came to stand between Artax and the Maiden, directly opposite Cordelia, who she seemed to drink in inch by inch. A desolate emptiness encroached upon Cordelia, an enveloping sadness that rapidly consumed all joy, all light.

"Blessed be the evening, High Priestess," the other three said in unison, bowing their heads towards her.

She inclined her chin ever so slightly in what seemed a bothersome effort.

"We can begin," the Maiden stated. Cordelia jerked, her heart hammering in her chest. *Begin? Begin what?* The Maiden's mouth, a jagged slit, parted and began to open, wider, wider, endless blackness emerging from within. And then, seemingly incongruously, a deep melodic sound rung out, a strange wordless chant, the other two joining in. Reinenoir continued to stand there, her wordless attention on Cordelia before she stepped back, melting into the shadows. But she was still there. Cordelia could feel her presence, cold and dark and deep as an Arctic chasm.

Cordelia couldn't run. She couldn't scream. She could only stare in horror as the other three raised their hands towards her in unison, the chanting growing louder, more urgent. They arched their backs, thrusting their chests forward and she felt herself swaying. She was disoriented, as though she were being pulled from every direction at once. Whatever they were doing to her, she couldn't break free. They were moving around her now in formation. What was visible of their faces swirled before her eyes, their cloaks a flap and flurry of plum, their chanting reaching a crescendo.

Light-headedness came fast and she suddenly felt tired; exhaustively, bone-crunchingly spent. She'd never felt more vulnerable and exposed. It took every ounce of strength to force her arms up, to draw them weakly over her chest.

Her teeth were chattering, her eyes desperately searching the deserted beach for help that wasn't coming. Her thoughts turned to Robbie. Maybe if she willed it enough, hoped it desperately enough, he would come for her. 'Robbie!' she silently screamed. *'I need you, Rob! Please help me!'*

She squeezed her eyes shut. And when she opened them, he was there.

His clothes were rumpled, his hair in disarray, but he was there.

Relief coursed through her body as Robbie reached out his long slender fingers and calmly took her shaking hand in his, so gently she could barely feel his touch. He took a step towards the edge of the circle, trying to pull her with him, but she couldn't move. Her legs were leaden, her feet stuck, sinking as though through quicksand.

"Rob," she mouthed, her eyes wide, begging, pleading. His brow furrowed and he tugged her hand again, although now she couldn't feel his in hers at all. "Robbie," she hoarsely whispered, as he tilted his head, regarding her, shadows gathering in his eyes as he looked from her to her cloaked tormentors. She was feeling woozy now, her knees beginning to tremble. She tried to cling to her brother, but she was fading fast.

And then, through the fog, she swore she heard someone yell her name from down the beach, but she was too drowsy, too dazed to respond. As quickly as he'd appeared, Robbie vanished. Maybe he was never there at all.

She heard her name again, and the voice seemed nearer now, and then she sensed something stream past her fast as lightning, something she couldn't see or hear but whatever it was, it caused the figures swaying and chanting around her to release her from their hold. They scattered as quickly as a handful of dirt thrown into the wind, fleeing back into the underbelly of shadow. With all the strength left in her body, she raised her head in the direction from which it had come, although she could barely focus.

"Let's see what he's got." Reinenoir's ice cold voice cut through the night. And then, even though no one was anywhere near Cordelia, a sudden sharp slicing pierced her throat. She fumbled a hand to her jugular, confused at the warm stickiness gushing between her fingers. She gasped for air as liquid began to fill her oesophagus, so a gurgling choking wracked her body.

Darkness was coming. Her legs gave way and she could feel herself falling.

"Cordelia!" the yell came again, this time louder, closer.

She knew that voice. It was a voice she'd know anywhere, strong and deep and comforting. A voice like home. But she was drowning, all air devoured by the molten waterfall cascading into her lungs with a tang of rusted iron.

She felt strong arms catch her.

And then, the black.

chapter twenty-nine

the flame

cordelia

Cordelia was dreaming. She was so tired, floating listlessly through that hazy dream, but she knew she needed to be scared, so scared… She *was* scared. Terrified, in fact. Petrified to her very soul. There was something bad. It wanted her. Wanted to hurt her. *Did* hurt her, agony in her throat. She was choking, drowning. And she was dying.

But then, Indigo.

Indigo?

Yes, Indigo had been there. And she'd seen him raise his palm to her attackers, and she swore she'd felt the temperature and force of the air around her shift, heat and viscosity streaming by her as if she were standing in the contrails of a fighter plane.

Her assailants had released her and scattered after that. But it hadn't been real. She'd dreamt it all…

Hadn't she?

She could hear someone speaking softly to her, and she could feel the protection of a warm embrace and she clung to that, clung to that as she felt herself fading further and further away.

robbie

Robbie stumbled towards the dark foyer, sleepy-eyed, his usually immaculate hair sticking up in every direction, his clothes creased and damp with perspiration.

He'd been dreaming. Of Cordelia. Of Cordelia and of something ghastly, terrible, terrifying — something he couldn't quite grasp. Nightmares like that weren't his bag and it had shaken him, woken him so abruptly his limbs flailed. And now there was a dreadful commotion, a door slamming, someone yelling his name loud enough to wake the dead.

He fumbled for the nearest lamp, flicking it on so it cast a meagre glow over the entryway. He was half asleep, so he wondered if he was still dreaming when he saw the hazy outline of an Adonis standing at the bottom of the stairs. He blinked, realisation dawning: it was Indigo. He blinked again. Cordelia was limp in Indigo's arms.

His eyes widened in shock and he instinctively followed Indigo as he moved past Robbie straight upstairs to Cordelia's bedroom, nudging the light switch on with his elbow and laying her gently on the bed. Indigo knelt down beside her and tenderly smoothed her hair back from her face.

Cordelia's room was revoltingly untidy as always, books and magazines spread over the white-washed dresser, discarded clothes strewn over the beige overstuffed armchair in the corner beside the white shuttered window. Brad Pitt looked down upon them in all his wounded magnificence from the *Legends of the Fall* poster, which hung above the desk with lumpy wads of Blu Tack. It was Cordelia's favourite movie. Not that Indigo knew that. He stopped knowing everything about her, her loves, her hates and everything in between, the day he left back in 1993. The other walls were adorned with framed collages of photos from Cordelia's life, friends and family – an assault of faces and smiles and hugs and beauty and sunshine. Indigo starred in many, tanned and smiling. But now Drew starred in more.

As Robbie moved into the bedroom, he caught his first proper look at Cordelia. Her neck and chest were smeared with what his brain computed had to be red paint.

"Hey what's that all over her?" he asked, stepping nearer, and that's when the smell hit him, metallic and acrid. "Oh my God, Indigo! Is that *blood?* What the in the name of Tarantino is going on?" Robbie cried. "How bad is she hurt?" Up close, the blood seemed to be tacky and coagulated and he could see no sign of a wound anywhere.

Indigo was peering worriedly into Cordelia's face, so stony and alabaster. Her skin had a strange sheen to it, an eerie translucence. And then Robbie realised Indigo's denim jacket was soaked with blood, that his face was smudged with crimson.

"Indigo!" Robbie demanded, hands flapping. "What's happened? Is she bleeding? Are *you?* Do I need to call someone?" He could hear himself growing high-pitched.

"No, no, it's not mine, it's hers, but it looks worse than it is. She's gonna be ok. I got it under control," he said with that arrogant confidence of his.

"Indigo!" Robbie strode to Cordelia's side and put a hand on her forehead. It was ice cold. "What's happened?"

Indigo's head snapped up. He stared at Robbie, then back at Cordelia. Robbie noticed he had a small scar on his face, a faint white line on the left side of his forehead that he'd obviously acquired in his new life. His life after them.

"She's gonna be fine," Indigo told him, far too calmly as he removed his blood-stained jacket, chucking it on the dresser.

"What in the hell is going on?" Robbie demanded, narrowing his eyes at Indigo, who was now covering Cordelia with a blanket. "I should call Dad."

"What?" Indigo murmured, still not tearing his eyes from Cordelia, then, "No. *No,* don't call anyone," he responded firmly. "Put the heating on, would you, Rob?" He rubbed his hands swiftly together as though trying to generate heat between his palms. "*Now,*" he commanded, looking Robbie directly in the eye with his *no arguments* stare. Robbie knew that stare well. Robbie had been coerced into many reckless adventures in the past because of that stare.

Robbie jumped up and ran to the hallway where he turned on the central heating, cranking it up high. He returned to Cordelia's room, where Indigo was kneeling beside the bed, holding her hands in his. Indigo's eyes were closed; he sat that way for some time. A lock of hair escaped from behind his ear and fell over his face as he leaned closer to her, opening his eyes.

Robbie was momentarily distracted. Except for the long hair, which Robbie wasn't quite sure about, Indigo hadn't changed a bit, even down to the same worn jeans and that sheepskin-collared denim jacket he'd removed to reveal a snug black v-neck t-shirt that showed off his killer frame to perfection. Actually, he'd put on a bit more muscle. He looked bloody good, still as sickeningly gorgeous as ever, although it wouldn't kill him to update his wardrobe.

Eventually, Indigo cocked his head to one side as though listening intently to something, then released Cordelia's hands and stood, his palms hovering over her rib cage. He took a deep breath, adjusted his position slightly, and narrowed his eyes.

Cordelia's whole body jerked and her torso rose up off the bed as though she'd been shocked with a defibrillator. She drew a deep gasping breath in. Her eyes flicked open, wild and searching, hands grappling at her throat.

"What the hell?!" Robbie cried, stumbling back, blinking. Holy moly, what did he just witness?

"Water, Rob, she needs water," Indigo ordered.

So many conflicting emotions were coursing through Robbie's body, so many questions jostling for position on the tip of his tongue, but he went downstairs to get Cordelia water, not before shooting Indigo a greasy look over his shoulder. When he returned, he took a deep breath and gathered himself before he strode back into the room. Cordelia was sitting up in bed, her blood-spattered face now flushed with glorious colour. She was gesturing to her throat, eyes narrowed at Indigo, who had dragged the armchair to her bedside, having shifted the piles of discarded clothing that previously adorned it to her dresser. He was sitting slumped forward, his head in his hands. They both looked up when Robbie entered the room and he gathered they'd been having words.

He knew he should give them some space, but whatever. At this point, his care factor was zero. He handed Cordelia the water, which she swallowed in one gulp, then perched himself on the foot of her bed.

"You guys need to tell me what the *fuck* is going on. What the hell have you done to my sister, Indigo?"

Cordelia glared at Robbie. "Are you *kidding* me, Rob? Before you get too comfy up there on that high horse you do realise you're not exactly blameless in this?"

Robbie felt the blood drain from his face. "Me?" he rasped.

"Do you not remember promising to pick me up from yoga?"

Robbie's stomach dropped. "Oh shit," he whispered, head in hands, "I fell asleep."

"Yeah, I gathered as much. And thanks to you, I had to walk home. In the *dark*. By *myself*."

Robbie raised his eyes slowly to meet hers.

"She was attacked, Rob," Indigo said solemnly. With those words, a series of haphazard images tumbled through Robbie's mind. Cordelia. The beachfront. A circle of cloaked figures swaying and chanting. But it had been a nightmare, hadn't it?

Robbie could feel the vomit rising. He staggered abruptly to his feet, ran to the bathroom, and retched into the toilet. When he had nothing left to bring up, he washed his face, then went downstairs where he poured a basin of warm soapy water, grabbing a couple of washcloths from the linen closet on his way back up.

He returned to Cordelia's room and sat down on the bed beside her. Balancing the basin on the nightstand, he dabbed a cloth into it then wrung it out, thrusting it to Indigo without looking at him, then dunking the second one. "I'm so sorry, Cora," he murmured, running the cloth gently over the sticky mess staining her neck. "I would never intentionally put you in danger."

"We know that, Rob," Indigo said, absently fingering the fang hanging low around his neck from a fine black leather string Robbie hadn't noticed 'til now. He abandoned it to begin wiping the blood from his face and hands with the washcloth.

Robbie glared venomously at Indigo. "We?" he spat. "*We?* You and her and I haven't been a *we* for a long time, mate!" He sprung up and stood over Indigo, glaring down at him menacingly.

Indigo hoisted his hands in surrender and leant back in the chair. Robbie sat back down and plunged the cloth aggressively into the soapy water, turning his attention back to Cordelia.

cordelia

When Robbie had cleaned her up as best he could, he leant over to cup her cheek, his eyes locked on hers and she knew he was searching for forgiveness. She smiled faintly and nodded at him, which drew a big exhale from him, followed by a relieved grin. He snatched up the soiled washcloths, chucked them in the basin, its contents now soupy red, and carried it carefully from the room. He shot Indigo one last dirty look as he left.

"How you feeling?" Indigo asked softly, his gaze so laden.

She shrugged her blood-stained sweatshirt off, dropping it on the floor. She didn't know how to act around him now. She was torn. On the one hand, she was furious with him for cutting her out of his life. But on the other hand, he'd been there when she really needed him tonight... and there was a dull ache of joy deep inside her at being in the same room as him again.

She'd forgotten.

She'd forgotten how it felt to be near him.

The exhilaration of his very presence.

His ability to captivate with one glance.

The way he lit up everyone around him.

Tears welled in her eyes. She glanced down, trying to blink them away. But the very nearness of him and all the emotion it brought, it was too much. The tears spilt over, hot, searing, humiliating. With every fibre of her being, all she wanted was for him to lie down beside her and take her in his arms, press his body to hers. She could barely catch her breath.

Robbie strode back into the room, balking when he saw the state of her. "Bloody hell, what've you done now, Indigo? Cordelia is *crying!*" Robbie snapped. "You know what it takes to make Cordelia cry in the presence of others? You're back all of five minutes and she's sobbing her dear little heart out!"

"Why are you yelling at me?" Indigo said, voice low.

"*Because you deserve it!*" Robbie shouted.

Indigo stared at him for a moment or two before exhaling shakily. "I know," he finally said, hanging his head, "I know you have every right to be pissed at me, but—"

"You left us," Cordelia interjected, quietly, fiercely.

Both boys looked at her.

"It might not have been your choice to leave here, but it was your choice to cut us out of your life. You left us in every sense of the word. And not just once. But twice. That night on the bridge, you chose to leave us again."

"Cora, I'm sor—" Indigo began.

"Nope." She held up her hand to shush him. "I don't want to hear 'I'm sorry'."

Indigo looked stricken.

"You were a part of our family. A part of us all. We welcomed you into our home and you used that charm of yours to force us all to… to *feel* something for you. You got us all used to having you around. And then you just left. *You just left without so much as a backwards glance!*"

Indigo opened his mouth to reply.

"Nope," Robbie said, holding his hand up in Indigo's face and waving at Cordelia to go on.

"You totally cut us off," Cordelia went on. "You didn't call, you didn't write. And all our calls and letters went unanswered. We didn't know if you were alive, dead, sick, hurt…! How were we meant to deal with that?"

Indigo looked at her, his eyes brimming with sorrow.

"Why?" she whispered. "Why would you do that to us? We loved you. We all loved you. *I* loved you." She heard his sharp intake of breath. "And you just threw it all back in our faces. Do you know how that made us feel?"

Indigo choked back a wracking breath, then composed himself. "I loved you, *love*, all of you. I never wanted to hurt you. You guys, you're family and—"

"How can you expect me to believe that?" she asked softly, closing her eyes for a beat.

He was gazing at her, seemingly unsure how to respond.

"You say you loved us, that we're family to you. But you know what? It's bullshit. If we were family, you would have turned to us when you needed us most."

"Touché," Robbie agreed.

"You know we would have been there in a heartbeat. And if you loved us, you wouldn't have cut us off." She was crying again now and she didn't even care. It was too much. Two-and-a-half years of hurting, of wondering, of feeling she'd never been enough for him.

All she'd ever wanted was to be his harbour in the storm.

"Cora, let me explain," he pleaded.

"What's to explain?" she sobbed. "What can you possibly say to make us feel better about the fact that we weren't enough? None of us were enough to stop you. To keep you." She took a deep breath and wiped at her eyes with the backs of her hands. "Did you even think of us? That night? On the bridge?"

"You don't understand," Indigo whispered. He'd gone deathly white.

"*I don't understand?* Really, Indigo? Well, whose fault is that? You could have picked up the phone anytime and talked to me, or Rob, or Mum and Dad… We were all there for you! We would have listened to you. We would have flown over and brought you back here. Back *home.*"

"Um, *actually,*" Robbie said, "if you recall, we *did* in fact attempt that. We jumped on a plane the minute we heard what you'd done, and you know how I hate to fly, Indigo. We came to see you in that quaint little hospital way out the back of bumfuck nowhere, but we were turned away and told you refused to see us. Some way to treat family, huh?"

"I-I was so ashamed," Indigo said, averting his eyes from theirs, his voice small. "I was… embarrassed. *Beyond* embarrassed. And I wasn't strong then. I couldn't bear to see the looks on your faces." He ran his hand through the back of his hair.

Robbie exhaled sharply.

"How can you still be so angry?" Indigo asked, and he looked so bewildered Cordelia's breath caught in her ribs.

"We're not angry," she said, attempting to reel her emotions back in. She glanced at Robbie, who was white-lipped and sullen. "*I'm* not angry," she reiterated, "I'm just… I'm just so sad," she said, her lip trembling, tears rushing to her eyes yet again. "It hurts my heart that you were so sad. That you felt so sad that you didn't want to be alive anymore and… and… You and me, we used to be able to talk about anything." She felt the tears rain down her face. She swiped at them with shaking hands. "I would have done anything, Indigo. Anything to help you."

"I know," he whispered, his eyes now glistening too. "I know it now. But then? I wasn't thinking rationally." He paused, staring down at the floor. "When I jumped off that bridge," he swallowed hard, "I honestly thought I was doing everyone a favour. I was so fucked up… I truly believed I was toxic and you'd all be better off without me, that the world would be better without me in it."

"So you didn't consider what you meant to us? That we'd be annihilated by what you did?" Robbie said.

"Shit, man, like, what do you want me to say?" Indigo said, raising his eyes to Robbie's. He took a deep breath. "Yeah, of course I knew you'd be upset, but honestly? I fully believed that my desperate yearning not to exist far outweighed what I told myself would be a temporary state of grief for you guys. I couldn't see past myself back then. I mean, look at the way I treated you all…" He sighed, covered his face with his hands, massaged his temples. "There was nothing good left." He dropped his hands, looked from Cordelia to Robbie. "And being around my father who constantly told me I was unwanted, that I was worthless, that I was nothing…"

"You're not nothing," Cordelia said fiercely. "You were *never* nothing."

"Yeah well, you hear it enough, it becomes the narrative in your head," he said with a sad smile. "I was constantly on edge and I was anxious all the time, so much so I could barely breathe. I hated — loathed — who I'd become, like, so, so much. And I didn't want you to see that person, didn't want anyone to see him. I-I was in a real bad way." His voice cracked.

Robbie blinked and looked away, lip trembling.

"I was so fucking tired all the time, no matter how much I slept. After I moved to New York, I was drunk or high like, every day. I just wanted it all to stop. I needed peace. I needed an escape. And I could see only one way to get it."

Cordelia couldn't stop herself. She reached out her hand and grasped his, warm and electric. "Oh, Inds," she breathed, feeling like her heart had been ripped from her chest, twisted and pummelled. She'd spent years wishing she could have been there for him that night. That night and the weeks and months and days leading up to it. She felt his pain so rawly. And then there was the guilt. She always felt if she'd gone sooner, if she'd listened to her instincts and just flown over there, she could have saved him.

"Please believe me, I honestly saw no other solution," Indigo choked. "All I wanted was to be free."

"I'm sorry, mate," Robbie said. "I guess it was easier to be mad at you for not wanting to be here than to think about *why* you didn't want to be here. I didn't know how bad it was for you."

"How could you?" Indigo shrugged. "As you said, I shut you guys out. I was convinced I was poison, and I guess in some way I was trying to protect the people I loved. From what I'd become."

"Inds?" Cordelia asked, guardedly, "Are... are you happy? That you survived?"

"Not at first. In the beginning, I was so full of shame and humiliation and devastation." Storm clouds gathered in his eyes. "But now? It's taken nearly two years of bloody hard work, but yes," he said, smiling gently and squeezing her hand, which was still burning in his. "Yes, I'm happy I survived. I'm so strong now – stronger than I've ever been. I know who I am, I know why I'm here, I know why I survived. I have peace, and I have purpose. And I'm thankful."

Without a thought in her head, Cordelia reached her arms out to him and pulled him onto the bed beside her, drawing him to her with all her might. He shuffled his arm around her and she curled into him, resting her head on his chest. She was engulfed by his warmth, his sandalwoody-sea-on-summer-breeze scent, by the steady beating of his heart, which certainly sounded as though it was no longer broken. Being in his arms felt like home. It was so late and she was suddenly so tired. Her eyelids were already drooping, she could barely keep them open.

"Hang on, I have questions," Robbie said, "about tonight."

Cordelia shuddered as images pushed at the recesses of her mind, battled to overtake her. Cloaked figures, obscured faces, plump blood-red lips, swirling tattoos, a forked tongue. She shook her head, pushing them out, knowing she'd get no sleep tonight if she gave in to them. She prayed they wouldn't translate into a resurgence of nightmares. She gripped tightly onto Indigo, balling fistfuls of his t-shirt in her palms as her heart hammered, her breath rapid. Clinging to him, focusing on him, on his steady breath, on the safety of his arms, it brought sanity; it brought a calmness that eased her very soul. She mirrored her breathing to his and it began to even out and the panic started to subside. Nothing could touch her when he was there.

"No more for tonight," she whispered. "It's time to sleep."

"We'll talk in the morning, man," Indigo said to Robbie, gently stroking her back. She began to relax.

"Fine," Robbie sighed. "I don't know about you two, but I'm gonna need a stiff drink after all this."

"That's not the only stiff thing you need," Cordelia murmured drowsily.

Robbie chuckled and stood up, leaning over to kiss them both on the forehead before moving to pull the curtains closed over the shutters. He picked up her sweatshirt and Indigo's jacket and quietly slipped from the room. On the periphery of her consciousness, Cordelia heard the washing machine starting up downstairs and then the liquor cabinet opening and closing and liquid being poured over ice.

Cordelia awoke disorientated. Her room was cave black, but with its double blackout curtains, it always was.

His name was on her lips: *Indigo*. He'd been here, right? She hadn't dreamed it. Her pillow still held the scent of him. She sat bolt up.

"Indigo?" she called into the darkness.

Nothing.

She swung her legs over the side of the bed and stood up. She swayed a little, feeling woozy. Everything that had happened last night rushed back to her and she grabbed the bedframe for support.

"Rob?" she said. She padded her way to the door and opened it a crack. She could hear the murmur of male voices floating up from downstairs.

The hallway clock said it was five past six. Early. She was still in her yoga clothes from last night; she needed a shower. She went into the bathroom and turned the taps on full blast. When she caught sight of herself in the mirror, she gasped. The lengths of her hair were matted with blood and a few dried flecks still peppered her neck and chest. She leant in close to the mirror, tilting her chin up, and she could see the faintest of silver lines ringing the right side of her throat. It was barely visible. She ran her fingers over it, it didn't hurt.

She stood under the shower for what seemed an eternity, letting the scalding water course over her body, her skin pink in its wake. She lathered up her hair and brushed her teeth, all the while replaying last night over and over in her head. The attack. Indigo. The things he'd done. The things he'd told them. And he was downstairs right now, in the kitchen with Robbie. Home again.

She dried off and returned to her room, where she slipped on a black denim mini dress, her mind still ticking as she adjusted the wide shoulder straps and fastened the buttons that ran down the front. She glanced out the window and saw it was overcast so she grabbed an oversized grey hoodie from the pile of clothes on the floor on her way out the door. It had 'The Bronx' emblazoned across the front in black block letters. She pulled it on but didn't bother to zip it up. It wasn't until she was at the bottom of the stairs that she remembered it had once been Indigo's. Her hair was still wet, but she'd managed to run a brush through it.

"Nice sweatshirt," Indigo commented from where he was sitting on the kitchen counter, munching on an apple. "I recall having one just like it myself." He winked. He was wearing the same jeans as last night but had on a clean grey-and-white striped t-shirt, and she remembered his nomad way of always keeping spare clothes in his car. His hair was damp and he had purple shadows beneath his eyes, as though he hadn't slept well.

"Finders keepers," she smiled shyly, taking the mug of fresh ginger and lemon tea Robbie handed her and sitting down at the kitchen table. She drew her knees up to her chest and blew on the hot tea cupped between her hands.

"How're you feeling?" Indigo asked.

"Fine," she replied, staring out the window into the backyard. In the back corner, small leaves were beginning to bud from the tips of the brown, ropey branches of the frangipani tree Indigo and his friends had congregated under at their thirteenth birthday party all those years ago. It would probably flower in a few weeks.

"Are you sure?" Robbie interjected. "Inds has been filling me in on what happened last night." He placed a bowl of fruit salad in front of her and squeezed her shoulder, then handed a second one to Indigo, who smiled in thanks.

Cordelia sighed and placed her mug on the table. She swung around to face the boys. In the light of day, she was ready to talk about it. "What *did* happen last night, Indigo?" she asked. "I've replayed it in my head over and over, but nothing makes sense." Her hand moved absently to her neck.

"What do you want to know?" he asked, examining the apple core in his hand before expertly tossing it into the bin.

"Well, for starters, who the hell attacked me?" She was trying to keep her voice calm and even.

Indigo and Robbie exchanged glances.

"I'm not some delicate little flower you need to protect!" she admonished. "Just tell me the truth!"

Indigo jumped down from the kitchen bench and walked across to the table where Cordelia sat, pulling out a chair so he could sit and face her. He straddled it backwards, resting his chin on his hands as he regarded her.

"Yeah, ok, look," he said, "I'll give it to you straight. Last night, you were attacked by warlocks."

"Warlocks?" she repeated, wrinkling her nose.

"They're like a type of witch. Powerful, with exceptional higher senses."

"O-kayyyyy… And higher senses are?"

"Well, you remember when we were kids, how I told you about those voices I could hear? And how I could pick up other people's feelings?"

"*You what now?*" Robbie balked, glancing from Indigo to Cordelia. "Oh, I get it," he sniped. "Secrets I wasn't privy to." He pursed his lips.

Indigo told him then. And after that he told the twins all about psychic abilities, about witches versus warlocks, about things Cordelia had never dreamt possible. The memory of the behemoth Artax summoning a flame to his palm out of nowhere flared bright. It was all flooding back to her. The chill down her spine, the paralysing fear, being frozen to the spot, unable to move or scream.

Cordelia plucked a blueberry from her bowl, rolling it between her fingers before placing it to the side. "Those warlocks, Inds, what did they want with me?"

"I-I'm not entirely sure." He picked up the discarded blueberry and popped it in his mouth. "Those warlocks last night, they were collectors."

"What the hell's a collector?" Robbie said, picking up the fruit salad Indigo had left on the bench and placing it in front of him. He hoisted himself to sit on the kitchen counter, leaning back on his hands and crossing his legs.

"Kind of like a vampire," Indigo explained.

Cordelia snorted. "*Vampires,* Inds? Seriously? You may have convinced me on the witches, but vampires? Ah, nope."

"Not some fictional undead blood-sucker like in the movies," Indigo said quickly, leaning to fish the blueberries from Cordelia's bowl, gathering them in his palm before tipping them into his. "A very much alive warlock who feeds off the life-force of others." He began transferring his raspberries to her bowl.

Cordelia stared at him, wondering if he was messing with her.

"But-but why?" she stammered.

"To increase their own power. And it gives them a major high."

"But they didn't do that to me, right?" she said, fingers travelling to her throat. "I mean, I feel totally fine today."

"No. If they'd done that to you, you'd be comatose right now. What they did to you…" he glowered, eyes hardening, "that was new. And unexpected."

"How can I feel so fine when there was so much blood?" She gazed at him indignantly.

"I told you last night, it seemed worse than it was," he murmured, averting his eyes.

She shifted in her seat. "How do they know who to target?"

Indigo thumbed his lip, staring into space.

"Earth to Inds?" she prompted.

"Oh," he said, glancing up at her, "um, sorry. Yeah, because they can see beyond the physical, they're able to go for people whose vibe they like."

"You've lost me," Cordelia said, arching a brow.

"Ok, so look at it this way," Indigo explained. "We're all made of matter and energy, right? So we have a physical body which is essentially just dense matter, but then we have an energy to us, and that energy is in us and around us and connects us all. Most people can't see that. But warlocks can, especially if they rely on it as a power source the way collectors do."

"What do they see?" Robbie asked.

"We-ell," Indigo replied thoughtfully, "that depends on their victim. If someone has a lot of baggage, well, their energy will reflect that. It will be dense and dark and heavy. Let's just say collectors go for those with less baggage."

"So why me?" Cordelia asked.

"I guess you have your shit sorted," Indigo said nonchalantly, dodging her gaze.

She pursed her lips, tapping her fork as she regarded him through narrowed eyes. "Tell me the truth, Inds," she said softly. She may not have seen him in years, but she still knew him, and she knew when he was avoiding telling her something.

He lifted his eyes to hers.

"Tell me," she repeated. "Why did they attack me?"

"I'm not sure."

"But you have a theory," she said accusingly.

"Yeah... I mean, maybe." He dropped his head into his hands, pressing his temples wearily. "I don't know yet, Cora. It's complicated."

"You owe me the truth," she said, her annoyance escalating.

"To ply you with unfounded theories at this stage would be irresponsible," he argued, linking his fingers and resting his head in his hands. "It's really complex. You wouldn't understand."

With those words, she was triggered. Anger rose up, exploded out of her. "That's *bullshit*, Indigo! All you do these days is keep secrets from me because you assume I won't understand! I'm not an idiot, you know."

He looked taken aback.

She pushed her chair back from the table with a screech. "If you can't be honest with me, then I'm outta here." She stormed towards the door. "I'm going for a surf."

"I-I don't really want you going out on your own," Indigo admitted quietly. And she stopped dead and wheeled around. "Not today, not when you might still be on their radar… They may target you again." He glanced at Robbie.

"Oh, really?" she snapped, hands on hips. "And how would you know that if you don't know why they targeted me in the first place?"

Indigo's face flushed. "Come on, Cora, now's not the time for games. Just come back and sit down. Let's talk."

"Nope," she said, glaring at him. "I'm done talking."

"Surely she's fine in broad daylight?" Robbie asked, looking from Cordelia to Indigo.

"If you want to go for a wave, I'll come with you," Indigo said.

"Whatever," she said, throwing her hands up in the air.

"Ok, grab your board. We'll take my car," he said.

"Fine," she retorted. "But we're going to Freshie."

indigo

Freshwater Beach. She knew how he felt about it. Back in the day, she'd always tried to wheedle it into their rotation. He pulled his black Landcruiser into the near-empty carpark and Cordelia was out before he'd even put the handbrake on. She'd turned his Red Hot Chilli Peppers CD way up and barely spoken a word to him on the short drive, and now she had her back to him as she wrapped a towel around herself and stripped off, emerging in a tiny black string bikini which she promptly pulled a wetsuit over. He exhaled shakily. Holy shit… her *body!*

She popped the boot and threw her clothes in, snatched her board out and strode towards the beach without a backwards glance.

He sighed heavily as he climbed out of the car, heading to the boot and flicking through the stack of surfboards inside until he found the one he wanted. Swathing a towel around his hips, he quickly changed into his wetsuit.

His board under one arm, he jogged down the sandy pathway that led through the dense shrubbery at the rear of the beach. Emerging through the dunes, he scanned the ocean, windswept today and gloomy green. He quickly spotted Cordelia out just past the choppy break, straddling her board, staring out at the horizon, her back to the beach, to him. It was a dim and blustery day, unseasonal for November. The grey cloud cover was heavy and the beach was deserted.

Indigo ran down the undulating sand, threw his board out into the frothy surf and leapt flat onto it. With powerful strokes, he paddled out past the break, reaching Cordelia swiftly.

"It's all or nothing with you," she said, not even turning around. Her voice was like ice. "I don't see you for over two years and now I can't seem to shake you."

"Surf's shit, Cora," he observed, eyeing the small messy whitecaps coming at them. It was mush out there.

"I don't care. I don't want to go back in."

The southerly wind whipped over them, Antarctic to the bone. Cordelia shivered. Her wet hair hung down her back like molten gold. Her black wetsuit clung to her curves, accentuating her tiny waist, her limbs strong and toned from all the time she'd clocked up on her board.

"Don't be so stubborn," he smiled. "Admit it's shit and let's go get warm."

"Fine," she sighed through chattering teeth. "It's shit. I'm going back in." She swung her board towards the beach. "Before you can accuse me of not understanding surf conditions either."

"Cora, please," he said, reaching out to grab the tip of her surfboard.

"Let *go*, Indigo," she said, ripping it from his grasp and paddling towards the shore.

"You know I didn't mean it the way it sounded," he called after her. "I hate you being mad at me."

She stopped paddling and swung back around, sitting up to stare at him. Their eyes met over the lapping waves, his large and pleading, hers searching, softening. His board was drifting towards hers, hers towards his; she made no move to stop it.

By the time their boards met with a clunk of fibreglass, she seemed to have let it go. She'd always been passionate, strong willed, yet quick to forgive. He'd never known her to hold a grudge, except maybe towards Tommy Monahagn who'd made Robbie's life hell in school and was supposedly now doing time. Her flesh was taut with goose bumps, her rosebud lips tinged blue. Indigo reached over and took her frigid hands in his. He rubbed a little colour back into them, then just sat, holding her hands between his.

"Forgive me?" he whispered, drinking her in.

She shrugged and lowered her gaze, breaking the intensity between them. She was silent for a while, staring out at the horizon. "Fine," she finally breathed, raising her eyes to meet his again. Those killer fucking eyes. "Ok."

He nodded and squeezed her hands, relief coursing through his body. He held her gaze and she softened, a slight flush spreading up her cheeks as the corners of her mouth turned up in the subtlest of smiles. Just being near her again awakened something inside of him. The way he felt about her was undeniable. She was lightning in his veins.

But then something in her shifted and she stiffened, yanking her hands from his almost guiltily. And just like that, the moment was gone. She was visibly shivering now, her teeth chattering uncontrollably.

"Let's get you warmed up," he ordered. They paddled in unison to the beach, the waves offering little assistance. They reached the shore and ran up the sand, the icy wind howling at their backs.

By the time they reached his SUV they'd both already stripped their frigid wetsuits to their waists. He popped the boot and chucked her her clothes and she quickly changed back into her mini dress and adopted sweatshirt behind a towel. She jumped into his car with its black rims and dark tinted windows where he sat in his jeans and t-shirt. He had the heating turned way up and they immediately began to thaw in the cosiness.

"New car smell," she breathed, inhaling deeply, "When did you get it?" she asked, ejecting the Chilli Peppers and flicking through radio stations. She stopped on Boys II Men, *End of the Road*.

"Bernadette made Lukas sell my car when I was away. Apparently, it was cluttering up the garage she never uses." A muscle in his jaw twitched. "I didn't want to drive her Porsche or the Maserati or the Bentley, so I bought this. It's a little more low profile," he smiled as he leaned over to retrieve a blanket off the back seat. He wrapped it around her.

"It smells like you," she said, holding it to her nose. "Edie must be glad to have you back?"

"Ah, yep," he grinned. Edita hadn't stopped fussing over him since he'd walked back through the door.

"Inds," she said softly, "I can't deal with all the secrets. You need to tell me what's been going on. Where have you been all this time? Why are you back?" Her fingers moved to the faint indent on the right side of her throat. "I know I was bleeding last night, worse than what you're making out, and now I barely have a scar. I mean, how is that possible?"

He didn't want her to know how bad it had been. He didn't want to scare her, for her to feel the churning fear he'd been feeling ever since. His instinct was to protect her at any cost. But after everything he'd put her through, he knew he owed her the truth. But all of it? He sure as shit knew that now wasn't the time to start delving into the truth about her childhood nightmares. That was something he needed to approach slowly, delicately.

"I don't even know where to start," he groaned, massaging his forehead with his fingertips.

"Why don't you start by telling me about New York?" she prompted, firmly holding his gaze with those coral-sea eyes.

This was Cordelia.

He'd always been able to tell her anything about himself.

He nodded, took a deep breath, and began.

chapter thirty

wicked game

cordelia

She shrugged the blanket from her shoulders. She'd warmed up while Indigo had been telling her about the years he'd been gone, regaining feeling in her hands and feet, her cheeks beginning to prickle with heat. But now she was too warm.

So much information in such a short space of time. Her head was spinning. She didn't know what to think, what to say. He'd spoken of New York and Sedona and Raf and Sasha and Nash and Aurora and Dawn. He'd explained he'd learnt of things he never knew existed, things that didn't sound possible, and that he'd discovered he could do things most people couldn't. Like how to heal a life-threatening wound with his bare hands.

He'd told her so much. So much to take in, to absorb.

He was sitting in the driver's seat, knee bent up, body turned towards her. He'd suddenly stopped talking and was gazing intently at her, his teeth hard on his lower lip as he absentmindedly ran his finger over a tear in the knee of his jeans.

"Why did you come back, Inds?" she asked gently. "I mean, why now?"

He glanced away and she could see there was something that was tearing him up inside. He looked so wretched. It took every ounce of her strength to not reach out for him, to touch that face of his, so indecently beautiful, even when marred by an expression so tortured.

"Please tell me." She hated seeing him like this.

He lifted his eyes to meet hers. "Lots of reasons. But mainly… because of you," he blurted, running a hand nervously through the back of his hair. "You, Cordelia, are where I belong."

A surge of adrenaline hit her veins. Her breath hitched in her chest as her heart thundered.

"The thing is," he said, his eyes locked so deep on hers, "I never stopped thinking about you. As hard as I tried to get you out of my mind, you were always there. Always have been, always will be." He flushed, a shy smile teasing at his lips. "I realise it's been a long time, that I can't just expect to pick up where we left off. And I *know* I hurt you." His throat bobbed. "I know I need to fix what I've broken. If I could turn back the clock, I swear I'd do it all differently. But I need you to know… I-I've always loved you, Cordelia. I never stopped. You're it for me." He shrugged with the resignation of the fact. "I came back because the longer I was away from you, the more I realised my life will never feel complete without you in it."

She was spiralling. It was what she'd always wanted to hear, what she'd dreamt of hearing, hoped, wished for every night, month after month. *Too little too late,* a little voice inside her said. *Too late. Too late. Too late.*

She looked away from him, pressing her hands shakily to her mouth. Chris Isaak was on the radio singing *Wicked Game* and she felt every lyric. Rudderless, she tuned in on that, closing her eyes for a moment, taking a deep breath in and slowly, slowly exhaling it.

He reached for her hand and she trembled as his fingers brushed hers. "Cora?" She refused to look at him. "Cordelia? Please look at me?"

She knew if she looked at him, she'd be done for. She couldn't look at him, couldn't look at him and not feel all those feelings she'd seen a moment ago reflected there, smouldering, burning deep in his eyes. For months now she'd shoved them down so far, she'd dug a hole, buried them… But she could feel them, those subterranean feelings, feel them rising, tumbling, bubbling up, rearing up right when she didn't want them to.

"Cordelia? Please, give me something?" he pleaded, gently grasping her chin and turning her face to his. She slowly, finally, raised her eyes to meet his. So familiar, so warm, flecked iridescent yellow and green and hazel and beautiful and brimming with hope. Yup, she was done for.

"Did you hear me?" he said, his knuckles caressing her cheek. "I love you, Cordelia. I'm in love with you."

When he looked at her that way, the rest of the world simply faded away.

"How long?" she whispered.

"Always, I think," he said, fingers skimming the fin of her collarbone. "It was always there, even when we didn't see it, even when I was too scared to put myself out there. I can't pretend anymore. Please tell me I'm him, Cora, the one who takes your breath away."

She closed her eyes for the beat of an exhale, snaring her quivering lip between her teeth. Stalling for time, she tentatively reached out, her fingers closing over the fang hanging from his neck by a black leather string. She noticed there were two small stones embedded in it, one black, the other yellow. "This is new," she murmured. "What is it?"

"A wolf's tooth," he replied distractedly, "It was a... a gift."

Her fingers travelled upwards to touch the faint scar that now resided on the left-hand side of his forehead, also new, and she wanted to cry.

"The darkness I defeated," he said, his voice catching, "it was because of you."

He was so near. She wanted to kiss him. Needed to kiss him. Felt as though she'd die if she didn't.

He moved to gently wipe a salty tendril of hair from her cheek, tucking it behind her ear. His hand slid to the nape of her neck and time seemed to stand still as he slowly drew her towards him. "I need you, Cora," he murmured, his voice cracking. "You're the reason I'm still breathing." And then his lips were brushing hers, whisper-soft at first, skin barely touching skin, but scorching all the same. The electricity throbbed between them so the breath left her body and she faltered to catch it. It was like he'd struck a match in the deepest recesses of her belly and the flame was slowly growing, rising up, up, up, the heat rapidly spreading throughout her body.

Soft fingers tangled in her hair as their kiss deepened, her arms finding their way around his neck as his tongue sought hers. She moulded herself against him, his body hard against hers as he slid his seat back and pulled her effortlessly to straddle him, his lips never leaving hers. They were both breathing heavily, his breath hers, her breath his, one and the same. She'd lost all sense of time and reason. All she knew right now was him, him, him, and she wanted him so much.

His hands were under her sweatshirt, strong and sure and gentle and firm and everywhere she wanted them to be. Her whole body was alive. She was feeling so much she didn't know which way was up. She arched back as his lips fluttered over her throat, her clavicle, fire where they touched. He drew aside the strap of her dress, layering kisses along the dip of her shoulder as he unfastened one button, then two, his hand sliding inside to cup her breast, his thumb moving back and forth over her nipple, and she gasped because his hands were on her body and nothing had ever, ever, felt so good.

A groan, deep and primal, escaped his mouth as it found hers again and she went molten. She grasped the hem of his t-shirt, pulling it up, up and off, her fingertips touring the ridges of his abdominals. His body was unbelievable. She needed to feel his skin against hers, the heat and weight of his body surging down on her, to explore every inch of him. Her body craved his desperately. Maybe if she pressed herself against him hard enough, she might push through his skin and pour herself inside of him.

"You are so beautiful," he breathed, pulling back to look at her, his chest rising and falling rapidly. He extracted his hand from inside her dress to trace the line of her cheek, then ran his thumb along her lower lip, plump from his kisses. He lent back in, parting her lips with his tongue. "I was so scared to come back here," he murmured between feverish kisses, "to tell you how I felt. I was terrified you might have met someone else, that you wouldn't want to see me…"

His words snapped her back to reality, to a reality she'd lost her head and momentarily forgotten, to a reality he wasn't going to like. Indigo was her kryptonite, hot molten kryptonite. She lost all control and sense of reason when she was around him. She pulled away half-heartedly before giving in and going back for more. She knew they had to stop, but she couldn't.

But they had to. "Stop," she finally panted. "We have to stop." It took every ounce of her resolve to pull back, to climb off him, to move back to the passenger seat, readjusting her dress, rebuttoning it. She felt like crying. Her body felt utterly incomplete when it wasn't touching his. She dropped her head into her palms, confused, spinning from what had occurred between them. What had she just done?

"What's wrong?" he asked, voice low. His eyes were full of concern, his pupils dilated. His fingertips caressed her back, sparks trailing down her spine. She shrugged him off, dropped her hands from her face.

"You're not good for me, Inds," she said, sighing deep and shuddery.

"Whaddaya mean?" he asked, searching her face. "If you ask me, I reckon we're pretty fucking great together." He reached for her hand.

"Stop it," she said, yanking away just as she felt herself being reeled back in. She sat on her hands, moved as far away from him as she could. "I can't do this. *We* can't do this. It's wrong."

"Wrong?" he repeated, confusion shadowing his eyes.

"I'm not thinking straight," she tried to explain. "I can't think straight around you. I totally lost my head right then. We shouldn't have done that. I shouldn't have kissed you…" She ran her hands through her hair and shook her head. "I can't be in this car with you," she said resolutely, opening the door and climbing out. The darkly tinted windows were completely fogged up, but she knew he'd just be able to make out her silhouette retreating towards the beach.

She glanced back to see him jumping out of the car, yanking his t-shirt back on. "Cordelia!" he called. "Wait up!" He jogged after her, reaching her as she hit the sand. He caught her hand, stopping her in her tracks. She spun to face him. The wind had picked up even more since they'd come in from their non-surf earlier in the day. Her hair whipped wildly in her face. Bruise-black clouds darkened the sky above them. Thunder rumbled menacingly in the distance.

"What's going on?" he asked, raising his voice so she could hear him over the squall. Her hand was still in his. She pulled it away, crossed her arms.

"Your timing is just atrocious, Inds," she said with a bitter half-laugh.

"What are you talking about?"

"I'm *so angry* with you!" she choked. Putting the blame on him was easier.

He took a step back, his eyes never leaving hers, hurt creeping into his.

"You kiss me, you tell me you love me, and then you just disappear… for *years!*" she railed. "Do you know how long I waited for you?" She stared at him, shaking her head. "For all your grand declarations, you just took off and left me! Well, you know what? I got sick of waiting around for someone who *never* called, *never* wrote, who *refused* to see me after I flew *halfway around the world* for him—"

"Cora, I said I was sorry—"

"You *broke* my *heart!*"

He reeled back as if she'd slapped him. And he just looked crushed.

"And now you're back," she continued, softer. "Of course you're back *now.*" She clenched her jaw.

"Now?" he asked, "What's wrong with now?"

She sunk down onto the sand, wrapping her sweatshirt tightly around herself and hugging her knees into her chest as she gazed out to sea. Tentatively, he sat down next to her, close, but not daring to touch her again. He waited patiently, silently, for her to continue.

"I waited for you, Indigo," she said stoically, her eyes never moving from the storm brewing on the horizon. "I believed in you… in… in *us.* I was convinced that what we had was once-in-a-lifetime and that you'd come back to me. But you didn't," she said, turning to stare him accusingly in the eye. "And it hurt like hell." Tears rushed to blur her vision.

"Robbie and Peyton, they got over me moping around, putting my life on hold for you. They were convinced you weren't coming back, and they convinced me, too… And you know what I realised? The world does *not* revolve around you, Indigo Wolfe," she said, her words laced with soft force. "At least mine doesn't." She paused for a moment before adding, "Well, it doesn't anymore, anyway."

"What are you saying?" he asked. His voice had dropped an octave.

She softened, giving up her anger. "I'm seeing someone," she said, so quietly she wondered if he'd heard her, but then she could see he wished he hadn't. She looked at the ground, refusing to meet his eyes, nervously twisting the fine band on her right ring-finger. "I didn't go looking," she explained. "It… it just kinda… happened."

"Who is it?" he asked. He'd taken a deep breath in, but she hadn't heard him exhale.

"Does it really matter?" she asked, finally raising her eyes to his, then wishing she hadn't. He looked terrible. He looked how she'd looked after New York.

"It does to me," he replied. "It's someone I know?"

She paused for a moment and then nodded. "It's not like you can plan who you fall for," she said, the words tumbling out. "We'd been friends for so long, and he tried so hard to cheer me up after you left. He was pretty hurt too, you know. We both really missed you, we were both pretty pissed at you… and I guess we bonded over that in the beginning."

"Please tell me it's not—"

"It's Drew, Inds," she finished gently.

"*Pres?* You're kidding me, right?" And he looked devastated. "I don't know what to say."

"There's nothing *to* say," she said softly. "You lost the right to have a say in my life a long time ago, Indigo. Drew's been mates with Robbie and me almost as long as you have. I don't owe you anything, Inds, neither does he. I-I don't belong to you."

Of course she was right, and his shoulders slumped as he gave up the fight. "Where is he now?"

"He's up in Byron with some of his uni mates," she explained. "He's meant to meet me in Surfers for Schoolies on Saturday."

"Does he know I'm back?"

"I haven't told him, no," she replied evenly. She didn't want to complicate the situation by telling Indigo she and Drew hadn't spoken in almost two weeks, that they were currently taking a bit of time out from one another. "I'll tell him when I see him." She felt sick when she realised she now had to add Indigo to the list of things she and Drew needed to talk about.

He stared at her brokenly. "Cora, the person I was two-and-a-half years ago, that fucked up, broken boy who went off the rails and shut you out, I look back and he's a stranger to me now." His voice wavered. "He wasn't well and he was so lost and hellbent on self-destruction." He cleared his throat, composed himself. "But that's not who I am today.

I've worked so hard to be the man I am now. Cora, I need to believe, *have* to believe, that you know that."

"I do," she whispered, "I really do." She knew him better than anyone in the whole world knew him and he truly had the best heart of anyone she'd ever met.

"So, if you really know that in your heart of hearts, why can't you forgive me? Why can't you give me another chance?" His voice was low.

"Indigo," she began, "When I'm with you, you make me feel things I didn't know were possible. And I know we could have been great together. But you left. You moved on. *I* moved on. What we had is in the past. And we can't go back. I'm with Drew now and he's my future. He loves me—"

"Do you love him?"

"I do," she nodded, her face softening as she thought of Drew with his outlandish conspiracy theories and his serious thoughtfulness, that adorable dimple that popped when he smiled just for her. Drew, who was so wounded, who needed her. "I do love him."

Indigo looked shattered. The tears welling in Cordelia's eyes spilled over. It broke her heart all over again to smash his to bits.

"And you're happy?" he choked, eyes glittering.

"I am," she nodded, smiling through her tears. Because despite their recent problems, Drew did make her happy.

He took a deep breath, a ragged breath and smiled back at her. Not his usual smile. A tired, faded version. "Well, that's all I want, for you to be happy." His lip trembled.

"I will love you all my life, Cordelia."

She swiped at her tears, swallowing back a sob. She looked at the ground, shaking her head, too overcome to respond. Thunder rumbled again, this time closer, and a jagged streak of lightning shot across the sky.

"Let's go," he said suddenly, jumping up, dusting the sand off his hands. "I'll take you home." He stalked off up the beach, back towards the carpark. One big fat solitary raindrop landed on Cordelia's face, then a staggered other and another slowly pattering after it.

"Inds?" she called after him.

"Yeah?" he asked, turning back to face her.

"You gonna be ok?"

He ran a hand through his hair. "Course," he grinned, a little too brightly. He turned and walked off, hands deep in his pockets. The rain started to come faster, heavier as she climbed to her feet and slowly followed him up the dunes.

They barely spoke on the way home, but she was vividly aware of him sitting there beside her, so palpably close yet so far. 1927 was on the radio singing *If I Could* and Indigo reached forward abruptly and turned it off, jaw set. The rain had let up a bit and the hollowness echoing through her heart was so deafening she wondered if he could hear it. She had to fight the overriding instinct to reach out and tuck the lock of hair that had fallen over his eye behind his ear. She could barely see straight, so deep was the desire to surrender to the raw ache coursing through her body. In another time, another place, she'd say to hell with everyone else, with the rest of the world.

But here and now... she couldn't. She never wanted to hurt Drew the way Indigo had hurt her.

"Come by the house tomorrow," she said quietly as they pulled up in her driveway, "Mum and Dad and Matty would love to see you."

He nodded gently as she climbed out and he shifted the car into reverse. "Bye, Cordelia," he smiled sadly. And his eyes! In his eyes, she could see she'd destroyed him. Once upon a time he'd been the person she'd have lain down and died to protect from hurt, and now she was the reason he was hurting. Turning away from him was like amputating a part of herself.

"Goodbye, Indigo," she whispered, her voice shaking. She closed the car door and turned her back so she didn't have to watch him drive away. As she walked slowly to the front door, the sky opened up again, rain pouring down to drench her in a matter of seconds.

Cordelia sunk down onto the porch step, dropped her head into her hands, and right there in the middle of that thunderstorm she sobbed her heart out.

chapter thirty-one

every breath you take

the covenstead, somewhere below north fort, manly

reinenoir

"Last night didn't exactly go as I'd hoped, but I knew that he would come," Reinenoir mused as she swept through the tunnel, robes fluttering.

The Maiden scurried in her wake holding a torch, its light bouncing off the damp concrete walls, their footsteps crunching on the floor below. "Yes, my lady," she said. "We did not foresee the early interference from the boy in the red car. His appearance prolonged the attack. We're fortunate she turned down the lift he offered."

Reinenoir didn't care about such trivial things. All she cared about was *him*. "His power," Reinenoir said, steering the topic back. She stopped in the dim passageway, spinning to eye her Maiden. "You could feel it, couldn't you? You know now I wasn't exaggerating." She leant forward in eager anticipation.

"He is powerful indeed. And they trained him well," the Maiden replied. "But they have protections on him. You saw what happened, how he repelled your magick. That was not all him."

Reinenoir tilted her head and shrugged. "At least now we know what we're dealing with." She gazed intently at her Maiden. "I want him," she said, narrowing her eyes, turning to climb the steps that would lead them back up to the storm raging above ground. "Now more than ever."

"Akasha to warlock. Has it ever been done?"

Reinenoir stopped dead and spun to give her a withering stare. The Maiden paled.

"Oh yes," the Maiden breathed, "of course." She cleared her throat. "Then we will need the full coven. If his power is hereditary and not collected, then he's not like anyone I've ever seen."

Reinenoir's lip curled in a dark smile. "Honestly, with his naivete, do you think he's any match for me right now?" she purred. "But we need to move quickly. We take him now while he's still green, we triumph."

"Will it be enough though, just to convert him? When he jumped and survived, he altered the whole timeline. Artax said we need to take him out to get us back on track," the Maiden said, wide-eyed.

"Let's try it my way first," Reinenoir said silkily. "It may well be enough."

"And if he won't come over?"

"If I can't have him, no one will. His threat is too great. You know as well as I do from where he's descended. If I cannot merge his line with mine, it dies with him. End of story."

chapter thirty-two

against all odds (take a look at me now)

manly, new south wales

indigo

Indigo raised his eyes in response to the quiet knock on his door.

"Indigo? Dinner's ready."

"I'm not hungry, thanks, Edie," he replied, rolling onto his side on his bed, curling into the foetal position. Thunder clapped in the distance as rain battered his windows.

"Indi, you must eat," she said gently.

"Maybe later." He heard her sigh and plod away. After what had happened with Cordelia that afternoon, his stomach felt like a lead balloon. When he closed his eyes, he could still feel her lips warm on his, her achingly beautiful body pressed up against him, her fingertips electric on his flesh.

But then she'd smashed his heart to smithereens.

He wasn't angry. It wasn't as though a part of him hadn't expected this, for her to have moved on. But it still hurt. It hurt like hell, in fact. He balled his hands into fists and drew them to his black-and-blue heart. He squeezed his eyes shut as a great shuddering breath left his body. He could feel a wave of emotion riding hot on its tail.

She was in love with someone else. She didn't want him anymore.

For everything he'd been through, all he'd achieved, the wholeness he'd found, it felt almost pointless if he couldn't share it with her.

And then there was the other thing. The thing he'd been avoiding dealing with since last night when Cordelia was attacked, the thing he'd pushed from his mind over and over and over again. After Cordelia had collapsed on the beach, he'd had to heal her neck wound. And then he was left to face the warlocks, three on one he'd thought, until the fourth had stepped forward, her satiny purple robes billowing around her, her blood-red lips twisted into a cruel grin...

He recalled it all so vividly because as he'd lain in Cordelia's bed the night before he'd dreamt it in such detail, not once, but twice, as though his mind was recreating every single little thing, ensuring it was cemented so deep in his temporal lobe that he would never forget.

But how could he?

He would never forget.

Could never forget.

He pressed his knuckles to his mouth and shuddered, trying to shake the memory from his mind, the image of her encroaching upon him, her expression as she'd lowered her hood, and he'd seen her face... And the power she'd demonstrated, the immense power...

Reinenoir.

That was what she went by now.

He was so weary. He'd barely slept last night and today had really taken it out of him. At least he knew now what she wanted, that Cordelia was safe, for now at least.

Please, he begged as his eyelids grew heavy and he felt himself drifting off, please don't let me dream of it... please don't let me dream of her... please...

"Cordelia!" he cried, running as fast as he could down the beach towards her. She was veiled in darkness, three cloaked figures surrounding her, their arms raised up high as they prowled around her in a circle. He was frantic. Nash had seen this happening in Manly, not all the way up here in Queenscliff. Something had altered the course of events.

He screamed her name again, but she didn't seem to hear him. He was close enough now to see her eyelids drooping, her legs trembling. As he ran, he held his arms out wide, raising his palms up in front of him and generating as much bioplasma as he could from his field. He fired then, both hands in unison, a warning shot never meant to hit the warlocks surrounding her. They weaved and scattered, releasing their hold on her.

"Cordelia!" he yelled again.

She lolled her head groggily to look at him, exposing her throat. No one was close enough to touch her, yet all of a sudden a streaming red line appeared at her jugular, slicing smoothly towards her windpipe as if cut by an invisible blade.

"Cordelia! NO!" he screamed as he saw her hand fumble clumsily to her neck, blood spurting between her fingers as a look of bewilderment crossed her face. Eyes wide with terror, she began to choke and splutter, drowning in her own blood.

Her legs buckled then and he saw her start to go down. In one swift movement, he skidded on his knees to catch her as she fell, cradling her gently. He clamped his hand over her throat to stem the blood, warm and slippery and everywhere. "I've got you, Cora," he choked. "Just stay with me, ok?" Instinct kicked in then as he closed his eyes and focused on her injury, seeing how deep it went, what was severed and how he could repair it, trying to concentrate on anything but the nagging thought that all his training meant nothing if he failed in this moment, that saving her meant everything. A wound that fresh was easy to work on and he put her back together quickly, doing all he could to stabilise her, aware they were not alone, not knowing how long he had.

Afterwards he sat with her clutched in his arms, smoothing the hair from her face and checking her pulse. It was weak, but it was there. He drew in a deep breath, trying to steady his shaking hands. Just as he was about to pick her up and carry her to his car, he heard it. His name.

"Indigo." The tone was teasing, sing-song.

The familiarity of the voice sent shivers down his spine. He looked up and saw the three warlocks standing watching him silently, arms by their sides, faces cloaked. "Which one of you did that to her?" He raised his hand, conjuring bioplasma to his palm so it writhed and streamed menacingly. "Next time I won't miss," he said, glaring up at them.

The largest warlock stepped forward, but that voice spoke again, "No, Artax, down boy," and Artax lowered his head and stepped back in line with the other two. "Hello, Indigo." He craned his neck to locate the source. And then he saw her, emerging through the darkness from behind the others, in a satin cloak of a brighter plum.

Indigo gathered Cordelia up and stood, drawing her protectively into his chest. He cradled her in the nook of his elbow, stretching his palm out in warning.

"Put that away, Indigo," she said, sauntering towards him, "There's no need for that tonight."

He took a step back and turned his body slightly to shield Cordelia from the woman now standing before him. But he didn't lower his hand. "Who are you?" he breathed, staring down at her, icy fear gripping his gut. Her face was hidden by her hood. All he could see was her mouth, shapely and painted red, now twisting into a condescending smile.

"You don't know me anymore?" she asked playfully.

He was aware Cordelia was growing colder in his embrace, her breathing shallower. She'd lost a lot of blood. If he didn't heal her further soon, it might be too late.

"I don't have time for games," he said, tentatively lowering his hand and using it to scoop Cordelia higher in his arms, nestling her head on his shoulder. "I'm walking away now." He began to back slowly away from her. He didn't know what else she was capable of, but he was poised and ready to put himself between her and Cordelia if she struck again.

"You're free to go," she said, "for tonight, anyway. I just wanted to see you. See how you've changed, see what you've become, mon chéri."

His heart froze. "What did you just call me?" he whispered. He could feel her eyes boring into him, drinking him in, assessing every inch of him.

She lifted her hand to her hood, slowly, slowly sweeping it back. Blonde hair fine as cornsilk unfurled to spill down her shoulders. His breath faltered in his lungs as he stared at her, the recognition instant. Her face was more angular now, she was older than when he'd known her, twenty now. But she still had the same sapphire blue eyes, the same pouty lips, the same perfect nose she'd gotten from her parents for her fourteenth birthday.

"Hello, Indi," she said, her grin broadening at his reaction.

"Harper?" he breathed, "Harper Valentine?" His heart was hammering.

"It's Reinenoir now," she purred.

"But… but why?" he spluttered. "Why Cordelia?" He glanced down at Cordelia, icy and wan and blood-soaked.

"So dramatic," she sighed. "It was just a scratch."

"A scratch?" he thundered. "You're psychotic! Answer my question. Why her?"

"I have my reasons."

"She was bait?" he cried, hoisted Cordelia higher in his arms.

"You flatter yourself," she smiled, her eyes lingering on Cordelia. "She wasn't just bait… Although I knew you'd come for her."

"What do you want with me?"

"You've grown up. Found yourself, come into your own. We were so good together once, Indi," she said. "Imagine what we could do together now?"

Cordelia's life force was weakening by the second. His head was reeling. Was Harper propositioning him?

'Yes,' he heard her voice in his head then, 'I am propositioning you.'

He shook his head, pushed her out of his mind, shut her out, shrouded it tightly. He turned his back on her and began to walk away, pressing his lips to Cordelia's forehead as he headed back towards the road where his car was parked.

"Join my coven, Indigo mon chéri," Harper called after him. "I can give you unfathomable power!"

'Never gonna happen!' he projected into her head as he walked. 'Va te faire foutre.'

"I'm only going to ask nicely once," she said, her voice drifting over the dunes. He just kept walking. "And then that power turns on you."

"Bring it," he muttered.

He wasn't expecting it, so when it hit him, he wasn't ready. A sonic boom of such black despair struck him hard in the back, radiating through him, knocking him to his knees. He curled his body over Cordelia's, protecting her as best he could as wave after wave of desolation washed over him. He bit his lip in agony, trying not to give her the satisfaction of crying out. It took all his strength to shield Cordelia's body. Just as he felt it penetrating him, sucking all joy and happiness from his very soul, a pulse of energy emerged from the top of his chest, an orb of white light that expanded to surround the both of them.

And as quickly as it started, it stopped, the black cloud receding. He was breathing heavily, his hands shaking as he raised his head to check his surroundings. There was no sign of Harper.

"That was just a taste," he heard her voice then, close by, although he couldn't see her, "Next time I won't be playing."

He staggered to his knees, clutching Cordelia tightly in his arms, shaken to his very core.

Indigo awoke then, drenched in sweat, fear gripping his belly.

Harper.

She was powerful.

The worst possible combination of powerful and ruthless.

And she would be coming for him.

But he would be ready.

Because he was Akasha.

gratitude list

Writing is an incredibly solitary task, the perfect hobby for an introvert like me. Or so I thought. The truth is, this book wouldn't exist without the input of so many others in so many different capacities. Where to begin? With my family because they always come first, second, and third.

I want to thank my boys, Xavier, Dash, Remy and Ted, for inspiring me every day. You guys are my muses and this series is a love letter of sorts to you. Thank you for allowing me the time away from you to write, for all those weekends and evenings I spent holed up in my room tapping away, for those nights I lay beside you in your beds illuminated by the glow of my laptop whilst you slept. You guys are my heart and soul and the best thing that's ever happened to me.

My surf-mad, petrol-head husband John, my one-man-cheer-squad and numero uno supporter… You believed in me even when I didn't, and you never let me give up when it all seemed insurmountable. Thank you for always being there through all the years of edits and re-writes, for telling me I'd always wonder if I didn't keep pushing. And as for all those drafts you read, for telling me they were great even when they really weren't… Love is blind, thanks, babe (you must be thrilled that finally, all those years spent immersing me in surfing and motorsports have come to fruition, if only on the page).

My mum, another person to plough through multiple drafts and give me feedback with the blunt honesty only she knows how to give. To all the professionals who told me, "Your mother is the worst person to read your manuscript because she's biased and will think anything you write is wonderful," you clearly haven't met my mother! She's always guaranteed to give it to you straight — if she thinks it's shit she'll tell you it's shit without even pausing to roll it in sugar to soften the blow. Mum, from draft one you've championed me and trusted I could do this and that is everything because I know you actually mean it.

My beautiful dad, who faithfully, unendingly believed in me because that's what fathers do. Thanks Dad, you've always taught us to put ourselves out there and give it a go. You and I have such opposing views of the world in so many ways yet our mutual respect knows no bounds. Hopefully you're as proud of me as I am of you.

My darling friends who beta read descended and helped make it better. In particular Alex Price-Randall — you've always pushed me to write to help others. Thank you for giving me a wealth of feedback, and for sharing your struggles for the sake of my 'art'. And of course Georgie Hookway, my touch stone and soul sister, your unwavering belief in me and this book buoys my effing heart, what would I do without you?

To all the professionals who had a hand in making descended what it is today: Virginia Lloyd, I thank you for Jenny-Craiging my flabby prose and for always telling me what I *needed* to hear. Alex Barba, who questioned everything and let nothing slide, Sherryl Clark who encouraged the art of showing not telling, and Samantha Elley, the queen of punctuation. Nicolee Payne, you're a genius with a paintbrush and I'll never get tired of staring at the beautiful artwork you created for my cover. Bea Brabante, readers do actually judge books by their covers, and I'm sure they'll have high hopes for mine thanks to you. Dave Loughnan, my tech genius (Liv he really is very clever!). Dan Blank for holding my hand so gently whilst forcing me to put myself out there… And of course my publicist, Juliet Potter, for believing in me and what I had to say from day one — let's always keep the faith, honey.

My two angels: Donna McCormick, (for always assuming my eventual success was a given. I probably would have fallen apart without you by now) and Lorelie Luna Ladiges, (you know what you do — I am so very grateful for all the magic that you weave).

Last but not least I want to thank all my dear friends (you know who you are), who lived my misguided youth alongside of me. We truly embodied the zeitgeist of the 90s and you've given me the ability to write it as we lived it (I'm sure you'll feel a sense of familiarity when reading parts of this). Sometimes I wonder how we're still alive, but I wouldn't change a thing... How glad are you there was no social media back then?!

I love my life and the people in it, and I'm grateful for you all.

X

Ingrid

Printed in Great Britain
by Amazon

41082610R00223